PENGUIN C

THE 120 DAYS OF SODOM

DONATIEN ALPHONSE FRANÇOIS, MARQUIS DE SADE, was born in Paris in 1740 into a distinguished Provençal family. Educated at the Louis-le-Grand Jesuit school and a military academy in Versailles, he fought in the Seven Years War with some distinction. In May 1763 he married Renée-Pélagie de Montreuil but in October of the same year was briefly incarcerated for committing sacrilegious acts with a prostitute. Further scandals followed, including an assault on a woman named Rose Keller in 1768 and an orgy with prostitutes in Marseille in 1772 which led to him being burned in effigy for poisoning and sodomy; he evaded the sentence by fleeing to Italy with his sister-in-law, with whom he was having an affair. Two years later, Sade and his wife spent the winter closeted away in his château in Lacoste with several female servants, giving rise to the so-called 'little girls affair'. At the behest of his mother-in-law, he was arrested in 1777 and spent the next thirteen years in prison – reading voraciously and writing several plays, short stories and novels, including *The 120 Days of Sodom*. After his wife divorced him upon his release in 1790, Sade began a relationship with a former actress, Marie-Constance Quesnet, that would last until his death. An active participant in revolutionary politics, Sade narrowly escaped the guillotine. Most of his major works were published in the 1790s, including *Justine, Philosophy in the Boudoir* and the *History of Juliette*. Wrongly suspected by Napoleon of writing an anti-Joséphine pamphlet, Sade was arrested in 1801 and later incarcerated at the mental asylum in Charenton, where he spent the rest of his life. He continued to write novels and plays, and organized the asylum's popular theatrical productions. He died in 1814 and was buried in an unmarked grave.

WILL MCMORRAN is Senior Lecturer in French and Comparative Literature at Queen Mary University of London.

THOMAS WYNN is Reader in French in the School of Modern Languages and Cultures at Durham University.

THE MARQUIS DE SADE

The 120 Days of Sodom
or
The School of Libertinage

Translated and with an Introduction by
WILL MCMORRAN AND THOMAS WYNN

PENGUIN BOOKS

PENGUIN CLASSICS

UK | USA | Canada | Ireland | Australia
India | New Zealand | South Africa

Penguin Books is part of the Penguin Random House group of companies
whose addresses can be found at global.penguinrandomhouse.com

This translation first published in Penguin Classics 2016

021

Translation and editorial material copyright © Will McMorran
and Thomas Wynn, 2016

Set in Sabon MT Std, 10.25/12.25 pt
Typeset by Palimpsest Book Production Limited, Falkirk, Stirlingshire
Printed in Great Britain by Clays Ltd, Elcograf S.p.A.

ISBN: 978-0-141-39434-3

www.greenpenguin.co.uk

MIX
Paper | Supporting
responsible forestry
FSC® C018179
www.fsc.org

Penguin Random House is committed to a
sustainable future for our business, our readers
and our planet. This book is made from Forest
Stewardship Council® certified paper.

Contents

Chronology

1740 2 June: Donatien Alphonse François de Sade born at the Hôtel de Condé in Paris. His father, Jean-Baptiste-François-Joseph, Comte de Sade (1702–67), from an old Provençal family, and his mother, Marie-Éléonore de Maillé de Carman (1712–77), a distant relative of the royal Condé family.

1744 Sent to Provence; stays initially with his aunts in Avignon, then with his uncle, the Abbé de Sade, in Saumane.

1748 *Thérèse the Philosopher*, a bestselling pornographic novel, published anonymously.

1750 Returns to Paris, educated by the Jesuits at Louis-le-Grand.

1754 Enrols at the academy of the Chevau-légers, an elite cavalry corps reserved for the oldest noble families.

1755–63 Military career begins as second lieutenant in the King's Infantry; commissioned as standard-bearer in the Comte de Provence's Carabiniers regiment, then as captain of the Burgundy regiment; demobilized at the end of the Seven Years War (1756–63) as cavalry captain.

1763 17 May: Marries Renée-Pélagie de Montreuil, daughter of a wealthy judge at the Cour des aides (a court concerned with financial matters).

18 October: Offers Jeanne Testard, fan-maker and occasional prostitute, two *louis* to take part in flagellation, sodomy and sacrilegious acts; she refuses. Eleven days later he is imprisoned in the Château de Vincennes, and in November transferred to the Château d'Échauffour, a property belonging to his in-laws.

1765 Affair with actress, Mlle de Beauvoisin, whom he takes to the family château of Lacoste, in Provence, and presents as his wife.

1767 Death of father. Birth of his first son, Louis-Marie, whose godparents are the Prince de Condé and the Princesse de Conti.

1768 First major public scandal. On Easter Sunday takes a beggar, Rose Keller, to his house in Arcueil, flogs her and commits sacrilegious acts; she escapes and goes to the police. Sade imprisoned at Saumur, Pierre-Encise and Lacoste.

1769 Birth of second son, Donatien Claude Armand. Travels to Low Countries.

1771 Birth of daughter, Madeleine-Laure. Imprisoned for debts.

1772 Organizes theatrical performances at Lacoste and Mazan. Affair with sister-in-law, Anne-Prospère.

June: Second major public scandal. Organizes orgy in Marseille with prostitutes and his valet, Latour. Charged with sodomy and poisoning, having given the prostitutes Spanish fly; sentenced to death *in absentia* and executed in effigy; flees to Italy with Anne-Prospère.

December: Arrested and imprisoned in the fortress of Miolans.

1773 April: Escapes from Miolans; on the run in the south of France and possibly Spain; returns to Lacoste.

1774 January: Police raid Lacoste; he escapes and goes into hiding.

May: Accession of Louis XVI (1754–93) to throne.

1774–5 Spends the winter in Lacoste with wife, fifteen-year-old male 'secretary', six newly recruited female servants of around the same age, and others – giving rise to the so-called 'little girls affair'.

January 1775: Children's families complain of abduction and seduction; human bones are found in garden – Sade dismisses this as a prank.

1775 July: Flees to Italy; visits Turin, Piacenza, Parma, Modena, Florence, Rome and Naples.

1776 July: Returns to Lacoste and writes the *Voyage to Italy*.

1777 January: Father of servant at Lacoste arrives to reclaim his daughter; during the altercation he shoots at Sade, but misses.

February: Arrives too late in Paris to see his dying mother; arrested by a *lettre de cachet* and imprisoned in Vincennes.

1778 Escapes from custody, recaptured after thirty-nine days and returned to Vincennes, where he spends the next six years.

1782 Writes *Dialogue between a Priest and a Dying Man*; starts work on *The 120 Days of Sodom, or the School of Libertinage*. Publication of Laclos's *Dangerous Liaisons.*

1784 29 February: Transferred to the Bastille.

1785 22 October: Begins writing *The 120 Days of Sodom*; finishes draft in thirty-seven days, written on a scroll.

1789 3 July: Caught shouting to passers-by that inmates at the Bastille are having their throats cut; transferred in the night to Charenton.

14 July: Storming of the Bastille. Scroll of *The 120 Days of Sodom* taken.

1790 2 April: Freed from Charenton.

9 June: Divorces wife at her request. Begins relationship with Marie-Constance Quesnet, with whom he remains until his death. Active participant in revolutionary politics.

1791 Anonymous publication of *Justine, or the Misfortunes of Virtue*. Performance of his play *Oxtiern, or the Misfortunes of Libertinage* at the Théâtre Molière.

1793 21 January: Louis XVI guillotined.

13 July: Charlotte Corday assassinates Jean-Paul Marat.

16 October: Marie-Antoinette guillotined.

8 December: Sade arrested under the Law of Suspects.

1794 27 July: Sade narrowly escapes the guillotine; Robespierre falls the same day.

15 October: Freed.

1795 *Aline and Valcour* and *Philosophy in the Boudoir* published.

1797–1801? *The New Justine* and the *History of Juliette, or the Rewards of Vice* published (exact years of publication uncertain).

1800 *Oxtiern* and *The Crimes of Love* published.

1801 Arrested and imprisoned in Sainte-Pélagie.

1803 March–April: After being accused of trying to seduce young inmates, transferred to Bicêtre, then to Charenton.

1804–13 Organizes theatrical performances at Charenton. Has sexual relationship with Madeleine Leclerc, a young laundress.

1807 Manuscript of *The Days of Florbelle or Nature Revealed* seized, and destroyed after his death.

1812–13 Writes the historical novels *Adélaïde de Brunswick, Princess of Saxony* and *The Secret History of Isabelle de Bavière, Queen of France*; publishes *The Marquise de Gange*.

1814 2 December: Dies; despite his wishes, given a Christian burial, but in accordance with his will no trace of his grave is left.

1904 Iwan Bloch (under pseudonym Eugène Dühren) publishes first edition of *The 120 Days of Sodom*.

1956–8 Jean-Jacques Pauvert prosecuted and condemned for publishing *The 120 Days of Sodom* and other works by Sade; judgement overturned in 1958.

1982 Scroll of *The 120 Days of Sodom* acquired by Swiss collector.

2014 Scroll returned to Paris and exhibited.

Introduction

The Scroll

On 3 July 1789, eleven days before the storming of the Bastille, the Marquis de Sade is taken from his cell in the prison's 'Liberty' tower in the middle of the night. Earlier that day, he had been caught shouting to the crowd outside through an improvised megaphone that the prisoners' throats were being cut. He is transported to Charenton, outside Paris, and obliged to leave all his personal effects behind. Among these is a copper cylinder, hidden in a crevice in the wall; it apparently remains there, untouched, for the next ten days. On the morning of 14 July, Madame de Sade heads to the Bastille to collect her husband's belongings, but is unable to get close to the prison – the Revolution has beaten her to it, and there is no more she can do. Sade is devastated, and it is the loss of the cylinder that grieves him most – it would lead him, he later said, to weep tears of blood. Inside was a scroll, twelve metres long and eleven centimetres wide, covered on both sides in tiny but perfectly neat handwriting: the manuscript of a novel entitled *The 120 Days of Sodom, or the School of Libertinage*.

Although Sade would never see his novel again, it had not been destroyed in the sacking of the Bastille: it had instead been taken by a young man named Arnoux de Saint-Maximin, who would subsequently sell it to a Provençal aristocrat, the Marquis de Villeneuve-Trans, in whose family it would remain in peaceful obscurity for three generations. Towards the end of the nineteenth century, however, whispers began to emerge of a privately held manuscript of a previously unknown work by the

Marquis de Sade; Henry Ashbee, the famous Victorian collector of erotica, offered a second-hand account of it in his *Index Librorum Prohibitorum* (1877), in which he described it as the tale of 'the doings of a certain community of libertines of both sexes'.[1]

When the scroll was sold by the Villeneuve-Trans family to a German collector at the turn of the twentieth century, the pioneering sexologist Iwan Bloch was granted access. In 1904, under the pseudonym Eugène Dühren, he published a private subscription edition of the text in Berlin, proclaiming it to be a great work of sexology. The scroll remained in Germany until 1929, when Sade's descendants, the Nouailles family, dispatched the leading Sade scholar, Maurice Heine, to reacquire it and bring it home to France. He did so, and in return was allowed the time and access required to produce a more rigorous edition of the text, which he published in another private subscription edition from 1931 to 1935. Heine would be the last of the novel's editors to see the original scroll, and all subsequent editions of the text are based on his transcription. The scroll itself stayed with the Nouailles family until, in 1982, they entrusted it to a family friend and publisher, Jean Grouet, who offered to have it valued. Grouet, however, smuggled the scroll over the border to Switzerland and sold it to a private collector, Gérard Nordmann. Despite decades of legal wrangling, it remained in Switzerland until 2014 (the bicentennial of Sade's death), when it was bought at a cost of €7 million by a private foundation and repatriated to France. The story of the scroll does not end there, however: its exhibition in Paris was cut short in December 2014 when the director of the foundation that had acquired the manuscript was charged with fraud. The scroll, which started its life in prison, is currently under lock and key once again, waiting for the courts to decide the next instalment of its turbulent history. It seems likely, however, that the French government will declare the scroll a national treasure to ensure it never leaves the country again.

As the final words on the scroll make clear, Sade began *The 120 Days of Sodom* on 22 October 1785 and finished thirty-seven days later. Although he wrote it in the Bastille, it was conceived a few years earlier in another prison, the Château de Vincennes. Sade's letters – like his cell – were subject to constant inspection, so generally give away little about his writing activities; his correspondence with his wife, however, does offer a few hints of the novel's beginnings. A letter from Madame de Sade dated 28 November 1782 reveals, for example, that some of her husband's manuscripts and notebooks have been confiscated, including some apparently compromising material: 'I don't know what you wrote in the papers that have been taken from you,' she writes, 'but it gives a bad impression of you, it seems to me, from what I've been told.' Her warning apparently falls on deaf ears, for in May the following year she tells him again, 'what you are writing is doing you a great wrong'.

While we cannot know for certain what Sade was writing, a letter railing against the political elite, which he sent on 26 April 1783 to his dear friend, Milli de Rousset, seems to anticipate the tone and rhetoric of the opening paragraph of the *120 Days*:

> By what right does this pack of leeches – which laps up the people's misfortunes, and which by its outrageous monopolies plunges this unfortunate class (whose sole crime is to be weak and poor) into the cruel necessity of losing either its honour or its life, and in the case of the latter leaving it no other choice than to lose it through poverty or on the scaffold – what right, I ask you, do these monsters have to demand virtues?

In June of the same year, Sade tells his wife of a 'great novelistic labour' that will keep him occupied for the whole of the coming autumn, while in November he offers her a taster of this new work: 'Here, my dear friend, is a small sample of a work I have spoken to you about; I have gathered almost two hundred similar character traits, all of which I have portrayed and arranged like the one I'm sending, so you can judge the whole thing.' He compares his project to a book he had recently acquired: the Abbé Bertoux's little-known compendium of *French Anecdotes, Since the Establishment of the Monarchy Until the Reign of Louis XV* (1767), a work structured chronologically with short anecdotes offered for each year included. Though he is dismissive of Bertoux's *Anecdotes*, he thereafter takes to calling his own work after it in his correspondence and thereby implies it has served as a kind of model.

Whether or not Sade did share early drafts of his most obscene and extreme novel with his wife, his correspondence at the time certainly suggests he has a grand design in mind. In a letter of 10 December 1783 he asks her for writing materials:

> I did not ask you for a cookery book but a nice manuscript. I'm returning your book to you – you can offer it as a present to your laundry girl. On the book's first page I give instructions as to how I want the manuscript. So that you can pass on this book if you wish, I prefer to describe the manuscript here. The cover must be extremely thin so that it can be rolled up, as this one already is. It must have precisely six hundred pages, all numbered in red.[2]

The need for a manuscript that could be rolled up, and that would include six hundred pages – a page, perhaps, for each of the 'passions' he would catalogue in the *120 Days* – suggests that Sade was formulating his work at least two years before he would write his 1785 draft. Some of the notes in this draft indeed refer to his careful planning of the novel's structure: he warns himself at the end of the manuscript, 'Do not deviate in the slightest from this plan, everything within it has been worked out several times and with the greatest precision' (p. 396). In the introductory section of the novel, another note refers to the coloured notebooks he had used for his early drafts: *'Place Durcet's portrait here as it is in notebook 18 bound in pink'* (p. 20). These notebooks do not appear to have survived.

It was Sade's extensive planning of the *120 Days* that allowed him to write the novel over such a short period of time, working between seven and ten in the evening over the thirty-seven days (thus taking a little under 120 hours to write 120 days). Created from dozens of slips of paper glued together, and covered in his minute handwriting, the manuscript's form as well as its content reflects and represents the horrors of incarceration; as a material object, it remains a unique example of prison art in its own right. While Sade declares the manuscript 'finished' at the end of the scroll, he clearly considered it an incomplete draft rather than a finished work. In a note to himself at the end of Part One, he warns, 'as I have been unable to reread myself, this must surely be teeming with other mistakes' and evidently envisaged a further period of writing up: 'When I make a fair copy, one of my first concerns should be to have a notebook nearby at all times, where I shall need to enter each incident and each portrait as I write them for without that I shall become horribly confused because of the multitude of characters' (p. 316).

It was not uncommon in the eighteenth century for novels, often published in instalments of one or two volumes at a time, to be left unfinished by their authors: Marivaux, for example, would eventually lose interest in two of his works, *La Vie de Marianne* (1731–45) and *Le Paysan parvenu* (1735), thus leaving his protagonists in perpetual limbo, while Sterne's *Tristram Shandy* (1759–67) seems to stop, rather than to conclude, after nine volumes. While these novels are driven less by plot than by digression, the *120 Days* offers a far more structured narrative, however, and one that builds slowly but inevitably to a bloody climax. We can only wonder why Sade never completed the fair copy he originally intended. Perhaps the unpublishable nature of the work led him to move on to other, less extreme projects such as *Aline and Valcour*, which he would begin the following year, or perhaps he planned to return to it once he had regained his freedom. Instead, the lost *120 Days* would linger in his imagination as a template for the libertine novels he would publish in the 1790s. The castle of Silling, the setting of the *120 Days*, would thus leave its trace in works such as *Justine* (1791) with its monastery buried in the forest and castle nestled in the mountains, and in the *History of Juliette* (1797–1801?), with the giant Minski's desolate palace, naturally fortified by the lake, woods and peaks that surround it.

The Life

By the time he wrote the *120 Days* Sade had already spent eight years in prison, first in Vincennes, then the Bastille. He had also been burnt in effigy, survived attempted murder and lived for months on the run as an outlaw. All this was a far cry indeed from the refined opulence in which his life had begun. He was born on 2 June 1740 at the Hôtel de Condé, one of the grandest princely residences in Paris, where his mother was lady-in-waiting to her distant relative, Princess Caroline-Charlotte de Condé; his father, a diplomat, belonged to an old and distinguished Provençal family. Sade's companion in early childhood was Prince Louis-Joseph de Bourbon, whose tutor was the Comte de Charolais – notorious for firing his musket at workmen, but shielded from prosecution by his rank. Sade's own fiery temperament became evident at an early age. When he was four years old he was sent away from Paris for reasons revealed in an apparently autobiographical passage from his epistolary novel, *Aline and Valcour*:

> Born and raised in the palace of the illustrious prince to whom my mother had the honour of being related, and who was about my age, I was keenly encouraged to consort with him, so that, being known by him since childhood, I should have his support throughout my life; but my vanity at the time, understanding nothing of such calculations, was one day wounded during our youthful games by a quarrel over some object or other to which he doubtless believed with very good reason his rank entitled him, and I avenged myself for his resistance with repeated blows – without a second thought holding me back, and with nothing but brute force able to separate me from my adversary.[3]

Sade spent the next few years living in the Provençal village of Saumane with his uncle, the Abbé de Sade, returning to Paris at the age of ten to attend the Jesuit school, Louis-le-Grand. When he turned fourteen he entered the academy of the Chevau-légers, an elite cavalry corps, in Versailles. He later joined the King's Infantry and the Comte de Provence's Carabiniers regiment before serving as a captain in the Burgundy regiment. Sade served with some distinction during the Seven Years War, but away from the battlefield he developed a reputation for excess. His commanding officer wrote to the Comte de Sade to warn him of the 'little follies' the Marquis had committed in Strasbourg.

The warning had little effect, however, as Sade admitted to his former tutor, the Abbé Amblet, in 1759: 'I rose every morning to go in search of pleasure and the thought of it made me oblivious to everything else.'

On 17 May 1763 Sade married Renée-Pélagie de Montreuil, the daughter of a wealthy judge. In October that same year he was briefly incarcerated in Vincennes for committing sacrilegious acts (including masturbating over an ivory statue of Christ) with an occasional prostitute, Jeanne Testard. A more public scandal followed on Easter Sunday 1768, when Sade took a beggar named Rose Keller to a house in Arcueil, where, according to her testimony, he cut her flesh with a knife and poured wax into her wounds; he denied using a knife, saying the cuts were from a cat-o'-nine-tails. In a doomed bid to minimize the scandal, Madame de Montreuil, Sade's mother-in-law, paid Keller off and had Sade imprisoned with a *lettre de cachet* signed by the king – less to punish him than to protect him from the judicial process to which he would otherwise have been subject.[4] Sade was freed after seven months and ordered to return to the family château of Lacoste in Provence. Four years later he was involved in another very public scandal in Marseille: an orgy with four prostitutes and his valet Latour went awry when two of the women fell violently ill after consuming chocolate-coated Spanish fly; he was accused of homosexual sodomy – a capital offence – and poisoning. While his wife did her best to appease the authorities, Sade fled to Italy with her sister, Anne-Prospère, with whom he had been having an affair. In their absence, Sade and Latour were convicted and burned in effigy. Upon his return from Italy, Sade was arrested in Chambéry and imprisoned at the fortress of Miolans; he managed to escape and spent the next few years hiding out in and around Lacoste, as well as venturing back to Italy.

A further scandal – the so-called 'little girls affair' – unfolded over the winter of 1774–5, which Sade and his wife spent at Lacoste with seven freshly recruited young servants aged about fifteen (and others in their twenties). In a letter written that November, Sade rather ominously tells his friend and lawyer Gaufridy to keep away: 'We have decided, for a thousand different reasons, to see very few people this winter. [. . .] When night falls, the château will be definitively locked shut.' The scandal broke in January when the servants' families filed complaints of abduction and seduction against Sade. In an effort to hide the evidence, the servants were prevented from returning home until the traces of their wounds had healed. When one of them, Nanon, gave birth to a daughter in May and threatened to tell all, she was falsely accused of theft by Madame de Sade and imprisoned; Nanon's child was taken from her and died of starvation. A judge in Aix declared that same month that the Marquis had given 'himself up to all kinds of excesses with young people of both sexes'. Sade fled to Italy once again, but a year later he was back in Lacoste. In January 1777 the father of another servant, Catherine Treillet, came to the château demanding that his daughter leave with him: she refused and, during the altercation, he fired a shot at Sade that narrowly missed. Sade travelled to Paris the following month to resolve the legal repercussions of the 'Treillet affair' and to see his dying mother; on the day of his arrival, however, he learned that she had died three weeks earlier. Worse was to follow for Sade: Madame de Montreuil seized on her errant son-in-law's presence in the capital to deal with him once and for all. She secured a *lettre de cachet* ordering his immediate incarceration. On 13 February he was arrested and, within an hour, locked up in Vincennes. So began thirteen years of imprisonment, with Sade held in Vincennes until 1784, when he was transferred to the Bastille.

Sade did not lose his aristocratic sense of entitlement in prison – indeed, he wrote to his wife in 1779, 'I am made to be served, and served I shall be.' He sent Madame de Sade on errands around Paris to buy luxury items such as eel pâté, apricot marmalade, fine bonnets and anal dildos made to precise measurements; he also requested the latest plays, novels and newspapers. He not only read voraciously in prison but wrote a great deal, including plays, short stories, the *Dialogue between a Priest and a Dying Man*, *The 120 Days of Sodom*, *Aline and Valcour* and *The Misfortunes of Virtue* (the first version of the story of Justine). His extensive prison correspondence with his wife reveals a complex relationship of humour, affection and vicious bullying – some of his letters contain death threats against her. Especially significant is his *grande lettre* of 20 February 1781 in which he defends his conduct towards the women he has abused: 'Yes I am a libertine, I admit; I have imagined everything that can be imagined of this kind, but I have surely not done everything I have imagined and will surely never do so. I am a libertine, but I am not *a criminal* or *a murderer.*' He signs the letter in blood.

Sade's physical health suffered in prison: his eyesight deteriorated, he was frequently denied exercise (partly due to his mistreatment of prison staff) and he became obese. In March 1784 he complained to M. Lenoir, the lieutenant general of police: 'It is not by such procedures that you will gain anything from my soul. You sour it, you revolt it by accumulating the feelings of hatred and vengeance with which this wretched and tormented soul ceaselessly suffers, and all that you will have gained – be quite sure of this – will be to have made me worse than I would ever have been in my life.' Sade's mental health also suffered, as he was only too aware. He wrote to his wife in late 1784 that 'prison is harmful because the solitude there gives greater force to one's ideas, and the disturbance that results from that force becomes infinitely more prompt and certain.' This mental strain led him to develop what he called a 'number system' that found him searching for clues as to the date of his release in the various letters, gifts and visits he received. Though he recognized this delirious arithmetic as 'an onset of madness', he continued to engage in it while preparing the *120 Days*, as a note from 1784 reveals: 'When the notary comes, I'll have been here for 7 weeks and 3 days, with 7 months and 3 weeks left, but nothing from 16 to 9 [. . .] That's 169 and forms 37. Now all the 37s have ended by making 169. That's sublime.' The same obsessiveness with numbers and dates, and the same leaps from reason to unreason, are evident in the *120 Days*.

Sade was freed from prison in the aftermath of the Revolution on 2 April 1790, but his wife refused to see him and divorced him two months later. Partly to create an appropriate public persona, and partly to earn much-needed money, Sade tried to establish himself as a playwright. His play *Oxtiern* was performed in 1791 at the Théâtre Molière, an establishment 'distinguished by its patriotism and love for the Revolution', according to the newspaper *Le Moniteur*; and in March 1792 the sole performance of his play *The Seducer* was interrupted by a riot in the theatre. None of his other plays were performed on the public stage, despite his repeated efforts. Fashioning himself as a revolutionary, he took the name 'Citoyen Louis Sade' and joined the radical Section Vendôme, later renamed the Section des Piques, becoming its elected president in July 1793. Sade was thus able to vote on the death penalty for those residents deemed to be counter-revolutionary. Among these were his former parents-in-law and (as his apologists have been keen to point out) Sade chose not to sign their death warrant, ensuring instead that their names were entered on a list that guaranteed their survival. In December of that year he was jailed under the Law of Suspects as an enemy of the Revolution. Whilst imprisoned in a former convent at Picpus, he was a direct witness to revolutionary violence: from his window he could see the guillotine's victims being buried in the garden; he later claimed he saw 1,800 people buried in thirty-five days. His own execution was scheduled for 27 July 1794, but he escaped the guillotine partly through the efforts of his companion, Marie-Constance Quesnet, a former actress. Their relationship would last until his death, and he dedicated *Justine* (1791) to her.

The revolutionary period saw the publication of Sade's major works, including *Justine, Aline and Valcour* (1795), *Philosophy in the Boudoir* (1795), *The New Justine* (1799) and the accompanying *History of Juliette* (1797–1801?). Wrongly suspected by Napoleon of writing an anti-Joséphine libel, *Zoloé and Her Two Acolytes* (1800), Sade was arrested at his publishers in early March 1801 and eventually incarcerated in the asylum at Charenton, where he spent the rest of his life. Dr Coulmier, the director of the asylum, granted Sade a significant degree of freedom, allowing him to organize the institution's popular theatrical activities, dramatized by Peter Weiss in *Marat/Sade* (1963) and by Doug Wright in *Quills* (1995, followed by a film version by Philip Kaufman in 2000). The plays at Charenton, some of which were written by Sade himself, were performed by inmates alongside professional actors. They drew audiences no doubt lured by the prospect of seeing a man likened by one visitor to 'one of those monstrous creatures that are displayed in cages [. . .] the all too famous Marquis de Sade'. Sade continued to write fiction in Charenton, including *The Days of Florbelle or Nature Revealed*, the manuscript of which was apparently destroyed by his son after his death, and three historical novels: *Adélaïde de Brunswick*, *The Secret History of Isabelle de Bavière* and *The Marquise de Gange*. In the last two years of his life, he had a sexual relationship with the young Madeleine Leclerc, a laundress or seamstress working at the asylum. He died on 2 December 1814.

The Afterlife

In his last testament, written in 1806, Sade requested that he be buried in the woods of his Malmaison property – so that 'the traces of my tomb may disappear from the surface of the earth just as I trust the memory of me will fade from the minds of men'.[5] Neither of these wishes would be granted: when Sade died he was given a Christian burial in the grounds of Charenton, and long after his death he continued to loom large in the public imagination. Immortalized as the most notorious libertine of the *ancien régime*, and as the author of the depraved *Justine*, Sade had already become a myth in his own lifetime, his crimes a work of fiction to rival his own novels. The Marseille episode, for example, had been transformed by one contemporary into a Roman orgy at which the women of the town were consumed by a 'uterine frenzy' and several participants died of their excesses.[6] According to *The Bastille Unveiled* (1789), meanwhile, Sade had been imprisoned for conducting 'human experiments' on live subjects in Provence. A few years later, the writer and politician Jacques-Antoine Dulaure compared Sade to the original Bluebeard, Gilles de Rais, and expressed horror that 'the Marquis de Sade, guilty of the same atrocities, is living peacefully among us'[7] – although Sade may well have been back in prison at the time. Twenty years after Sade's death, the critic Jules Janin went even further, claiming that Sade's works had killed more children than twenty Gilles de Rais ever could, and that his villainy was all the greater as 'these are books and consequently crimes that will not perish'.[8] Janin even offered the cautionary tale of 'poor little Julien', a young boy of his acquaintance who aged twenty years in a single night and became epileptic after reading *Justine*.

The line separating fact from fiction is often blurred in these early pieces on Sade, as his crimes are turned into stories and his stories into crimes. Each adds to the horror inspired by the other, and, as Janin puts it, Sade becomes 'a name that everyone knows and no one pronounces', a name that makes his fiction unreadable other than in the occasional, clandestine editions circulating discreetly among French literary circles. As the nineteenth century drew to a close, however, bibliophiles and admirers of *curiosa* began to publish Sade's works in expensive private editions, starting tentatively with some of his literary essays before taking the plunge with works such as *Justine*. They were soon joined by a new generation of sexual scientists, and the pioneering sexologist Richard von Krafft-Ebing devoted a section of his foundational *Psychopathia Sexualis* (1886) to the newly coined perversion of 'sadism':

> The notorious Marquis de Sade, after whom this combination
> of lust and cruelty has been named, was such a monster. Coitus
> only excited him when he could prick the object of his desire
> until the blood came. His greatest pleasure was to injure naked
> prostitutes and then dress their wounds.[9]

Sade may still be a monster for Krafft-Ebing, but now he is a monster to be studied rather than feared; there is, for the first time, a legitimate, scientific reason to study his fiction.

While Krafft-Ebing's definition of sadism was based on Sade's biography (and in particular the Rose Keller affair), works of sexology at the turn of the twentieth century often drew on fiction for their case studies – real case studies in the sexual domain were, after all, hard to come by.[10] If the line between fact and fiction is often as blurred in this period as it had been in Sade's own lifetime, this ambiguity works in Sade's favour when Iwan

Bloch publishes the inaugural edition of the *120 Days* in 1904, presenting it not as a novel but as a work of science:

> the principal work of the Marquis de Sade, in which he gathered all his observations and ideas on the sexual life of man, and on nature and the varieties of sexual perversions. It is composed according to a systematic plan, with the aim of a scientific grouping of the examples cited.[11]

The six hundred 'passions' are described as 'cases reported' – rather than created – and Bloch thereby transforms Sade from a psychopath into a psychopathologist, and indeed into a precursor to Krafft-Ebing himself. As extraordinary as Bloch's claim will soon appear to any reader who delves into the following pages, more extraordinary still is the fact that such a claim was taken seriously, and indeed endlessly perpetuated, by the eclectic mix of scientists and Surrealists who took up the Sadean cause in the first half of the twentieth century. The poet Guillaume Apollinaire, who publishes an edition of 'selected pages' of Sade in 1909, thus hails the *120 Days* as 'a rigorously scientific classification of all the passions in their relationship to the sexual instinct', and as the founding work of 'sexual psychopathology'.[12] As sexology ceded ground to psychoanalysis, Sade was moreover hailed as a precursor to Freud as well as Krafft-Ebing. This indeed would be the fate of Sade throughout the twentieth century: to be perpetually recast in the image of those seeking his cultural rehabilitation, whether they be sexologists, psychoanalysts, Surrealists, structuralists or even feminists.

For all the interest in Sade in French intellectual circles between the wars, the so-called *divin marquis* remained more talked about than read. The editions of his works published by Heine in the 1920s and 1930s, like the bibliophilic editions of the previous century, were produced in very modest numbers for a private readership of wealthy subscribers – only 360 copies of Heine's *120 Days* were printed. These editions were nonetheless read by the generation of intellectuals that included Georges Bataille, Pierre Klossowski, Maurice Blanchot and Simone de Beauvoir, all of whom went on to write important essays on

Sade after the Second World War. Even before the outbreak of war, however, the rise of National Socialism had provided a chilling new context for the reading of Sade's fiction: writing in exile in 1944, the German philosophers Max Horkheimer and Theodor W. Adorno trace the rise of fascism back to an Enlightenment they identify as totalitarian – and which they claim Sade's works expose as such: 'the strict regime of the libertine society of the *120 Days of Sodom* [. . .] prefigures the organization, devoid of any substantial goals, which was to encompass the whole of life' under totalitarianism.[13]

While many of Sade's exegetes after the war sought to 'de-nazify' Sade, others made the connection between the castle of Silling and the Nazi concentration camps: writing in November 1945, Raymond Queneau describes Sade as 'a hallucinatory precursor of the world ruled by the Gestapo, its tortures, its camps',[14] a suggestion echoed in Albert Camus's remark that 'from Sade's lurid castle to the concentration camps, man's greatest liberty consisted only of building the prison of his crimes'.[15] If reading Sade would never be the same again, this did not deter those determined to bring Sade to a broader public. In the 1950s Jean-Jacques Pauvert brought out the first 'complete works' of Sade in French, and the Olympia Press in Paris immediately followed up with English translations of most of the major works. In 1956, however, Pauvert's edition led to his prosecution and conviction for committing an 'outrage aux bonnes mœurs' (offence against public decency), although the verdict was later overturned on appeal. Ever since the Pauvert trial, it has remained an offence to display Sade's works in shop windows in France – an honour he shares with Adolf Hitler. Nevertheless, in little over a decade Sade's works started to appear in mass-market paperbacks in France, a sign they were entering the French literary canon. Sade also crossed the Atlantic in the 1960s when the Grove Press in New York acquired the rights to the Olympia translations and released revised versions under its own imprint.

For a while it looked as if Sade would find a place in British culture too. In the wake of the trial of D. H. Lawrence's *Lady Chatterley's Lover* in 1960, a test case for the Obscene Publications Act passed a year before, English publishing houses were emboldened to publish Sade for the first time. In 1965 a Corgi paperback appeared purporting to be *Justine* (actually a translation of *The Misfortunes of Virtue*, the earlier version of the Justine story).[16] More of Sade's works would no doubt have followed had it not been for the Moors Murders trial of 1966. In 1923 Louis Perceau had confidently challenged Sade's opponents to 'cite a single sadistic crime inspired by the reading of his works';[17] with the child murders committed by Ian Brady and Myra Hindley, Perceau's confidence suddenly seemed premature. It came out during the trial that Brady had among his books a copy of Sade's *Justine* – the Corgi edition – as well as *The Life and Ideas of the Marquis de Sade* (1933) by the anthropologist Geoffrey Gorer. Brady's reading of Sade fired the public imagination – a fire stoked by commentators who confidently asserted a causal connection between Brady's reading of Sade in 'fairly recent paperback'[18] and his crimes. George Steiner, for example, alluded to the 'high probability that the reading of Sade and related material was a significant factor' in the case, while Pamela Hansford Johnson fretted about the 'most fantastic growth of a semi-literate reading public' and insisted, 'There are some books that are not fit for all people and some people who are not fit for all books.'[19] Neither critic seemed to notice that the Corgi *Justine* had not appeared in print until after Brady had committed two of the three murders of which he had been convicted (and two further murders to which he and Hindley would later confess). In any case, a ban on the publication (and importation) of Sade's works swiftly followed the trial and remained in force until 1989, when Arrow Books reprinted the old Grove Press translations published in the 1960s.

While the British agonized over the moral threat posed by violent and pornographic fiction, in France a new generation of literary critics was doing its best to extract Sade from the kind of moral debates that had led to the Pauvert trial. Of these the most influential by some margin was Roland Barthes, who advocated an approach to Sade that eliminated any need to address the violence within his works by making it a matter of words alone:

'the only Sadean universe,' he claimed, 'is the universe of discourse' – or, as he would put it more bluntly a few years later, 'written down, shit does not smell'.[20] Since the 1970s a long line of Sade scholars has echoed Barthes's assertion that the violence in Sade is purely linguistic – a matter of form rather than content.[21] Rather like the sexologists who championed Sade earlier in the century, such an approach casts the critic as a clinician dissecting the Sadean text with scientific objectivity, but leaves no place for reflecting on the visceral experience of reading Sade. And while Barthes's excremental dictum may seem logical in the abstract, the reader of certain passages in the first part of the *120 Days* may well find the written word can offer a far more pungent experience than Barthes allows. This indeed is the problem with the narrowly linguistic approach to Sade: it does not survive one's first encounter with the text. Although it has since the 1980s ceded ground to an historicist approach that situates Sade firmly in his own period as an Enlightenment writer and thinker, the latter has proved no more conducive to exploring the visceral power of Sade's fiction: the violence previously confined within language has simply been confined to the past instead. There is a pressing need in Sade scholarship for approaches that engage more effectively – and affectively – with the actual experience of reading an œuvre defined by its violence.

The Libertines

Ironically, perhaps, the *120 Days* reflects on the very questions of affect or response that critics working on Sade have generally been reluctant to address. The libertines listen to the prostitutes' narrations and act out their own versions of the scenes they hear described – a case of monkey hear, monkey do. Throughout the novel, the reader is reminded of the power of words: one of the four libertines, Curval, is described in the introduction as the author of 'several works whose effects had been prodigious', while we hear on the fourth day of a churchman with extraordinary powers of persuasion: 'in just two hours of conversation he was sure to make a whore out of the most virtuous and most prudent of girls' (p. 112). On the thirtieth day Duclos also offers a portrait of the Comte de Lernos, a libertine who uses books as part of his seductions.

The belief that fiction had the power to corrupt readers was widely held in the eighteenth century: Rousseau, in the preface to his novel *Julie, or the New Heloise* (1761), proclaims with little discernible irony, 'No chaste girl has ever read a novel.'[22] If this may seem naive to a twenty-first-century reader, it is not because we have left this fear of fiction behind – it has simply shifted from the novel to more recent (and visual) forms of storytelling, from horror movies and pornographic films to video games. It is difficult to know whether Sade believed in the power of his own fiction to influence or corrupt – rather than simply arouse – his readers. His novels contain endless examples of stories that trigger sexual responses in those who listen to them, but there are very few instances of anyone ever being changed or converted by what they hear; as one of the libertine monks in *Justine* asks rhetorically, 'Can we become anyone other than who we are?'[23] For all their openness to new experiences, the libertines of the *120 Days* are utterly set in their tastes and powerless to change them – they leave the castle of Silling just as they were when they arrived. There is something both dispiriting and reassuring about this immutability: on the one hand everyone is doomed to be as they are, but on the other no one can ever be corrupted by what they see or hear – for all the immoral pedagogy implied by Sade's School of Libertinage.

Are Sade's readers as immune to words as his libertines? Jean Paulhan argues that reading Sade may affect readers in unpredictable ways. In his deposition at the Pauvert trial, he cites the example of Alphonse de Lamartine, who said he would never have become a poet had he not read Sade as a nineteen year old.[24] Paulhan also mentions the case of a young girl of his acquaintance whose reading of Sade persuaded her to enter a convent.[25] As apocryphal as both these examples may be, Paulhan is right to challenge the assumption that depravity necessarily depraves. Indeed, Sade does little to encourage the reader to identify with the four 'heroes' of the *120 Days*: in marked contrast to other libertine works – such as Laclos's *Dangerous Liaisons* (1782) or Sade's own *Philosophy in the Boudoir* – there is nothing

glamorous or seductive about the libertines of Silling. Aged
between forty-five and sixty, two of the four are more or less
impotent and one is in faltering health; only the Duc de Blangis
is virile and handsome, if 'astonishingly hirsute'. Nor will many
readers be seduced by their particular peccadilloes. Even one of
Sade's most ardent admirers, Gilbert Lely, complained of the
disproportionate space given to coprophilic practices in the *120
Days* – in part a result of the unfinished nature of the manuscript,
but a reflection nonetheless of a marked scatological bias in the
first part of the text. For the Sadean libertine, eroticism and
disgust are not antithetical but intertwined. The more disgusting
the object, the more intense the sensation and the greater the
thrill: 'Beauty, freshness only strike one in a simple way,' observes
the narrator in the introduction, 'ugliness, degradation deliver a
much firmer blow – the shock is far stronger, the excitation must
therefore be more intense' (p. 41).

The intensity the libertine seeks – and, indeed, requires if he
is to overcome his infirmities – is gained by violating conventions
and customs. Sex in the *120 Days* is fundamentally transgressive:
sodomy becomes the new norm; genders are bent as the libertines
become wives as well as husbands; the female body becomes an
object of repulsion and a site of violence; and boys and girls
aged between twelve and fifteen provide harems for the libertines. The presence of children in Silling and in the prostitutes'
narrations is doubtless the most disturbing aspect of the *120
Days* for modern readers sensitized to issues of child sexual
abuse. Even by the standards of the time, the youngest of the
boys and girls imprisoned in Silling are still children. In France
in the eighteenth century the age of puberty was around fourteen
for boys and sixteen for girls;[26] although girls as young as twelve
and boys as young as fourteen could be married, the average
age for first marriages was far higher.[27] To add to the reader's
unease, the Silling harems recall the so-called 'little girls affair'
– particularly as one of the servant girls closeted away in Lacoste
was called Rosette, a name Sade later used for one of the victims
in the *120 Days*. While Sade scholars generally avoid drawing
parallels between Sade's biography and his works, the realities
of Lacoste undeniably cast a shadow over the fantasies of Silling.

If Lacoste represented a lost idyll for Sade, then it is tempting to view Silling as his attempt to recapture and recreate that idyll on a grander, more fantastic scale. But Silling is a site of pain as well as pleasure, of submission as well as liberation, and in this respect Sade's experience of *ancien régime* justice and incarceration without trial evidently casts a shadow of its own over the *120 Days*. An element of satire clearly underpins his four grotesque libertines – a bishop, a judge, a nobleman and a financier – and the novel may also be read as an assault on the institutions they represent. Sade, after all, saw himself as the victim of injustice, persecuted beyond reason for what were in his view petty offences. Paulhan argues that the heroine of Sade's *Justine*, abused by every man she encounters, represents Sade far more than any libertine, and reveals him to be a masochist rather than a sadist.[28] There are certainly moments in Sade's fiction – from *Justine* to *The Marquise de Gange* – when he seems to identify with the plight of his prisoners and to rail against those who abuse their power. As plausible as it may be to read the *120 Days* as a prisoner's fantasy of absolute power, it is therefore simplistic to identify the author too closely with his libertines, or to see in the latter some sort of collective alter ego; like Flaubert in *Madame Bovary*, Sade seems to be 'present everywhere but visible nowhere'[29] in the *120 Days*.

The Classic

For all the attempts of its early readers to present it as a work of science, *The 120 Days of Sodom, or the School of Libertinage* is rooted in the literary – and sub-literary – culture of its time. While its title reflects a debt to the great storytelling collections of the European tradition, such as Boccaccio's *Decameron* (1349–51) and Marguerite de Navarre's *Heptameron* (1559), its subtitle declares it to be a work of eroticism. It is not the only one of Sade's works to announce a pedagogic theme: ten years later he would give his *Philosophy in the Boudoir* the subtitle *The Immoral Teachers*, and advertise it on its title page as a series of 'Dialogues destined for the education of young ladies'. In both instances, Sade is nodding to the earthier European tradition of the so-called whore dialogue, a form conceived by Pietro Aretino in his *Ragionamenti* (1534–6), which many regard as the first work of modern pornography; the reference to a school in the subtitle to the *120 Days* also evokes Michel Millot's influential example of the genre, *L'Ecole des filles* (1655) (translated into English in 1680 as *The School of Venus*). This genre of erotic fiction, in which an older, sexually experienced woman would teach a young novice about sex, flourished in England as well as France in the second half of the seventeenth century, and paved the way for the popular whore biographies of the eighteenth century, such as John Cleland's *Memoirs of a Woman of Pleasure* (1748–9), better known as *Fanny Hill*, and Fougeret de Monbron's *Margot la ravaudeuse* (1753). By embedding its four whore biographies within a storytelling frame, the *120 Days* stages the erotic reception implied in these earlier texts to make the audience a part of the performance.

The libertine tradition to which Sade alludes in his subtitle constitutes a distinct strand of erotic fiction within French literature, although one which increasingly overlaps with whore dialogues and biographies in the eighteenth century. The term *libertin* had primarily been associated with heretical religious opinion in the sixteenth and seventeenth centuries, but by the eighteenth century it had connotations of sexual debauchery; it was used to describe erotic fiction ranging from straightforwardly pornographic texts, such as La Touche's *History of Dom Bougre* (1740), to more cerebral and sophisticated works, such as Crébillon fils's *The Wayward Head and Heart* (1736–8), Vivant Denon's *No Tomorrow* (1777) and Laclos's *Dangerous Liaisons*. Like the *Bildungsroman* they anticipate, these stories about a young person's entrance into society are narratives of education, as the protagonist discovers social and philosophical – as well as sexual – truths.

The novel that most closely anticipates Sade's blend of pornography and philosophy is the anonymously published *Thérèse the Philosopher* (1748). Of particular significance to the *120 Days*, *Thérèse the Philosopher* contains a tale told by a prostitute, Madame de la Bois-Laurier, in which various encounters with clients of unusual tastes are described – a template in miniature for the storytelling in Silling. The eponymous heroine of Sade's *History of Juliette* may be speaking for the author when she describes *Thérèse the Philosopher* as 'a charming work [. . .] the only one to have shown what the goal is, without, however, quite reaching it'.[30] The *120 Days* was perhaps Sade's first attempt to reach that goal, although his narrator is keen to stress the originality of his own undertaking, hailing it as 'the most impure tale ever written since the world began, for no such book may be found among either the ancients or the moderns' (p. 59).

As important as it is to understand the context in which Sade was writing, it is just as important to recognize the context in which we are reading his fiction today. When Sade's place in the French literary pantheon was signalled by his publication in the prestigious Bibliothèque de la Pléiade collection in the 1990s, not everyone was delighted: 'Shall we receive among our literary classics,' Roger Shattuck asked, 'the works of an author who desecrates and inverts every principle of human justice and decency developed over four thousand years of civilized life?'[31] While Shattuck treats Sade as if he might infect the ranks of the classics, some of Sade's supporters have conversely worried that their author may be diminished by his newly acquired literary status. Annie Le Brun, for example, has complained that literary criticism on Sade has 'made him respectable by neutralizing him'.[32] In some ways these contrasting anxieties are well founded: when a work like the *120 Days* becomes a classic, both the *120 Days* and the idea of what makes a classic change a little in the process. On the one hand, the arrival of this novel among the ranks of Penguin Classics marks a significant step in its canonization outside France as a work of world literature – a reassuring badge of respectability that may allow it to circulate more freely and widely. On the other, when the *120 Days* becomes a classic, the literary canon may seem a little less respectable, a little less safe, than it did before. The humanist belief that the canon is, as Wayne Booth simply puts it, 'the good stuff'[33] – the kind of reading that morally improves its readers – seems difficult to cling on to when a novel like the *120 Days* is allowed into the fold. This may be no bad thing, for such a view of the canon is arguably based on a rather naive idea of what literature is – or should be. Literature is not a matter of 'rose-coloured window panes',[34] as Henry James put it. As Franz Kafka once observed, rather melodramatically, literature at its most powerful can be a terrible thing:

> If the book we are reading does not wake us, as with a fist hammering on our skull, why then do we read it? So that it shall make us happy? Good God, we would also be happy if we had no books, and such books as make us happy we could, if need be, write ourselves. But what we must have are those books which come upon us like ill-fortune, and distress us deeply, like the death of one we love better than ourselves, like suicide. A book must be an ice-axe to break the sea frozen inside us.[35]

It is difficult to imagine a book that fits this description better than the *120 Days*. And, as unlikely as it may at first seem, Kafka's remarks suggest that such a work may, after all, be profoundly moral in its effects. By assaulting our senses and our values the *120 Days* may, in fact, revive them. Sade himself makes the argument in several of his works that 'examples of virtue in distress, offered to a corrupt soul in which there remain some decent principles, can restore that soul to goodness just as surely as if one had shown dazzling prizes and the most flattering rewards.'[36] As disingenuous as Sade's defence of his methods certainly is, the reader may well find some inadvertent truth in this apparent lie – that the spectacle of the suffering victim is more likely to inspire compassion than cruelty.

Simone de Beauvoir has argued, perhaps counter-intuitively, that Sade deserves to be regarded as a *moraliste* for the ethical reflection he inspires in his readers:

> Sade drained to the dregs the moment of selfishness, injustice, misery, and he insisted upon its truth. The supreme value of his testimony lies in its ability to disturb us. It forces us to re-examine thoroughly the basic problem which haunts our age in different forms: the true relation between man and man.[37]

Reading Sade, as Beauvoir suggests, can be – should be – a troubling, uncomfortable experience. *The 120 Days of Sodom* is perhaps the most challenging text ever written, its incomplete state only adding to the difficulties faced by the reader. In three of the novel's four parts we find only the lists of the passions the storytellers would have told, interspersed with brief summaries of the increasingly violent events unfolding in the castle. It is left to the reader to add flesh to the bare bones of the narrative – and some may feel that to engage with the text in this way is to enter into an uncomfortable complicity with the brutality at its heart. While it may be easier to read this text passively – or indifferently – to do so risks another form of complicity: to ignore the violence is to leave it unchallenged, to tolerate the intolerable. As difficult as it may be, the *120 Days* needs to be read actively, and thoughtfully, because for all the horrors it contains, there are relatively few that have not been perpetrated at some point in our history – and, at times, on a far greater scale than that imagined by Sade. This is why Apollinaire's prediction in 1909 that 'this man who seemed to count for nothing throughout the nineteenth century might well dominate the twentieth'[38] now seems prescient, and why the *120 Days* retains the 'perpetual modernity'[39] that Frank Kermode identifies as the hallmark of a classic: it is a work that is impossible to ignore.

NOTES

1. 'Pisanus Fraxi' [Henry Ashbee], *Index Librorum Prohibitorum: Being Notes Bio- Biblio- Icono- graphical and Critical, on Curious and Uncommon Books* (London: Privately Printed, 1877), p. 423.
2. Sade repeats this request for a 'notebook of 600 hundred pages with margins, of fine Dutch paper, bound in a flexible cover' in a letter written on 16 February 1784, in which he declares he will copy out his '*Anecdotes*'.
3. Sade, *Aline et Valcour, ou le Roman philosophique*, in *Œuvres*, ed. Michel Delon, vol. 1 (Paris: Gallimard, 1990), p. 403.
4. Prisons in *ancien régime* France were not conceived primarily as correctional facilities; as the jurisconsult Daniel Jousse noted, 'prison is intended not to punish criminals, but to hold them', and *lettres de cachet* could be used to hold particularly recalcitrant individuals indefinitely without trial (*Traité de la justice criminelle de France*, 4 vols (Paris: Debure père, 1771), 2.223).
5. Sade, 'Testament', in *Œuvres complètes du Marquis de Sade*, vol. 11 (Paris: Pauvert, 1991), pp. 158–9.
6. Louis Petit de Bachaumont, *Mémoires secrets pour servir à l'histoire de la république des lettres en France, depuis 1762 jusqu'à nos jours; ou Journal d'un observateur* (London: John Adamson, 1777–89), 6.187.
7. Jacques-Antoine Dulaure, *Collection de la liste des ci-devant ducs, marquis, comtes, barons, etc.* (Paris: Year 2 [1793–4]), p. 4.
8. Jules Janin, *Le Marquis de Sade: la vérité sur les deux procès criminels du marquis de Sade par le Bibliophile Jacob* (Paris: Les marchands de nouveauté, 1834), p. 33.
9. Richard von Krafft-Ebing, *Psychopathia Sexualis, with Especial Reference to the Antipathic Sexual Instinct: A Medico-Forensic Study*, trans. F. J. Redman (New York: Redman, 1906), pp. 105–6.
10. Inspired by the fiction as well as the life of Leopold von Sacher-Masoch, Krafft-Ebing would also coin the term 'masochism'

in his *Psychopathia Sexualis* (much to Sacher-Masoch's horror).

11. 'Eugène Dühren' [Iwan Bloch], Preface to Marquis de Sade, *Les 120 Journées de Sodome, ou l'école du libertinage* (Paris: Club des Bibliophiles, 1904), p. iii.

12. Guillaume Apollinaire (ed.), *L'Œuvre du Marquis de Sade* (Paris: Bibliothèque des Curieux, 1909), p. 24.

13. Max Horkheimer and Theodor W. Adorno, *Dialectic of Enlightenment: Philosophical Fragments* (Stanford, CA: Stanford University Press, 2002), p. 69.

14. Raymond Queneau, 'Lectures pour un front', in *Batons, chiffres et lettres* (Paris: Gallimard, 1965), p. 215.

15. Albert Camus, *L'Homme révolté* (Paris: Gallimard, 1951), p. 134. Three decades later, Pier Paolo Pasolini would echo these readings of Sade by setting *Salò* (1975), his film adaptation of the *120 Days*, in Fascist wartime Italy.

16. Sade, *Justine, or the Misfortunes of Virtue*, trans. Alan Hull Walton (London: Corgi, 1965); a reprint of a hardback edition published a year earlier by Neville Spearman.

17. 'Helpey' [Louis Perceau], 'Le Marquis de Sade et le Sadisme', in Sade, *La Philosophie dans le boudoir* ('Sadopolis: aux dépens de la Société des études sadiques' [Paris: Maurice Duflou, 1923]), p. 36.

18. Pamela Hansford Johnson, *On Iniquity: Some Personal Reflections Arising Out of the Moors Murder Trial* (London: Macmillan, 1967), p. 115.

19. George Steiner, Letter, *Times Literary Supplement* (26 May 1966), quoted in Hansford Johnson, *On Iniquity*, pp. 115, 28. See John Sutherland, *Offensive Literature: Decensorship in Britain 1960–1982* (London: Junction Books, 1982) and Lisa Downing, *The Subject of Murder: Gender, Exceptionality and the Modern Killer* (Chicago and London: University of Chicago Press, 2013).

20. Roland Barthes, 'L'arbre du crime', *Tel Quel*, 28 (1967), p. 37; *Sade, Fourier, Loyola* (Paris: Seuil, 1971), p. 141.

21. Lawrence Lynch, for example, has declared that 'Sade's violence is indeed that of language' (*The Marquis de Sade* (Boston: Twayne, 1984), p. 129), while Geoff Bennington has insisted that 'the only "real" cruelty in Sade is that worked in the body of a language' ('Sade: Laying Down the Law', *Oxford Literary Review*, 6. 2 (1984), p. 54).

22. Jean-Jacques Rousseau, Preface to *Julie, ou la Nouvelle Héloïse*, ed. Michel Launay (Paris: Garnier-Flammarion, 1967), p. 3.

23. Sade, *Justine, ou les Malheurs de la vertu*, in *Œuvres*, ed. Michel Delon, vol. 2 (Paris: Gallimard, 1995), p. 261.

24. In an earlier essay, written in 1945, Paulhan claims Lamartine had once said that reading Sade had made him 'more tender' ('Sade, ou le pire est l'ennemi du mal', *Labyrinthe*, 11 (1945), p. 1).

25. This case rather suspiciously resembles one of the passions of the *120 Days*, according to which a young woman's response to being severely browbeaten by a libertine is to enter a convent (see below, p. 292).

26. In the *120 Days* Sade makes no such distinction between boys and girls, describing fourteen as 'the age at which Nature customarily showers her favours upon us' (p. 269).

27. The average age for first marriages was around twenty years for men and eighteen for women among the aristocracy, and around twenty-seven for men and twenty-six for women among the rest of the population. An age of consent of eleven years old was established in France in 1832, rising to thirteen in 1863 and fifteen in 1945. See Philippe Ariès, *Histoire des populations françaises et de leurs attitudes devant la vie depuis le XVIIIe siècle* (Paris: Seuil, 1971).

28. See *Le Marquis de Sade et sa complice ou Les Revanches de la pudeur* (Brussels: Editions Complexe, 1987).

29. Gustave Flaubert, letter of 9 December 1852, in *Correspondance*, ed. Jean Bruneau, 2 vols (Paris: Gallimard, 1973–80), 2. 204.

30. Sade, *Histoire de Juliette*, in *Œuvres*, ed. Michel Delon, vol. 3 (Paris: Gallimard, 1998), p. 591.

31. Roger Shattuck, *Forbidden Knowledge: From Prometheus to Pornography* (San Diego: Harcourt Brace, 1997), p. 269.

32. Annie Le Brun, *Soudain un bloc d'abîme, Sade* (Paris: Gallimard, 1993), p. 11.

33. Wayne C. Booth, *The Company We Keep: An Ethics of Fiction* (Berkeley and Los Angeles: University of California Press, 1988), p. 294.

34. Henry James, 'The Art of Fiction', in *The Art of Criticism: Henry James on the Theory and Practice of Fiction*, ed. William Veeder and Susan M. Griffin (Chicago: University of Chicago Press, 1986), p. 177.

35. From a letter to Oskar Pollak (27 January 1904). Quoted by George Steiner in 'To Civilize our Gentlemen', in *Language and Silence: Essays 1958–1966* (London: Faber, 1967), p. 88.

36. Sade, *Justine, ou les Malheurs de la vertu*, p. 132.

37. Simone de Beauvoir, 'Must We Burn Sade?', trans. Annette Michelson, in Sade, *The 120 Days of Sodom and Other Writings*, trans.

Austryn Wainhouse and Richard Seaver, (New York: Grove Press, 1966), pp. 63–4.

38. Apollinaire (ed.), *L'Œuvre du Marquis de Sade*, p. 17.

39. Frank Kermode, *Forms of Attention: Botticelli and Hamlet* (Chicago: University of Chicago Press, 1985), p. 62.

Further Reading

SELECTED FRENCH EDITIONS

Collected Editions

Œuvres complètes du Marquis de Sade, ed. Gilbert Lely, 16 vols (Paris: Cercle du livre précieux, 1966–7). Remains the standard scholarly edition for those works not included in the Bibliothèque de la Pléiade edition (see below).

Œuvres complètes du Marquis de Sade, 15 vols, eds Jean-Jacques Pauvert and Annie Le Brun (Paris: Pauvert, 1986). Still in print and contains Sade's plays, which are not available elsewhere in French.

Œuvres, ed. Michel Delon, 3 vols (Paris: Gallimard, 1990–98). Part of the canonical Bibliothèque de la Pléiade collection, this edition includes Sade's major works, some of which are now unavailable elsewhere (such as *La Nouvelle Justine, ou les Malheurs de la vertu* and the *Histoire de Juliette, ou les Prospérités du vice*).

Individual Editions

Les 120 journées de Sodome, ed. Gilbert Lely (Paris: Union générale d'éditions, 1998).

Aline et Valcour, ou le Roman philosophique, ed. Jean-Marie Goulemot (Paris: Librairie générale française, 1994).

Contes étranges, ed. Michel Delon (Paris: Gallimard, 2014).

Contes libertins, ed. Stéphanie Genand (Paris: Garnier-Flammarion, 2014).

Les Crimes de l'amour, ed. Michel Delon (Paris: Gallimard, 2014).
Dialogue entre un prêtre et un moribond, ed. Jérôme Vérain (Paris: Fayard, 1997).
Écrits politiques, ed. Maurice Lever (Paris: Bartillat, 2009).
Histoire secrète d'Isabelle de Bavière, reine de France, ed. Gilbert Lely (Paris: Gallimard, 1992).
Les Infortunes de la vertu, ed. Béatrice Didier (Paris: Gallimard, 2014).
Justine, ou les Malheurs de la vertu (Paris: Librairie générale française, 1973).
Lettres à sa femme, ed. Marc Buffat (Paris: Actes Sud, 1997).
La Marquise de Gange, ed. Jean Goldzink (Paris: Autrement, 1993).
La Philosophie dans le boudoir, ed. Jean-Christophe Abramovici (Paris: Flammarion, 2007).

SELECTED ENGLISH TRANSLATIONS

A number of Sade's works have yet to be translated into English, including *La Nouvelle Justine, ou les Malheurs de la vertu*, (Sade's much-expanded version of *Justine, ou les Malheurs de la vertu*), *Aline et Valcour, ou le Roman philosophique*, and two of his historical novels – *La Marquise de Gange* and the *Histoire secrète d'Isabelle de Bavière* (completed in 1813; published posthumously in 1953).

Adelaide de Brunswick, trans. Hobart Ryland (Washington: The Scarecrow Press, 1954).
The Crimes of Love, trans. David Coward (Oxford: Oxford University Press, 2005).
Dialogue between a Priest and a Dying Man, in *Justine, Philosophy in the Bedroom and Other Writings*, trans. Richard Seaver and Austryn Wainhouse (New York: Grove Press, 1990).
Juliette, trans. Austryn Wainhouse (New York: Grove Press, 1990).
Justine, or the Misfortunes of Virtue, trans. John Phillips (Oxford: Oxford University Press, 2012).
Letters from Prison, trans. Richard Seaver (New York: Arcade, 1999).

The Misfortunes of Virtue and Other Early Tales, trans. David
   Coward (Oxford: Oxford University Press, 1999).
Philosophy in the Boudoir, or The Immoral Mentors, trans. Joachim
   Neugroschel (New York: Penguin, 2006).
Rape, Incest, Murder! The Marquis de Sade on Stage, trans.
   John Franceschina, 3 vols (Albany, GA: BearManor Media,
   2013).
Voyage to Italy, trans. James A. Steintrager (Toronto: University
   of Toronto Press, forthcoming).

BIOGRAPHIES

Lever, Maurice, *Marquis de Sade: A Biography*, trans. Arthur Gold-
   hammer (London: HarperCollins, 1993).
du Plessix Gray, Francine, *At Home with the Marquis de Sade*
   (London: Chatto & Windus, 1999).
Schaeffer, Neil, *The Marquis de Sade: A Life* (London: Hamish
   Hamilton, 1999).
Thomas, Donald, *The Marquis de Sade* (London: Allison & Busby,
   1992).

GENERAL WORKS ON LIBERTINE FICTION

Cusset, Catherine, *No Tomorrow: The Ethics of Pleasure in the
   French Enlightenment* (Charlottesville and London: University
   Press of Virginia, 1999).
—— (ed.), *Libertinage and Modernity*, special issue of *Yale French
   Studies*, 94 (1998).
Cryle, Peter, *Geometry in the Boudoir: Configurations of French
   Erotic Narrative* (Ithaca, NY, and London: Cornell University
   Press, 1994).
—— *The Telling of the Act: Sexuality as Narrative in Eighteenth-
   and Nineteenth-Century France* (Newark: University of
   Delaware Press, 2001).
Darnton, Robert, *The Forbidden Best-Sellers of Pre-Revolutionary
   France* (New York and London: W. W. Norton, 1995).

DeJean, Joan E., *Literary Fortifications: Rousseau, Laclos, Sade* (Princeton, NJ: Princeton University Press, 1984).

Feher, Michel (ed.), *The Libertine Reader: Eroticism and Enlightenment in Eighteenth-Century France* (New York: Zone Books, 1997).

Goulemot, Jean Marie, *Forbidden Texts: Erotic Literature and its Readers in Eighteenth-Century France* (Philadelphia: University of Pennsylvania Press, 1994); first published as *Ces livres qu'on ne lit que d'une main: lecture et lecteurs de livres pornographiques au XVIIIe siècle* (Aix-en-Provence: Alinéa, 1991).

Kavanagh, Thomas M., *Enlightened Pleasures: Eighteenth-Century France and the New Epicureanism* (New Haven, CT: Yale University Press, 2010).

Hunt, Lynn (ed.), *The Invention of Pornography: Obscenity and the Origins of Modernity, 1500–1800* (New York: Zone Books, 1993).

Miller, Nancy K., *The Heroine's Text: Readings in the French and English Novel, 1722–1782* (New York: Columbia University Press, 1980).

——— 'Libertinage and Feminism', in *Libertinage and Modernity*, ed. Catherine Cusset, special issue of *Yale French Studies*, 94 (1998), pp. 17–28.

——— *French Dressing: Women, Men and Ancién Régime Fiction* (London and New York: Routledge, 1995).

Saint-Amand, Pierre, *The Libertine's Progress: Seduction in the Eighteenth-Century French Novel*, trans. Jennifer Curtiss Gage (Hanover, NH, and London: University Press of New England, 1994).

Steintrager, James A., *The Autonomy of Pleasure: Libertines, License and Sexual Revolution* (New York: Columbia University Press, 2015).

Wynn, Thomas, 'Libertinage', in *The Cambridge History of French Literature*, eds. William Burgwinkle, Nicholas Hammond and Emma Wilson (Cambridge: Cambridge University Press, 2011), pp. 412–19.

Young, Paul J., *Seducing the Eighteenth-Century French Reader: Reading, Writing and the Question of Pleasure* (Aldershot: Ashgate, 2008).

GENERAL WORKS ON SADE

Allison, David B., Roberts, Mark S. and Weiss, Allen S. (eds), *Sade and the Narrative of Transgression* (Cambridge: Cambridge University Press, 1995).

Barthes, Roland, *Sade/Fourier/Loyola*, trans. Richard Miller (New York: Farrar, Straus and Giroux, 1976).

Beauvoir, Simone de, 'Must We Burn Sade?', trans. Annette Michelson, in Sade, *The 120 Days of Sodom and Other Writings*, trans. Austryn Wainhouse and Richard Seaver (New York: Grove Press, 1966); first published as 'Faut-il brûler Sade?' *Les Temps modernes*, 74 (December 1951), pp. 1002–1033, and 75 (January 1952), pp. 1197–230.

Carter, Angela, *The Sadeian Woman* (London: Virago Press, 1979).

Dworkin, Andrea, *Pornography: Men Possessing Women* (London: Women's Press, 1981)

Edmiston, William F., *Sade: Queer Theorist*, in *Studies on Voltaire and the Eighteenth Century*, 2013:03 (Oxford: Voltaire Foundation).

Frappier-Mazur, Lucienne, *Writing the Orgy: Power and Parody in Sade*, trans. Gillian C. Gill (Philadelphia, PA: University of Pennsylvania Press, 1996); first published as *Sade et l'écriture de l'orgie* (Paris: Nathan, 1991).

Laugaa-Traut, Françoise, *Lectures de Sade* (Paris: Armand Colin, 1973).

Le Brun, Annie, *Sade: A Sudden Abyss*, trans. Camille Naish (San Francisco: City Lights Books, 1991); first published as *Soudain un bloc d'abîme, Sade* (Paris: Pauvert, 1986).

McMorran, Will, 'The Sound of Violence: Listening to Rape in Sade', in *Representing Violence in France, 1760–1820*, ed. Thomas Wynn, *Studies on Voltaire and the Eighteenth Century*, 2013:10 (Oxford: Voltaire Foundation).

Parker, Kate and Sclippa, Norbert (eds), *Sade's Sensibilities* (Lewisburg, PA: Bucknell University Press, 2015).

Phillips, John, *Sade: The Libertine Novels* (London, and Sterling, VA: Pluto Press, 2001).

——— (ed.), *Sade and his Legacy*, special edition of *Paragraph*, 23.1 (2000).

Roger, Philippe, *Sade: la philosophie dans le pressoir* (Paris: Grasset, 1976).

St-Martin, Armelle, *De la médécine chez Sade: disséquer la vie, narrer la mort* (Paris: Champion, 2010).

Shattuck, Roger, *Forbidden Knowledge: From Prometheus to Pornography* (New York: St Martin's Press, 1996).

Thomas, Chantal, *Sade, la Dissertation et l'orgie*, 2nd edn. (Paris: Payot & Rivages, 2002).

Warman, Caroline, *Sade: From Materialism to Pornography*, in *Studies on Voltaire and the Eighteenth Century*, 2002:01 (Oxford: Voltaire Foundation).

Wynn, Thomas, *Sade's Theatre: Pleasure, Vision, Masochism*, in *Studies on Voltaire and the Eighteenth Century*, 2007:02 (Oxford: Voltaire Foundation).

ON *THE 120 DAYS OF SODOM*

Cryle, Peter M., 'Taking Sade Serially: *Les Cent vingt journées de Sodome*', *SubStance*, 20.1, issue 64 (1991), pp. 91–113.

DeJean, Joan E., 'Inside the Sadean Fortress: *Les 120 journées de Sodome*', in *Literary Fortifications: Rousseau, Laclos, Sade* (Princeton, NJ: Princeton University Press, 1984), pp. 263–326.

Fradinger, Moira, 'Riveted by the Voice: The Sadean City at Silling', *French Forum*, 30.2 (Spring 2005), pp. 49–66.

McMorran, Will, 'Behind the Mask? Sade and the *Cent vingt journées de Sodome*', *Modern Language Review*, 108.4 (2013), pp. 1121–34.

Sauvage, Emmanuelle, *L'œil de Sade: Lecture des tableaux dans Les Cent vingt journées de Sodome et les trois Justine* (Paris: Honoré Champion, 2007).

Tort, Michel, 'L'effet Sade,' *Tel Quel*, 28 (1967), pp. 66–83.

Translators' Note

This translation is based on Maurice Heine's edition of *Les 120 journées de Sodome* (Paris: Stendhal et Cie, 1931–5). This was the second edition of the novel, following the sexologist Iwan Bloch's inaugural edition of 1904, and the last to be based on the original scroll. No subsequent editors, including Jean-Jacques Pauvert, Gilbert Lely and Michel Delon, have ever had access to the scroll, and all have chosen to offer modernized and corrected versions of the Heine text. Ever since the 1950s, readers of the *120 Days* have thus encountered versions of the novel that are rather more polished and refined than the text that Heine's transcription of the scroll reveals – versions in which the punctuation is elegant, the paragraphing consistent, abbreviations are given in full, missing words are added, and all numbers are given as words. Arguably misled by this editorial taming of the original manuscript, some critics have even suggested recently that the *120 Days* is not an incomplete text after all, but a finished work. This translation, by contrast, aims to offer English readers an insight into Sade's text as it really is, rather than as it might have been – in other words as an incomplete and uncorrected draft, with all the little mistakes, clumsy repetitions, awkward phrasing and scribbled notes one would expect to find in any such draft. One of Sade's notes at the end of Part One moreover suggests he had not even had time to reread what he had previously written, so all these signs of a text awaiting revisions that would never be carried out should come as no surprise.

To give the reader as much of a sense of the original as possible, we have kept corrections to a bare minimum. In contrast to recent French editions, for example, we have not written

numbers as words unless Sade has done so, nor changed the
Provençal term of address 'Milli' to the standard 'Mlle'. We have
also retained Sade's abbreviations for certain forms of address
('M.' and 'Mr.' for 'Monsieur', and 'Md.' for 'Madame'), and for
months of the year ('8^{ber}', '9^{ber}' and 'X^{ber}' for October, November
and December respectively). To avoid confusion we have,
however, made Sade's spelling of various names consistent (anno-
tating these inconsistences when they arise), and we have followed
Heine in correcting verb endings. The original punctuation of
the *120 Days* is very much that of an eighteenth-century draft:
haphazard, with very long sentences broken up by commas alone,
with no speech marks or question marks (and only the very
occasional semicolon or exclamation mark). We have tried to
convey a sense of these long – almost Proustian – sentences,
although this has required the introduction of semicolons, colons
and dashes to prevent syntactical collapse. The limited access to
the scroll we have enjoyed suggests that Sade – writing in a
minute script – was more concerned with creating a compact
manuscript than one with regular paragraphing; indeed, long
sections of the scroll seem to be written in a continuous script
with no discernible paragraphs whatsoever. We have generally
followed Heine's edition in this regard, but have introduced new
paragraphs to distinguish more clearly between the storytellers'
narrations and the conversations and actions that interrupt them.
Where missing words have been added to the original manuscript
we have indicated these using square brackets.

The 120 Days of Sodom
or
The School of Libertinage

[Introduction]

The extensive wars that Louis 14 had to wage throughout the course of his reign, while exhausting the state's finances and the people's resources, nevertheless uncovered the secret to enriching an enormous number of those leeches always lying in wait for the public calamities they provoke rather than quell in order to profit from them all the more. The end of this reign, so sublime in other respects, is perhaps one of the periods of the French Empire that saw the most of those hidden fortunes that dazzle only by an extravagance and debauchery that are just as well concealed. It was towards the end of this reign and shortly before the Regent had attempted, through that famous tribunal known by the name of the Chamber of Justice,[1] to force this multitude of tax-collectors to return their ill-gotten gains, that four among them[2] conceived the unique feat of debauchery we are about to describe. It would be wrong to assume that the commoners alone were responsible for this extortion: at its head were some very distinguished noblemen. The Duc de Blangis and his brother, the Bishop of ***, both of whom had made immense fortunes by it, constitute indisputable evidence that the nobility knew just as well as the rest how to line their pockets in this way; these two illustrious personages, intimately bound both in their pleasures and their business affairs to the renowned Durcet and the Président[3] de Curval, were the first to conceive of the debauchery whose story we are telling here, and, having discussed it with their two friends, these four comprised the cast of these famous orgies.

For more than six years these four libertines, brought together by the conformity of both their riches and their tastes, had imagined strengthening the ties between them by marriages that owed far more to debauchery than to any of the other motives that ordinarily inspire such ties – and these were the arrangements they made. The Duc de Blangis, widower to three wives of whom one had left him with two daughters, having recognized that the Président de Curval had some interest in marrying the elder of the two girls, despite the liberties he knew full well her father had taken with her – the Duc, as I say, conceived all at once of this triple marriage. 'You want Julie for your wife,' he said to Curval. 'I give her to you without hesitation and set only one condition: that you will not be jealous if she continues, even as your wife, to offer me the same favours she always has in the past; and moreover that you will support me in persuading our mutual friend Durcet to give me his daughter Constance, for whom I confess I have more or less the same feelings you have developed for Julie.' 'But,' said Curval, 'you realize no doubt that Durcet, as libertine as yourself . . .' 'I know all there is to know,' replied the Duc. 'Do such things come to an end at our age and with our way of thinking? Do you imagine I want a wife to be my mistress? I want her to satisfy my whims, to veil – to conceal – an infinite number of small, secret depravities the cloak of marriage hides marvellously well. In a word, I want her just as you want my daughter – do you think I'm unaware of your intentions and your desires? We fellow libertines, we take women to be our slaves – their position as wives renders them more submissive than mistresses, and you know the value of despotism in the pleasures we taste.'

At that moment Durcet entered, the two friends apprised him of their conversation and the tax-collector, enchanted by an overture that allowed him to declare the feelings he too had conceived for Adélaïde, the Président's daughter, accepted the Duc as his son-in-law on condition that he would become the same for Curval. The 3 marriages did not take long to settle, the dowries were immense and the conditions commensurate; the Président, as culpable as his two friends, had without putting Durcet off confessed his secret little affair with his own daughter; accordingly, the 3 fathers, each wishing to retain his rights, agreed in order to extend them still further that the three young ladies, uniquely bound both in assets and in name to their husbands, would as far as their bodies were concerned belong no more to any one of the three than to any other but equally to all of them, on pain of the most severe punishment should they dare to breach any of the conditions to which they were subject. They were on the cusp of concluding these arrangements when the Bishop of ***, already bound in his pleasures to his brother's two friends, proposed adding a fourth subject to their pact should they be willing to let her join the 3 others. This subject, the Duc's second daughter and thus the Bishop's niece, was more closely related to the latter gentleman than was commonly supposed: the Bishop had indulged in liaisons with his sister-in-law, and the two brothers knew without a doubt that the existence of this young person, who was named Aline, certainly owed far more to the Bishop than to the Duc. The Bishop, who had taken care of Aline since the cradle, had more-over not, as one may well imagine, seen her charms blossom without wishing to enjoy them himself; he was in this respect on a par with his fellow libertines and the asset he proposed for exchange was thus similarly damaged or degraded. However, as her graces and her tender youth surpassed those of her three companions, his offer was accepted without hesitation; the Bishop, like the 3 others, both ceded and retained his rights, and each of our four personages thus bound together became husband to four wives. It so followed from this arrangement, worth recapitulating for the reader's ease,

    that the Duc, Julie's father, married Constance, Durcet's daughter,

    that Durcet, Constance's father, married Adélaïde, the Président's daughter,

    that the Président, Adélaïde's father, married Julie, the Duc's eldest daughter,

    and that the Bishop, Aline's uncle and father, married the three others while offering Aline to his friends, notwithstanding the rights he continued to reserve over her. These happy nuptials were celebrated at a magnificent estate owned by the Duc in the Bourbonnais, and I leave it to our readers to imagine the orgies that took place there – the need to depict others precludes the pleasure we would have taken in depicting these. Upon their return the alliance between our four friends only gained in strength, and as it is important to introduce them properly, a short description of their lubricious arrangements will serve, it seems to me, to shed some light on the character of these lechers until the time comes for us to return to them one by one in their proper place and deal with them more fully.

This company had established a common purse that each of them took turns to administer for six months, but the funds of this purse, intended for pleasure alone, were immense. Their excessive wealth enabled the most extraordinary exploits on this score, and the reader should not be surprised to hear that two million a year were allocated to good cheer and lubricity alone.

Four renowned bawds dealing in women, and the same number of pimps dealing in men, had no other task than to find for them, both in the capital and in the provinces, all that either sex could offer the better to sate their sensuality. It was their custom to gather each week for four suppers in four different country houses located at four different points on the outskirts of Paris. At the first of these suppers, exclusively reserved for the pleasures of sodomy, only men were allowed. One would commonly see 16 young men aged between 20 and 30 whose enormous proportions allowed our four heroes, taking the part of women, to taste the most sensual of pleasures; these men were selected purely according to the size of their members, and it was more or less required for these to be too magnificently proportioned ever to have penetrated any woman – this was an essential condition and, as no expense was spared, it was very rare that it was not met. However, in order to taste all pleasures at once these 16 husbands were joined by the same number of much younger boys who were there to serve as wives. These were aged from 12 to 18, and in order to be admitted had to possess a freshness, countenance, grace, bearing, innocence, and candour far superior to anything our own brushes could paint. No woman was to be present at these male orgies in which all the most lascivious acts conceived by Sodom and Gomorrah were performed. The second supper was devoted to girls of polite society, who, obliged to give up their vain preening and the usual arrogance of their demeanour, were obliged because of the sums they had received to surrender to the most uncommon whims and even indignities that it often pleased the libertines to inflict on them. There were usually 12 of these girls present, and as Paris could not have provided enough variety of this kind as often as was required, such evenings alternated with others at which the same number of women of the right sort were drawn from the finest judicial and military families; there are more than four or five thousand women in Paris from one or the other of these classes who are obliged, by necessity or greed, to take part in these kinds of gatherings – all that is required is a little help to find them, and as our libertines were admirably well served they often made miraculous finds among this particular rank. No matter how respectable a lady might be, her total submission was required, and this libertinage, which never respects any limits, was considerably inflamed by inflicting atrocities and abominations upon those whom nature and social convention had apparently dictated should be spared such ordeals. They would arrive, they would have to submit to everything, and as our 4 villains all had a taste for the most depraved and flagrant debauchery, this total acquiescence to their desires was no trivial matter. The 3rd supper was devoted to the vilest, filthiest creatures one could ever meet. For those who know the excesses to which debauchery can lead this refined taste will seem perfectly straightforward: it is utterly sensual to wallow, so to speak, in the mire with creatures of this class; one discovers therein the most complete abandon, the most monstrous depravity, the most complete degradation, and these pleasures, compared either to those tasted the previous evening or to the distinguished creatures with whom they were tasted, add considerable spice to each of these excesses. As the debauchery on such evenings was more comprehensive, nothing that might add to its variety and piquancy was forgotten. A hundred whores would appear over the course of six hours and all too often fewer than a hundred would leave in one piece – but let us not get ahead of ourselves: this particular refinement requires details we are not yet ready to relate. The 4th supper was devoted to maidens. Only those between the ages of 7 and 15 were admitted. Their rank was of no importance: all that mattered was their countenance, which had to be alluring, and the certainty of their maidenhead, which had to be absolute – an unbelievable libertine refinement! It was not that they definitely wanted to pluck all these roses – indeed, how could they given they were always offered in groups of 20, and of our four libertines only two were in any condition to carry out such an act; of the other two, the tax-collector could no longer achieve any erection at all and the Bishop could only climax in a manner that may, admittedly, dishonour a virgin but that nevertheless leaves her quite intact. It mattered not: the 20 maidenheads were required regardless, and those that were not ravaged by the friends themselves fell prey in their presence to some equally debauched valets who were always kept close at hand for more than one reason. Aside from these four suppers there was another held every Friday, secretly and exclusively – a smaller but no doubt far more expensive affair. Only 4 young and noble ladies, abducted from their parents by hook or by crook, were admitted. Our libertines' wives almost always took part in these orgies, and their extreme submission, their efforts and their ministrations added yet more piquancy to the occasion. As regards the fare offered at these suppers it goes without saying that it was as refined as it was plentiful: none of these meals cost less than ten thousand *francs*, and all the most rare and exquisite delicacies that France and foreign climes had to offer were brought to the table; the same elegance and abundance applied to the wines and liqueurs, while the fruits of all seasons could be found there even in winter; we may affirm in a word that not even the table of the greatest monarch on earth was served with such opulence and magnificence. Let us retrace our steps and paint as best we can for the reader each of these four characters in detail – not to flatter them, nor to seduce or captivate, but with the simple brushstrokes of Nature, who despite all her disorderliness is often quite sublime, even when she is at her most depraved. For, dare we say in passing, if crime does not possess the same delicacy one finds in virtue, is it not more sublime, does it not have a grandeur and sublimity that surpasses – and always will – virtue's monotone and effete attractions? Would you argue the utility of one rather than the other? Is it for us to scrutinize the laws of Nature, is it for us to judge whether or not, vice being as necessary to her as virtue, she inspires in us an equal penchant for one or the other, according to her respective needs? But let us continue.

The Duc de Blangis, master at 18 years old of an already immense fortune, and one which he greatly increased later through his extortions, encountered all the difficulties that beset a young man of wealth and influence who need deny himself nothing: almost always in such cases the measure of one's powers becomes that of one's vices, and one denies oneself all the less when one is able to procure everything with ease. Had the Duc received from Nature some primitive qualities, perhaps these would have made up for the dangers of his position, but this bizarre Mother, who sometimes seems to conspire with Fortune for the latter to favour all the vices she gives to certain individuals from whom she expects very different efforts than those that virtue implies, and because [she] needs these just as she needs the others – Nature, as I say, in singling out Blangis for immense wealth had endowed him with every inclination and inspiration required to abuse them. As well as a very dark and wicked mind, she had given him a most malevolent and implacable soul, together with irregular tastes and whims that inspired the terrifying libertinage to which the Duc was so singularly inclined. Born deceitful, obdurate, imperious, barbaric, selfish, as extravagant in his pleasures as he was miserly when it came to doing any good, a liar, a glutton, a drunkard, a coward, given to sodomy, incest, murder, arson and theft – not a single virtue compensated for all these vices. Indeed it was not just that he revered no virtues, but that he regarded them with horror, and was often heard to say that to be truly happy in this world a man had not just to give himself to every vice but always to refuse himself a single virtue, and that it was not just a question of always doing evil but also of never doing good. 'There are many people,' the Duc said, 'who are driven to evil only when their passion drives them to it; once returned from their waywardness, their tranquil soul calmly resumes the path of virtue, and thus spending their life flitting from doubt to misdeed and misdeed to remorse, they end their days no closer to knowing exactly what part they played on this earth. Such individuals,' he continued, 'must be unhappy – always drifting, always irresolute, their entire life is spent despising in the morning what they did the previous evening. Quite sure they will repent of the pleasures they taste, they tremble in allowing themselves these delights, so that they become at once virtuous in crime and criminal in virtue. My firmer character,' added our hero, 'will never deny itself in that way: I never hesitate in my choices, and as I am always sure to find pleasure in those I make, remorse will never dull their appeal; steadfast in the principles I formed in my tender youth, I always act in accordance with them; they have revealed to me the emptiness and nullity of virtue; I loathe it and shall never be caught returning to it; these principles have convinced me that vice alone allows man to experience that moral and physical vibration which is the source of the most sensual delights – I surrender myself to it. From an early age I set myself above the monstrous fantasies of religion, being perfectly convinced that the existence of the creator is a revolting absurdity in which not even children believe any more; there is no need for me to restrain my tastes in order to please Him, it is from Nature that I received these tastes, and I should offend her by resisting them – if they are wicked, it is because they serve her purposes. In her hands I am nothing but a machine for her to operate as she wishes, and there is not a single one of my crimes that fails to serve her; the greater her need, the more she spurs me on – I should be a fool to resist her. Only the law stands in my way, but I defy it – my gold and my influence place me beyond the reach of those crude scales meant only for the common people.' Were one to object to the Duc that all men nonetheless had notions of what was just and unjust that could only have come from Nature, as these ideas were found in all peoples and even among the uncivilized,[4] he would affirm that these notions were only ever relative, that the strongest always considered just what the weakest regarded as unjust, and if these two were to change places they would also change their ways of thinking. The Duc concluded from this that nothing was truly just other than that which gave pleasure, and nothing was unjust except that which caused pain: that in taking one hundred *louis* from a man's pocket, he was doing something very just for himself, even though the man he had robbed would surely view this act quite differently; that as all these ideas were simply arbitrary, anyone who allowed himself to be bound by them was nothing but a fool. It was by reasoning of this kind that the Duc justified all his crimes, and because his was the sharpest of wits his arguments seemed irrefutable. Modelling his conduct on his philosophy, the Duc had since the first flush of youth unreservedly abandoned himself to the most shameful and extraordinary excesses; his father, dying young and leaving him, as I have said, master of an immense fortune, nevertheless stipulated that the young man was to let his mother receive the benefit of a great part of this fortune for the rest of her days. A condition of this kind soon began to rankle with Blangis: and as this scoundrel saw poison as the only way around it, he promptly decided to make use of it. But this traitor, only just starting out on his career of vice, did not dare take action himself: he enlisted one of his sisters, with whom he was living in criminal intimacy, to execute the plan, giving her to understand that if she succeeded he would give her a share of the fortune this death would bring him. But the young lady was horrified by this proposal, and the Duc, seeing that his ill-confided secret would perhaps be betrayed, decided there and then to condemn the very person he had intended to be his accomplice to the same fate as his victim; he brought them both to one of his estates, from which the two unfortunates never returned. Nothing is as encouraging as a first crime that goes unpunished. After this trial, the Duc broke free from all restraints: if anyone showed the least opposition to his desires, poison was employed at once; from murders of necessity he soon moved on to murders of sensuality; he conceived that wretched vice that makes us find pleasure in the sorrows of others; he sensed that a violent blow dealt to any adversary triggers in the mass of our nerves a vibration that, by exciting the animal spirits flowing through the concavity of those nerves, forces them against the erectile nerves to create from this tremor something known as a lubricious sensation. Consequently he began to commit rapes and murders solely according to a principle of debauchery and libertinage, just as another man, to arouse these same passions, would content himself with frequenting whores. At 23 years of age, he and three of his companions in

vice, whom he had indoctrinated with his philosophy, banded
together to hold up a public coach on the open road, rape the
male and female travellers alike, kill them afterwards, and seize
the money, which they certainly did not need; all three[5] were
then to attend the ball at the Opéra that very night to secure
their alibi. This crime was executed only too well: two charming
young ladies were raped and slaughtered in their mother's arms;
countless other horrors were also committed of which no one
dared suspect him. Weary of a charming wife given him by his
father before his death, the young Blangis did not delay in sending her to join the spirits of his mother, his sister and all his other
victims so that he could marry a girl who was quite wealthy
though publicly disgraced, and whom he knew without doubt
to be his brother's mistress – this was the mother of Aline, a
character in our novel whom we have mentioned above. This
second wife was soon sacrificed like the first, and was replaced
by a third, who was soon treated like the second; rumour had
it that the immensity of his build had killed all his wives, and
because this tall story was indeed accurate at least in its grasp
of proportion, the Duc allowed this conjecture to take root in
order to veil the truth. This terrifying colossus did indeed resemble Hercules or a centaur: the Duc was five feet eleven inches
tall, with such strong and powerful limbs, such sturdy joints,
such supple sinews . . . Add to this a masculine and proud face,
very large black eyes, handsome brown eyebrows, an aquiline
nose, beautiful teeth, an air of health and vigour, broad shoulders, a substantial yet trim frame, splendid thighs, superb
buttocks, the finest legs in the world, an iron will, the strength
of a horse, hung like a mule, astonishingly hirsute, gifted with
the ability to spill his sperm as often as he wished in a day, even
at the age of 50 as he was then, an almost continually erect
member precisely 8 inches around by 12 inches long, and you
will have as accurate a portrait of the Duc de Blangis as if you
had drawn it yourself. But if this masterpiece of Nature was
violent in his desires, what became of him – good God! – when
the intoxication of his senses triumphed over him: he was no
longer a man, but a raging tiger – pity the poor soul then serving
his passions! Dreadful roars, atrocious blasphemies burst from

his swollen chest, flames seemed to shoot from his eyes, he
frothed at the mouth, neighed like a horse – one would have
taken him for the very god of lubricity himself; however he took
his pleasure, his hands would inevitably stray, and on more than
one occasion he was seen to strangle a woman to death at the
very moment of his perfidious climax. Once recovered, the most
complete insouciance towards the abominations he had just
allowed himself soon succeeded his delirium, and from this indifference, from this kind of apathy, new sparks of sensuality were
soon ignited. In his youth the Duc had come as many as 18 times
in a single day without ever seeming any more exhausted after
the final spurt than he had after the first. Seven or 8 times in a
row still posed him no difficulty, despite his fifty years. For
almost twenty-five years he had indulged in passive sodomy and
he withstood such assaults with the same vigour he would show
when inflicting them actively himself a moment later whenever
it pleased him to change role. For a wager he had withstood as
many as 55 assaults in the same day. Gifted as we have said with
prodigious strength, he could pin a girl down with one hand in
order to rape her – he had proved this several times. One day
he wagered he could suffocate a horse between his legs, and the
beast breathed its last at the very moment he had predicted. His
excesses at the dining table surpassed, if that is possible, those
of the bedroom: it was impossible to imagine what became of
the immense amount of food he devoured; he regularly ate three
meals a day, all of which were long and plentiful, always accompanied by ten bottles of burgundy; he had in the past drunk up
to thirty and would wager against anyone that he could drink
as many as 50, but as his drunkenness resembled his passions,
as soon as the liqueurs and wines had inflamed his soul he would
fly into a rage – he would have to be tied down. And for all that
– who would have thought it? – as the soul so often fails to
match the strength of the body, a resolute child would have
terrified this colossus, and when he could no longer rely on
cunning or treachery to dispatch his enemy, he became meek
and cowardly, and the very thought of the most innocuous
confrontation, if fought on equal terms, would have made him
flee to the ends of the earth. He had nevertheless followed

convention and fought one or two campaigns, but had so dishonoured himself that he had left the service immediately after;
defending his depravity with as much wit as brazenness, he
openly declared that, as cowardice was simply the desire for
self-preservation, it was perfectly impossible for reasonable
people to condemn it as a failing.

Retaining absolutely the same moral traits and adapting them
to a physical constitution infinitely inferior to the one just
traced, one had the very portrait of the Bishop of ***, brother
of the Duc de Blangis. The same darkness in his soul, the same
penchant for crime, the same contempt for religion, the same
atheism, the same treachery, with a more supple and cunning
wit, however, and a greater skill for plunging his victims into
misfortune, but a slender and delicate waist, a small and slim
body, faltering health, very delicate nerves, greater refinement
in the pursuit of pleasure, mediocre faculties, a most ordinary
member – small even, but containing himself so expertly and
always spilling so little that his endlessly inflamed imagination
allowed him to taste pleasure as frequently as did his brother;
in addition, sensations of such delicacy, nerves of such prodigious susceptibility, that he would often swoon the moment he
came and would almost always lose consciousness as he did so.
He was 45 years old, with a very fine physiognomy, rather pretty
eyes, but a revolting mouth and revolting teeth, a pale, hairless
body, a small but shapely arse, and a prick 5 inches around by
6 inches long. An idolater of active and passive sodomy, but of
the latter above all, he spent his life being buggered, and this
pleasure, which never requires a great expenditure of energy,
was perfectly suited to the paltriness of his powers; we shall
speak elsewhere of his other tastes. As regards those of the
dining table, he took them almost as far as his brother but added
a little more sensuality to them. His Lordship, as much a scoundrel as his older brother, moreover possessed qualities that
doubtless led him to rival the renowned exploits of the hero we
have just described. We shall content ourselves with citing one
of these – it will suffice to show the reader what such a man
was capable of, and what he could and would do once he had
done what we are about to read.

One of his friends, an extremely wealthy man, had once had an affair with a young noblewoman with whom he had had two children, a girl and a boy; he had never been able to marry her, however, and the young lady had become another man's wife. This unfortunate woman's lover died young, but in possession nonetheless of an immense fortune; as he did not care for any of his relatives, he decided to leave all his worldly goods to the two wretched fruits of his affair. On his deathbed he confided his plan to the Bishop and entrusted him with these two immense bequests, which he divided into two equal trusts and which he commended to the Bishop, charging him with the education of these two orphans and with giving each of them their due upon reaching the age prescribed by law; at the same time he enjoined the prelate to invest his pupils' funds so as to double their capital; at the same time he confirmed his intention to leave the mother in eternal ignorance of what he was doing for her children and insisted that this matter should absolutely never be broached with her; these arrangements settled, the dying man closed his eyes, and his Lordship found himself master of almost a million in banknotes, and two children. The scoundrel did not take long to make up his mind: the dying man had spoken to him alone, the mother knew nothing about it, the children were only four or 5 years old; he publicly declared that his dying friend had left his worldly goods to the poor, and the very same day the rogue seized them for himself. But bringing ruin on these two unfortunate children was not enough: the Bishop, who never committed one crime without immediately conceiving another, went, bearing proof of his friend's approval, to remove the children from the remote boarding school where they were being raised, and placed them with people in his employ, resolving at once to have them both serve his perfidious pleasures. He waited until they were 13 years old: the little boy reached this age first, he made use of him, bent him to all his debauches and as he was extremely pretty had his way with him for a week. But the little girl did not turn out so well: she was very ugly when she reached the prescribed age, without this in the least hindering our scoundrel's lubricious frenzy, however; his desires sated, he feared that if he were to let these children live they might uncover something of the secret that concerned them; he took them to one of his brother's estates and, confident of rediscovering in a new crime the sparks of lubricity his pleasures had extinguished, he sacrificed them both to his ferocious passions, and accompanied their deaths with such piquant and cruel scenes that his sensuality was reborn amidst the torments he inflicted on them. This secret is unfortunately all too true, and there is no libertine even slightly steeped in vice who does not know the hold murder has over the senses and how sensually it determines a climax; it is a truth with which the reader should be forearmed before embarking upon a work that will go to such lengths to elaborate this system.

Unconcerned thereafter about any eventualities, his Lordship returned to Paris to enjoy the fruits of his crimes, and without the slightest remorse at having betrayed the intentions of a man no longer in a position to feel either pain or pleasure.

The Président de Curval was the most senior member of this company: almost 60 years of age, and singularly worn down by debauchery, he was barely more than a skeleton; he was tall, wizened, gaunt, with sunken and dimmed eyes, a livid and sickly mouth, a prominent chin, a long nose. As hirsute as a satyr, with a flat back and flabby buttocks that sagged so much they seemed more like two dirty rags flopping over his thighs – the skin there so withered by lashes of the whip one could wind it around one's finger without his noticing; in the middle of all this one could see, without having to spread the cheeks apart, an immense orifice whose enormous diameter, smell and colour made it resemble a chamber pot rather than an arsehole; and, to crown it all, this swine of Sodom's little habits included always leaving this part in such a filthy state that one could see without fail a layer of muck two inches thick around it. Beneath a belly as wrinkly as it was livid and flabby, one could discern amidst a forest of hair a tool which in its erect state might have been about 8 inches long by 7 around, but this state was now most rare, and a frenzied series of acts was required to induce it; this still occurred two or three times a week, however, and the Président would then indiscriminately screw all holes, though that of a young boy's backside was infinitely the most precious to him. The Président had had himself circumcised so that the head of his prick was never covered – a ceremony that greatly enhances pleasure and to which all voluptuaries should submit, but one of its purposes is to keep this part as clean as possible: this was very far from being the case with Curval for, as filthy in this part as in the other, his unhooded head – already naturally very large – gained at least an inch in circumference. Equally unclean about the rest of his body, the Président, whose tastes were at least as squalid as his body, was a character whose rather malodorous presence might not have been to everyone's liking, but his fellow libertines were not the sort to be scandalized by such trifles and the subject was never even broached with him. Few men had been as cavalier and as debauched as the Président, but completely jaded, utterly torpid, all he was left with now was the depravity and turpitude of libertinage. More than three hours of excess, and of the vilest excess at that, were required to produce a sensual tingling in him; as for his climax, though he experienced this far more often than an erection and almost once a day, it was, however, so hard to come by, or only came through such peculiar and often such cruel or unclean acts, that those serving his pleasures would often give up, and this would spark in him a kind of lubricious rage, the effects of which would sometimes succeed better than his own efforts. Curval was so utterly engulfed in the mire of vice and libertinage that he had become incapable of speaking in any other terms – he always had the filthiest expressions on his lips and in his heart, and he energetically interspersed these with blasphemies and curses inspired by the genuine horror he shared with his fellow libertines for everything pertaining to religion; this disorder of mind, further increased by the almost continuous state of drunkenness he liked to maintain, had for some years given him an air of imbecility and torpor that was, he claimed, his dearest pleasure. Born as much a glutton as a drunkard, he alone could vie with the Duc, and in the course of this story we shall see them both perform feats of this kind that will undoubtedly astonish our most celebrated gourmands. Curval had not fulfilled the duties of his office for the last 10 [years] – not only was he no longer in any fit state to do so any more, but even if he had been I think he would have been asked to recuse himself for the rest of his life.

Curval had led a very libertine life – every kind of excess was familiar to him – and those who knew him well strongly suspected he owed his immense fortune entirely to two or three despicable murders. In any event, the following story distinctly suggests that this kind of excess was apt to move him profoundly, and it is to this adventure, which unfortunately caused something of a scandal, that he owed his banishment from the courts; we shall report it here to give the reader an idea of his character.

In the vicinity of Curval's mansion there lived an unfortunate porter who, father to a charming young girl, was ridiculous enough to be a man of feeling: twenty times already messages of all sorts had arrived aiming to corrupt this poor man and his wife with proposals regarding their young daughter – all of which failed to shake their resolve; and Curval, responsible for these missives, and whose irritation only increased as their refusals mounted, was at a loss as to how to have his way with the young girl and subject her to his libidinous whims – until it dawned on him quite simply to get the daughter into his bed by having her father broken on the wheel.[6] The plan was no sooner conceived than executed: two or three rascals in the Président's pay intervened, and by the end of the month the unfortunate porter was embroiled in an imaginary crime that appeared to have been committed at his door and that led him directly to the Conciergerie's dungeons;[7] as one may well imagine, the Président soon took charge of this [case] and as he did not wish it to drag on. Thanks to his mischief and money, within three days the wretched porter was condemned to be broken alive on the wheel, without ever having committed any crime other than wanting to defend his honour and to protect that of his daughter. At that point the solicitations resumed – the mother was summoned, she was told that she alone could save her husband, that if she were to satisfy the Président, then he would certainly wrest her husband from the dreadful fate awaiting him. There was no time to waver, the wife sought advice – it was known full well to whom she would turn, their counsel was bought, and they replied without equivocation that she should demur not a moment longer. In tears, the wretched woman herself brings her daughter to her judge's feet: he promises everything they could hope for, but had no intention of keeping his word – he not only feared that if he were to keep it, the reprieved husband would cause a scandal when he saw the price placed on his life, but the scoundrel took an even more piquant pleasure in obtaining what he wanted without having to keep his word. He then indulged his imagination with some acts of villainy which fuelled his perfidious lubricity, and this is how he went about investing the scene with the greatest possible infamy and piquancy. His mansion faced a spot where criminals are sometimes executed in Paris, and as the crime had been committed in that district, he managed to arrange for the execution to be carried out in this very square; at the appointed time, he had the wretch's wife and daughter brought to his house; all the windows overlooking the square were shuttered up so that nothing could be seen of the events unfolding below from the rooms where he was holding his victims. The scoundrel, who knew the exact time of the execution, chose that very moment to deflower the young girl in her mother's arms and everything was arranged with such skill and precision that the scoundrel came in the girl's arse at the very moment her father expired. As soon as the deed was done – 'Come see,' he said to his two princesses as he opened a window on to the square, 'come see how I have kept my word to you.' And the poor women saw, the first her father, the second her husband, expiring under the executioner's cudgel. They both collapsed in a faint, but Curval had planned everything: this fainting was their mortal agony – they had both been poisoned and never opened their eyes again. For all the care he took to cloak this whole affair in the shadows of the deepest of mysteries, some of it came to light nonetheless: the women's deaths passed unnoticed, but he was strongly suspected of prevarication in the husband's case; his motive was known in part, and all this ultimately led to his retirement. From that moment on Curval, no longer obliged to keep up appearances, plunged headlong into a fresh ocean of crimes and vices – he had victims sought from all around to be sacrificed to the perversity of his tastes; through an atrocious refinement of cruelty, and one which is nonetheless easy to understand, it was above all among the ranks of the most unfortunate that he enjoyed unleashing the effects of his perfidious rage. He had several women searching day and night in garrets and hovels for all the most forlorn creatures that penury had to offer, and under the pretext of offering succour he either poisoned them, which was one of his most delightful pastimes, or lured them to his house, where he sacrificed them to the perversity of his tastes. Men, women, children – they all served his perfidious rage and this led him to commit excesses that would have sent his head to the scaffold a thousand times were it not for his influence and his gold, which saved him from this fate a thousand times. One may well imagine that such an individual cared no more for religion than his two fellow libertines; no doubt he despised it just as intensely, but in the past he had done more to root it out from people's hearts, for, using the wit he once had to write against it, he was the author of several works whose effects had been prodigious, and these successes, which he would constantly recall, were still among his dearest pleasures.

The more we multiply the objects of our arousal . . . *Place Durcet's portrait here as it is in notebook 18 bound in pink, then having finished the portrait with these words from the notebooks . . . the impotent years of childhood, resume thus:*[8]

Durcet is 53 years of age: he is small, short, fat, very stocky, with a pleasant and fresh face, very fair skin, his whole body and particularly his hips and buttocks exactly like a woman's; his arse is fresh, fleshy, firm and plump, but gapes excessively from habitual sodomy; his prick is extraordinarily small, barely 2 inches around by 4 inches long; he absolutely never gets hard any more, his climaxes are rare and very painful, far from plentiful and always preceded by spasms which throw him into a kind of frenzy that drives him to crime; he has a woman's bust, a sweet and pleasant voice, and is most polite in society though his mind is at least as depraved as those of his fellow libertines; an old school friend of the Duc's, the two of them enjoy themselves together every day, and one of Durcet's great pleasures is to have his anus tickled by the Duc's enormous member.

These are, in a word, dear reader, the four scoundrels with whom I shall have you spend a few months – I have described them for you as best I can so that you may know them inside and out, and so that nothing should surprise you in the tale of their various excesses. It has been impossible for me to enter into the precise detail of their tastes – I would have ruined the interest and principal design of this work in divulging these to you. But as this tale takes its course, the reader will only have to follow them closely to discover their habitual little sins and the particular kind of sensual mania that appeals to each of them. For now all that can be said in broad terms is that they shared a taste for sodomy, that all four had themselves buggered regularly and that all four idolized arses. The Duc, however, due to the immensity of his build and no doubt out of cruelty rather than taste, still fucked cunts with the greatest pleasure, as did the Président on occasion albeit more rarely. As for the Bishop, he despised them so intensely that the very sight of them would have made him droop for 6 months; he had only ever fucked one in his life (his sister-in-law's) and this in order to have a child who might one day provide him with the pleasures of incest – we have seen how he succeeded in this. As regards Durcet, he idolized the arse with at least as much ardour as the Bishop, but enjoyed it rather more incidentally: his favoured assaults were aimed at a 3rd temple. This mystery will be unveiled in due course – let us complete the portraits essential to an understanding of this work by now giving our reader an idea of the four wives of these respectable husbands.

What a contrast! Constance, the Duc's wife and Durcet's daughter, was a tall, slim woman, pretty as a picture and as shapely as if the Graces had delighted in beautifying her, but the elegance of her figure in no way diminished her freshness, she was no less fleshy and plump, and the most delicious curves, visible beneath skin whiter than a lily, led one to imagine Cupid himself had fashioned her. Her face was a touch long, her features exceptionally noble, more majesty than sweetness and more grandeur than finesse; her eyes were large, black and full of fire, her mouth extremely small and adorned with the most beautiful teeth imaginable, her tongue was slender, narrow, exquisitely pink and her breath sweeter even than the scent of a rose. She had a full, well-rounded bust, as white and firm as alabaster; her exceptionally curvaceous loins led down delectably to the most perfectly and exquisitely shaped arse that Nature had produced in a long while – it was perfectly round, not too large but firm, white, plump and parting only to reveal the neatest, prettiest and most delicate little hole; a hint of the daintiest pink suffused her arse, that charming sanctuary of the sweetest lubricious pleasures. But, good God! How fleetingly it retained all these charms: four or five of the Duc's assaults soon withered all these graces, and after her marriage Constance was soon little more than the image of a beautiful lily whose leaves have been stripped by the storm. Two round and perfectly sculpted thighs supported another temple, no doubt less delectable, but which offered the devotee so many charms that my quill would strive in vain to do justice to them. Constance was more or less a virgin when the Duc married her, and her father – the only man she had known – had, as we have said, left her utterly intact on that side. The most beautiful black hair, tumbling in natural curls over her shoulders and, if so desired, all the way to the pretty down of the same colour that shaded this voluptuous little cunt, added a further adornment it would have been wrong of me to omit, and lent this angelic creature of around 22 years of age all the charms Nature can bestow upon a woman. Constance combined all these graces with a discerning and pleasant mind – nobler indeed than it should have been, given the sad situation in which fate had placed her, for she felt it in all its horror, and she would doubtless have been much happier had her powers of perception been less refined. Durcet, who had raised her more as a courtesan than as his daughter, and whose sole concern had been to provide her with talents rather than manners, had, however, never been able to destroy in her heart the principles of decency and virtue it had seemingly pleased Nature to engrave there. She had no religion, no one had ever spoken to her about it, she had never been allowed to observe its rites, but none of this had extinguished in her that humility, that natural modesty, which owes nothing to religion's monstrous fantasies and which, in a decent and sensitive soul, is so difficult to efface. She had never left her father's house, and the scoundrel had, since she was twelve years old, made her serve his depraved pleasures; she found those the Duc now tasted with her to be on an altogether different scale – her body was appreciably altered by this immense disparity, and the day after the Duc had sodomitically deflowered her, she fell dangerously ill: her rectum was thought to be completely perforated but her youth, her health and the effect of some salutary ointments soon restored the use of that forbidden path to the Duc, and the unfortunate Constance, compelled to inure herself to this daily torture (which was not the only one), made a full recovery and became accustomed to all his demands.

Adélaïde, Durcet's wife and the Président's daughter, was perhaps a superior beauty to Constance but of an entirely different type: she was twenty years of age, small, slim, extremely slender and delicate, pretty as a picture, with the most beautiful blonde hair one could ever hope to see; an alluring air of sensibility suffused her whole body and her face in particular, giving her the air of a heroine from a romance; her extraordinarily large eyes were blue – they conveyed tenderness and modesty all at once; two long, fine, yet strikingly shaped eyebrows adorned a forehead that was rather low, but of such nobility and grace one would have [thought] it the very temple of modesty; her narrow nose, somewhat pinched at the top, descended imperceptibly into a semi-aquiline shape; her lips were thin, bordered by the most vibrant pink, and her rather large mouth (this was the only flaw in her heavenly physiognomy) opened to reveal 32 pearls that Nature appeared to have sown amidst roses; she had a rather long, beautifully turned neck, and she would quite naturally always tilt her head over her right shoulder, especially when she was listening – but what graces this alluring pose lent her! She had a small bust, perfectly round, very firm and pert, but there was barely enough for a handful – it was like two little apples a playful Cupid had brought from his mother's garden; her chest was a little compressed, and was also very delicate; her belly was as smooth as satin; a little blonde crotch unadorned with much down served as a peristyle to the temple where Venus seemed to demand her tribute – this temple was so narrow that not even a finger could be inserted without making her cry out, and yet, thanks to the Président, the poor child had not been a virgin for almost two

lustres[9] on either this side or that delightful side we have yet to
trace. What charms did this second temple possess! The curve
of her loins! The shape of her buttocks! That combination of
whiteness and rosiness! But taken as a whole all this was on the
small side: delicate in all her proportions, Adélaïde was the
sketch rather than the model of beauty – it seemed that Nature
had wanted merely to suggest in Adélaïde what she had
announced so majestically in Constance. Were one to part this
delectable arse, a rosebud would offer itself to you that Nature
wished to show in all its freshness and in the most tender of
pinks – but how tight! How small! It was only with immeasurable effort that the Président had prevailed, and he had been
able to renew these assaults only two or three times ever since;
Durcet, not so demanding, troubled her less on this score, but
since becoming his wife how many other cruel surrenders, how
many other dangerous concessions had been required to earn
this one small kindness, and besides, offered up to the four
libertines according to the arrangements made, what cruel
assaults had she yet to bear – both of the kind Durcet spared
her and all the rest. Adélaïde had the sensibility her face suggested
– that is to say, straight out of a romance: the places she sought
with the greatest pleasure were solitary and there she would
often shed tears despite herself – tears which we do not study
enough and which a sense of foreboding seems to wrest from
Nature. She had recently lost a friend whom she idolized and
this terrible loss perpetually haunted her imagination: as she
knew her father so well, and understood just how far he took
his waywardness, she was convinced her young friend had fallen
victim to the Président's wickedness (for he had never been able
to persuade her to grant him certain things) and this was not
implausible; she imagined she would suffer much the same fate
one day, and this was far from improbable. The Président had
not in her case taken the same precautions in matters of religion
as Durcet had with Constance – he had let this prejudice take
root and thrive, imagining that his pronouncements and books
would easily destroy it. He was mistaken – religion provides
sustenance for a soul of the complexion of Adélaïde's: no matter
how much the Président preached, and no matter how much he

made her read, the young lady remained devout, and all these excesses which she did not share, which she despised, and of which she was the victim, in no way disabused her of the monstrous fantasies that were the only happiness in her life; she would hide herself away to pray to God, she would steal away to fulfil her Christian duties, and would inevitably be very severely punished by either her father or her husband as soon as one or the other noticed.

Adélaïde suffered all this with patience, quite convinced that one day the heavens would reward her. Her temperament was, in any case, as gentle as her sensibility, and her beneficence – one of the virtues for which her father most despised her – bordered on excess. Curval, incensed against the vile ranks of the destitute, sought only to humiliate them, to demean them still further or to find victims among them; his generous daughter, by contrast, would have gone without sustenance herself in order to provide for the poor and she had often been seen secretly taking them all the sums intended for her pleasures. In the end Durcet and the Président reprimanded and disciplined her so thoroughly that they corrected her of this error and utterly deprived her of the means to reoffend; Adélaïde, with only tears to offer the wretched, would nonetheless weep over their misfortunes and her impotent but still sensitive heart could not refrain from virtue. One day she learnt that a poor woman was about to prostitute her daughter to the Président because her desperate plight left her no choice: the delighted lecher was already preparing himself for one of his favourite pleasures; Adélaïde secretly had one of her dresses sold, sent the money immediately to the mother and by means of this modest succour, and some sermon or other, dissuaded her from the crime she was about to commit; when the Président discovered this (as his daughter was yet to marry) he was driven to such violence against her that she spent 2 weeks in bed, but none of this could put a stop to the actions inspired by this sensitive soul's tender impulses.

Julie, the Président's wife and the Duc's eldest daughter, would have eclipsed the two previous ladies had it not been for what in many people's eyes would be a decisive failing, but which may perhaps have been the only reason for Curval's passion for her,

so true it is that the effects of the passions are inconceivable and
that their waywardness – the fruit of disgust and satiety – is only
matched by their excess. Julie was tall, shapely, although very
fleshy and very plump, with the most beautiful brown eyes possible, a charming nose, striking and graceful features, the loveliest
chestnut hair, a white and delightfully chubby body, an arse that
might have served as the model to the one sculpted by Praxiteles,[10] a warm, narrow cunt as pleasurable as this spot can be,
fine legs and charming feet, but the most appallingly adorned
mouth, the most rotten teeth, and an inveterate filthiness about
the rest of her body and particularly about the two temples of
lubricity, which no one – I repeat – no one other than the Président (subject to the same failings himself and doubtless
enamoured of them), absolutely no one else would have put up
with despite all of Julie's charms. But as for Curval, he was mad
about her: his most divine pleasures were plucked from this
stinking mouth – kissing it sent him into delirium and, far from
reproaching her for her natural uncleanliness, on the contrary
he egged her on and ultimately succeeded in making her bid a
final farewell to water. Julie combined these failings with doubtless less unpleasant ones: she was very greedy, she had a tendency
to drunkenness, and scant virtue, and I believe that if she had
dared, whoring would have held few fears for her. Brought up
by the Duc in total abandonment of principles and morals, she
adopted much of his philosophy and, all in all, she doubtless
had what it took to be a subject, but by a still stranger effect of
libertinage it often happens that a woman who shares our failings gratifies us far less in our pleasures than one who possesses
only virtues: the first resembles us, and is not scandalized by us;
the second is terrified and that certainly offers an added charm.
The Duc, despite the enormity [of] his build, had already had
his way with his daughter, though he had been obliged to wait
until she was 15 years of age and even so had not been able to
prevent her from being seriously injured by this exploit – and
so much so that, wishing to marry her off, he had been obliged
to put an end to these delights and to content himself with
pleasures that were less dangerous, if no less exhausting. Julie
fared little better with the Président, whose prick as we know

was very large, and besides, as unclean as she may have been from her own neglect, she simply could not bear the foulness of the debauchery so beloved by the Président, her dear husband.

Aline, Julie's younger sister and in truth the Bishop's daughter, was very far from sharing her sister's habits, character and failings. The youngest of the four, she was barely 18 years of age; she had a lively little physiognomy – fresh and almost mischievous, with a dainty upturned nose, vivacious and expressive brown eyes, a delectable mouth, a fine figure though not very tall, chubby, a somewhat dark but soft and fine complexion, a rather fat but shapely arse, the most voluptuous pair of buttocks a libertine could hope to see, a pretty, brown crotch, the cunt a little low – *à l'anglaise*, as they say – but perfectly narrow, and when it was offered up to the company she was very much a maiden; she still was at the time of the expedition whose story we are now writing and we shall see how these first fruit were destroyed. As regards her arse, the Bishop had been quietly enjoying it every day for the last 8 years, but without inspiring a taste for this in his dear daughter, who, despite her impish and lascivious air, only submitted out of obedience and had yet to show the slightest pleasure in joining in the abominations of which she was the daily victim. The Bishop had left her in profound ignorance: she barely knew how to read and write, and had absolutely no conception of religion; her native wit was childish, her replies were amusing, she played, loved her sister very much, utterly despised the Bishop and feared the Duc as she did fire itself; on her wedding day, when she saw herself naked and surrounded by 4 men, she wept, and yet did everything demanded of her, without pleasure and without petulance. She was abstemious, very clean and with no other failing than her considerable laziness – indifference reigned over her every act and over every aspect of her person, despite the air of vivacity promised in her eyes. She abhorred the Président almost as much as her uncle, and Durcet, who did not go easy on her, was nonetheless the only one who seemed not to revolt her in any way.

Such were the 8 principal characters with whom we shall have you live, my dear reader; it is now time to reveal to you the purpose of the singular pleasures the friends proposed for themselves.

It is accepted among true libertines that the sensations communicated by the organ of hearing excite more than any others and produce the most vivid impressions; consequently our four scoundrels, who wanted sensuality to flood their hearts as thoroughly and as deeply as it could penetrate, had to this end conceived of something rather peculiar.

The plan was, once they had first surrounded themselves with everything that could best satisfy the other senses through lubricity, to have in this setting all the different excesses of debauchery, all its branches, all its offshoots – in a word, and in the language of libertinage, all its passions described to them in order and in the greatest detail. One cannot imagine the degree to which men vary these when their imaginations are set ablaze: the difference between men – extreme in all their other manias, in all their other tastes – is even more marked in this particular sphere, and the man who could identify and describe these depravities would perhaps produce one of the finest works on customs one could ever hope to see, and perhaps one of the most interesting. First of all they therefore had to find subjects who could describe all these excesses, analyse them, elaborate them, detail them, graduate them, and invest all this with the appeal of a story. They consequently made the following decision: after countless searches and investigations, they found four women already past their prime, which is exactly what was needed, experience being the most essential thing here – four women, as I say, who, having spent their lives in the most excessive debauchery were well placed to give an exact account of all their findings. And as the friends had endeavoured to choose women gifted with a certain eloquence and with a turn of wit appropriate to what was required of them, once these four had shared and discussed their stories with each other they were able to include among their lives' adventures all the most remarkable excesses of debauchery – and ordered such that the first woman, for example, would include in the story of her life the 150 simplest passions and the least refined or most ordinary excesses; the second, within the same constraints, an equal number of more peculiar passions involving one or more men with several women; the third would likewise include in her story 150 of the most criminal manias – and the most outrageous to law, nature and religion; and since all these excesses lead to murder, and murders committed through libertinage vary infinitely (and with every different torment devised by the libertine's inflamed imagination), so the fourth was to combine the events of her life with the detailed account of 150 of these different tortures. Meanwhile our libertines, surrounded as I said earlier by their wives and then by other objects of all kinds, would listen, would become inflamed and – with either their wives or these different objects – would finally extinguish the blaze ignited by these storytellers. Nothing could be more sensual in this plan than the lascivious manner in which [it] was carried out, and it is this manner and these diverse tales that together will form this work – which in the light of this revelation I advise any devout individual to abandon at once if he does not wish to be scandalized, for he can see its plan is far from chaste and we venture to forewarn him that its execution will be even less so. As the four actresses concerned here play a most essential role in these memoirs, we believe ourselves obliged – even if we must beg the reader's indulgence – to paint their likeness: they will tell stories, they will act – would it be possible, given all this, to leave them unknown? Do not expect to find portraits of great beauties, though there were doubtless plans to make use of the bodies as well as the minds of these four creatures; it was nonetheless neither their charms nor their age that mattered here, just their wit and their experience, and it was in this respect impossible to be better served.

Md. Duclos was the name of the woman entrusted with the telling of the 150 simple passions: she was forty-eight years of age, still quite youthful, retaining much of her former beauty, with very beautiful eyes, very white skin and one of the finest and plumpest arses one could ever hope to see; a fresh and clean mouth, a magnificent bust and pretty brown hair, a large but high waist and the airs and graces of a high-class whore; she had spent, as we shall see, her life in places where she could freely study what she was about to relate, and one could tell she would set about her task with wit, skill and enthusiasm.

Md. Champville was a tall woman of around 50 years of age – slim, shapely, with the most sensual look in her eyes and bearing; a faithful follower of Sappho, as even her slightest movements, her simplest gestures and her merest words revealed – she had brought ruin on herself by keeping various women and, were it not for this taste, to which she had sacrificed almost everything she could earn about town, she would have been most comfortably off. She had been a common whore for a very long time and in recent years had gone on to assume the role of procuress, though she limited herself to a certain number of clients – all indisputable lechers of a certain age; she never entertained young men, and this prudent and lucrative conduct restored her finances a little. She had been blonde, but a wiser tint was beginning to colour her hair; her eyes were still very pretty – blue and delightfully expressive. Her mouth was beautiful, still fresh and with perfect teeth; no bust but a fine belly (she had never caused a port-wine stain),[11] a slightly raised mons and a clitoris that jutted out more than 3 inches when aroused – if she was tickled there she was sure to swoon before long and particularly if a woman provided this service; her arse was very flabby and worn, utterly slack and withered and so toughened by the libidinous habits her story will reveal that one could do whatever one wanted to it without her even noticing. One thing that was rather peculiar – and certainly very rare in Paris of all places – was that she was on this side as much a virgin as a girl fresh out of a convent, and perhaps if she had not hired herself out for this accursed expedition, and hired herself out to people who desired only extraordinary things and therefore found her appealing – perhaps, as I say, if it had not been for this expedition that peculiar virginity would have gone to the grave with her.

Madame Martaine, a stout matron of 52 years of age, very hale and hearty, blessed with the fattest and finest backside one could ever hope to find, offered an entirely contrary proposition: she had spent her life in sodomitical debauchery and had become so used to it indeed that she could taste pleasure only that way. As a natural deformity – her vagina was obstructed[12] – had prevented her from exploring other avenues, she had abandoned herself to this kind of pleasure, driven both by the impossibility of doing otherwise and by her first experiences; as a result she confined herself to this lubricious practice, for which she still had a delightful reputation – braving all, fearing none. Even the most monstrous tools caused her no alarm – indeed she preferred them, and the rest of these memoirs may well reveal her still valiantly fighting under the banners of Sodom like the most intrepid of buggers. She had quite elegant features, but an air of languor and ruin was beginning to wither her charms, and without her plumpness to sustain her, she might already have appeared very decrepit.

As for Madame Desgranges, she was vice and lechery incarnate: tall, thin, 56 years of age, pale and emaciated, lifeless eyes, dead lips, she was the very image of crime at death's door; she had once had brown hair – it had even been claimed she used to have a beautiful body, but before long she was little more than a skeleton that could inspire nothing but disgust; her withered, worn, scarred and lacerated arse looked more like marbled paper than human skin, and the hole was so large and wrinkly that the largest of tools could enter her dry without her feeling a thing. To crown these charms, this noble athlete of Cythera,[13] wounded in several battles, had one breast missing and three fingers cut off, she limped, and was also missing six teeth and one eye; we shall perhaps learn of the kind of attacks which had seen her so mistreated. What is quite certain is that nothing had led her to mend her ways, and if her body was the image of ugliness, her soul was the repository of all the most unspeakable vices and crimes – an arsonist, a parricide, a sodomite, a tribade,[14] a murderer, a poisoner, she was guilty of incest, rape, theft, abortion and sacrilege; one could say in all truth that there was not a single crime in the world this hussy had not committed or had others commit. Her current trade was bawdry – she was one of the company's appointed purveyors and, as she combined a wealth of experience with quite a pleasant turn of phrase, she had been chosen to fulfil the role of fourth storyteller, namely the one whose story would contain the greatest atrocities and abominations. Who better to play that part than a creature who had committed them all?

Once these women had been found, and found to meet their
every requirement, it was time to take care of the minor roles.
The friends had at first wished to surround themselves with a
great number of lascivious objects of both sexes, but when they
realized that the only setting where this lubricious episode might
comfortably take place was that same castle in Switzerland
which belonged to Durcet and in which he had dispatched little
Elvire,[15] that this rather modest castle could not house such a
number of occupants, and that in any case it might be indiscreet
and dangerous to bring along so many people, they limited themselves to 32 subjects in all, including the storytellers, thus making
four of this rank, eight young girls, eight young boys, eight men
endowed with monstrous members for the pleasures of passive
sodomy, and four servants. But all this required some refinement:
an entire year was devoted to these details, immense sums were
spent, and the following measures were employed for the eight
young girls in order to acquire the very finest delights France
had to offer. Sixteen knowledgeable bawds, each accompanied
by two deputies, were sent into the 16 principal provinces of
France, while a 17th carried out the same task in Paris alone.
Each of these procuresses was told to meet at one of the Duc's
estates near Paris, and they were all to arrive there in the same
week, exactly 10 months after their departure – this was the
time they had been given for their search; each one was to bring
nine subjects, making a total of 144 girls, and from these 144,
only 8 were to be chosen. The bawds were urged to consider
only birth, virtue and the most delightful of faces; they were to
conduct their searches principally in respectable families, and
no girl was allowed whom they could not prove to have been
snatched from either a convent of noble boarders or from the
bosom of her family (and a distinguished family at that); anyone
not from a higher class than the bourgeoisie,[16] and anyone from
among these upper classes who was not also very virtuous, very
virginal and very beautiful, was mercilessly rejected; spies
watched over these women's activities and promptly informed
the company about their progress. They were given thirty thousand *francs* – all expenses paid – for each subject found to their
liking (it is extraordinary how much all of this cost); as regards

the girls' age, this was fixed between 12 and 15 and anything above or below was ruthlessly rejected. Meanwhile, with the same requirements, by the same means and at the same cost – with the age also set between 12 and 15 – 17 agents of sodomy roamed the capital and provinces alike, and their meeting with the friends was set for a month after the selection of the girls; as for the young men whom we shall henceforth designate by the name of fuckers, all that mattered was the size of their members – nothing less than 10 or 12 inches long by 7 and a half around was acceptable. Eight men worked to this end throughout the kingdom, and their meeting was set for a month after that of the young boys. Although the story of these choices and these meetings is not our concern, a word or two about them here would not be amiss, the better to convey the genius of our four heroes; it seems to me that anything that serves to reveal their character and to shed light on an episode as extraordinary as the one we are about to describe cannot be regarded as out of place.

When the time for the meeting with the young girls had arrived, everyone gathered at the Duc's estate. With some bawds unable to reach their complement of 9, and some others losing subjects on the way either through illness, or escape, only 130 girls arrived at the meeting – but what charms, good God! Never, I believe, have so many been seen in one place; 13 days were devoted to their inspection, and each day 10 were examined. The four friends would form a circle in the middle of which the young girl would appear, dressed initially as she had been at the time of her abduction: the bawd who had led her astray would tell her story (if any of the conditions of nobility or virtue were not met, the young girl would, without further question, be dismissed that instant – with no assistance and no one to accompany her – and the procuress would lose all the expenses she might have incurred in acquiring her); next, the bawd would withdraw, once she had given the details of the case, and they would interrogate the young girl to see if all that had just been said about her was true; if it was, the bawd would return and hitch the girl's skirts up from behind to expose her arse to the company – this was the first thing they wanted to examine. The slightest flaw in this part would lead to her immediate dismissal; if, on the contrary, nothing was found wanting with such charms, she would be stripped naked, and paraded in this state back and forth five or six times from one of our libertines to the next; they would turn her this way and that, touch her, smell her, spread her legs, examine her two virginities – but all this with great sangfroid and without the spell cast by the senses disrupting this examination in the least. Once this was done, the child would withdraw and her examiners would put *approved* or *dismissed* by her name when signing the ballot; next, these ballots would be placed in a box without them sharing their thoughts with each other. When all the girls had been examined, the box was opened: for a girl to be approved, her ballot had to have the four friends' names in her favour; if a single name was missing, she was immediately dismissed, and, as I have said, all such cases were inexorably sent away on foot, without assistance or a guide – except for perhaps a dozen or so with whom our libertines entertained themselves once they had made their choices, and whom they later returned to their bawds. In this first round 50 subjects were excluded; the other 80 were paraded again, but with far greater rigour and severity. The slightest flaw was reason enough for immediate exclusion: one girl as lovely as the day was rejected because she had a tooth slightly out of line with the rest; more than 20 others were rejected because their parents were bourgeois; 30 more were thrown out during this second round, leaving only 50. The friends resolved to proceed to the third examination only once they had spilled their come at the hands of these fifty subjects, so that the perfect serenity of the senses might result in a more composed and considered choice. Each of the friends surrounded himself with a group of 12 or 13 of these young girls: each group was different – these were overseen by the bawds; so exquisitely did the girls vary their poses, so well did they perform, there were in a word such lubricious scenes that sperm ejaculated, heads cooled, and another 30 of their number disappeared after this round, leaving only 20. This was still 12 too many; the friends found relief in new ways – in all those ways one might imagine would provoke disgust – but the 20 remained, and how were they to whittle down this number of creatures who were so utterly celestial one would have thought them the very work of the divine? As they were alike in beauty, something within them had to be found that could establish for 8 of them at least some kind of superiority over the other 12, and what the Président proposed in this regard was truly worthy of all the disorderliness of his imagination – no matter, his solution was accepted. It was to see which of the girls would best perform something that would often be demanded of them; four days were sufficient to provide a satisfying answer to this question, and 12 girls were finally rejected, though not unscathed as the others had been. They were for a week the friends' complete and utter playthings; then, as I said, they were returned to the bawds, who soon grew rich prostituting such distinguished subjects. As for the 8 who were chosen, they were placed in a convent until the day of departure, and in order to save the pleasure of possessing them until the appointed time, the friends did not so much as touch them beforehand. I dare not paint these beauties – they were all so equally exceptional that my brushstrokes would inevitably become monotone; I shall content myself with naming them and with honestly declaring that it is utterly impossible to imagine such a collection of graces, charms and perfections – and should Nature wish to give man an idea of the most inspired of her creations, she would offer him no other models.

The first was named Augustine: she was 15 years old; she was the daughter of a baron from Languedoc and had been abducted from a convent in Montpellier. The second was named Fanny: she was the daughter of a judge at the Courts of Justice in Brittany and was abducted from her father's château. The 3rd was named Zelmire: she was 15 years old; she was the daughter of the Comte de Terville, who idolized her; he had taken her out hunting with him on one of his estates in Beauce and, when he left her alone in the forest for a moment, she was abducted there and then; she was his only daughter and with a dowry of four hundred thousand *francs* was to have married a very great lord the following year. She was the one who wept and despaired the most at the horror of her fate. The 4th was named Sophie: she was 14 years old and the daughter of a gentleman who was rather comfortably off and living on his estate in Berry; she had been abducted whilst out walking with her mother, who, attempting to defend her, was hurled into a river where she perished before her daughter's very eyes. The 5th was named Colombe: she was from Paris and the daughter of a judge at the Courts of Justice; she was 13 years old and had been abducted one evening while returning with her governess to her convent from a children's ball; the governess had been stabbed. The 6th was named Hébé:[17] she was 12 years old; she was the daughter of a noble cavalry captain living in Orléans; the young lady had been enticed and abducted from the convent where she was being raised; two nuns had been bribed. It was impossible to behold anything more alluring and more adorable. The 7th was named Rosette: she was 13 years old; she was the daughter of the lieutenant general of Chalon-sur-Saône; her father had just died, she was at her mother's house in the countryside, near the town, and she was abducted in full view of her relatives by kidnappers disguised as robbers. The last was called Mimi or Michette: she was 12 years old; she was the daughter of the Marquis de Senanges[18] and had been abducted from her father's estate in the Bourbonnais during an open-top carriage ride, which she had been allowed to take with just two or 3 women from the château who were murdered. As one can see, the preparations for these pleasures came at a high price in terms of both money and crime; these immense sums meant little to such people, and as for these crimes, this was an age when there was little danger of these being investigated and punished as they have been since. As a result, everything turned out well – so well indeed that our libertines were never troubled by any repercussions, and barely any searches were conducted.

The moment came for the examination of the young boys: as they were easier to procure, they were greater in number. The panderers presented 150 of them, and it would certainly be no exaggeration on my part to declare that they were the equals of the group of young girls for their delightful faces as much as for their childlike graces, candour, innocence and nobility. Thirty thousand *francs* were paid for each one (the same price as for the girls) but those who undertook this task had nothing to lose because, as this game was both more refined and more to our devotees' taste, it had been decided that the pimps would not lose their fees – that those boys deemed unsuitable would indeed be dismissed, but that since they would be put to some use their fees would be paid just like the others. This examination was conducted just as that of the young ladies had been: 10 were inspected each day, with the very wise precaution that had been neglected a little too often with the girls – with the precaution, as I say, of always coming at the hands of the 10 boys presented before proceeding to the examination itself. They were tempted to exclude the Président: they were wary of the depravity of his tastes – they felt they had been duped by his accursed penchant for infamy and degradation when choosing the girls; he promised not to succumb to this, and if he kept his word it was in all likelihood not without difficulty, for once a damaged and depraved imagination has become accustomed to these kinds of outrages against good taste and nature – outrages that excite it so deliciously – it is very difficult to bring it back to the straight and narrow. It seems that the imagination's desire to satisfy its tastes deprives it of the ability to exercise judgement; scorning what is truly beautiful and cherishing only what is ghastly, the imagination decrees as it fancies, and a return to more honest sentiments would strike it as an offence against principles it would be utterly loath to abandon. One hundred subjects had been unanimously approved by the close of the first sessions, and these judgements had to be revisited five times in a row in order to arrive at the small number that was to be admitted; three times in a row 50 still remained, whereupon the friends were obliged to resort to peculiar methods to break in some way the beautiful spell cast by these idols and thereby reach the requisite number. They thought of dressing them up as girls: 25 departed as a result of this trick, which, by lending the sex they idolized the appearance of the one to which they were indifferent, demeaned them and almost entirely broke the spell, but nothing could be done to vary the votes cast for the final twenty-five – whatever they tried, whether it was spilling their come, or waiting until the very moment they came before writing the names on the ballots, or trying the same method they had used with the young girls, the same 25 still remained, and so they decided to draw lots. Here are the names they gave[19] to those who remained, their age, their birth and the summary of their story. As for their portraits, I admit defeat – the features of Cupid himself were surely no more delightful, and the models in whom Albani[20] sought the features of his divine angels were certainly far inferior.

Zélamir was 13 years of age: he was the only son of a gentleman from Poitou who raised him with the greatest care on his estate; he had been sent to Poitiers, escorted by a single servant, to see a female relative, and our blackguards, who were lying in wait, murdered the servant and seized the child. Cupidon was the same age: he was at the school in La Flèche;[21] the son of a gentleman from the outskirts of that town, he was studying there; he was stalked and abducted one Sunday whilst out walking with his fellow pupils; he was the prettiest boy in the school. Narcisse was 12 years of age: he was a Knight of Malta;[22] he had been abducted in Rouen, where his father held an honorary post in keeping with his nobility; the boy was being sent to Louis-le-Grand[23] in Paris; he was abducted on the way. Zéphire,[24] the most delightful of the 8 (had their excessive beauty made such a distinction possible), was from Paris: he was studying there at a famous boarding school; his father was a general officer who moved heaven and earth to get his son back, but without any success; the schoolmaster had been bribed, and had handed over seven boys of whom 6 were discarded. He had turned the Duc's head and the latter protested that had he been obliged to pay a million to bugger that child, he would have handed over the money in an instant; he reserved the boy's first fruit for himself, and these were unanimously granted him. O tender and delicate child! What a mismatch, and what a dreadful fate lay in store for you! Céladon[25] was the son of a magistrate from Nancy: he was abducted in Lunéville, where he had gone to see an aunt; he had just turned fourteen; he was the only one seduced by means of a young girl his own age, who was introduced to him somehow; the little minx lured him into the trap by pretending to be in love with him; he was not closely watched over, and the ruse succeeded. Adonis was 15 years of age: he was abducted from the Collège du Plessis[26] where he was studying; he was the son of a Président at the Supreme Court who protested and remonstrated in vain, for such precautions had been taken that he was unable to find any trace of his son. Curval, who had been mad about the boy for two years, had met him at his father's house, and was the one who had provided the means and information necessary to lead him astray; his fellow libertines were most astonished by such reasonable taste in such a depraved mind, and Curval, terribly proud of himself, used this episode to show them that, as they could see, he was still on occasion capable of good taste. The child recognized him and wept, but the Président consoled him with the assurance that he would be the one to deflower him and, as he offered this extremely touching consolation, he bounced his enormous tool against the boy's buttocks; he did indeed ask those assembled for the boy and secured him without difficulty. Hyacinthe[27] was 14 years of age: he was the son of an officer who had retired to a small town in Champagne; he was taken whilst out hunting, which he loved more than anything, and which his father imprudently allowed him to do unaccompanied. Giton[28] was 13 years of age: he was abducted in Versailles, from among the pages of the king's Great Stables; he was the son of a nobleman from the Nivernais, who had brought him there no more than 6 months earlier; he was abducted quite straightforwardly whilst out walking alone on the Avenue de St. Cloud.[29] His first fruit were reserved for the Bishop, who had developed a passion for him. Such were the masculine deities our libertines prepared for their lubricity – we shall see at the appropriate time and place what use they made of them. 142 subjects remained, but there was no toying with this prey as there had been with the other – no one was dismissed without having first been of service; our libertines spent a month with them at the Duc's château. As it was the eve of their departure, they had already broken with all the usual daily arrangements, and this kept them entertained until the moment came for them to set off. When they had more than had their fill of the boys, they came up with an amusing way of getting rid of them – this was to sell them to a Turkish pirate. By this means no trace was left, and they recovered some of their costs; the Turk came to collect them near Monaco, where they had been sent in small batches, and forced them into slavery – a dreadful fate no doubt, but one that was nonetheless perfectly amusing to our four scoundrels.

The moment came to choose the fuckers; those who were discarded from this group posed no difficulties – taken when they were old enough to see reason, they were paid for their travel and their trouble and headed back home. The 8 panderers employed for these had, moreover, been handed a much easier task, since the measurements were by and large fixed and there were no other conditions to meet. Thus fifty of them arrived: of the 20 largest of these, the 8 youngest and prettiest were chosen, and as only the four largest of these 8 will be mentioned in any detail, I shall content myself with naming these. Hercule, truly built like the god whose name he was given, was 26 years old and endowed with a member 8⅙ inches around by 13 inches long; never had anything quite as fine or majestic as this tool been seen – almost always aloft and (as they had proved) able to fill a pint glass to the brim in 8 ejaculations. He was moreover very sweet and had the most alluring physiognomy. Antinoüs, so named because, like Hadrian's catamite,[30] he had both the finest prick in the world and the most voluptuous arse (a very rare combination), wielded a tool 8 inches around by 12 inches long; he was 30 years old and had the prettiest face in the world. Brise-cul[31] had a rattle so amusingly shaped it was almost impossible for him to bugger anyone without splitting their arse, and this is how he came by his name. The head of his prick resembled an ox heart and was 8¼ inches around; his shaft was only 8 inches around, but this crooked shaft was so curved it tore apart the anus as it penetrated, and this feature was so precious to libertines as jaded as ours that he had been much sought after. Bande-au-ciel,[32] so named because he was perpetually erect no matter what he was up to, was equipped with a tool eleven inches long by 7¹¹⁄₁₂ around; bigger pricks than his had been rejected because they had trouble getting hard whereas his would spring aloft at the slightest touch no matter how many times he came in a day. The four others were of more or less the same size and bearing. The friends entertained themselves for a fortnight with the 42 discarded subjects and, having had their fill of them and worn them to the bone, they sent them away richly rewarded.

All that remained was to pick the four servants, and this was without doubt the most colourful choice of all. The Président was not the only one with depraved tastes: his three friends, and Durcet in particular, were all rather smitten with this accursed mania for turpitude and debauchery that causes one to find a more piquant charm in old, disgusting and filthy objects than in the most divine of Nature's creations. It would doubtless be difficult to explain this fantasy, though many people share it – Nature's disorders bring with them a kind of piquancy that acts upon the nervous system with perhaps as much if not greater force than her most flawless charms. It is moreover proven that it is horror, foulness – something ghastly – that we want when we are hard, and where better to find this than in a corrupt object? Certainly, if it is filth that gives pleasure in the lubricious act, then the greater the filth, the deeper the pleasure, and the corrupt object is evidently filthier than the untouched or perfect object. There is not the slightest doubt about this – besides, beauty is the simple thing, ugliness is the extraordinary thing, and all ardent imaginations doubtless prefer the extraordinary thing in lubricity to the simple thing. Beauty, freshness only strike one in a simple way; ugliness, degradation deliver a much firmer blow – the shock is far stronger, the excitation must therefore be more intense. One should not be surprised therefore if a great many people favour an old, ugly, even stinking woman for their pleasures over a pretty young girl – no more surprised by this, as I say, than we should be by a man who prefers walking in the arid and rugged terrain of the mountains to the dreary paths of the plains. All these things depend upon our constitution, our organs, the manner in which these react, and we are no more able to command our tastes to change in this than we are to vary the shape of our bodies. In any case, this was as we have said the Président's predominant taste and more or less in truth that of his three fellow libertines, for they had been unanimous in their choice of servants – a choice which, as we shall see, clearly betrayed the kind of disorder and depravity we have just depicted. Orders were thus given to scour Paris for the four creatures required to fulfil this task, and as disgusting as their portraits may be, the reader will nonetheless permit me to trace them – they are too essential to those matters of custom whose elaboration is one of this work's principal aims.

The first was called Marie: she had been servant to a famous brigand only recently broken on the wheel, and for her part had been flogged and branded; she was 58 years old, with barely any hair left, a crooked nose, dull and rheumy eyes, a large mouth furnished with 32 teeth, it is true, but these were as yellow as sulphur; she was tall, scraggy, having had 14 children – all 14 of whom she had, so she said, smothered for fear they would turn out bad; her belly rippled like the waves of the sea, and one of her buttocks had been eaten away by an abscess. The second was named Louison: she was 60 years old, short, hunchbacked, one-eyed, with a limp, but with a fine arse for her age and quite good skin. She was as wicked as the devil and always willing to commit any of the horrors and excesses one might demand of her. Thérèse was 62 years old: she was tall, thin, skeletal, without a hair left on her head, without a tooth in her mouth and exhaling from this orifice a stench that could bowl one over backwards; her arse was riddled with wounds and her buttocks so prodigiously slack one could roll the skin around a stick; the hole of this fine arse resembled the mouth of a volcano in size, and as for its smell it was a veritable close stool;[33] Thérèse had never in her life, so she said, wiped her arse, and it was perfectly evident there was still shit there from her childhood; as for her vagina, it was the repository of every filth and horror, a veritable sepulchre whose fetidness would cause one to faint; she had a crooked arm and a limp. Fanchon was the name of the fourth: she had been hanged 6 times in effigy[34] and there was not a single crime on this earth she had not committed; she was 69 years old, pug-nosed, short and fat, with a squint, barely any forehead, with only two old teeth ready to drop from her stinking maw; an erysipelas[35] covered her backside, and haemorrhoids the size of a fist hung from her anus; a ghastly canker was devouring her vagina and one of her thighs was all burnt; she was drunk for three quarters of the year and with her weak stomach would vomit everywhere when drunk. Her arsehole, despite the bunch of haemorrhoids lining it, was naturally so large that she trumped and farted and often more besides without noticing. In addition to their household duties at this lascivious retreat, these four women also had to take [part] in all the orgies and attend to the various lubricious needs and services one might demand of them.

With all these preparations complete and summer now begun, attention turned to the transportation of the various items that would make the friends' stay at Durcet's estate comfortable and pleasant throughout their four months there. A great stock of furniture and mirrors, provisions, wines, liqueurs of every kind was dispatched; workmen were sent there, and Durcet – who had already gone ahead – received, lodged and installed the subjects as they arrived, little by little. But the moment has now come to give the reader a description of the celebrated temple destined for so many wanton sacrifices in the four months to come. He will see the care with which this remote and solitary retreat had been chosen, as if silence, isolation and tranquillity were potent vehicles of libertinage, and as if the very same qualities that wreak religious terror upon the senses inevitably lent an additional charm to lust. We shall paint this retreat not as it was before, but newly transformed by the efforts of the four friends into a place of great beauty and still more perfect solitude. To reach there one first had to get to Basel; one then crossed the Rhine, beyond which the road narrowed so much one had to leave the carriages behind; a little later one entered the Black Forest,[36] then plunged further in about 15 leagues along an arduous and tortuous road that was absolutely impracticable without a guide. A dilapidated hamlet of colliers and foresters[37] came into view at these heights: this is where the territory of Durcet's estate begins, and the hamlet belongs to him; as the inhabitants of this little village are almost all thieves or smugglers, it was easy for Durcet to befriend them, and the first order he gave them was an explicit instruction to let no one approach the castle after the 1st of 9ber,[38] the date the entire company would be gathered together. He armed his faithful vassals, granted them some privileges they had long solicited, and the barrier was closed; the following description will indeed show how difficult it was, once the gate was bolted shut, to reach

Silling – the name of Durcet's castle. Once one had passed the charcoal oven, one began to climb a mountain almost as high as the Mont St. Bernard[39] and with an infinitely more difficult approach, for it is only possible to reach the summit on foot; it is not that mules cannot pass there, but that the path one must take is so flanked by precipices on every side that one places oneself in great peril when riding them – six of those carrying the provisions and crew perished there, as did 2 of the workmen, who had chosen to ride two of them. Almost five long hours are needed to reach the peak, which offers an oddity of a different kind that, because of the precautions taken, became a new barrier so utterly insurmountable that only birds could traverse it. This peculiar whim of Nature is a crevasse more than one hundred and eighty feet across that divides the peak's northern and southern faces and makes it impossible, once one has scaled the mountain, to descend again without the aid of some crafts-manship. Durcet had these two faces – between which a precipice plunges over a thousand feet deep – linked by a very handsome wooden bridge that was destroyed as soon as the last crews had arrived, and from this moment on there was no possible means of communication with the castle of Silling. For, descending the northern face again, one comes to a little plain of about four acres, utterly surrounded by rocky crags whose summits reach the heavens – crags which envelop the plain like a screen, with-out leaving the slightest gap between them; this pass, named the bridge path, is thus the only one leading down to the little plain, and once it has been destroyed there is not a single creature on earth of any species one could name that can reach this little plain. And there in the middle of this plain – so well surrounded, so well defended – is Durcet's castle: a wall thirty feet high encircles it; beyond this wall, a very deep moat full of water protects one last enceinte forming a circular gallery; a low and narrow postern finally leads into a large inner courtyard around which all the lodgings have been built; these lodgings, vast and well furnished indeed after the most recent alterations, give on to a very large gallery on the first floor. Note that I shall describe the apartments not as they may once have been, but as they had just been transformed and laid out in accordance with the new plans. From the gallery one entered a very pretty dining room fitted with tower-shaped cabinets, which, communicating directly with the kitchens,[40] allowed the food to be served hot, promptly and without the need for a valet. From this dining room, furnished with carpets, stoves, ottomans, the finest armchairs and everything that could make it as comfortable as it was pleasant, one went through to a simple, plain drawing room, which was extremely warm and appointed with very nice furniture. This drawing room led to an assembly room, intended for the storytellers' narrations – this was, so to speak, the battlefield for the combats to come, the headquarters for the lubricious gatherings, and, as it had been decorated accordingly, it merits a short description of its own: it was in the shape of a semicircle; in the curved part of the room were four alcoves lined with vast mirrors and each adorned with a splendid ottoman; these four alcoves were built directly facing the diameter, cutting the circle in half; a throne raised four feet high was set against the wall forming the diameter – this was for the storyteller, a position which not only meant she was facing the four alcoves intended for her listeners but also, as the circle was small, ensured she was not too far from them, and indeed that they would not miss a word of her narration, for she was placed there like an actor on a stage and the listeners in the alcoves looked on as if from the stalls. At the foot of the throne were tiers where the subjects of debauchery, brought there to sooth the excitation of the senses produced by the tales, would sit; these tiers, like the throne, were covered in black velvet fringed with gold, and the alcoves were decked in a similar fabric and trim, but in dark blue. At the foot of each alcove was a little door opening into an adjoining dressing room,[41] intended to accommodate any subjects the friends wished to summon from the tiers on those occasions they did not wish to carry out in front of all and sundry the pleasure for which the subject had been summoned; these dressing rooms were provided with sofas and all the other accoutrements necessary for abominations of every kind. On either side of the throne was a free-standing column reaching up to the ceiling – these two columns were intended to restrain those subjects in need of correction due to some offence or other; all the instruments necessary for this correction were hanging from the columns, and this imposing sight served to ensure a subservience most essential in episodes of this kind – a subservience from which almost all the appeal of sensuality springs in the soul of the tormenter. This chamber led to a closet which formed the furthest extent of this part of the building. This closet was a kind of boudoir from which no sound nor secret could escape; it was very warm, very dark throughout the day, and was intended for face-to-face combat or for certain other secret pleasures that will be explained in due course. To reach the other wing one had to retrace one's steps, and, once back in the gallery, at the end of which was a very beautiful chapel, one entered the parallel wing which closed the circuit of the inner courtyard. Here there was a very pretty antechamber leading to four exquisite apartments, each with its own boudoir and privy; very beautiful Turkish beds – decked in three colours of damask silk – and matching furniture graced these quarters, whose boudoirs offered all that the most sensual and refined lubricity could ever desire. These four bedrooms, very warm and very comfortable, were intended for the four friends, who were thus perfectly well accommodated; as their wives were to share, according to the arrangements made, the same quarters as themselves, they were given no rooms of their own.

The second floor contained more or less the same number of apartments, but these were laid out differently: on one side, there was first of all an enormous room complete with 8 alcoves, each furnished with a small bed, and these were the young girls' quarters, next to which were 2 small bedrooms for 2 of the old women who were to look after them; beyond these were two charming, identical rooms intended for two of the storytellers; retracing one's steps, one came across a similar apartment with 8 recessed alcoves for the 8 young boys and two adjoining bedrooms for the 2 duennas charged with watching over them, and beyond, two more identical bedrooms for the two other storytellers. Eight charming monastic cells finer than those we have just seen formed the quarters for the 8 fuckers, though they were to sleep very little in their own beds. On the ground floor were the kitchens, with six cells for the 6 individuals charged with this work, among whom were three women renowned for their cooking; they had been chosen over men for an episode such as this, and rightly so, I do believe. The cooks were assisted by three robust young girls, but none of these six was to appear at the entertainments, none of these six was intended for that purpose – and should the rules the friends had set themselves in that regard be breached, this would only be because nothing can contain libertinage, and the surest way of prolonging and multiplying its desires is to try to impose limits upon it. One of these three maids was to take care of the several livestock that had been brought to the castle, for aside from the four old women intended for domestic service, there were absolutely no servants other than these three cooks and their assistants. But depravity, cruelty, disgust, infamy, all these passions anticipated or tasted had prepared another place that urgently requires sketching (for the laws essential to the interest of the narrative prevent us from painting it in its entirety). Beneath the steps leading to the altar of the small Christian temple glimpsed from the gallery a fateful stone could be mechanically raised to reveal a very narrow and very steep spiral staircase that descended three hundred steps into the bowels of the earth and led to a kind of vaulted dungeon, sealed behind three iron doors and containing every horror that the cruellest art and most refined barbarity could conceive – as much to terrify the senses as to commit atrocities. And how peaceful it was there! How reassuring it must have been for the scoundrel, driven there by crime, alone with his victim! He was in his own home, far from France, in a land where he had nothing to fear, in the depths of an uninhabitable forest, in a refuge within this forest, which, through the measures taken, only birds of the air could reach, and there he was – deep in the bowels of the earth. Woe! A thousand times, woe to the wretched creature left thus to the mercy of a lawless and godless scoundrel – a man amused by crime, with no other concern but his passions and no other constraints but the imperious laws of his perfidious pleasures! I do not know what will happen there, but what I can say at this moment without spoiling the story is that when it was described to the Duc, he came 3 times in a row. At last – with everything ready, everything perfectly in place, the subjects already installed – the Duc, the Bishop, Curval and their wives, followed by the four subaltern fuckers, set off (Durcet and his wife, along with all the others, had already gone ahead, as we have said) and it was not without tremendous difficulty that they arrived at the castle on the evening of 29th 8ber.[42] Durcet, who had headed out to meet them, had the mountain bridge destroyed as soon as they had crossed it, but that was not all: when the Duc surveyed his surroundings he decided that, as the provisions were all within and there was no longer any need to leave, it was necessary both to prevent attacks from outside (of little concern) and escapes from inside (of greater concern) – it was necessary, as I say, to wall up all the doors through which one might penetrate within, and to shut themselves completely away in this fortress as if in a besieged citadel, without leaving the slightest breach for either enemies or deserters. His order was executed: they barricaded themselves in to such an extent that it was no longer possible to see where the doors had been, and they installed themselves within, according to the arrangements we have just read. In the two days that remained until the 1st of 9ber the subjects were rested, so they would appear refreshed when the scenes of debauchery began, and the four friends worked on a code of laws, which they signed and promulgated to the subjects as soon as it was drafted. Before we proceed it is essential we share these laws with our reader, who, following the exact description we have given him in all matters, will now have only to follow the story, effortlessly and sensually, with nothing to confuse his understanding or trouble his memory.

Regulations.

Everyone shall rise each day at 10 o'clock in the morning: at this time the four fuckers who have not been employed overnight shall come pay the friends a visit and shall all bring a little boy along with them; they shall go from one bedroom to the next, acting according to the will and desires of the friends, but in the beginning the little boys they bring shall be there only for show, as it has been decided and arranged that the 8 virginities of the young girls' cunts shall be taken only in the month of X[ber 43] and those of their arses, as well as those of the arses of the 8 young boys, shall be taken only during the month of January; and this is to allow a burgeoning desire, endlessly inflamed but never sated, to excite the senses – a situation that must inevitably lead to the kind of lubricious frenzy the friends are endeavouring to provoke as one of the most delectable states of lubricity.

At eleven o'clock the friends shall head to the young girls' quarters; it is there that breakfast, consisting of hot chocolate, or toast dipped in Spanish wine or other restorative tonics, shall be served. This breakfast shall be served by the 8 naked girls, assisted by the two old women, Marie and Louison, who are posted at the girls' harem, with the two others to be posted at the boys' harem. Should the friends wish to commit indecent acts with the girls over breakfast, or indeed before or after, the girls are to lend themselves to these with the resignation required of them, and without which they shall be severely punished. But it has been agreed that there shall be no secret or private trysts at this time of day, and should anyone fancy a little frolic it must be among friends and in front of everyone present at breakfast.

These girls shall adopt the general rule of kneeling each time they see or meet a friend, and they shall stay thus until they are told to rise; only these girls, the wives, and the old women shall be subject to these laws – all the others shall be exempt, but everyone shall be obliged to address each of the friends only as *my Lord*. Before leaving the girls' bedroom, the friend charged with hosting that month (the intention being that each month one friend shall oversee every detail, and that each shall take his turn in the following order, namely Durcet during 9[ber], the Bishop during X[ber], the Président during January, and the Duc during February) – the friend whose month it shall thus be, before leaving the girls' quarters, shall inspect each of them, one after the other, to see if they are in the state they have been ordered to be in; the old women shall be informed each morning of the need for the girls to be in such and such a state. As it is strictly forbidden to go to the privy other than in the chapel, which has been furnished and set aside for this purpose, and forbidden to go there without express permission, which is often refused and with good reason, the friend in charge that month shall carefully inspect all the girls' individual privies immediately after breakfast, and should there be any contravention of these two aforementioned articles, the offender shall be sentenced to corporal punishment.

From there the friends shall go to the boys' quarters in order to conduct the same inspections and to condemn offenders likewise to capital punishment;[44] the four little boys who did not visit the friends in the morning shall receive them now when they come into their bedroom, and shall drop their breeches before them; the four others shall stand still and wait for their orders. Messieurs may or may not frolic with these four, whom they shall not have seen that day, but whatever they get up to shall be in public – there shall be no tête-à-tête at these times of day. At one o'clock those boys or girls – young or old – who have obtained permission to answer an urgent call of nature, that is to say of the more weighty kind (and this permission shall be granted only very selectively and to a third at most of the subjects) – those boys and girls shall, as I say, go to the chapel where everything has been expertly prepared for the pleasures such matters afford; there they shall find the four friends, who shall wait for them until two o'clock and no later, and who shall employ them as they see fit for those pleasures they wish to enjoy. From two to three o'clock, the first two tables shall be served and have lunch at the same time, one in the girls' spacious quarters, the other in the little boys' quarters; the 3 kitchen maids shall serve these two tables, the first of which shall include the 8 little girls and the four old women, the second the four wives, the 8 little boys and the 4 storytellers. During this lunch, Messieurs shall go to the drawing room, where they shall chat among themselves until 3 o'clock; shortly before this time, the 8 fuckers shall appear there in the smartest and most resplendent attire possible. At 3 o'clock the masters' lunch shall be served and the 8 fuckers shall be the only ones to enjoy the honour of an invitation. This lunch shall be served completely naked by the four wives, with the help of the four old women dressed as sorceresses; the latter shall take the dishes from the towers where the maids, down below, shall have left them, and hand them over to the wives, who shall lay them on the table; during the meal the 8 fuckers may grope the wives' naked bodies as much as they like without the latter being able to spurn their advances or defend themselves – they may even go as far as insulting them and raising the rod to them, hurling as much abuse as they see fit.

Everyone shall rise from the table at five o'clock, at which time only the 4 friends (the fuckers shall withdraw until the hour of the general assembly) – the four friends, as I say, shall go through to the drawing room, where 2 little boys and 2 little girls (different ones each day) shall serve them coffee and liqueurs naked; it shall still be too soon for the friends to indulge in any pleasures that might sap their strength – they shall instead have to confine themselves to mere trifles. Shortly before 6 o'clock the 4 children who just served dinner shall withdraw, so they may quickly get dressed. At six o'clock precisely Messieurs shall enter the great chamber destined for the narrations described above. They shall each take their places in their alcoves and the rest shall arrange themselves in the following manner: on the aforementioned throne shall be the storyteller; the tiers beneath her throne shall be adorned with the 16 children arranged so that four of these, namely two girls and two boys, shall be facing an alcove; likewise the rest, so that each alcove shall have an identical quartet[45] before it. This quartet shall be exclusively assigned to the alcove it faces, without the alcove to the side being able to form any designs upon it, and these quartets shall be changed each day – no alcove shall have the same one twice. Each of the quartet's children shall wear a chain of artificial flowers tied around their arm and leading all the way to the alcove so that when the proprietor of that alcove wants some or other child from his quartet, he shall simply have to tug on the garland and the child shall come running. Seated above each quartet there shall be an old woman assigned to that quartet, and under the orders of the head of the alcove. The three storytellers not on duty that month shall be seated on a banquette at the foot of the throne without any particular assignment but

nonetheless ready to take orders from everyone. The four fuckers destined to spend the night with the friends may absent
themselves from this gathering; they shall be busy in their
bedrooms preparing themselves for the exploits each night shall
demand of them. As regards the four others, they shall be at the
feet of the four friends in their alcoves, each of whom shall take
his place on the sofa next to the wife whose turn it happens to
be. This wife shall always be naked, the fucker shall wear a pink
taffeta vest and drawers, the storyteller of the month shall be
dressed as an elegant courtesan, as shall her three companions,
and the little boys and little girls of the quartets shall always be
differently and elegantly costumed, with one quartet in Asiatic
style, one in Spanish, another in Turkish, a fourth in Greek, and
the following day other styles, but all of these clothes shall be
made of taffeta and gossamer; the lower half of the body shall
never be constrained in any way and the removal of a single pin
shall be enough to bare all. As regards the old women, they shall
be variously dressed as Grey Sisters,[46] nuns, fairies, sorceresses
and sometimes widows. The doors of the closets adjoining the
alcoves shall always be left ajar, and these closets well heated
by stoves and decorated with all the furnishings necessary for
various kinds of debauchery; four candles shall burn in each of
these closets and fifty more in the chamber. At 6 o'clock precisely
the storyteller shall begin her narration, which the friends may
interrupt at any moment they see fit; this narration shall last
until 10 o'clock in the evening and during this time, as its purpose
is to inflame the imagination, all forms of lubricity shall be
permitted except, however, those that would disturb the order
and arrangement agreed for the deflorations, as these shall
always be strictly observed, but as for the rest each friend shall
do whatever he wishes with his fucker, his wife, the quartet and
the quartet's old woman – and even the storytellers, if the whim
should take him – and may do so either in his alcove or in the
adjoining closet. The narration shall be suspended for as long
as it takes to satisfy the friend whose needs interrupt it, and shall
resume as soon as he is done. At 10 o'clock supper shall be
served: the wives, the storytellers and the 8 little girls shall
promptly leave to sup among themselves separately – no women

shall ever be admitted to the men's supper – and the friends shall sup with the four fuckers not on night duty and four little boys; the four others shall serve with the help of the old women. After supper the friends shall go through to the assembly room for the celebration of the so-called orgies; there, everyone shall gather, both those who have supped separately, and those who have supped with the friends, but still with the exception of the 4 fuckers on night duty. The chamber shall be especially warm, and illuminated by chandeliers alone; everyone shall be naked there – storytellers, wives, young girls, young boys, old women, fuckers, friends – everyone pell-mell, everyone sprawled over cushions on the floor, and like animals everyone shall change places, switch roles, incestify,[47] adulterate, sodomize, and (still with the exception of any deflorations) surrender themselves to all the excesses and debauchery that may best fire the imagination. When the time comes for these deflorations, then and only then shall the friends proceed, and, once the child is deflowered, they may have their way with it whenever and however they wish; at precisely two o'clock in the morning the orgies shall end. The four fuckers destined for night duty shall enter in elegant nightshirts to fetch the friend with whom each is to spend the night, the friend also taking with him one of the wives, or one of the deflowered subjects (once they have been), or a story-teller or an old woman, so that he may spend the night between her and his fucker – and in all this he shall do as he likes on condition that he obeys the sensible arrangements that allow the friends to change companions every night if they so wish. This shall be the order and arrangement of each day. In addition to this, each of the 17 weeks spent at the castle shall be marked by festivities: at first these shall be weddings (an account of these shall be given at the appropriate time and place), but as the first of these weddings shall take place between the youngest children, who shall not be able to consummate them, these shall not disturb the order established for the deflorations; as the weddings between the adults shall take place only after the deflorations, their consummation shall not do any harm as they shall be enjoying only what has already been plucked.

The four old women shall answer for the conduct of the 4

children – should these commit any offences, the old women shall report them to the friend in charge that month, and the corrections shall be meted out together every Saturday evening at the time of the orgies. An exact record shall be kept in the meantime. As regards any offences committed by the storytellers, these shall be punished half as severely as those of the children, because their talent is of service and talent always deserves respect; as for those meted out to the wives or the old women, these shall always be double those of the children. Any subjects who refuse something that is asked of them, even if it is impossible, shall be very severely punished: it is up to them to anticipate and prepare accordingly. The slightest laugh, or the slightest lack of attention, respect or submission at any of the orgies shall be one of the gravest and most cruelly punished offences. Any man caught in the act with a woman shall be punished with the loss of a limb if he has not been granted permission to have his way with this woman. The slightest religious act on the part of any of the subjects, whoever it may be, shall be punished by death. The friends are expressly enjoined to use in all their gatherings only the most lascivious, the most debauched language, and the most foul, the most shocking and the most blasphemous expressions.

The name of God shall only be pronounced accompanied by insults and curses, and shall be repeated as often as possible; as regards their tone, it shall always be at its most brutal, most severe and most imperious with the women and the little boys, but submissive, whorish and depraved with the men, whom the friends, when playing the role of wives to these, must regard as their husbands. Should one of Messieurs be found lacking in any of these respects, or dare to show even a glimmer of reason or, indeed, to end a single day without going to bed drunk, he shall pay a fine of 10 thousand *francs*. Whenever a friend has to relieve himself of a heavy burden, a woman of the rank he deems appropriate shall be obliged to accompany him and attend to his needs – of which she shall be informed during the act.

None of the subjects – man or woman – shall be allowed to attend to any matters of cleanliness, whatever these may be, particularly after a heavy burden has been relieved, without the express permission of the friend in charge that month, and if that permission is refused and these matters are attended to regardless, the punishment shall be of the utmost severity. The four wives shall have no prerogatives of any kind over the other women – on the contrary, they shall always be treated with greater rigour and inhumanity, and shall very often be charged with the most vile and arduous tasks, such as, for example, the cleaning of the communal and individual privies established in the chapel; these privies shall be emptied only once a week, but always by the wives, who shall be severely punished if they show any reluctance or do a poor job. If any subjects attempt an escape in the course of this gathering, they shall immediately be sentenced to death, whoever they may be. The cooks and their assistants shall be treated with respect, and any of the friends who break this law shall pay a fine of a thousand *louis*. As for these fines, these shall all be specially set aside upon the friends' return to Paris to provide the initial funds for a new episode either of this kind or another.

With these matters settled and regulations promulgated during the day of the 30th, the Duc spent the morning of the 31st checking everything, having all the regulations recited aloud, and above all inspecting the fortress thoroughly to ensure there was no risk of attack, nor any easy means of escape. Having recognized one would have to be a bird or a devil to leave or to enter, he gave a full account of his findings to the company, and spent the evening of the 31st haranguing the women, all of whom gathered on his orders in the chamber of stories; and, having mounted the rostrum or throne intended for the storytellers, here, more or less, is the speech he made to them.
    'Feeble, fettered creatures, destined solely for our pleasures, you shall not I hope have flattered yourselves that the power – as absurd as it is absolute – that you are allowed in the outside world shall be granted you in these surroundings. A thousand times more submissive than any slaves would be, you should expect nothing other than humiliation, and obedience is the only virtue I advise you to practise – it is the only one suited to the situation in which you find yourselves. Above all, do not imagine

you can rely on your charms: too jaded for those snares, you must see that such bait shall not succeed with us. Remember at all times that we shall make use of all of you, but that not one of you should flatter herself that she has the power to inspire in us any feeling of pity: outraged by those altars that have succeeded in wrenching a few grains of incense[48] from us, our pride and our libertinage shatter these as soon as the illusion has satisfied our senses, and contempt, almost always followed by hatred, instantly succeeds the spell cast by the imagination. What could you offer in any case that we do not already know by heart? What could you offer that we would not trample underfoot, often at the very moment of ecstasy? There is no point in hiding it from you, your service shall be harsh, it shall be painful and demanding, and the slightest offences shall immediately be met with corporal or physical punishment. I must therefore advise meticulousness, submission and your complete self-abnegation as you listen only to our desires: let these be the only laws you follow – fly ahead of them, anticipate them, inspire them, not because you have much to gain from conducting yourself in this way, but just because you would have so much to lose by not doing so. Consider your situation, what you are, what we are, and let these reflections make you tremble: here you are far from France in the depths of an uninhabitable forest, beyond steep mountains, the passes through which were cut off as soon as you had traversed them; you are trapped within an impenetrable citadel; no one knows you are here – you have been taken from your friends, your families, you are already dead to the world and it is only for our pleasures that you are breathing now. And who are the individuals to whom you now find yourselves subordinate? Inveterate and infamous scoundrels with no God other than their own lubricity, no laws other than their own depravity, no limit other than their own debauchery – Godless rakes, without principles, without religion, the least criminal of whom is sullied with more abominations than you could count, and in whose eyes the life of one woman – did I say of one woman? of all the women inhabiting the earth's surface – is as insignificant as the swatting of a fly. There shall doubtless be few excesses we will not pursue – let none of these revolt you, lend yourself to them without batting an eyelid and face them all with patience, submission and courage. If one of you should suffer the misfortune of succumbing to the intemperance of our passions, let her bravely accept her fate – we are not in this world to live for ever, and the best thing that can happen to a woman is to die young. We have read you some very sensible regulations, devised both for your safety and our pleasures – follow them blindly and be prepared for anything on our part if you irritate us with your poor conduct. Some among you have ties to us, I know, which may perhaps make you arrogant, and which may lead you to hope for indulgence – you shall be sorely mistaken if you count on this: no ties are sacred in the eyes of people like us, and the more they seem so to you, the more their severance shall tickle the perversity of our souls. Daughters, wives, it is therefore to you that I am speaking now: do not expect any privileges from us; we must warn you that you shall be treated with even greater severity than the others, and this is precisely to show you how contemptible in our eyes are the ties you may think bind us together. Moreover, do not expect us always to specify the orders we wish you to execute: a gesture, a glance, often simply an inner feeling on our part shall indicate these, and you shall be as severely punished for not having guessed and anticipated these as you would have been had you been notified of them and shown signs of disobedience; it is for you to decipher our movements, our looks, our gestures, to decipher their meaning and above all not to misread our desires. Let us suppose, for example, that this desire was to see one part of your body and that you were clumsily to reveal another – you must see how deeply such an error would disturb our imagination, and the great risk one takes in cooling a libertine's ardour if, say, when he was expecting an arse to come into, one were idiotically to present him with a cunt. As a rule, offer your fronts to us only very rarely – remember that the rancid part of your body which Nature only formed in a moment of madness is always the one that revolts us the most. And as for your arses, there are further precautions to take, as much to hide that foul neighbouring lair when offering them up as to avoid showing these arses at certain times in the very state other people would always wish to see them in; you understand me, no doubt, and you shall in any case receive from the four duennas instructions later that shall explain everything. In a word, tremble, guess, obey, anticipate, and if you do all this, even if you are far from being fortunate, perhaps you shall not be entirely wretched. In any case, there shall be no affairs among you, no liaisons, none of that idiotic, girlish friendship, which, in softening up the heart on the one hand, renders it on the other both more sour and less amenable to the sole and simple humiliation to which we have condemned you. Remember that it is not at all as human beings that we see you, but purely as animals fed for intended service, and heavily beaten when they refuse such service. You have seen the extent to which we have forbidden anything that might resemble an act of religion – I warn you that few crimes shall be punished more severely than this one. We know only too well that there remain among you some imbeciles who cannot take it upon themselves to abjure the idea of that vile God and to renounce religion: I will not hide from you that these girls shall face a thorough examination, and that there shall be no limit to how far we will go with them should they have the misfortune to be caught in the act – let them be persuaded, these foolish creatures, let them be convinced, therefore, that the existence of God is a folly that has no more than twenty followers in the world today, and that the religion that invokes Him is no more than a fable absurdly invented by tricksters whose interests in deceiving us are only too evident these days. In a word, decide for yourselves: if there were a God, and that God had some power, would He allow the virtue that honours Him, and that you profess, to be sacrificed as it shall be here to vice and libertinage? Would He, this all-powerful God, allow a feeble creature such as I, who would be no more to Him than an insect is in the eyes of an elephant – would He allow, as I say, this feeble creature to insult Him, mock Him, defy Him, stand up to Him and offend Him, as I do to my heart's content every second of the day?'

This little sermon concluded, the Duc stepped down from his pulpit and, except for the four old women and the four storytellers, who were well aware they were there as sacrificers and priestesses rather than victims – except for these 8, as I say, all the rest burst into tears, and the Duc, whom this did not bother in the slightest, left them to speculate, to jabber away, to complain among themselves – knowing full well that the 8 spies would provide a full account of it all – and went to spend the night with Hercule, one of the band of fuckers who had become his most intimate favourite as his lover, though little Zéphire still had pride of place in his heart as his mistress. As they wanted all the arrangements for the following day to be in place by the morning, each of them continued their preparations into the night and on the stroke of ten o'clock the next morning the curtain rose on a scene of libertinage that was not to be disturbed in any way, nor any of its regulations breached, until and including the 28th of February.

The time has come, friendly reader, for you to prepare your heart and mind for the most impure tale ever written since the world began, for no such book may be found among either the ancients or the moderns. Understand that any decent pleasures, or any prescribed by that beast you endlessly invoke without knowing and that you call Nature – that any such pleasures, as I say, shall be expressly excluded from this collection, and should you stumble across them by chance it shall only be in cases where they shall be accompanied by some crime, or tainted by some infamy. No doubt many of the various excesses you shall see depicted shall displease you, we know, but there shall be others that inflame you to the point of spilling your come, and that is all we require – if we had not said everything, analysed everything, how do you think we could have guessed what appeals to you? It is for you to take what you want and leave the rest – someone else shall do the same and, little by little, everything shall have found its rightful place. This is the story of a magnificent feast where 600 different dishes are offered for your delectation – do you eat them all? Of course not, but such a prodigious number broadens the limits of your choice, and, delighted by this heightening of your powers, nor do you dream of berating the host who so regales you. Do the same here – choose, and leave the rest without declaiming against it simply because it does not have the ability to please you; remember that others shall enjoy it, and be philosophical. As for the variety, rest assured it is accurate: study closely the passion that seemed to you to resemble another without the least difference, and you shall see that this difference does exist and, as slight as this may be, this passion is the only one to have that refinement – that subtlety – that distinguishes and defines the kind of libertinage that concerns us here. We have moreover blended these 600 passions into the storytellers' tales – this too is something the reader should know in advance; it would have been too monotonous to describe them otherwise, one by one, without introducing them into the body of a narrative. But as a reader unfamiliar with such matters might perhaps confuse the passions described with the straightforward adventures or events of the storyteller's life, each of these passions has been carefully marked by a line in the margin, above which is the name that may be given to the passion;[49] this mark is beside the very line upon which the tale of this passion begins, and the end of the paragraph always marks the end of the passion. But as there are many characters in action in a drama of this kind (notwithstanding the efforts we have made in this introduction to portray and describe them) we shall include a table containing the name and age of each actor, with a brief sketch of his likeness, so that when one encounters an unfamiliar name in the course of a tale, one will be able to refer to the table, and to the extended portraits above, should the brief sketch not offer a sufficient reminder of what has previously been said.

Cast of the Novel of the School of Libertinage.

The Duc de Blangis, 50 years old, the build of a satyr, endowed with a monstrous member and prodigious strength; he may be regarded as the repository of all vices and all crimes; he killed his mother, his sister and three of his wives.

The Bishop of *** is his brother; 45 years old, thinner and more delicate than the Duc, with a revolting mouth; he is treacherous, cunning, a loyal devotee of active and passive sodomy; he utterly scorns any other form of pleasure; he cruelly arranged the deaths of two children for whom a friend had left a considerable fortune in his hands; he has nerves of such sensitivity he almost faints when he comes.

The Président de Curval, 60 years old, is a tall man, wizened and gaunt; sunken, dimmed eyes, a sickly mouth, the walking image of debauchery and libertinage, a dreadful squalor about his person that he finds sensual; he has been circumcised, his erections are rare and only achieved with difficulty, but they do happen and he still ejaculates almost every day; his tastes lead him to prefer men, nevertheless he does not scorn a maiden; he has the peculiar taste of cherishing both old age and anything that resembles his own foulness; he is endowed with a member almost as large as the Duc's; in recent years debauchery has made him torpid, and he drinks a great deal. He owes his fortune to murders alone and is in particular guilty of a dreadful one that can be found in his more detailed portrait. When he comes he experiences a kind of lubricious rage which drives him to acts of cruelty.

Durcet, a financier, 53 years old, great friend and former class-mate of the Duc; he is small, short and stocky, but his body is youthful, handsome and fair; he has a woman's build and all her tastes; deprived of the ability to please women by his lack of firmness, he has imitated them instead and has himself fucked at any time of day; he is quite fond of the mouth – this is the only way he can enjoy himself as the active party. His only divinities are his pleasures and he is always willing to sacrifice everything for them; he is shrewd, cunning and has committed many crimes. He poisoned his mother, his wife and his niece to safeguard his fortune; his soul is rigid and stoical, utterly impervious to pity. He no longer gets hard and his ejaculations are very rare. His moments of climax are preceded by a kind of spasm that sends him into a lubricious rage danger-ous to those of either sex who happen to be serving his passions at the time.

*

Constance is the Duc's wife and Durcet's daughter; she is 22 years old, a Roman beauty, more majesty than finesse, a little plump but shapely, a splendid body, a perfectly sculpted arse that could serve as a model, and jet black hair and eyes; she is intelligent and senses only too well the horror of her fate. A great depth of natural virtue that nothing has been able to destroy.

Adélaïde, Durcet's wife and the Président's daughter; a pretty doll, she is 20 years old, blonde, with very tender, animated, pretty blue eyes; she has all the allure of a heroine from a romance. A long, well-turned neck, a mouth a little on the large side – this is her only flaw. A small bust and a small arse, but all of this, though delicate, is white and shapely; a romantic sensibility, a tender heart, virtuous and devout to excess, and she hides away in order to fulfil her Christian duties.

Julie, the Président's wife and the Duc's eldest daughter; she is 24 years old, fleshy, plump, with lovely brown eyes, a pretty nose; striking and pleasant features, but a ghastly mouth; she has very little virtue and indeed a great inclination to uncleanliness, drunkenness, greed, and whoring; her husband loves her for the foulness of her mouth: this peculiarity suits the Président's tastes. She has never been taught any principles or religion.

Aline, her younger sister, the Duc's supposed daughter, although in truth the daughter of the Bishop and one of the Duc's wives; she is 18 years old, with a lively and pleasant physiognomy, very fresh-faced, brown eyes, an upturned nose, a mischievous look despite her fundamentally indolent and lazy disposition; she does not appear to have any carnal desires as yet, and most sincerely detests all the abominations of which she is the victim; the Bishop deflowered her backside when she was 10 years old; she has been left in crass ignorance – she does not know how to read or write; she despises the Bishop and is deeply afraid of the Duc. She loves her sister very much, is abstemious and clean, replies amusingly and childishly; her arse is delightful.

*

Madame Duclos, 1ˢᵗ storyteller; she is 48 years old, retains much of her former beauty, still very youthful – one could not have a finer arse. Brunette, a full waist. Very chubby.

Madame Champville is 50 years old; she is slim, shapely, with lubricious eyes; she is a tribade, as everything about her proclaims; her current trade is that of a bawd; she used to have blonde hair, she has pretty eyes, a long and ticklish clitoris, an arse well worn from years of service, although she is still a virgin there.

Madame Martaine is 52 years old; she is a bawd; a matronly figure, hale and hearty; her vagina is obstructed and she has only ever known the pleasures of Sodom, for which she seems to have been specially created as, despite her age, she has the finest possible arse – it is very fat and so accustomed to penetration that she can withstand the largest tools without batting an eyelid. She still has pretty features, but these are beginning to fade nevertheless.

Madame Desgranges is 56 years old; she is the greatest villainess ever to have lived; she is tall, slim, pale, and used to have brown hair; she is the very image of crime incarnate. Her withered arse resembles marbled paper, and its orifice is enormous. She has one breast, three fingers and is missing six teeth – *fructus belli*.[50] There is not a single crime she has not committed herself or had others commit; she has a pleasant manner of speaking, some wit, and is currently one of the company's appointed bawds.

Marie, the first of the duennas, is 58 years old; she has been flogged and branded; a former servant to thieves; dull and rheumy eyes, a crooked nose, yellow teeth, with one buttock eaten away by an abscess; she has borne and killed 14 children.

Louison, the second duenna, is 60 years old; she is short, hunchbacked, one-eyed, with a limp, although she still has a very pretty arse; she is always ready for any crime and is extremely wicked. These first two duennas are assigned to the girls and the next two to the boys.

*

Thérèse is 62 years old, resembles a skeleton, with neither hair nor teeth, a stinking mouth, an arse riddled with wounds, and an excessively large hole; she is appallingly filthy and foul-smelling; she has a crooked arm and a limp.

Fanchon, 69 years of age, has been hanged 6 times in effigy, and has committed all imaginable crimes; she has a squint, and is pug-nosed, short, fat, with no forehead and only 2 teeth; an erysipelas covers her arse, a bunch of haemorrhoids hangs from her arsehole, a canker devours her vagina, she has a burnt thigh and a cancer eating away at her breast; she is always drunk, vomits, farts and shits all over the place and at any time without even noticing.

Harem of young girls.

Augustine, daughter of a baron from Languedoc, 15 years old, a lively and delicate little face.
Fanny, daughter of a judge from Brittany, 14 years old, a sweet and tender air.
Zelmire, daughter of the Comte de Tourville,[51] a nobleman from Beauce, 15 years old, a noble air and a very sensitive soul.
Sophie, daughter of a gentleman from Berry, charming features, 14 years old.
Colombe, daughter of a judge at the Courts of Justice in Paris, 13 years old, very fresh-faced.
Hébé, daughter of an officer from Orléans, a very libertine air and alluring eyes; she is 12 years old.
Rosette and Michette, both an air of beautiful virgins; one is 13 years old and the daughter of a magistrate from Chalon-sur-Saône; the other is 12, and the daughter of the Marquis de Senanges; she was abducted from her father's estate in the Bourbonnais.
Their figures, the rest of their charms, and above all their arses are beyond all expression. They have been picked from *130*.

Harem of young boys.

Zélamir, 13 years old, son of a gentleman from Poitou.

Cupidon, the same age, son of a gentleman from La Flèche.

Narcisse, 12 years old, son of an important man from Rouen; a Knight of Malta.

Zéphire, 15 years old, son of a general officer from Paris; he is reserved for the Duc.

Céladon, son of a magistrate from Nancy; he is 14 years old.

Adonis, son of a Président of the Supreme Court of Paris, 15 years old, reserved for Curval.

Hyacinthe, 14 years old, son of a retired officer living in Champagne.

Giton, a King's page, 12 years old,[52] son of a gentleman from the Nivernais.

No quill can do justice to the graces, features and secret charms of these 8 children – beyond anything that one could possibly describe, and picked, as we know, from a very great number.

Eight fuckers.

Hercule, 26 years old, quite pretty, but a very bad character – the Duc's favourite; his prick is 8⅙ inches around by 13 inches long. Comes a great deal.

Antinoüs is 30 years old, a very handsome man; his prick is 8 inches around by 12 inches long.

Brise-cul, 28 years old, the air of a satyr; his prick is crooked, its head or glans is enormous – it is 8¼ inches around, and the shaft of the prick 8 inches around by 13 inches long. This majestic prick is completely curved.

Bande-au-ciel is 25 years old, he is very ugly, but hale and hearty; a great favourite of Curval; he is 25 years old, always aloft, and his prick measures 7¹¹⁄₁₂ inches around by 11 inches long.

The four others, from 9 or 10 to 11 inches long by 7½ to 7¾ inches around, and from 25 to 30 years old.

End of the introduction.

Omissions I have made in this introduction:
1st must say that Hercule and Bande-au-ciel are very knavish[53]
and very ugly respectively, and that none of the 8 has ever been
able to have his way with either a man or a woman.
2nd that the chapel serves as a latrine, and describe how it is put
to this use.
3rd that the bawds and pimps during their expeditions were
accompanied by cut-throats under their orders.
4th describe the servants' busts briefly and speak of Fanchon's
cancer. Give a little more detail about the faces of the 16 children
as well.

The 120 Days of Sodom
or the School of Libertinage

Part One.

The 150 simple passions, or passions of the first class, comprising the thirty days of November filled by Duclos's narration, interwoven with the scandalous events of the castle in the form of a journal during this month.

1st Day.

Everyone rose on the 1st of 9ber at 10 o'clock in the morning as prescribed in the regulations, from which the four friends had mutually sworn not to deviate in any way. The four fuckers who had not shared a bed with the friends overnight brought Zéphire to the Duc, Adonis to Curval, Narcisse to Durcet, and Zélamir to the Bishop first thing in the morning. All four of these boys were very timid and still very awkward, but spurred on by their guides they performed their duties very well and the Duc came – the 3 others, more reserved and less profligate with their come, had as much pumped into them as he did, but without spending any of their own. At 11 o'clock they entered the women's quarters, where the 8 young sultanesses appeared naked and served the hot chocolate thus. Marie and Louison, who presided over this harem, assisted and supervised them. There was much groping and kissing, and the 8 poor little unfortunate victims of the most signal lubricity blushed, hid themselves behind their hands, tried to protect their charms, before revealing them as soon as they realized their modesty irritated and angered their masters. The Duc, who was very soon hard again, measured the circumference of his tool against Michette's slim little waist and the difference was no more than 3 inches. Durcet, in charge that month, conducted the prescribed examinations and inspections: Hébé and Colombe were at fault, and their punishment was immediately prescribed and scheduled for the hour of orgies on the following Saturday. They wept, but moved no one. From there the friends headed to the boys' quarters: the four who had not appeared that morning – namely Cupidon, Céladon, Hyacinthe and Giton, removed their breeches as ordered and the friends briefly enjoyed the sight; Curval kissed all four on the mouth and the Bishop frigged their pricks for a moment while the Duc and Durcet were otherwise occupied. The inspections were carried out – no one was at fault; at one o'clock the friends took themselves off to the chapel, where, as mentioned, the privies had been installed. As the needs anticipated for that evening had led to many permissions being refused, only Constance, Madame Duclos, Augustine, Sophie, Zélamir, Cupidon and Louison appeared. All the rest had asked, but had been ordered to save it for the evening; our four friends, stationed around a seat constructed for that purpose, had these seven subjects placed on the seat, one after another, and withdrew once they had enjoyed their fill of this spectacle. They came down to the dining room, where, while the women had their lunch, they chatted among themselves until the moment they were served. The four friends each placed themselves between two fuckers, following the rule they had imposed upon themselves never to allow any women at their table, and the four naked wives, assisted by the old women dressed as Grey Sisters, served the most magnificent and succulent meal it was possible to prepare; there was no one more refined and skilful than the cooks they had brought with them, and they were so well paid and so well supplied that everything was bound to go marvellously well. As this meal was to be lighter than the supper, the friends contented themselves with four splendid courses, each comprising twelve

dishes: burgundy accompanied the hors d'œuvre, bordeaux was
served with the starters, champagne with the roasts, hermitage
with the entremets, tokay and madeira with the desserts. Bit by
bit their minds became inflamed; the fuckers, who had this very
moment been granted all rights over the wives, mistreated them
a little – Constance was even pushed about a little – beaten a
little – for failing to bring a plate promptly enough to Hercule,
who, seeing that he was well and truly in the Duc's good graces,
felt he could push his insolence so far as to beat and maul the
latter's wife, at which the Duc merely laughed. Curval, very tipsy
over dessert, hurled a plate at his wife's face that would have
split her head open had she not dodged[1] out of its path; Durcet,
seeing one of his neighbours was hard, without further ceremony
– despite being at the dining table – simply unbuttoned his
breeches and presented his arse; his neighbour screwed it and,
once this operation was over, they carried on drinking as if
nothing had happened. The Duc, with Bande-au-ciel, soon
emulated his old friend's little abomination and wagered that
he could coolly drink three bottles of wine while being buggered,
despite the enormity of Bande-au-ciel's prick. What experience,
what composure, what sangfroid in libertinage! He won his
wager, and as these were not his first drinks of the day, for these
three bottles had come after 15 others, he was a little groggy
as he stood up. The first object to appear before him was his
wife, weeping at her ill-treatment by Hercule, and this sight
excited him to such a degree that he was driven to excesses with
her there and then that we cannot possibly relate yet. The reader,
who can see that we are at pains in these opening stages to
impose some order upon these matters, will excuse us for drawing a veil over many small details. Finally, our champions
adjourned to the drawing room, where new pleasures and new
thrills awaited them. There, coffee and liqueurs were presented
to them by a charming quadrille[2] comprising Adonis and
Hyacinthe from among the handsome young boys and Zelmire
and Fanny from among the girls. Thérèse, one of the duennas,
supervised them, as it was the rule that wherever two or three
children were brought together a duenna was required to guide
them. Our four libertines, half-drunk but determined to observe

their laws, contented themselves with kissing and fondling,
which their libertine wits nevertheless knew how to season with
all the refinements of debauchery and lubricity. From the
extraordinary things he demanded of Hyacinthe, they thought
for a moment the Bishop was about to spill his come while
Zelmire was frigging him. Already his nerves were quivering and
the spasms of his climax were beginning to take hold of his body,
but he contained himself, forcing the tempting objects about to
triumph over his senses far from him and, knowing there was
more work to be done, saved himself until the end of the day at
least. They drank six different sorts of liqueur and three kinds
of coffee, and the hour sounding at last, the two couples withdrew to get dressed. Our friends had a nap for a quarter of an
hour, then went to the throne room – the name given to the room
destined for narrations; the friends took their places on their
sofas, the Duc with his dear Hercule at his feet, Adélaïde (Durcet's
wife and the Président's daughter) naked at his side, and for his
quadrille before him – with garlands of flowers leading all the
way to his alcove as has been explained – Zéphire, Giton, Augustine and Sophie, dressed as shepherds and shepherdesses, presided
over by Louison as an old peasant, playing the role of their
mother. Curval had Bande-au-ciel at his feet, Constance (the
Duc's wife and Durcet's daughter) on his sofa, and for his
quadrille four young Spaniards, both sexes wearing their
costumes with the greatest possible elegance – namely Adonis,
Céladon, Fanny and Zelmire, presided over by Fanchon as a
duenna. The Bishop had Antinoüs at his feet, his niece Julie on
his sofa and four almost naked savages for his quadrille – namely
Cupidon and Narcisse from among the boys, and Hébé and
Rosette from among the girls, presided over by an old Amazon
played by Thérèse. Durcet had Brise-cul as his fucker, Aline (the
Bishop's daughter) near him, and before him four little sultanesses, with the boys dressed as girls, their outfits showing off
to the utmost the enchanting figures of Zélamir, Hyacinthe,
Colombe and Michette; an old Arab slave, played by Marie,
directed this quadrille. The three storytellers, magnificently
dressed in the style of high-class Parisian whores, sat at the foot
of the throne on a sofa placed there especially, and Md. Duclos,

the narrator of the month, dressed in a very delicate and elegant
negligée, with plenty of rouge and diamonds, having taken her
place on her rostrum, began thus the story of her life's events,
in which she was to incorporate the details of the first 150
passions, designated under the name of *simple passions*.

'It is no small venture, Messieurs, to speak before a circle such
as yours – accustomed to all the most elegant and refined productions of the world of letters, how will you tolerate the shapeless
and coarse tale of an unfortunate creature such as myself, who
never received any education other than the one libertinage gave
me? But your indulgence is reassuring – you demand just the
unadorned truth, and no doubt on these grounds shall I dare lay
claim to your praise. My mother was 25 years old when she
brought me into the world, and I was her second child – the first
was a girl 6 years older than me. Her origins were not illustrious:
an orphan, she had lost both her father and mother when she
was very young, and as her parents had lived near the Recollect
friars in Paris,[3] when she found herself abandoned and with no
means of her own she gained permission from these good Fathers
to come to their church and ask for alms; but as she was still
quite young and sweet, she soon caught their eye and, little by
little, she went from the church up to the bedrooms and before
long came back down again pregnant. It was to adventures of
this kind that my sister owed her existence, and it is more than
likely that my own birth had no other origin. Nevertheless, the
good Fathers, happy with my mother's docile nature and seeing
how much she brought to the community, compensated her for
her work by placing her in charge of hiring chairs at their church,
a post that my mother had no sooner gained than, with the
permission of her superiors, she married a water-carrier from the
friary, who promptly adopted my sister and me without baulking
in the slightest. Born in the church, I lived so to speak more at
the church than at our own house. I helped my mother put out
the chairs, assisted the sextons in their different tasks; I would
have served Mass had the need arisen, even though I had only
turned five. One day, as I was returning from my holy occupa-
tions, my sister asked me if I had not already met Father Laurent

... "No," I said. "Well," she said to me, "he has his eye on you,
I know it: he wants to show you what he showed me. Don't run
away, look at him and don't be scared – he won't touch [you],
but he will show you something that's very funny, and if you let
him do this he'll pay you well. There are more than fifteen of us
from around here that he has shown as much – he loves this more
than anything and he has given us all presents." You can well
imagine, Messieurs, that I needed no further encouragement, not
only not to run away from Father Laurent but indeed to seek
him out; modesty speaks only in hushed tones at the age I was
then, and is not its silence when one leaves Nature's arms absolute proof that this false sentiment owes much less to that first
Mother than it does to our education? I promptly flew to the
church and, as I was crossing a little courtyard between the
entrance to the church on the friary side and the friary itself, I
came face to face with Father Laurent. He was a friar of around
40 years of age with a very handsome physiognomy; he stops me
– "Where are you going, Françon?" he asks me. "To put the chairs
out, Father." "Fine, fine, your mother will put those out. Come,
come into this closet," he tells me as he leads me into a little
cubbyhole that was there, "I shall show you something you've
never seen . . ." I follow him in, he closes the door behind us and,
having placed me right in front of him – "Look, Françon," [he]
says to me, taking from his breeches a monstrous prick that
almost bowled me over backwards with fear. "Look, my child,"
he continued as he frigged himself, "have you ever seen the likes
of this before . . . ? It's what we call a prick, my little one, yes, a
prick . . . it's used for fucking, and what you're about to see, what
will soon flow, is the semen with which you're made – I showed
it to your sister, I show it to all the little girls your age: bring me
more, bring me more, be like your sister who's introduced me to
more than twenty . . . I'll show them my prick and make my come
fly in their faces . . . That is my passion, my child, I have no other
. . . and you shall see it." And at that moment I found myself
completely covered with a white dew that stuck to me all over
and some drops of which had flown up into my eyes, as my little
head was at the same height as the buttons on his breeches.
Meanwhile, Laurent was gesticulating – "Oh, the beautiful come

. . . the beautiful come I spill," he exclaimed, "look how covered in it you are!" And calming down little by little, he quietly slipped his tool back in its place and made himself scarce, slipping 12 *sols*[4] into my hand and encouraging me to bring him some of my little friends. I could not have been in a greater hurry, as you can well imagine, to go and tell all to my sister, who wiped me down all over with the greatest care so that no trace was left, and who, for procuring me this small good fortune, did not fail to ask for half my earnings. Learning by this example, I did not fail, in the hope of a similar share of the spoils, to seek out as many little girls as I could for Father Laurent, but, when I brought him one he already knew, he rejected her, and giving me 3 *sols* to encourage me – "I never see them twice, my child," he told me, "bring me ones I don't know and never any who tell you they've already had dealings with me." I did a better job after that: in three months I introduced Father Laurent to over twenty new girls, with whom he delighted in following exactly the same routine he had with me. Along with the condition that they be unknown to him, there was another I followed regarding their age that he had endlessly impressed on me: they had to be no younger than 4 years old, and no older than 7. And my little stash was going better than ever when my sister, realizing I was treading on her turf, threatened to tell my mother everything if I did not put an end to this tidy little business, and so I parted ways with Father Laurent.

'However, as my duties were always bringing me into the vicinity of the friary, the very day I turned 7 I met a new lover whose mania, though very childish, was nonetheless a little more serious. This one was called Father Louis: he was older than Laurent and there was a certain *je ne sais quoi* about his bearing that was far more libertine. He grabbed me at the church door as I entered and entreated me to go up to his room; at first I demurred somewhat, but having assured me that my sister, 3 years earlier, had indeed gone up there too and that every day he received little girls of my age there, I followed him. No sooner were we in his cell than he shut it carefully and, pouring some syrup into a goblet, he promptly made me drink three large glassfuls in a row. These preliminaries completed, the reverend, more tactile than his fellow friar, began to kiss me and, playfully untying my petticoat and pulling my shift up beneath my stays, despite my modest attempts to defend myself, he grabbed hold of all of the front parts he had just uncovered and, having fondled and considered them thoroughly, asked me whether I wanted to piss. In desperate need to do so because of the large dose of drink he had just made me swallow, I assured him that my need was as considerable as could be, but that I did not want to do so in front of him. "Oh, by God, yes, you little minx!" added the lecher. "Oh, by God, yes! You'll do it in front of me and worse than that – on me! Look," he said to me as he took his prick from his breeches, "here's the tool you will drench – you must piss on it." So picking me up and standing me on two chairs, with a foot on each one, he spread my legs as wide as he could, then told me to squat: holding me in position, he placed a chamber pot beneath me, sat himself on a little stool the same height as the pot, his tool in hand right beneath my cunt; one of his hands supported my hips, with the other he frigged himself, and as this position brought my mouth level with his own, he kissed it. "Come, my little one, piss!" he told me. "Right now! Flood my prick with that enchanting liqueur whose warm flow has such a hold on my senses! Piss, my sweet, piss and try to drench my come." Louis became animated, he became excited – it was easy to tell that this peculiar operation was the one that most delighted all his senses. The sweetest ecstasy crowned him at the very moment the waters swelling my stomach poured from me most abundantly, and the two of us filled the pot at the same time – he with his come, and I with my urine. This operation complete, Louis delivered more or less the same speech that Laurent had; he wanted to make a bawd out of his little whore, and this time, caring little about my sister's threats, I brazenly procured for Louis all the children I knew. He asked the same of all who came to him, and as he would willingly see them 2 or three times without baulking, and as he always paid me on the side – regardless of what I took from my little friends – within six months I found myself with a little sum to enjoy at my leisure as long as I took care to hide it from my sister.'

*

'Duclos,' interrupted the Président at this point, 'did we not warn you that your tales must include the greatest and most extensive detail? That we can only judge how the passion you describe relates to the customs and character of each man as long as you hide none of the circumstances? That the slightest circumstances are besides infinitely helpful to that excitation of our senses we demand of your tales?' 'Yes, my Lord,' said Madame Duclos, 'I was warned to neglect no detail and to enter into the slightest minutiae whenever they might help to shed light on characters or types. Have I been guilty of some omission of this kind?' 'Yes,' said the Président, 'I have no sense of your second Recollect's prick, and no sense of his climax – besides, did he frig your cunt, and did he have you touch his prick? You see? Nothing but neglected details!' 'Forgive me,' said Madame Duclos, 'I shall atone for these errors and watch my step in future. Father Louis had a very ordinary member, longer than it was wide and gener-ally of a very common appearance – I even remember he had some difficulty getting hard and would only gain a little firmness at the moment of climax. He didn't frig my cunt, he contented himself with stretching it as much as he could with his fingers the better to let the urine flow; he brought his prick very close to it two or three times and his climax was intense, brief, and with no wild words on his part other than "Oh, fuck! Go on, piss, my child! Piss, my pretty fountain, piss, piss! Can't you see I'm coming?" And he interspersed all this with kisses on the mouth that had nothing too libertine about them.' 'That's it, Duclos!' said Durcet. 'The Président was right: I could not picture anything for myself during your 1st tale, but now I can imagine your man.'

'One moment, Duclos,' said the Bishop, seeing she was about to resume. 'For my part I have a need somewhat more pressing than the need to piss – it's had me in its grip for a while and I feel it needs to let fly.' And at the same moment he pulled Narcisse closer: flames shot from the prelate's eyes, his prick was glued to his belly, he was frothing at the mouth, his pent-up come was desperate to escape and could do so only by violent means; he led his niece and the little boy into the closet. Everything stopped – they regarded a climax as something too important not to suspend everything the moment it was to happen, and not to concentrate all efforts to make it a delicious one. But Nature on this occasion did not meet the prelate's wishes, and a few minutes after he had shut himself away in the closet he emerged from it furious, in the same erect state, and, addressing Durcet, who was in charge that month – 'You will put that little rascal down for punishment on Saturday,' he told him, violently hurling the child away from him, 'and let it be a severe one, I beg you.' One could thus tell the young boy had doubtless been unable to satisfy him, and Julie very quietly told her father what had happened. 'Oh, for God's sake! Take another one,' the Duc said to him. 'Pick one from our quadrilles if yours does not satisfy you.' 'Oh, my satisfaction now would be too far from what I wanted before,' said the prelate. 'You know where a thwarted desire leads us – I prefer to contain myself, but let's not go easy on the little rascal,' he continued, 'that's all I have to say . . .' 'Oh, I assure you he shall be reprimanded,' said Durcet. 'It's right that the first to be caught out sets an example to the others. I'm sorry to see you in this state; try something else – have yourself fucked.' 'My Lord,' said Madame Martaine, 'I feel greatly inclined to satisfy you, and if Your Grace would like . . .' 'Oh, no! No, by God!' said the Bishop. 'Don't you know there are all sorts of occasions when one doesn't want a woman's arse? I'll wait, I'll wait . . . Let Duclos continue, it will let fly this evening – I'll have to find one that suits me. Continue, Duclos.' And the friends, having laughed heartily at the libertine candour of the Bishop – *there are all sorts of occasions when one doesn't want a woman's arse* – the storyteller resumed her tale in these terms.

'I had just turned 7 when one day, as I brought Louis one of my little friends as usual, I found one of his fellow friars in his cell with him; as this had never happened before I was surprised, and wanted to leave, but once Louis had reassured me, we boldly entered, my little companion and I. "Look, Father Geoffroi," Louis said to his friend, pushing me towards him. "Didn't I tell you she was pretty?" "Yes, indeed," said Geoffroi, taking me on his knee and kissing me. "How old are you, my little one?" "Seven, Father." "That's 50 years younger than me," said the

good Father, kissing me again; and during this little monologue
the syrup was prepared as usual and both of us were given three
glassfuls to swallow. But as I was not accustomed to drinking
this when I brought fresh game to Louis (for he would give it
only to the girl I would bring him, while I would not usually
stay but leave immediately) I was on this occasion taken aback
by this step and, with a tone of the most naive innocence I asked
him, "And why are you having me drink, Father? Is it that you
want me to piss?" "Yes, my child," said Geoffroi, who was still
holding me between his thighs and whose hands were already
wandering over my front. "Yes, we want you to piss – and it's
with me that this adventure shall take place, perhaps a little
differently to the one that happened to you here. Come to my
cell – leave Father Louis with your little friend and let's take care
of our own business. We'll meet up again when our work is
done." We left – Louis told me quietly to be very obliging with
his friend and said I would not regret it. Geoffroi's cell was not
far from Louis's and we reached it without being seen: no sooner
had we entered than Geoffroi, having locked us in tight, told me
to untie my apron strings; I obeyed; he lifted my shift up over
my navel himself and, having sat me on the edge of his bed,
spread my thighs as wide as he could as he pushed me back, so
my whole belly was revealed and my body was resting on my
rump. He ordered me to hold this pose and to start pissing the
moment he gently slapped one of my thighs with his hand; so,
contemplating me for a moment in this pose, and still striving
with one hand to part the lips of my cunt, he unbuttoned his
breeches with the other and, with swift and violent movements,
started to tug on a dark and stunted little member that did not
seem very inclined to respond to what was apparently being
demanded of it; in order to persuade it with greater success, our
man set about procuring the greatest sensation possible for it
by proceeding with his favourite little routine. He thus kneeled
between my legs, inspected a moment longer the interior of the
little orifice that was revealed to him, brought his mouth to it
several times, growling some lascivious words under his breath
that I cannot recall as I never understood them at the time, and
continued to play with his member, which still did not stir; he

finally sealed his lips hermetically to those of my cunt, I received
the agreed signal, and immediately unleashing the surfeit of
water from my guts, I inundated him with floods of urine that
he swallowed as quickly as they spurted into his gullet. This time
his member unfurled, and its imperious head soared as high as
my thigh – I felt him proudly showering it with the sterile proofs
of his depleted strength; everything had been timed so well that
he swallowed the last drops at the precise moment his prick,
overwhelmed by its moment of triumph, wept over it with tears
of blood. Geoffroi staggered up, and I thought I could tell he no
longer had the same devoted religious fervour for his idol once
his incense had burnt itself out as he had while his delirium,
inflaming his tribute, was still casting its spell. He gave me 12
sols rather brusquely, let me out without asking me, as the others
had, to bring him girls (apparently he had supplies of his own),
and pointing the way to his friend's cell told me to leave, adding
that as the time for his service was fast approaching he could
not accompany me himself, and shutting the door without giving
me time to reply.'

'Oh, but indeed,' said the Duc, 'there are a great many people
who absolutely cannot bear the moment the spell breaks – it
seems one's pride suffers when one allows oneself to be seen by
a woman in such a weakened state, and a sense of disgust arises
from one's embarrassment.' 'No,' said Curval, whom Adonis
was frigging on his knees, and whose hands were wandering all
over Zelmire. 'No, my friend, pride has nothing to do with it,
but the object that essentially has no value other than the one
our lubricity lends it, reveals itself absolutely as it is when our
lubricity is spent; the more violent the excitation, the uglier the
object becomes when this excitation no longer sustains it (just
as we are more or less tired according to whether we have taken
more or less exercise) and the disgust we then experience is
simply the feeling of a soul that has had its fill and no longer
appreciates the happiness that has just worn it out.' 'But from
this disgust, nevertheless,' said Durcet, 'thoughts of vengeance
are formed that have seen dire consequences.' 'That's something
else, however,' said Curval, 'and as the rest of these narrations

will perhaps offer us examples of what you're talking about, let's not rush the dissertations such events will naturally inspire.' 'Président, tell the truth,' said Durcet. 'On the verge of losing control yourself, I believe that at the present moment you would rather prepare yourself for pleasure than hold forth on disgust.' 'Not at all . . . not a bit,' said Curval. 'I could not be calmer . . . There is no doubt,' he continued, kissing Adonis on the mouth, 'that this child is charming . . . but we cannot fuck him – I know of nothing worse than your laws; one is reduced to such things . . . such things . . . Go on, go on, continue, Duclos, for I feel I might do something silly, and I want the spell to hold at least until I go to bed.' The Président, who saw his tool was beginning to rise up, sent the two children back to their places and, reclining once again beside Constance, who as pretty as she was did not inflame him as much, he urged Duclos a second time to continue, and she promptly obeyed in these terms.

'I returned to my little friend. Louis's operation was over, and with neither of us particularly happy we left the friary, myself almost resolved never to return there. Geoffroi's tone had hurt my youthful pride and, without delving into where this disgust came from, I enjoyed neither its effects nor its consequences. It was, however, written in the stars that I would have a few more adventures in this friary, and the example of my sister (who had had dealings, so she told me, with more than fourteen there) was enough to convince me I was not at the end of my escapades. I realized this three months after my last adventure, in the overtures made to me by one of these good reverends, a man of about 60 years of age; there was no end to the ruses he would dream up to persuade me to enter his bedroom – one succeeded so well at last that I found myself there on a fine Sunday morning without knowing how or why. The old lecher, who was called Father Henri, shut me in with him the moment he saw me enter, and embraced me wholeheartedly. "Aha, little minx!" he cried out, giddy with joy. "I've got you now – you won't escape me this time." It was very cold; my little nose was full of snot, as is often the case with children – I wanted to blow my nose. "Oh! No, no!" said Henri, protesting. "I'll do that! I'll do that for you, my

little one." And having laid me down on his bed with my head
tilted back a little, he sat beside me, pulling my upturned head
on to his knees; positioned thus, he seemed with his eyes to be
devouring this cerebral secretion. "Oh! The pretty little snot-
face!" he said, swooning. "How I'm going to suck her!" Then,
bending over my head and putting my nose entirely in his mouth,
he not only devoured all the snot that covered me, but even
lubriciously darted the tip of his tongue into first one nostril
then the other – and so skilfully that he prompted two or three
sneezes that redoubled the streaming he desired and devoured
with such eagerness. But regarding this one, Messieurs, do not
ask me for details: nothing popped out, and whether he did
nothing or whether he did his business in his breeches, I didn't
see a thing, and among the multitude of his kisses and licks there
was nothing that betrayed a more intense ecstasy, so I do not
believe he came. He didn't hitch up my skirts, nor did his hands
stray, and I assure you this old libertine's fantasy could be carried
out on the most decent and inexperienced girl in the world
without her suspecting the slightest lubricity.

'The same could not be said of the one offered me by chance
the very day I turned nine. Father [Etienne], as the libertine was
called, had already told my sister several times to bring me to
him, and she had persuaded me to go see him (without, however,
wanting to take me herself, for fear our mother, who already
suspected something, would find out about it) when I found
myself face to face with him at last in a corner of the church
near the sacristy. He went about it with such good grace, he used
such winning arguments, that I did not take much convincing.
Father Etienne was around forty years old: he was hale, hearty
and vigorous; we were barely in his bedroom when he asked me
if I knew how to frig a prick. "Alas!" I said to him blushing, "I
don't even know what you mean." "Well then! I'll teach you, my
little one," [he] said to me, kissing me devotedly upon my mouth
and eyes. "My sole pleasure is to educate little girls, and the
lessons I teach them are so excellent they never forget them. Start
by untying your apron strings, for if I am to teach you how to
go about giving me pleasure, it is only fair I should teach you
at the same time how to receive it, and nothing must get in our

way for this particular lesson. Come on, let's begin with you –
what you see there," he said to me, placing my hand on my mons,
"is called a cunt, and here's what you need to do to elicit delicious sensations there: you have to rub that little bump you feel
there, and which is called the clitoris, lightly with your finger."
Then, as he made me do it . . . "There, see, my little one, like
that – while one of your hands is busy there, introduce a finger
of your other hand gradually into that delicious slit . . ." Then,
placing my hand there . . . "Like that, yes . . . Well then, don't
you feel anything?" he added as he had me put his lesson into
practice. "No, Father, I assure you," I replied innocently. "Oh!
Of course, it's because you are still too young, but two years
from now you'll see the pleasure this will give you." "Wait," I
said to him, "I think I can feel something now, though." And I
rubbed as much as I could those places he had told me about
. . . Sure enough, some faint, sensual tingles began to convince
me that his recipe was no mere fancy and the great use I have
since made of this reliable method has succeeded in persuading
me more than once of my teacher's expertise. "And now to me,"
Etienne told me, "for your pleasures excite my senses, and I must
share them, my angel. Look," he said to me as he had me grab
a tool so monstrous my two little hands could barely reach
around it, "look, my child – this is called a prick, and this movement here," he said as he guided my wrist with quick tugs, "this
movement is called frigging, so right now you are frigging my
prick. Go on, my child, go on! Go on, with all your strength –
the more rapid and urgent your movements, the sooner the
moment of my intoxication will come – but make sure of one
essential thing," he added as he continued to guide my tugs.
"Make sure always to keep the head uncovered – never cover it
with the fold we call the foreskin. If this foreskin were to cover
that part we call the glans, all my pleasure would evaporate.
Come, now, my little one," continued my teacher, "now let me
do to you what you're doing to me." And pressing against my
chest as he said this, while I continued to work away, he placed
his two hands so expertly, moved his fingers so skilfully, that
pleasure finally took hold of me, and it is thus unquestionably
to him I owe my first lesson. And so, my head beginning to reel,

I abandoned my task and the reverend, who was not yet ready for it to end, agreed to sacrifice for a moment his own pleasure in order to concentrate on mine alone. And once he had me taste it completely, he made me resume the task my ecstasy had forced me to interrupt, and ordered me very clearly not to get distracted again and to concentrate on him alone. I did so with all my soul, it was only fair – I certainly owed him some gratitude; I worked away so willingly and followed all his orders so exactly that the monster, overcome by such urgent tugs, finally spewed up all its rage and covered me with its venom. Etienne seemed transported by the most sensual delirium: he kissed my mouth with ardour, touched and fondled my cunt, and the wildness of his words reflected his lack of control even more clearly. His F's and B's,[5] interlaced with the most tender names, marked this delirium, which lasted a very long time and from which the chivalrous Etienne, quite unlike his fellow friar, the drinker of urine, emerged only to tell me I was charming, to beg me to come see him again and to tell me he would always reward me as he was about to at that moment. Slipping a little *écu*[6] into my hand, he took me back to the place from which he had taken me, and left me utterly amazed and utterly enchanted with a change of fortune that, reconciling me with the friary, left me determined to return frequently in future, as I was convinced that the more I advanced in years the more I would encounter pleasant adventures there. But my destiny now lay elsewhere: more important events were waiting for me in a new world, and when I returned home I learned news that would soon trouble the giddiness prompted by the pleasant turn of events in my last story.'

At this point a bell was heard to ring in the dining room: it was the one that announced that supper was served. As a result Duclos, roundly applauded for the interesting small beginnings of her story, descended from her rostrum and the friends, once they had attended to the dishevelled state in which they found themselves, turned to new pleasures as they hastened after those that Comus[7] now offered. This meal was to be served naked by the 8 little girls; they were ready and waiting as the friends changed room, having taken the precaution of leaving a few

minutes earlier. Those attending the supper were to number 20:
the 4 friends, the 8 fuckers and the 8 little boys, but the Bishop,
still furious with Narcisse, did not want to let him attend the
feast, and as the friends had agreed to be mutually and reciproc-
ally indulgent towards each other, it did not occur to any of them
to ask for the charge to be rescinded, and the little fellow was
locked up alone in a dark closet until it was time for the orgies,
when his Lordship would perhaps make it up with him. The
wives and storytellers quickly ate their supper among themselves
to be ready for the orgies; the old women supervised the 8 little
girls' service, and the friends sat down to eat. This meal, far more
substantial than the lunch, was served with much greater
opulence, lustre and splendour. There was first of all a course of
bisque soup and 20 dishes of hors d'œuvre; twenty entrées
followed and were soon succeeded themselves by 20 further light
entrées, comprising nothing but white poultry and game dressed
in all sorts of ways. These were followed by a course of roast
meats that featured the rarest dishes imaginable, then a course
of cold pastries arrived that soon gave way to 26 entremets of
all shapes and sizes. The table was cleared and the dishes that
had just been removed were replaced with a full complement of
sweet pastries – hot and cold; finally came the dessert, which
included a prodigious variety of fruit despite the season, then the
ice creams, hot chocolate and liqueurs that were taken at the
table. As regards the wines, they varied with each course: for the
first there was burgundy, for the second and third two different
kinds of Italian wine, for the 4th a wine from the Rhine, for the
5th wines from the Rhône, for the 6th sparkling champagne, and
two kinds of Greek wine with two further courses. The friends'
minds were prodigiously inflamed; they did not have permission
at supper, as they did it at lunch, to discipline those serving to
the same degree – as these were the very quintessence of what
their company had to offer, they had to be handled a little more
carefully, but they were nevertheless subject to a frenzied dose
of foulness. The Duc, half-drunk, said he only wanted to drink
Zelmire's urine from then on, and swallowed two large glasses
of it, which he had her fill by getting her to climb on to the table
and squat over his plate. 'What a great feat it is,' said Curval, 'to

swallow a maiden's piss!' And calling Fanchon to him: 'Come, you slut!' [he] said to her. 'It is from the source itself that I want to draw.' And tilting his head back between the legs of this old witch he greedily swallowed the foul floods of poisoned urine she spurted into his stomach; at last the conversation became more inflamed – various questions of custom and philosophy were debated and I leave it to the reader to ponder how refined the moral lesson may have been. The Duc offered an encomium of libertinage, and proved that it was part of Nature and that the more its excesses were multiplied the better she was served; his opinion was universally accepted and applauded, and everyone rose to put into practice the principles that had just been established. Everything was ready in the chamber of orgies: the wives were already there, naked, reclined over cushions piled on the floor, pell-mell with the young catamites, who had left the table shortly after dessert especially; our friends staggered in, two of the old women undressed them, and they fell upon the flock like wolves attacking a sheepfold. The Bishop, whose passions were cruelly excited by the obstacles they had encountered when they had first reared their head, grabbed hold of Antinoüs's sublime arse as Hercule screwed him and, overcome both by this latter sensation and doubtless by the vital and much desired service that Antinoüs was providing him, he finally disgorged floods of semen with such force and of such pungency that he swooned in ecstasy; the fumes of Bacchus triumphed over senses numbed by this excess of lechery and our hero drifted from his swoon to a sleep so deep he had to be carried to bed. As for the Duc, he also had a marvellous time; Curval, remembering the offer Madame Martaine had made to the Bishop, ordered her to carry it out and gorged himself on her arse as he was buggered himself. A thousand other horrors, a thousand other abominations accompanied and followed this one, and our three brave champions, as the Bishop was dead to the world – our valiant athletes, as I say, escorted by the four fuckers on night duty (who had not been present, but now came to fetch them), retired with the same wives they had sat with on their sofas during the narration – unfortunate victims of their brutality, upon whom it is only too likely they inflicted more indignities than caresses, and in whom they

no doubt inspired more disgust than pleasure. Such was the story
of the first day.

2nd Day.

Everyone rose at the usual time. The Bishop, entirely recovered
from his excesses, and since four o'clock that morning utterly
scandalized at having been left to sleep alone, had rung for Julie
and the fucker assigned to him to take up their posts; they
promptly arrived, and the libertine fell back into their arms to
wallow in fresh abominations. Once breakfast had been taken
as usual in the girls' quarters, Durcet conducted his inspection
and, despite all that had been said, new offenders appeared
before him. Michette was guilty of one type of offence and
Augustine, whom Curval had ordered to remain in a particular
state the whole day, was discovered in the absolutely contrary
state; she had completely forgotten, she apologized profusely
and promised it would never happen again, but [the] quadrum-
virate was implacable and they were both added to the list of
punishments set for the first Saturday. Singularly discontented
with the clumsiness of all these little girls in the art of masturbation and irritated by their experience on this score the
previous evening, Durcet proposed to set aside an hour in
the morning for lessons to be given on this subject, and each of the
friends would take it in turns to rise an hour earlier. As this
exercise was scheduled from 9 to 10 o'clock – each of them, as
I say, would take it in turns to rise at nine o'clock to make
themselves available for this exercise. It was decided that the
one who performed this function would sit quietly in an armchair
in the middle of the harem and each little girl, accompanied and
guided by Madame Duclos, the finest masturbatrix within the
castle walls, would try her hand with him; that Madame Duclos
would direct their hands, their movements, would teach them
the speed – faster or slower – with which they had to tug according to the state of the patient, would dictate their postures, their
poses, during the operation, and fixed punishments would be
set for those who by the end of a fortnight could not perfectly

succeed in this art without the need for further lessons. Above
all they were very specifically advised, in accordance with the
Recollect's principles, always to keep the glans uncovered
throughout the operation and to have their other, free hand busy
itself at the same time with tickling the area around, according
to the different fancies of those with whom they would be dealing. The financier's plan was universally welcomed; Madame
Duclos, when summoned, accepted the commission and from
this day forth put a dildo in the girls' quarters on which they
could at any time exercise their wrist to maintain the degree of
agility required. Hercule was given the same job among the boys,
who are always far more adept in this particular art than girls,
because all it involves is doing to others what they do to themselves – and these boys needed only a week to become the most
delectable friggers one could ever hope to meet. No one was at
fault among them on this particular morning, and as the example of Narcisse the previous evening had led to almost all
permissions being refused, the only ones in the chapel were
Duclos, the 2 fuckers, Julie, Thérèse, Cupidon and Zelmire.
Curval was very hard: he had become extraordinarily inflamed
with Adonis that morning while inspecting the boys, and it was
thought he would spill his seed watching Thérèse and the 2
fuckers in action, but he contained himself. Lunch passed by as
usual, but the dear Président, having singularly drunk and frol-
icked throughout the meal, became inflamed once again as coffee
was served by Augustine and Michette, Zélamir and Cupidon,
supervised by old Fanchon, who had just this once been ordered
to be naked along with the children; this contrast gave rise to
Curval's latest lubricious frenzy and he indulged in a few choice
excesses with the old woman and Zélamir, the latter finally costing him his come. The Duc, his prick aloft, held Augustine very
tight; he bellowed, he swore, he raved, and the poor little thing,
trembling all over, kept backing away like the dove before the
bird of prey that stalks her, ready to pounce; he contented himself
nevertheless with a few libertine kisses and with giving her a
first lesson in advance of those she was to begin the following
day; and as the two others, rather less lively, had already begun
their naps, our two champions followed suit, and the four only

woke at 6 o'clock to go through to the chamber of stories. The subjects and costumes for all the quadrilles from the previous evening were changed, and our friends had as their companions on the sofas: the Duc – Aline, the Bishop's daughter and consequently at the very least the Duc's niece; the Bishop – his sister-in-law, Constance, the Duc's wife and Durcet's daughter; Durcet – Julie, the Duc's daughter and the Président's wife; and Curval, to rouse (and arouse) himself a little – Adélaïde, his daughter and Durcet's wife, one of the creatures he enjoyed goading most of all, because of her virtue and devoutness. He began with a few crude pleasantries and, having ordered her to maintain throughout the session a pose that was most appealing to his tastes but most humiliating for this poor little woman, he threatened her with all the consequences of his anger were she to abandon it for one moment; as everything was ready, Duclos mounted her rostrum and took up the thread of her narration thus.

'My mother had not been seen at home for three days when her husband, more concerned about his belongings and money than the creature herself, decided to go to her bedroom, where they used to store their most precious possessions; but imagine his astonishment when, instead of what he was looking for, he found only a note from my mother telling him to come to terms with the loss he had incurred, as, having decided to separate from him for ever, and having no money, she had no choice but to take all she could with her – besides he had no one but himself and his rough treatment of her to blame for her departure, and she was leaving him two girls worth quite as much as everything she had taken with her. But the fellow was far from agreeing that the former was worth as much as the latter, and the notice he graciously gave us – asking that we leave without staying another night at home – offered incontrovertible proof that he did not tally in the same way as my mother. Not particularly wounded by a compliment that offered my sister and me complete freedom to indulge ourselves as we wished in the particular way of life we were starting to enjoy so much, we thought only of packing up our few belongings and taking leave of our dear stepfather as swiftly as he had given us notice. We promptly found a small room nearby, my sister and I, while we decided where our destiny lay; there our thoughts first turned to our mother's fate. We did not doubt for a minute she was at the friary, having decided to live secretly with some Father, or to be kept by one of them in some spot nearby, and we had settled without much concern on this opinion when a Brother from the friary arrived bringing a note that changed our view; this note essentially said we would be best advised to come to the friary as soon as it was dark, to the Father Superior himself (whose note it was), and that he would wait in the church until 10 o'clock in the evening and take us to the place where we would find our mother – in whose new-found happiness and tranquillity he would let us share with pleasure. He urged us in the strongest terms to come, and above all to cover our tracks with the greatest care, as it was vital our stepfather should have no idea of everything they were doing, both for our mother and for ourselves. My sister, who by this time had turned fifteen, and who consequently had more wit and reason than I did at only nine, having dismissed the bearer of the note with the reply that she would reflect on the matter, could not help but be astonished at all these machinations. "Françon," she said to me, "let's not go – there's something behind this. If this proposal were genuine why would my mother not have added a note of her own to this one, or not have signed it at least? And with whom would she be at the friary, my mother? Father Adrien, her closest friend, hasn't been there for three years. Ever since then she only ever goes in passing, and has no long-standing affairs there any more – what could have led her to choose such a refuge? The Father Superior is not and has never been her lover. I know she entertained him two or three times, but he isn't the kind of man to be taken with a woman just because of that, for there is no one more fickle or even brutal towards women once his whim has been satisfied – so why would he have taken such an interest in our mother? There is something behind this, as I say – I never liked that old Father Superior: he's wicked, he's hard, he's brutal – he once lured me into his bedroom, where there were three others with him, and after what happened next I swore later never to set foot there again. If you trust me on this, let's leave

all these wicked monks[8] behind. There's no need for me to hide
it from you any more, Françon, I have an acquaintance, a good
friend I dare say, known as Md. Guérin. I've been visiting her
place for two years now and she hasn't let a week pass by without offering me a nice little trick, but not the 12 *sol* variety that
we used to turn in the convent: not one of them has earned me
less than 3 *écus*. Look, here's the proof," my sister continued as
she showed me her purse, in which there were more than ten
louis.[9] "As you see I've enough to live off. So then, if you want
to follow my advice, do as I do: Madame Guérin will take you
in, I'm sure – she saw you a week ago when she came to collect
me for a tryst, and she told me to propose this to you too, and
even if you are a little young, she'll always be able to find work
for you. Do as I do, I tell you, and we'll soon be raking it in.
Anyway that's all I can say as, except for tonight when I'll pay
your way, you mustn't count on me, my little one – it's every
man for himself in this world. I earned this with my body and
my fingers, do as much yourself, and if prudery has you in its
grip to the devil with you – and above all don't come looking
for me, for after what I'm telling you now, if I saw your parched
tongue hanging two feet out your mouth I wouldn't offer you
a single glass of water. As for my mother, far from being upset
about her fate, whatever it may be, I assure you I couldn't be
happier, and my only wish is that the whore is so far away I
never see her again as long as I live – I remember how much she
got in the way of my work, and all the pretty advice she gave
me while she got up to three times worse. May the devil take
her, my girl, and above all never bring her back – that's all I wish
for her." Not having, to tell the truth, a heart more tender or a
soul much more honourable than my sister's, I wholeheartedly
joined in all the insults she aimed at this excellent mother, and,
thanking my sister for the introduction she had offered me, I
promised to follow her to this woman's place and – once I had
been taken in there – to be a burden to her no longer. As for
refusing to go to the friary, I was of the same mind as my sister
– "If she really is happy, good for her," I said. "As for ourselves,
we can be too, in that case, without needing to go and share her
fate – and if it's a trap they're laying for us it's one we must

avoid at all costs." Whereupon my sister embraced me. "Right then," she said, "I see now you're a good girl – come now, you can be sure we'll make a fortune. I'm pretty and so are you – we shall earn as much as we want, my girl, but you must not get attached. Remember: one today, another tomorrow – you have to be a whore, my child, a whore in your heart and your soul. As for me," she continued, "I am one myself – you can see now there is no confession, no priest, no counsel, no appeal that could tear me away from vice. Good God! I would show my arse on a highway milestone as serenely as I would drink a glass of wine. Do as I do, Françon: we get everything we want from men by our acquiescence – the work is a little tough at first, but you get used to it. There are as many tastes as men – you need to be prepared for this before you start. One wants one thing, another wants something else, but so what? We are there to obey, we submit, it's over before long and the money remains." I was astonished, I must admit, to hear such dissolute words from the mouth of such a young girl, and one who had always seemed to me so proper, but as my heart was of the same caste, I let her know soon enough that I not only intended to follow her example in all matters, but even to outdo her if the need arose. Delighted with this, she embraced me once more and, as it was beginning to get late, we called for some poulard[10] and some nice wine; we ate and slept together, having decided to call in at Madame Guérin's the very next morning and ask to be admitted into the ranks of her boarders. It was over supper that my sister taught me everything I had yet to discover about libertinage. She showed herself to me completely naked and I can assure you she was one of the most beautiful creatures in Paris at the time: the most exquisite skin, the most delightful plumpness, yet the most supple and alluring figure nonetheless, the prettiest blue eyes, and all the rest just as becoming. I also learned later how much Madame Guérin prized her and the pleasure with which she pimped her to her clients, who never tired of her and were endlessly asking to see her again. We were no sooner in bed than we realized we had carelessly forgotten to reply to the Father Superior, who would perhaps be angered by our oversight, and whom we needed to placate at least while we remained in this part of town – but how to make amends for our omission? It was past eleven o'clock, so we decided to leave things as they were. Clearly this affair was close to the Father Superior's heart, and it was thus easy to infer that he was acting more for himself than for our supposed happiness as he claimed, for no sooner had midnight sounded than there was a gentle knock on the door: it was the Father Superior himself. He had been waiting, he told us, for two hours and we should at least have replied to him; and, sitting down by our bed, he told us that our mother had resolved to spend the rest of her days in a small, secret apartment they had at the friary, where she was enjoying the finest fare in the world, enriched with the company of all the friary bigwigs who came to spend half the day with her and another young woman, a female companion of hers; that all it needed to make up the numbers was us, but as we were too young to settle there permanently, he would take us on for only three years, at the end of which he swore he would grant us our freedom, and a thousand *écus* each; that he had also been instructed by my mother to assure us we would be doing her a great kindness to come and share her retreat with her. "Father," said my sister brazenly, "we thank you for your proposal but at our age we have no desire to shut ourselves away in a cloister to become the whores of priests – we have already been so far too often." The Father Superior renewed his entreaties, which became more and more heated – which showed how much he wanted his plan to succeed; realizing at last that he would not get his way, he threw himself almost in a frenzy upon my sister: "Well then, little whore," he said to her, "satisfy me one more time at least before I take my leave of you." And, unbuttoning his breeches, he straddled her: she did not resist, convinced that by letting him sate his lust she would be rid of him sooner, and the lecher, pinning her beneath him with his knees, started to tug on his hard and rather sturdy tool a third of an inch from the surface of my sister's face. "That beautiful face!" he exclaimed. "That pretty little whore's face – how I'm going to drench it with come! Oh, good God!" And at that very moment the floodgates opened, the sperm ejaculated and my sister's physiognomy, and particularly her nose and mouth, was wholly covered with

the proof of the libertinage of this man, who would perhaps not
have been satisfied so cheaply had his plan succeeded. The friar,
calmer now, thought only of getting away, and, having thrown
an *écu* for us on to the table and relit his lantern, told us, "You
little imbeciles, you little beggars, you are missing out on your
fortune – may the heavens punish you by having you fall into
penury, and, for my revenge, may I have the pleasure of seeing
it happen – these are my last wishes." My sister, who was wiping
her face, soon returned all his nonsense with interest, and with
our door closed until morning, the rest of our night at least was
peaceful. "What you saw there," my sister told me, "is one of
his favourite passions: he loves to come over a girl's face more
than anything – if only he left it at that . . . So be it, but the rascal
has many other tastes, and some so dangerous that I fear . . ."
But my sister, overcome by tiredness, fell asleep without finish-
ing her sentence, and as the next day brought further adventures
we gave no more thought to this one.

   'As soon it was morning we got up and, straightening our
clothes as best we could, we headed over to Md. Guérin's: this
heroine resided on the Rue Soli,[11] in a very neat first-floor apartment she shared with six rather tall ladies of 16 to 22 years of
age, all very fresh and pretty, but whom I shall describe, if it
pleases you, Messieurs, only as and when it becomes necessary
to do so. Madame Guérin, delighted by the plan that had brought
my sister to her, as she had indeed wanted for so long, received
and lodged the two of us with the greatest pleasure. "As young
as this girl may seem to you,"[12] my sister said as she introduced
me, "she'll serve you well – I'll vouch for her. She is sweet, pretty,
has a very good temperament, and the most decided whorishness
in her soul. You have many lechers among your acquaintances
who want children – here's one who is just what they are after
. . . put her to work." Madame Guérin, turning towards me,
asked me if I was ready for anything. "Yes, Madame," I replied
with a somewhat brazen air that pleased her, "anything to earn
money." We were introduced to our new companions, who
already knew my sister very well and who, out of friendship for
her, promised to take care of me. We all ate together and this,
in a word, Messieurs, was the first time I set myself up in a

brothel. It did not take long for me to find work there: that very
evening an old merchant bundled up in a coat arrived and
Madame Guérin paired me off with him to break me in. "Oh,
as for this one!" she said to the old libertine as she introduced
me to him. "You like them hairless, Mr. Duclos – I guarantee this
one does not have a hair on her." "Indeed," said the old eccentric
as he leered at me, "she seems quite the child – how old are you,
my little one?" "9 years old, Monsieur." "Nine years old . . . well,
well, Md. Guérin, you know this is just how I like them, or
younger still if you've got any – I'd damn well take them from
their wet nurse's arms." And as Madame Guérin withdrew, laughing at this, the door was closed on the two of us. Then the old
libertine approached, kissing me two or three times on the mouth;
with one of his hands guiding mine, he had me pull from his fly
a tool that was not remotely hard, and, carrying on without
saying too much, he untied my petticoats, laid me on the sofa
with my shift hitched up to my chest and, straddling my thighs,
which he had spread as wide as possible, he opened up my cunt
as much as he could with one hand while manualizing[13] himself
over it with the other with all his might. "The pretty little bird!"
he said, exciting himself and sighing with pleasure. "How I would
tame her if I still could, but I can't any more. I could try for four
years – this bugger of a prick would still not get hard. Open up,
open up, my little one, spread them wide." And finally, after a
quarter of an hour, I noticed my man sighing more heavily – a
few *Good God's* lent his words a little more energy, and I felt the
area around my cunt flood with the warm and scummy sperm
that the rascal, unable to release inside me, strived to push in
with his fingers. He was no sooner done than he left in a flash,
and I was still busy wiping myself down as my gallant was
opening the door to the street below. This is the provenance,
Messieurs, which earned me the name Duclos: it was the practice
in this house for each girl to adopt the name of her first client
and I followed their custom in this regard.'

'One moment,' said the Duc. 'I did not want to interrupt before
you came to a pause, but now you have, explain two things to
me a little more: the first, whether you ever had news of your

mother and if you ever discovered what happened to her; and
the second, whether the causes of the antipathy both you and
your sister had for her were naturally within you or whether
they had another cause. This is important to the history of the
human heart, and it is this in particular we are studying.' 'My
Lord,' replied Duclos, 'neither my sister nor I ever had the slightest news of that woman.' 'Well, then,' said the Duc, 'in that case
it is clear, is it not, Durcet?' 'Incontestably,' replied the financier.
'There is no reason to doubt it for a second, and you were very
fortunate not to fall into the trap, for you would never have
escaped from it.' 'It is remarkable,' said Curval, 'how this particular mania is catching on.' 'My word! That's because it's so
delectable!' said the Bishop. 'And the second point?' asked the
Duc, addressing the storyteller. 'As for the second point, my Lord,
the reason for our antipathy – I would indeed find it difficult to
account for this, but it was so violent in both our hearts that we
mutually swore we would have been capable of poisoning her
had we not managed to rid ourselves of her by other means. Our
aversion was of the greatest intensity, and as she had given us no
grounds for this, it is more than likely that this sentiment within
us was nothing other than Nature's handiwork.' 'And who could
doubt it?' said the Duc. 'Every day she happens to inspire in us
the most violent inclination for that which men call crime, and
you might have poisoned her twenty times without this action
being anything other than the result of this penchant for crime
she inspired in you – a penchant she revealed when she endowed
you with such intense antipathy. It is madness to imagine one
owes anything to one's mother, and on what, therefore, would
such gratitude be founded? On the fact she came when she was
fucked?[14] Rightly so, no doubt! As for me I see only reasons for
hatred and contempt – does she bring us happiness when she
brings us into the world? . . . Far from it, she hurls us into a world
full of dangers and it is up to us to survive them as best we can.
I remember I had one myself long ago who inspired in me more
or less the same sentiments Duclos felt for hers – I despised her.
As soon as I was able I dispatched her into the next world, and
I have never in all my days since tasted a thrill as intense as the
one I felt when she closed her eyes, never to open them again.'

At that moment dreadful sobs were heard coming from one of the quadrilles – it proved to be from the Duc's. Upon closer inspection, young Sophie was seen melting into tears: blessed with a different heart than these scoundrels, their conversation had awoken in her mind the cherished memory of the woman who had brought her into the world – perishing to protect her as she was abducted – and it was not without floods of tears that this cruel image offered itself to her tender imagination. 'Oh, by God!' said the Duc, 'this is excellent – it's your mummy you're weeping for, my snotty little one, isn't it? Come closer, come closer, so I can console you.' And the libertine, inflamed by these preliminaries, by these words, and by their effect, revealed a fearsome prick that seemed eager to come. Meanwhile, Marie, the duenna of this quadrille, brought the child out: her tears were flowing abundantly, the novice's outfit she was wearing that day only seemed to add to the charms of the sorrow that graced her; she could not have been prettier. 'Damn and bugger!' exclaimed the Duc, springing up like a madman. 'This morsel looks good enough to eat! I want to do what Duclos has just described – I want to smear her cunt with come . . . undress her!' And everyone awaited the outcome of this minor skirmish in silence. 'Oh, Monsieur, Monsieur!' Sophie cried out as she threw herself at the Duc's feet. 'Have some respect for my grief at least: I'm bemoaning the fate of a mother who was very dear to me, who died defending me and whom I shall never see again – take pity on my tears, and grant me at least this one evening of rest.' 'Oh, fuck!' exclaimed the Duc as he fondled a prick that was threatening the heavens. 'I would never have thought this scene could be so sensual – undress her! Undress her!' he told Marie in a frenzy. 'She should already be naked!' And Aline, who was on the Duc's sofa, wept warm tears as did gentle Adélaïde, who could be heard moaning in Curval's alcove as he, far from sharing in this beautiful creature's pain, scolded her brutally for abandoning the pose in which he had placed her, and moreover observed the outcome of this delightful scene with the keenest interest. Meanwhile, Sophie is undressed without the slightest regard for her grief, she is placed in the attitude Duclos had just depicted, and the Duc announces he is about to come. But how to go about it? What Duclos had just described was carried out by a man without an erection and the come from his flaccid prick could be directed wherever he wanted; this was not the case here – the menacing head of the Duc's tool would not turn away from the heavens it seemingly threatened. It would have required, so to speak, placing the child on top of it; they did not know how to go about this and all the while the greater the obstacles the more the irate Duc swore and blasphemed. Madame Desgranges finally came to the rescue – there was nothing in the way of libertinage that was unknown to this old witch: she grabbed the child and placed her so adeptly on her knees that, no matter what position the Duc adopted, the end of his prick always brushed against her vagina. Two servants come over to pin down the child's legs and, had it been time for her to be deflowered, she could not have been more prettily displayed. But this was not all: a skilful hand was needed to let the torrent gush forth, and to steer it straight to its destination; Blangis did not want to take a risk on a clumsy child's hand for such an important operation. 'Take Julie,' said Durcet. 'You'll be well pleased with her – she's beginning to frig like an angel.' 'Oh, fuck!' exclaimed the Duc, 'she'll blow it, the little slut – I know her! It's enough that I'm her father – she'll be terribly frightened.' 'Indeed, I recommend a boy,' said Curval. 'Take Hercule, he has a supple wrist.' 'I want only Madame Duclos,' said the Duc. 'She is the finest masturbatrix we have – let her abandon her post for a moment and come here.' Duclos steps forward, beaming with pride at having been favoured so emphatically; she pulls her sleeve up to her elbow and, taking hold of his Lordship's enormous instrument, she starts to tug on it, keeping the head uncovered, to rub it with such skill, to excite it with such quick thrusts and at the same time so favoured in keeping with the state of her patient, that at last the bomb explodes over the very hole it is meant to cover: it is flooded; the Duc yells, swears, raves; Duclos does not waver, her movements guided by the degree of pleasure they produce. Antinoüs, placed at the ready, delicately works the sperm into the vagina as it flows and the Duc, overcome by the most delicious sensations, collapses with pleasure as he sees his fevered member, whose ardour had just inflamed him so potently, soften between the fingers of his masturbatrix. He flops back on to his sofa, Madame Duclos returns to her place, the child cleans herself up, consoles herself and returns to her quadrille, and the tale continues, leaving the spectators convinced of a truth I believe they had already embraced quite some time ago – that the idea of crime was always able to inflame the senses and drive us to lubricity.

'I was utterly astonished,' said Duclos, taking up the thread of her oration, 'to see all my companions laughing when they saw me afterwards, asking me if I had cleaned myself up, and count-less other comments that proved they knew very well what I had just been doing. I was not left in the dark for long, and my sister, leading me to a room next to the one in which the trysts usually took place and in which I had just been closeted myself, showed me a hole that directly overlooked the sofa and through which one could easily see everything that was going on. She told me that these young ladies entertained themselves by having a look at what the men were doing to their companions, and that I was free to come there myself whenever I wanted, as long as it was not occupied – for it often happened, she said, that this respect-able hole was privy to mysteries they would teach me about in due course. It took less than a week for me to partake of this pleasure, and when a girl called Rosalie, one of the most beau-tiful blondes you could hope to find, was asked for one morning, I was curious to see what was about to happen to her; I hid myself away and here is the scene I witnessed. The man she had business with was no more than twenty-six to thirty years old: as soon as she entered he had her sit down on a very high stool designed for this ceremony; once she was seated he removed all the pins holding her hair in place, and the forest of magnificent blonde tresses gracing this beautiful girl's head tumbled to the floor; he took a comb from his pocket, combed them, untangled them, stroked them, kissed them, interlacing each gesture with an encomium for this beautiful hair that captivated him so pecu-liarly; finally, he pulled from his breeches a small prick, withered and very stiff, which he promptly wrapped in his Dulcinea's hair and, manualizing himself in her chignon, he came; putting his other hand around Rosalie's neck, and clasping her mouth to his kisses, he roused his dead tool once more. I saw my companion's hair all sticky with come – she cleaned it up, put the pins back in and our lovers parted.

'One month later, my sister was summoned for a character our young ladies told me to go and watch, as he had a rather baroque fantasy: he was a man of about 50 years of age; no sooner had he entered than, without any preamble, without a caress, he showed his backside to my sister, who, familiar with this ceremony, has him bend over a bed, grabs his slack and wrinkly old arse, thrusts five fingers into his orifice, and starts to shake it about so furiously the bed creaks. Meanwhile, our man, without revealing any more of himself, excites and fondles himself, keeps up with her movements, lends himself to them with lubricity and cries out that he is coming and that he is enjoying the greatest of pleasures. The exertion had been violent indeed, for my sister was drenched in sweat, but what meagre scenes and what sterility of imagination.

'If the one who was introduced to me soon after added little in terms of complexity, he at least seemed more sensual and his mania had in my view more of a libertine hue. He was a fat man of around 45 years of age, short, stocky, but hale and hearty; having not encountered a man of his taste before, my first act as soon as I was with him was to hitch my skirts up to my navel. A dog threatened with a rod could not have a longer face: "Oh, golly, sweetheart! Keep your cunt to yourself, I beg you," and at the same time he pulls my skirts down more hurriedly than I had raised them. "These little whores," he continued moodily, "only have cunts to show you. Thanks to you I might not be able to come all evening . . . not until I've got that fucking cunt out of my head." And as he said this, he turned me around and lifted my petticoats up methodically from behind; parading me around in this attitude, holding my skirts up all the while to see my arse move as I walked, he led me to the bed where he laid me down flat on my stomach. He then examined my backside with the most scrupulous attention, shielding himself all the while with his hand from the sight of my cunt, which he seemed to fear more than fire; at last, having warned me to conceal as best I could that shameful part, to use his expression, he lubriciously fondled my backside at length with both hands; he stretched it, squeezed it, sometimes he brought his mouth [to it], and once or twice I even felt it directly pressing against my hole, but he did not touch himself yet – nothing popped out. Apparently feeling a greater sense of urgency, however, he readied himself for the denouement of his operation: "Lie down flat on the floor," he told me, throwing a few cushions on to it. "There, yes, like that ... legs well spread, arse raised a little and the hole as wide open as possible – that's perfect," he continued as he saw how meek I was; and so, taking a stool, he placed it between my legs, and sat upon it in such a manner that his prick, which he pulled from his breeches at last and tugged on, was so to speak at the exact height of the hole he worshipped. His movements then quickened – with one hand he frigged himself, with the other he spread my buttocks – and all he said were some words of praise, seasoned with plenty of curses. "Oh, good God! What a fine arse!" he roared. "What a pretty hole! And how I'm going to flood it!" He was as good as his word: I felt all wet; the libertine seemed overwhelmed by his ecstasy – so true it is that the tribute paid at this temple is always more ardent than the incense burned at the other, and he left after promising to come and see me again as I satisfied his desires so well. He did indeed return the next day, but his fickleness led him to prefer my sister; I went to watch them and saw that he followed exactly the same procedures, and that my sister lent herself to them with the same acquiescence.'

'Did she have a fine arse, your sister?' asked Durcet. 'One small detail will allow you to judge, my Lord,' said Duclos. 'A famous artist, charged with painting a Venus with beautiful buttocks, asked for her the following year to be his model – having visited, so he said, all the bawds in Paris without finding her equal.' 'But in that case, as she was 15 years old, and as we have girls here of the same age, compare her backside for us,' continued the financier, 'with some of the arses you see before you.' Duclos cast her eyes on Zelmire and said that it would be impossible to find anyone who resembled her sister more closely in every respect – not just her arse, but even her face. 'Come then, Zelmire!' said the financier, 'come and show me your buttocks.'

She was indeed part of his quadrille. The charming girl approaches, trembling: she is placed at the foot of the sofa, lying on her belly; her rump is raised with cushions, the little hole fully revealed; the lecher, stiffening a little, kisses and fondles all that is exposed to him; he orders Julie to frig him, she does so, as his hands stray elsewhere; lubricity intoxicates him – his little instrument seems to stiffen for a moment with Julie's sensual tugs. The lecher swears, the come flows and supper sounds.

As the same abundance reigned at every meal, to describe one is to have described them all, but as almost everyone had come, the friends needed to recover their strength at this one and consequently drank a great deal. Zelmire, whom they were calling Duclos's sister, was extravagantly feted and everyone wanted to kiss her arse – the Bishop left his come on it, the 3 others got hard again, and they all went to bed as they had the previous evening, that is to say, each with the wife they had sat with on the sofas and the four fuckers who had not appeared since lunch.

3rd Day.

The Duc rose at nine o'clock: he would be the first to lend himself to the lessons Madame Duclos was to give the young girls; he planted himself in an armchair and submitted for an hour to the various touches, manipulations, caresses, and the various poses of each of these little girls, led and guided by their teacher; and as one can well imagine his fiery temperament was wildly excited by such a ceremony – he had to show incredible restraint not to spill his come, but master enough of his passions, he was able to contain himself and returned triumphant, boasting that he had just withstood an assault that he challenged his friends to sustain with the same composure. This led to the setting of forfeits, and a fine of fifty *louis* was imposed on anyone who came during the lessons. Instead of the usual breakfast and inspections, this particular morning was spent drawing up a table for the 17 orgies planned for the end of each week, as well as finalizing the deflorations which the friends felt better placed to decree now that they were more familiar with the subjects than they had been previously. As this table set out in a decisive manner all the operations to be undertaken in the campaign, we have thought it necessary to provide a copy to the reader. It seemed to us that, once he had read and discovered the fate of each subject, he would take a greater interest in these subjects in the remaining operations.

Table of plans for the rest of the expedition.

On the 7th of 9ber, at the end of the 1st week, the wedding of Michette and Giton shall proceed in the morning, and the bride and groom, whose age no more allows them to consummate their marriage than the next three couples, shall be separated that same evening, and without any further regard for a ceremony which served simply as entertainment during the day; the correction of those subjects entered on the list of the friend in charge that month shall proceed that same evening.

On the 14th the wedding of Narcisse and Hébé shall proceed likewise, with the same conditions as above. On the 21st likewise with that of Colombe and Zélamir, on the 28th likewise with that of Cupidon and Rosette. On the 4th of December, once Champville's narrations have paved the way for the following exploits, the Duc shall deflower Fanny. On the 5th the said Fanny shall be married to Hyacinthe, who shall enjoy his wife in front of the whole company; these shall be the festivities of the fifth week, and the corrections shall take place as usual that evening because the weddings shall be celebrated in the morning.

On the 8th Xber Curval shall deflower Michette.

On the 11th the Duc shall deflower Sophie; on the 12th, to celebrate the festivities of the 6th week, Sophie shall be married to Céladon, and with the same conditions as the marriage above. This shall not be repeated for the following.

On the 15th Curval shall deflower Hébé.

On the 18th the Duc shall deflower Zelmire, and on the 19th, to celebrate the festivities of the 7th week, Adonis shall marry Zelmire.

On the 20th Curval shall deflower Colombe. On the 25th,

Christmas day, the Duc shall deflower Augustine, and on the 26th, for the festivities of the 8th week, Zéphire shall marry Augustine. On the 29th Curval shall deflower Rosette, and the arrangements above have been made so that Curval, less well endowed than the Duc, shall have the youngest for his share.

On 1st January, the first day that Madame Martaine's narrations shall have paved the way for imagining new pleasures, the sodomitical deflorations shall proceed in the following order. On 1st January the Duc shall bugger Hébé; on the 2nd, to celebrate the 9th [week], Hébé, having been deflowered in front by Curval and behind by the Duc, shall be handed over to Hercule, who shall enjoy her in front of the whole company as prescribed. On the 4th Curval shall bugger Zélamir.

On the 6th the Duc shall bugger Michette and on the 9th, to celebrate the festivities of the 10th week, the said Michette, whose cunt shall have been deflowered by Curval and her arse by the Duc, shall be handed over to Brise-cul for him to enjoy &c. On the 11th the Bishop shall bugger Cupidon.

On the 13th Curval shall bugger Zelmire.

On the 15th the Bishop shall bugger Colombe. On the 16th, for the festivities of the 11th week, Colombe, whose cunt shall have been deflowered by Curval and her arse by the Bishop, shall be handed over to Antinoüs, who shall enjoy her &c. On the 17th the Duc shall bugger Giton.

On the 19th Curval shall bugger Sophie, on the 21st the Bishop shall bugger Narcisse. On the 22nd the Duc shall bugger Rosette. On the 23rd, for the festivities of the 12th week, Rosette shall be handed over to Bande-au-ciel.

On the 25th Curval shall bugger Augustine.

On the 28th the Bishop shall bugger Fanny. On the 30th, for the festivities of the 13th week, the Duc shall take Hercule as his husband and Zéphire as his wife, and the wedding, like the 3 others that follow, shall take place in front of everyone. On 6th February for the festivities of the 14th week Curval shall take Brise-cul as his husband and Adonis as his wife.

On 13th February for the festivities of the 15th week the Bishop shall take Antinoüs as his husband, and Céladon as his wife.

On 20th February for the festivities of the 16th week Durcet shall take Bande-au-ciel as his husband, and Hyacinthe as his wife.

As regards the festivities of the 17th week, which fall on the 27th of February, the eve of the conclusion of the narrations, these shall be celebrated by sacrifices among which Messieurs shall reserve *in petto*[15] their choice of victims. According to these arrangements, from 30th January all the virginities shall be taken, except those of the 4 young boys whom Messieurs are to take as wives and whom they are keeping intact until then in order to ensure their entertainment lasts until the end of the expedition. As the objects are deflowered, they shall replace the wives on the sofas during the narrations and by Messieurs' sides during the night, alternating as desired with the 4 remaining catamites whom Messieurs are saving to be their wives in the last month. From the moment a deflowered girl or boy replaces a wife on the sofa, this wife shall be repudiated. From this moment on she shall be utterly disgraced, and shall be ranked below even the servants. As regards Hébé, 12 years of age, Michette, 12 years of age, Colombe, 13 years of age, and Rosette, 13 years of age, as soon as they are handed over to the fuckers and seen to by them, they too shall fall into disgrace, shall only be summoned for harsh and brutal pleasures, shall rank alongside the repudiated wives and shall be treated with the utmost severity; and from 24th January all four shall find themselves on the same footing in this regard.

From this table one can see that the Duc shall have deflowered the cunts of Fanny, Sophie, Zelmire, Augustine, and the arses of Hébé, Michette, Giton, Rosette and Zéphire,

that Curval shall have deflowered the cunts of Michette, Hébé, Colombe, Rosette, and the arses of Zélamir, Zelmire, Sophie, Augustine and Adonis,

that Durcet, who does not fuck at all, shall have deflowered only Hyacinthe's arse, and shall take him as his wife,

and that the Bishop, who only fucks up the arse, shall have sodomitically deflowered Cupidon, Colombe, Narcisse, Fanny and Céladon.

*

The whole day having been spent drawing up these arrangements as much as chatting about them, and with no one being found to be at fault, nothing of interest happened until the hour of storytelling, where the arrangements being the same, though always varied, the celebrated Duclos mounted her rostrum and resumed in these terms her narration of the previous evening.

'A young man whose mania, though hardly libertine at all in my opinion, was nonetheless quite peculiar appeared at Md. Guérin's very soon after the last adventure I spoke of yesterday. He required a young and wholesome wet nurse; he suckled at her breast and came over the thighs of this good woman as he gorged on her milk. His prick seemed measly to me and he was a puny individual in every respect – and his climax was as meek as his habits.

'The next day in the same room another man appeared whose mania you will no doubt find more amusing. He wanted the woman to be wrapped up in a sheet that hermetically sealed her whole bosom and her whole face within it. The only part of the body he wished to see, and the most perfect specimen of which had to be found for him, was the arse; all the rest was of no interest to him and it was clear he would have been very upset to have even glimpsed it. Md. Guérin summoned for him a woman from outside, of rank ugliness, and of almost 50 years of age, but whose buttocks were shaped like those of Venus – there was no more beautiful sight. I wanted to see this operation: the old duenna, well wrapped up, immediately placed herself flat on her stomach upon the edge of the bed; our libertine, a man of around 30 years of age and who appeared to me to be a gentleman of the bench, lifts her skirts above her loins, and is sent into raptures at the sight of the charms offered to satisfy his tastes; he touches, he spreads her buttocks apart, kisses them ardently, and his imagination is far more inflamed by what he pictures for himself than it would doubtless have been had he seen the woman uncovered – however pretty she may have been. He imagines he is with Venus herself, and before very long his tool, stiffened by his tugging on it, spurts gentle raindrops all over the splendid buttocks before his eyes; his climax was intense and forceful; he sat there before the object of his worship, one of his hands opening it up while the other fondled it, and he yelled out ten times – "What a fine arse! Oh, what a delight it is to drench such an arse in come!" He got up as soon as he was done and made himself scarce without showing the slightest desire to know with whom he had just been.

'A young Abbé[16] asked for my sister some time afterwards: he was young and handsome, but his prick so small and limp one could barely see it. He laid her out almost naked on a sofa, kneeled down between her thighs, supporting her buttocks in his two hands and tickling the pretty little hole in her backside with one of them; meanwhile, his mouth drew close to my sister's cunt; he tickled her clitoris with his tongue, and did it so skilfully, making such precise and equal use of these two motions, that in three minutes he plunged her into delirium; I saw her head loll, her eyes roll wildly, and the minx cried out, "Oh, my dear Abbé, you are making me die of pleasure!" The Abbé's custom was to swallow every last drop of the liqueur his libertinage caused to flow; he did so, and pulling and tugging away on himself as he approached the sofa upon which my sister lay, I saw him spray the sure proofs of his virility over the floor. I had my own turn with him the following day and can assure you, Messieurs, that it is one of the sweetest practices I have encountered in my life: that rogue of an Abbé had my first fruit, and the first come I ever spilled was in his mouth;[17] keener than my sister to repay him for the pleasure he was giving me, I instinctively seized his raised prick and my little hand repaid him for all those delights his mouth was giving me.'

Here the Duc, singularly inflamed by the caresses to which he had lent himself that morning, could not refrain from interrupting; he thought this form of lubricity, executed with the delectable Augustine, whose keen and impish eyes heralded the most precocious temperament, would relieve him of the come that was causing his balls to prickle unbearably. She was in his quadrille, he liked her well enough – she was destined to be deflowered by him. He called her over: she was dressed that evening as a Savoyarde[18] and was charming in this disguise. The duenna hitched her skirts up and placed her in the position Duclos had described; the Duc grabbed hold of her buttocks first of all, kneeled down, introduced a finger to the rim of her anus, which he gently tickled, gripped the clitoris, which was already very noticeable in this lovely child, and sucked it. Languedoc girls are lascivious – Augustine was the proof of this: her pretty eyes sparkled, she sighed, she instinctively raised her thighs, and the Duc was fortunate enough to receive youthful come that was no doubt flowing for the first time. But one stroke of luck never follows another: there are libertines so hardened in their vices that the simpler and sweeter the act in which they are engaged, the less it excites their accursed minds; our dear Duc was of this number – he swallowed this delectable child's sperm[19] without his own wanting to flow. One could see the moment coming, for there is no one as fickle as a libertine – the moment, as I say, that he would blame this poor little wretch, who, utterly embarrassed at having yielded to nature, hid her head in her hands, and looked to flee back to her place. 'Let another take her place,' said the Duc, casting a furious glance at Augustine. 'I would rather suck them all than fail to come.' Zelmire, the second girl in his quadrille (and also reserved for him) was brought over: she was the same age as Augustine, but the anguish of her situation shackled within her any capacity for a pleasure that, in other circumstances perhaps, Nature would have allowed her to taste as well; her skirts are hitched up – above two slender thighs whiter than alabaster, she reveals a rounded little mons covered in a light down which had barely begun to grow. She is put in position: obliged to submit, she obeys without thinking, but, however hard the Duc tries, nothing comes; he gets up, furious, after a quarter of an hour and, storming into his closet with Hercule and Narcisse – 'Oh, fuck!' he exclaims. 'I can see that's not the prey I need,' he adds, referring to the two girls, 'and that I'll only succeed with this kind.' We do not know the excesses to which he was driven, but after a while screams and roars could be heard that proved he had won the battle and that boys always offered a far more dependable vessel to come into than even the most adorable girls. Meanwhile, the Bishop, too, had closeted himself away with Giton, Zélamir and Bande-au-ciel, and once the outbursts of his climax had also rung out, the two brothers, who had in all likelihood indulged in the same excesses, returned to listen more calmly to the rest of the tale, which our heroine resumed in these terms.

'Almost two years passed by without any other characters appearing at Madame Guérin's, or at least only those with tastes too common to be told here (or with the same tastes I have just described), when I was told to tidy myself up, and above all to wash my mouth thoroughly. I do as I'm told and go downstairs when instructed. A man of about fifty years of age, fat and stocky, was with Guérin – "There she is, Monsieur," she said. "Only 12 years old and as spick and span as if she had come straight from her mother's belly, that much I can vouch for." The client examines me, has me open my mouth, inspects my teeth, inhales my breath, and no doubt happy with everything, accompanies me to the temple destined for our pleasures. The two of us sit down directly facing each other and very close; no one could be more serious than my gallant, no one could be more composed or more phlegmatic; he ogled me, watched me with eyes half-closed, and I could not understand where all this was leading until, breaking the silence at last, he told me to collect as much saliva in my mouth as I could. I do as I'm told. As soon as he judges my mouth to be full, he throws himself passionately upon my neck, puts his arm around my head to fix it in position and, sealing his lips to mine, he pumps, he draws, he sucks and eagerly swallows all I had collected of that enchanting liqueur that seemed to overwhelm him with ecstasy; he draws my tongue in just as frenziedly, and as soon as he feels it to be dry and sees there is nothing left in my mouth, he orders me to begin my task again; he in turn begins his own again, I do mine again, and so on eight or even ten times in a row. He sucked in my saliva so frenziedly I felt my chest constrict; I thought a few sparks of pleasure at least would crown his ecstasy – I was wrong. His composure, which only unravelled a little in the midst of his passionate sucking, returned the moment he had finished, and, as soon as I told him I could stand it no longer, he fell to ogling me once again, staring at me as he had at the start; he then got up without saying a word to me, paid Madame Guérin and left.'

*

'Oh, good God! Good God!' said Curval. 'So I'm more fortunate than he, for I'm coming!' Everyone raises their heads to see the dear Président doing to his wife Julie – his companion on the sofa that day – the very thing Duclos had just described; they knew this passion was rather to his liking, aside from a few details that Julie could expertly provide, and which the young Duclos had doubtless not been able to match with her gallant, if indeed the refinements this man had demanded – and which the Président was far from desiring – are to be believed.

'One month later,' said Duclos, who had been ordered to continue, 'I had an encounter with the sucker of an absolutely contrary avenue: he was an old Abbé, who, having kissed me beforehand and caressed my backside for over half an hour, thrust his tongue into my hole, penetrated it, darted it about, turned it this way and that with such art I almost thought I could feel it deep in my guts; but this Abbé, less phlegmatic than the last one as he spread my buttocks with one hand, frigged himself very sensually with the other, and came, drawing my anus into his mouth so violently, tickling it so lubriciously that I shared his ecstasy. When he was done he examined my buttocks again for a moment, stared at the hole he had just enlarged, could not stop himself from smothering it with kisses once more, then made himself scarce, assuring me that he would often come back to ask for me and that he was very pleased with my arse. He kept his word and for nearly 6 months he came to me three or four times a week to carry out the same operation, one to which he had so accustomed me that he never failed to leave me expiring with pleasure – a detail which in any case seemed quite irrelevant to him, for as far as I could tell he neither inquired nor seemed to care about it. Who knows indeed – so extraordinary are men's ways – if this might not have displeased him?'

Here Durcet, whom this tale had just inflamed, wanted like the old Abbé to suck an arsehole, but not that of a girl; he summons Hyacinthe, of all of them the one he liked best; he puts him in position, kisses his arse, frigs his prick, gamahuches[20] him. From the quivering of his nerves, from the spasm that always preceded his coming, everyone thinks his vile little sprat, which Aline was tugging on as hard as she could, was finally about to disgorge its seed, but the financier was not so profligate with his come – he was not in the least bit hard. They come up with a change of objects: Céladon is offered but to no avail; a timely bell announcing supper comes to rescue the financier's honour . . . 'It is not my fault,' he said, laughing to his friends. 'As you could see, I was about to win the battle – it's this damned supper that's delaying it. Come, let's exchange one pleasure for another: I shall return with even greater ardour to our amorous skirmishes once Bacchus has crowned me.' The supper, as succulent as it was merry, and as lubricious as ever, was followed by orgies where many little abominations were carried out: many mouths and arses were sucked, but one of the things they delighted in the most was hiding the faces and breasts of the young girls and placing wagers on whether they could recognize them simply by examining their buttocks. The Duc got it wrong a few times, but the 3 others were such connoisseurs of arses that they did not make a single mistake. Everyone went to bed and the following day brought new pleasures, and some new reflections.

Fourth Day.

As the friends were eager to identify at any hour of the day those youths, among both the girls and the boys, whose virginities were deemed to belong to them, they decided to have them wear with all their various outfits a ribbon in their hair that would indicate to whom they belonged: as a result, the Duc opted for pink and green, and the cunts of all who wore a pink ribbon to the front would thus belong to him, as would the arses of all who wore a green one to the rear; from this moment Fanny, Zelmire, Sophie and Augustine each wore a pink bow in their hair to the side, and Rosette, Hébé, Michette, Giton and Zéphire wore a green one in their hair to the rear as evidence of the rights the Duc enjoyed over their arses. Curval chose black for the front, and yellow for the rear, so that from then on Michette, Hébé, Colombe and Rosette always wore a black bow to the front, and Sophie,

Zelmire, Augustine, Zélamir and Adonis a yellow one in a chignon; Durcet only singled out Hyacinthe, with a lilac ribbon to the rear, and the Bishop, who had the rights to only five sodomitical virginities, ordered Cupidon, Narcisse, Céladon, Colombe and Fanny to wear a violet one to the rear. No matter what they wore, these ribbons were never to be removed and, at a glance, spying one of these young people with such and such a colour to the front and another to the rear, they could immediately identify who had rights over the arse and who had them over the cunt. Curval, who had spent the night with Constance, complained bitterly about her the next day; we are not sure what lay behind his complaints – it takes so little to offend a libertine – but whatever it may have been he was about to have her put down for punishment the following Saturday when this beautiful creature announced she was pregnant. As Curval, the only party who could be suspected aside from her husband, had only known her carnally since the beginnings of this expedition, that is to say for the last four days, such news greatly amused our libertines for the clandestine pleasures they foresaw themselves enjoying all too clearly. The Duc could not get over it – in any case, in his eyes this event merited exemption from the punishment she should otherwise have suffered for having displeased Curval. They wanted to let the fruit ripen: the idea of a pregnant woman entertained them and the promise of what was to follow amused their perfidious imaginations even more lubriciously; she was excused from the lunch service, from punishments, and from some other little duties that her condition now made it less appealing to see her fulfil, but was still obliged to be present on the sofa and, until ordered otherwise, to share the bed of whoever it pleased to choose her. On this morning it was Durcet who lent himself to the masturbation lessons and, as his prick was extraordinarily small, he posed more difficulties for the schoolgirls; they worked away on him nonetheless, but the little financier, who had done a woman's job all night, could never take on that of a man; he was as tough as old leather, insensible, and all the skill of these eight charming schoolgirls, guided by the most skilful of teachers, failed to raise even his nose. He left utterly triumphant, and as impotence always results in a little of that humour called *spite*[21] in matters of libertinage, his inspections were astonishingly severe: Rosette among the girls and Zélamir among the boys were the victims – one was not in the state she had been told to be in (this enigma will be revealed) and the other had unfortunately relieved himself of that which he had been told to retain. At the communal privies only Duclos, Marie, Aline and Fanny, two second-class fuckers and Giton were present; Curval, who was very hard that day, became very inflamed with Duclos – the lunch, at which there were some very libertine exchanges, did nothing to calm him, and the coffee served by Colombe, Sophie, Zéphire and his dear friend Adonis, set his imagination completely ablaze. He grabbed the last of these four and, pitching him over a sofa, placed his enormous member, swearing as he did so, between the young boy's thighs from behind, and as this enormous tool stuck out more than 6 inches the other side, he ordered him to frig the protruding part vigorously while he himself frigged the child over the piece of flesh with which he had skewered him. Meanwhile, he displayed to the whole company an arse as filthy as it was large, the foul hole of which was all too tempting to the Duc: seeing this arse within reach, he aimed his skittish instrument at it as he continued to suck Zéphire's mouth, an operation he had already begun before the idea he was now putting into action had occurred to him. Curval, who had not been expecting such an assault, blasphemed with delight – he stamped his feet, spread himself wider and yielded to it; at this point the youthful come of the charming boy he was frigging dripped on to the enormous head of his raging instrument; the warm come he feels wetting him, the repeated thrusts of the Duc, who was also starting to come, it all drives him on, it all brings matters to a head and floods of foaming sperm come and drench Durcet's arse – he had posted himself in front, as he said, so that none of it would be wasted, and his plump white cheeks were gently soaked in an enchanting liqueur he would have much preferred in his bowels. Meanwhile, the Bishop had not been idle: he was sucking the divine arseholes of Colombe and Sophie one after the other; no doubt tired, however, from some nocturnal exertions, he gave little sign of life, and like all libertines who are made unjust by capriciousness and disgust, he took out on these delightful children the all

too merited deficiencies of his feeble constitution. The friends
dozed for a few moments and, as the hour of storytelling had
arrived, they went to listen to the lovely Duclos, who resumed
her tale in the following manner.

'There had been a few changes in Md. Guérin's house,' said our
heroine. 'Two very pretty girls had just found dupes to support
them and to betray, as we all do. To make up for this loss, our
dear Mother[22] had cast her eyes on the daughter of a tavern-
keeper from the Rue St. Denis, a girl of 13 years of age and one
of the prettiest creatures one could ever hope to find. But the
little lady, as prudent as she was devout, resisted all her seductions until Madame Guérin, having used a clever ruse to lure
her to our house one day, placed her in the hands of the peculiar
character whose mania I shall describe for you. He was a churchman of 55 to 56 years of age, but so youthful and vigorous one
would have thought him under forty. No one in the world had
a more singular talent than this man for luring young girls into
vice, and as it was his most sublime gift, he made it his one and
only pleasure; all his delight lay in uprooting those childhood
prejudices, in making virtue contemptible, and in draping vice
in the most beautiful colours. No effort was spared: seductive
images, flattering promises, delightful examples, everything was
brought to bear, everything was adeptly handled, everything
was skilfully adapted to the age, to the particular wit of the child,
and he never missed his mark – in just two hours of conversation
he was sure to make a whore out of the most virtuous and most
prudent of girls, and for thirty years he had plied his trade in
Paris. He had confessed to Md. Guérin, one of his closest friends,
that according to his register he had seduced and plunged more
than 10 thousand young girls into libertinage; he offered such
services to more than 15 bawds, and when these were not required
he conducted research on his own account, corrupting all he
encountered and dispatching them afterwards to his procuresses
– for what is most extraordinary, and indeed the very reason,
Messieurs, I am telling the story of this unique character, is that
he never enjoyed the fruits of his labour himself: he would shut
himself away with the child, but for all the opportunities his wit

and eloquence brought him, he would leave very inflamed. We were absolutely certain this operation excited his senses, but it was quite impossible to know where, or how, he satisfied them: the closest examination revealed nothing other than a prodigious fire in his eyes as he finished his speech, a few hand movements over the front of his breeches that revealed a pronounced erection provoked by the diabolical work he carried out, but no more. He arrived, and was shut away with the young barmaid. I watched him: the tête-à-tête was lengthy, the seducer employed the most extraordinary pathos, the child cried, became animated, seemed to become possessed by a kind of enthusiasm – this was the moment our character's eyes were at their most inflamed, and we observed his hand moving over his breeches; he got up shortly after, the child stretched out her arms as if to embrace him, he kissed her as a father would and without the slightest hint of lubricity; he left, and three hours later the little girl arrived at Md. Guérin's with her things.'

'And the man?' asked the Duc. 'He'd vanished straight after his lesson,' replied Duclos. 'Without returning to see the result of his labour?' 'No, my Lord, he was so sure of it – he had never failed, not even once.' 'This is a quite extraordinary character,' said Curval. 'What do you make of it, M. le Duc?' 'What I make of it,' this gentleman replied, 'is that he was aroused by this seduction alone, and that he came in his breeches as a result.' 'No,' said the Bishop, 'you haven't got it: this was just a preliminary to his depravities, and upon leaving I wager he went on to commit much greater ones.' 'Greater ones?' asked Durcet. 'And what more delectable pleasure could he have procured for himself than that of enjoying his own handiwork as he was its lord and master?' 'Well,' said the Duc, 'I wager that I have guessed it: this, as you have said, was just a preliminary, his mind would become inflamed by corrupting girls, and he would then go off and bugger boys . . . He was a bugger, I wager.' Duclos was asked whether she had any evidence for such a supposition and whether he also seduced little boys; our storyteller replied that she had no such evidence and, despite the Duc's very plausible assertion, each nevertheless remained in suspense as to the character of this strange evangelist, and once it was universally agreed his mania was truly delectable, but that one had either to consume one's own creation or do something worse afterwards, Duclos took up the thread of her storytelling thus.

'The very next day after the arrival of our young novice, who was named Henriette, there arrived a fanciful lecher who put the two of us to work at the same time; this new libertine's only pleasure was to observe through a hole all the rather peculiar delights taking place in an adjoining room – he used to enjoy secretly watching these and thus found in the pleasures of others divine sustenance for his own lubricity. He was put in the room I spoke of before, and where I used to go so often, like my companions, to spy on and enjoy the passions of libertines. I was to entertain him as he looked on, and the young Henriette went into the other room with the gamahucher of arseholes I spoke of yesterday. That lecher's very sensual passion was the spectacle we wished to provide for our observer, and to inflame the former all the more, and to ensure his performance would be more torrid and more pleasing on the eye, he was told that the girl chosen for him was a novice who was to make her debut with him; he was readily persuaded of this by the little barmaid's modest and childlike air, and so he was as ardent and as lubricious as could be in his libidinous pursuits, which he had no idea were being observed. As for my man, his eye glued to the hole, one hand on my buttocks, the other on his prick, which he rubbed little by little, he seemed to attune his ecstasy to the one he was secretly watching. "Oh, what a spectacle!" he said from time to time ... "What a fine arse that little girl has and how well that bugger is kissing it!" When at last Henriette's lover came, mine took me in his arms and, having kissed me for a moment, turned me around, fondled, kissed, licked my behind lubriciously and drenched my buttocks with the proofs of his virility.'

'As he frigged himself?' asked the Duc. 'Yes, my Lord,' replied Duclos, 'and as he frigged a prick of such extraordinary minute [ness] it is not worth describing.'

*

'The character who appeared next,' continued Duclos, 'would perhaps not merit a place on my list had he not seemed to me worthy of citing to you for the quite peculiar circumstance he added to his pleasures, which were in other respects quite simple, and which will show you the degree to which libertinage destroys in men all feelings of modesty, virtue and decency. This one did not want to see, he wanted to be seen; and knowing there were men whose fantasy was to watch in secret the pleasures of others, he asked Madame Guérin to have a man of such tastes hidden so he could offer him the spectacle of his pleasures. Madame Guérin approached the man I had entertained just a few days earlier at the peephole, and without telling him that the man he was about to see knew very well he was being watched, as this would have spoiled his pleasure, she had him believe he would indeed be secretly watching as he pleased the spectacle he was to be offered. The observer was shut away with my sister in the room with the hole and I went in with the other one, a young man of twenty-eight, handsome and youthful; informed as to the whereabouts of the hole, he placed himself facing it without ostentation, and positioned me next to him. I frigged him: as soon as he was erect, he got up, revealed his prick to the observer, turned round, showed his arse, hitched my skirts up, showed him mine, kneeled before it, nuzzled my anus with the end of his nose, spread it apart firmly, revealed it all with great pleasure and precision and came as he frigged himself, holding me from behind, with my skirts hitched up, in front of the hole, so that the man who had stationed himself there could see all at once at this crucial moment both my buttocks and my lover's raging prick. As much as the latter had revelled in this, God knows what the other must have felt; my sister said he was in seventh heaven and that he swore he had never experienced such pleasure – and her buttocks were afterwards drenched at least as much as mine had been.'

'If the young man had a fine prick and a fine arse,' said Durcet, 'that was reason enough for a pretty climax.' 'In that case it must have been delightful,' said Duclos, 'for his prick was very long, quite sturdy, and his arse as soft, as plump, as prettily shaped as that of Cupid himself.' 'Did you spread his buttocks?' asked the Bishop. 'Did you show his hole to the observer?' 'Yes, my Lord,' said Duclos, 'he showed mine and I revealed his – he could not have presented it more lubriciously.' 'I have seen a dozen scenes like this in my life,' said Durcet, 'which have cost me plenty of come – there are few that are more delightful to carry out. I am talking about both perspectives, for it is as lovely to spy as it is to be spied upon.'

'A character with more or less the same taste,' Duclos continued, 'took me to the Tuileries[23] a few months later: he wanted me to entice passing men and frig them right under his very nose, as he hid among a pile of chairs; and once I had frigged seven or eight for him thus, he sat on a bench on one of the busiest paths, hitched up my skirts from behind, showed my arse to passers-by, took out his prick and ordered me to frig it in front of all these passers-by – which, though it was dark, caused such an uproar that by the time he brazenly[24] spilled his come there were more than ten people surrounding us and we had to run off to avoid being shamed.

'When I told Madame Guérin the story, she laughed and told me she had known a man in Lyon, where young boys pander for a living – a man, as I say, whose mania was just as peculiar: he dressed up as a street pimp, bringing custom himself to two whores he paid and kept for this purpose, then hid in a corner to watch his patrons in action, while the whore, whom he bribed to this end, would show him the prick and buttocks of the libertine she was with – this was the only pleasure that suited our fake pimp's tastes and that could make him spill his come.'

As Duclos had finished her tale early, they spent the rest of the evening on a few choice lubricious acts until supper was served, and as their minds had been inflamed by acts of brazenness, the friends did not head to their closets, but each took his pleasure in front of the others: the Duc had Madame Duclos strip naked; he then had her bend over and rest against the back of a chair and ordered Madame Desgranges to frig him over her friend's buttocks, so that the head of his prick would brush against

Duclos's arsehole with each thrust. They added some other
details that the order of contents does not yet allow us to unveil,
so many indeed that the storyteller's arsehole was left utterly
drenched, and the Duc, very well served and entirely surrounded,
came with great roars that showed how inflamed his mind had
been. Curval had himself fucked, the Bishop and Durcet for their
part did some very strange things with both sexes, and supper
was then served. After the meal there was dancing: the 16 young
people, four fuckers and the 4 wives were able to form three
contre-dances,[25] but all the players at this ball were naked, and
our libertines, nonchalantly reclined on the sofas, entertained
themselves deliciously with all the charms displayed in turn by
the various poses the dancers were required to assume; they had
beside them the storytellers, who manualized them quickly or
slowly, according to the pleasures they were taking, but,
exhausted by the day's delights, no one came and each took to
his bed to recover the strength required to indulge in new abominations the following day.

Fifth Day.

It was Curval that morning who went off to lend himself to the
school's masturbations, and as the young girls were starting
to make progress, he had considerable difficulty resisting the
repeated tugging and the varied and lubricious poses of these
eight charming little girls, but as he wanted to contain himself,
he abandoned his post. Breakfast was taken, and it was decreed
that morning that Messieurs' four young lovers – namely Zéphire
(the Duc's favourite), Adonis (Curval's beloved), Hyacinthe
(Durcet's companion), and Céladon (the Bishop's) – would
henceforth attend all meals at their lovers' sides, and would as
a rule sleep in their bedrooms each night, a privilege they would
share with the wives and fuckers; this would allow them to
dispense with the customary morning ceremony, according to
which the 4 fuckers who had not slept would bring them 4 boys.
The latter now arrived on their own, and when Messieurs entered
the young boys' quarters, they would now be received only by

the remaining four with the prescribed ceremonies. The Duc, who over the last two or three days had become smitten with Madame Duclos, whose arse he thought splendid, and whose conversation he found pleasant, insisted she sleep in his bedroom too, and, once this precedent was set, Curval followed by inviting the aged Fanchon, with whom he was besotted, into his bedroom; the two others waited a little while longer before filling this fourth position of privilege in their quarters at night. They also ruled that same morning that the 4 young lovers who had just been chosen would ordinarily wear, whenever their character costumes were not required (such as when they were in quadrilles) – would, as I say, wear the clothes and attire I shall now describe: a kind of small surcoat,[26] very tight-fitting, light, and open like a Prussian uniform, but far shorter and reaching no lower than halfway down the thigh; this little surcoat, fastened at the waist and tails as with all uniforms, was to be of pink satin lined with white taffeta; the facing and cuffs were of white satin, and beneath was a kind of short jacket or waistcoat, also of white satin, with matching breeches that had a heart-shaped opening below the waist at the back, so that reaching through this slit one could grab the arse without the slightest difficulty; a ribbon tied in a large bow fastened the flap, and when one wanted this part of the child to be completely bare all one had to do was pull on the bow, which was of a colour chosen by the friend to whom the virginity belonged; their hair, casually dressed with a few curls to the side, was completely free and loose at the back and tied simply with a ribbon of the prescribed colour; a highly perfumed powder, somewhere between grey and pink in tone, added colour to their locks; their eyebrows, perfectly trimmed and generally painted black, combined always with a delicate hint of rouge upon their cheeks, brought out their dazzling beauty; their heads were bare, their legs in white silk stockings embroidered with pink, their feet delightfully shod in grey slippers tied with a large pink bow. A sumptuously tied cravat of cream gauze was paired with a small lace ruffle, and examining all four of them one could doubtless be assured there was no more charming sight in the world. The moment they were adopted in this manner, all permissions of the kind sometimes granted in the

morning were absolutely refused them, though they were granted
as many rights over the wives as the fuckers enjoyed: they could
mistreat them as they pleased not only during the meals but even
at any other time of the day, certain that they would never be
condemned for it. These tasks complete, the usual inspections
were carried out: beautiful Fanny, whom Curval had ordered to
remain in a particular state, was in the contrary state (all this
will be explained below); her name was entered into the book of
corrections; among the young ones, Giton had done what it was
forbidden to do; his name was put down too, and once the chapel
duties were carried out, with few matters arising, it was time
to eat. This was the first meal at which the four lovers were
in attendance: each took his place beside the friend who was
smitten with him, the latter seating him to his right with his
favourite fucker to his left; the addition of these charming little
guests enlivened the meal – all four were very well behaved,
terribly sweet, and beginning to enter fully into the spirit of their
new home. The Bishop, on very good form that day, did not stop
kissing Céladon for almost the whole meal, and as this child was
required to join the quadrille serving coffee, he left shortly before
dessert; when his Lordship, whose mind had just been inflamed
by the boy, saw him again quite naked in the drawing room next
door, he could not contain himself. 'Good God!' he said, all
ablaze. 'As I can't bugger him, at least I can do to him what Curval
did yesterday to his own catamite.' And grabbing the little fellow,
he lay him down on his belly as he said this and slipped his prick
between his thighs. The libertine was in seventh heaven: the hair
of his prick rubbed against the sweet hole he would very much
have liked to pierce; with one hand he fondled the buttocks of
this delectable little Cupid, with the other he frigged his prick;
he glued his mouth to that of this beautiful child, pumped the
air from his chest, swallowed the saliva from it; the Duc, to excite
him with the spectacle of his own libertinage, placed himself
before him as he gamahuched Cupidon, the second of the boys
serving coffee that day, from behind; Curval had himself frigged
by Michette in full view of the Bishop and Durcet offered the
latter Rosette's spread buttocks. Everything conspired to procure
the Bishop the ecstasy one could see he craved: it arrived, his

nerves quivered, his eyes blazed – he would have been a fearful
sight for anyone who did not know the terrible effects such thrills
had on him; his come escaped at last and dripped on to Cupidon's
buttocks – the boy had carefully been placed at the last moment
beneath his little friend to receive proofs of virility which were
nevertheless not his due. The time for the narrations came, everyone took their places – by a rather peculiar arrangement all the
fathers had their daughters on their sofas this day; this caused
no concern and Duclos continued in these terms.

'As you have not demanded, Messieurs, that I provide you with
an exact account of what happened to me day by day at Md.
Guérin's, but simply of the more peculiar events that may have
marked some of these days, I shall pass over in silence various
uninteresting childhood anecdotes that would offer you nothing
but monotonous repetitions of what you have already heard,
and tell you that I had just turned sixteen, not without considerable experience of the profession I was practising, when there
fell to my lot a libertine whose daily fantasy deserves to be told:
he was a sober judge of almost fifty years of age and if Md.
Guérin (who told me she had known him for many years) was
to be believed, he carried out without fail each morning the
fantasy I shall now share with you. His usual bawd, who had
just retired, had recommended him beforehand to our dear
Mother, and it was with me that he began at her house. He
stationed himself alone at the hole I spoke of before: in the
adjoining room there was a porter or Savoyard,[27] a commoner
at any rate, but clean and healthy – this was all he required, age
and appearance did not matter to him; in full view, and as close
to the hole as possible, I frigged this honest peasant, who had
been briefed beforehand and was delighted to be earning money
this way. Having lent myself without holding back to everything
the dear fellow could desire of me, I had him come into a porcelain saucer and, ditching him there as soon as he had spilled his
last drop, I hastened into the other room. My man is waiting
for me in ecstasy: he pounces on the saucer, swallows the nice
warm come; his own flows; with one hand I spur on his ejaculation, with the other I collect it carefully as it falls and, swiftly

raising my hand to the lecher's mouth with every spurt, as nimbly and deftly as I can, I have him swallow his come as he spills it. This was all there was to it – he neither touched nor kissed me, nor even hitched up my skirts, and rising from his armchair with a coolness to match the fervour he had just shown, he took his cane and withdrew, saying that I frigged very well, and that I had grasped his tastes very well. The following day another man was brought in, as they had to be changed every day along with the women: my sister looked after him, he left, content to begin afresh the next day, and throughout the time I spent at Md. Guérin's I never saw him miss this ceremony at precisely nine in the morning – without him ever hitching up the skirts of any of the girls, even though he was shown some charming ones.'

'Did he want to see the porter's arse?' asked Curval. 'Yes, my Lord,' replied Duclos, 'the girls had to take care, when entertaining the man whose come he'd eat, to turn him this way and that, and the peasant himself also had to turn the girl this way and that in every direction.' 'Ah! Now I see,' said Curval, 'but I couldn't make sense of it otherwise.'

'Soon after,' Duclos continued, 'we saw a girl of about 30 years of age, quite pretty but with hair as red as Judas, arrive at the harem; we thought at first she was a new companion, but she soon put us straight, telling us she had come for just one tryst. The man for whom this new heroine was destined, a stout financier of healthy complexion, soon arrived himself, and the peculiarity of his taste – as it was for him that a girl surely no one else would have wanted was destined – this peculiarity, as I say, gave me a burning desire to go and watch them. No sooner were they in the usual room than the girl stripped naked and showed us a very white and plump figure. "Come on! Jump! Jump!" the financier told her. "Warm yourself up, you know full well I want you to sweat." And there the redhead was, skipping and running around the bedroom, leaping like a young goat, and our man observing her as he frigged himself – and all this without my being able to fathom where this adventure was heading. When the poor creature was dripping with sweat, she approached the libertine, raised an arm and had him smell her armpit, where the sweat was dripping from every hair. "Ah! That's it! That's it!" said our man, staring fervently at the sticky arm beneath his nose. "What a smell! How ravishing!" Then, kneeling before her, he smelled her and breathed her in, his nose inside her vagina and by her arsehole, but always returning to her armpits, either because that part delighted him the most, or because the aroma was at its strongest there – it was there his mouth and nose always returned with the greatest eagerness. At last a fairly long if not very sturdy prick, which he had been tugging on vigorously for more than an hour without any success, deigns to raise its head, the girl positions herself, the financier approaches from behind to bury his sprat in her armpit, she squeezes her arm, forming it seems to me a very tight spot in this place; meanwhile, in this position he enjoys the sight and smell of her other armpit, grabs hold of it, shoves his snout right into it, and comes as he licks it, devouring that part of the body which gives him so much pleasure.'

'And this creature,' asked the Bishop, 'absolutely had to be a redhead?' 'Absolutely,' said Duclos. 'These women, as you well know, my Lord, have in that part of the body an infinitely more violent aroma, and his sense of smell was doubtless the one that, once pricked by something strong, best awakened in him the organs of pleasure.' 'So be it,' resumed the Bishop, 'but by God it seems to me I would rather have smelled that woman's arse than sniff under her arms.' 'Oho!' exclaimed Curval. 'They both have their attractions, and I assure you that if you gave it a try you would find it quite delectable.' 'Meaning, Mr. le Président, this little dish amuses you too?' 'Well I've tried it,' said Curval, 'with a few details added here or there, and I assure you I've never done so without it costing me some come.' 'Well, I can guess what those details were, can I not?' the Bishop responded. 'You smelled the arse too . . .' 'Oh! Come, come,' the Duc interrupted, 'don't make him give confession, my Lord – he would tell us things we should not hear yet. Continue, Duclos, and do not let these chatterboxes tread on your turf.'

*

'It had been,' our narrator resumed, 'more than 6 weeks since Madame Guérin had absolutely prohibited my sister from washing, and had demanded she keep herself in the most rank and foul state possible, without our being able to fathom her motives, when an old and florid lecher appeared, apparently half-drunk, rudely asking Madame whether the whore was truly filthy. "Oh, you can count on it!" said Madame Guérin. They are introduced, shut away, and I fly to the hole: I no sooner reach it than I see my sister, naked, astride a large bidet full of champagne, and our man armed with a big sponge, washing and soaking her, carefully collecting every drop that dripped from her body or the sponge. It had been so long since my sister had cleaned any part of herself, as she had been strictly forbidden even to wipe her backside, that the wine immediately acquired a dirty brown colour and indeed a smell that could not have been very pleasant, but the more this wine was tainted by the muck it absorbed, the more it delighted our libertine: he tastes it, finds it delicious, grabs a glass and, filling it half a dozen times, swallows the disgusting and putrefied wine in which he has just washed a body caked so long in filth. Once he has finished drinking, he grabs my sister, lays her on the bed flat on her stomach and disgorges all over her buttocks and gaping hole the shameless seed that frothed with the foul particulars of his disgusting mania.

'But another mania, far dirtier still, was immediately to reveal itself to me: we had in the house one of those women called walkers in brothel parlance, whose job it is to fly about night and day to unearth fresh game. This creature, more than 40 years of age, combined withered charms which had never been very seductive with the dreadful failing of having feet that stank; this was the very subject required by the Marquis de ... He arrives, is introduced to Lady Louise, as our heroine was called, finds her delightful, and as soon as he is with her in the sanctuary of pleasures, has her take off her shoes. Louise, who had been told to change neither her stockings nor her shoes for more than a month, offers the Marquis a rancid foot that would have made anyone else throw up, but it was precisely what was most dirty and disgusting about the foot that most inflamed our man: he grabs it, kisses it ardently, his mouth parts one toe after another and in the gaps between his tongue gathers with fervent enthusiasm that blackish, stinking filth that nature leaves there and that a lack of cleanliness allows to accumulate; he not only draws it into his mouth but swallows it, savours it, and the come he spills as he frigs himself during this escapade offers unequivocal proof of the excessive pleasure it gives him.'

'Oh! As for that one, I don't get it,' said the Bishop. 'Then I'll have to try to make you understand,' said Curval . . . 'What? You have a taste for that?' asked the Bishop. 'Watch me,' said Curval. They get up, surround him, and see this extraordinary libertine, who embraced every taste of the most depraved lechery, taking Fanchon, that dirty and aged servant described above, by her disgusting foot and swooning with lust as he sucks on it. 'As for me, I understand all that,' said Durcet. 'One needs only to be somewhat jaded to grasp all such abominations – satiety inspires them in libertinage, which then promptly tries them out. One tires of the simple thing, the imagination is piqued, and the poverty of our means, the weakness of our faculties, the corruption of our minds leads us to abominations.'

'Such was no doubt the case,' said Duclos as she resumed, 'of the old Commandeur des Carrières, one of the finest of Madame Guérin's clients. He only wanted women physically impaired either by libertinage, or by nature, or by the hand of justice: in a word, he accepted only the one-eyed, blind, lame, hunchbacked, legless, one-armed, toothless, those with mutilated limbs or those whipped and branded or clearly scarred by some act of justice or another, and always moreover of a ripe old age. For the scene I secretly observed, he had been given a 50-year-old woman, branded as a public thief, who was also one-eyed. This double degradation was for him something to be treasured: he shuts himself away with her, has her strip naked, delightedly kisses the unmistakeable signs of her disgrace upon her shoulders, passionately sucks every ridge of the wound he called a mark of honour. Once this was done, all his ardour was brought to bear on her arsehole: he parted her buttocks, voluptuously kissed the withered hole they

concealed, sucked it for a very long time, and then, straddling [*Say this*
the whore's back, he rubbed his prick against the scars inflicted *better.*][28]
by justice, praising her for having merited this triumph, and,
leaning over her backside, he consummated his sacrifice, kissing again the altar at which he had just paid such a lengthy
tribute, and spilling his abundant come over those seductive
marks that had so inflamed his mind.'

'Good God!' said Curval, whose lubricity that day was warping
his imagination. 'See, my friends – see from this hard prick how
the tale of this passion inflames me!' And calling Madame
Desgranges – 'Come, you foul bitch!' he said. 'Come! You who
so resemble the one who's just been described, come give me the
same pleasure she gave the Commandeur.' Madame Desgranges
approaches; Durcet, an ally in these excesses, helps the Président
strip her naked; at first she demurs, as they knew she would, and
they scold her for concealing something that will further endear
her to their company; finally her withered back is bared and a V
and an M[29] reveal that she twice suffered the ignominious operation whose traces nevertheless fire our libertines' shameless
desires. The rest of that worn and withered body – that arse of
taffeta chiné,[30] that gaping, rancid hole in the middle, those muti-
lations to the breast and to three fingers, that stunted leg that
makes her limp, that toothless mouth – all of this inflames, excites
our two libertines: Durcet sucks her from in front, Curval from
behind, and while objects of the most exquisite beauty and utmost
freshness are there before them, ready to satisfy their slightest
desires, it is with something that Nature and crime have defiled,
have withered, it is with the filthiest and most disgusting object
that our two ecstatic lechers will taste the most delectable pleasures . . . And who can explain man after that? The two of them,
seeming to fight over that cadaver-in-waiting like two ferocious
mastiffs over a corpse, and indulging in the vilest excesses,
disgorge their come at last, and, though exhausted by this pleasure, they would perhaps have continued at that moment with
some related act of depravity and infamy had supper not
prompted them to attend to other pleasures. The Président,
disconsolate at having spilled his come and able to revive himself

in such circumstances only by guzzling and drinking to excess, swelled up like a veritable hog. He wanted little Adonis to frig Bande-au-ciel, and made him swallow the come; and, not content with this last abomination, which was carried out there and then, he got up, said his imagination was suggesting yet more delectable things to him than this and, without further explanation, took Fanchon, Adonis and Hercule off with him, shut himself away in the far boudoir with them and only reappeared for the orgies, though on such sparkling form that he was still capable of a thousand other horrors each more peculiar than the rest (but that the essential order we have set ourselves prevents us from describing at this stage to our readers). Everyone went to bed and Curval, that reckless Curval who had that night been allotted the divine Adélaïde, his daughter, and who could thus have enjoyed the most delightful of nights with her, was found the next morning slumped over the revolting Fanchon, with whom he had carried out further horrors throughout the night, while Adonis and Adélaïde, deprived of his bed, were in a small bunk far removed and on a mattress on the floor respectively.

Sixth day.

It was his Lordship's turn to appear at the masturbation classes, and off he went. Had Duclos's disciples been men, his Lordship would in all likelihood have been unable to resist, but a little slit below the belly was an outrageous flaw in his eyes and, had the Graces themselves surrounded him, the sight of that accursed slit would have been enough to mollify him; he thus resisted heroically – I do not think he so much as stiffened – and the operations continued. It was clear to see that the friends were very keen to find fault with the 8 young girls in order to procure for themselves the following day, the fateful Saturday of corrections – to procure for themselves on that occasion, as I say, the pleasure of punishing all 8 of them. There were already 6 on the list, and beautiful Zelmire made it 7 – did she in all good faith truly deserve it? Or did the pleasure of the punishment they had in mind for her prevail over all sense of fairness? We shall leave this case to the conscience of the wise Durcet and content ourselves with telling the story. A very beautiful lady swelled the numbers on the list of offenders – the gentle Adélaïde; her husband Durcet wanted, so he said, to set an example by showing her less forgiveness than the others, and it was indeed with him that she had been found wanting. He had taken her to a certain place where the services she was to render him after certain necessities were not absolutely flawless. Not everyone is as depraved as Curval, and even though she was his daughter she in no way shared his tastes: either she baulked, or conducted herself poorly, or perhaps it was simply spite on Durcet's part; in any case she was put down in the book of penances to the great satisfaction of those assembled. As the inspection of the boys' quarters passed without incident, they moved on to the secret pleasures of the chapel, pleasures all the more piquant and all the more peculiar in that even those who asked to attend were refused permission to come and provide them. That morning only Constance, 2 of the subaltern fuckers and Michette were to be seen there.

At lunch Zéphire, with whom the friends were more and more pleased with every passing day, both for the charms that seemed to make him more beautiful each day and the appetite for libertinage he [showed] – Zéphire, as I say, insulted Constance, who, even though she was no longer serving, had nevertheless appeared at lunch: he called her a baby breeder and gave her a few slaps across her belly to teach her a lesson, so he said, for laying eggs with her lover, then he kissed the Duc, caressed him, frigged his prick for a moment, and succeeded so well in inflaming his skull that Blangis swore he would douse him with come before the afternoon was up, and the young fellow taunted him and said he dared him to do so. As he was required to serve the coffee, he left as dessert arrived and reappeared naked to serve it to the Duc as soon as the latter rose from the table; the Duc, very animated, began with a little horseplay – he sucked the boy's mouth and prick, placed him on a chair in front of him with his backside at the height of his mouth, and gamahuched him in this manner for a quarter of an hour. His prick rose up at last, raised its proud head, and the Duc saw only too well that his tribute finally required some incense; however, everything other than what they

had done the previous day was forbidden. The Duc resolved therefore to follow his friends' example: he bends Zéphire over a sofa,
aims his tool between his thighs, but the same thing happened to
him that had happened to Curval – his tool protruded by 6 inches.
'Do as I did,' said Curval, 'frig the child over your prick, spray his
come over your glans.' But the Duc thought it would be more
enjoyable to screw two at a time: he begs his brother to put
Augustine in position for him; her buttocks are glued against
Zéphire's thighs, and the Duc, fucking so to speak a girl and a
boy at the same time, adds even more lubricity by frigging
Zéphire's prick over Augustine's pretty, round, white buttocks,
flooding them with that childish little come which, as one can
well imagine, soon flows in abundance when excited by something
so pretty. Curval, who found this situation amusing and who
could see the Duc's arse gaping and yawning for a prick, as all
buggers' arses do when their pricks are hard, came over to repay
him in kind for what he had received himself two days earlier,
and the dear Duc had no sooner felt the sensual thrusts of this
intromission than his come, letting fly at almost the same moment
as Zéphire's, flooded the sides of the temple from behind while
Zéphire sprayed its pillars. But Curval did not come and, withdrawing his proud and spirited tool from the Duc's arse, he
threatened the Bishop (who was frigging himself in the same
manner between Giton's thighs) with the very fate to which he
had just subjected the Duc; the Bishop dares him to do so, the
battle commences, the Bishop is buggered and deliciously spills,
between the thighs of the pretty child he caresses, some sensually
provoked libertine come. Meanwhile Durcet, a benign spectator,
having for his part only Hébé and the duenna, was far from idle
though almost dead-drunk, and silently indulged in abominations
over which we are obliged to draw a veil; at last everything was
calm, everyone fell asleep, and when 6 o'clock came to awaken
our actors, they headed for the new pleasures Duclos had in store
for them. That evening the sexes of the quadrilles were reversed,
with all the little girls as sailors, and all the little boys as grisettes[31]
– it was a ravishing sight. Nothing inflames lust like this sensual
little switch: one is pleased to find in a little boy that which makes
him resemble a little girl, and a girl is much more alluring when,

in order to please, she borrows from the sex one would prefer her to have. That day they all had their wives beside them on the sofas – they congratulated each other on such a religious arrangement and, as everyone was ready to listen, Duclos resumed, as we shall see, the telling of her lubricious stories.

'There was at Md. Guérin's a whore of around 30 years of age, blonde, a little portly but unusually fair and youthful; she was named Aurore. She had a charming mouth, pretty teeth and a sensual tongue, but – who would have thought it? – whether it was from a failure of schooling or a frailty of stomach, that adorable mouth had the failing of constantly allowing a prodigious quantity of wind to escape, and, particularly when she had eaten a great deal, she would burp incessantly for an hour with enough force to turn a windmill. It is said with good reason that every failing finds a devotee, and because of hers this beautiful girl had a most ardent one – a wise and serious Sorbonne scholar who, weary of arguing the existence of God to no avail in his academy, sometimes came to the brothel to convince himself of the existence of one of His creatures instead. He gave notice and, on this particular day, Aurore stuffed herself. Curious about this devout tête-à-tête, I rush to the hole and, after a few preliminary caresses between our lovers all aimed at the mouth, I see our rhetorician delicately place his dear companion upon a chair, take a seat facing her and, placing his pitiful relics in her hands – "Begin," he told her, "begin, my pretty little one. You know how to save me from this languid state – take them now, I beg you, for I am desperate for satisfaction." With one hand Aurore took the scholar's limp tool, with the other she grabbed his head, sealed her mouth to his, and off she went, disgorging sixty burps one after the other between his jaws. No words can convey the ecstasy of this servant of God – he was in seventh heaven: he breathed in, he swallowed all that was hurled at him – it was as if he would have been sorry to miss out on the slightest waft, and meanwhile his hands strayed over my friend's breasts and beneath her petticoats. But these caresses were only incidental: the one and only object of his attention was that mouth, which overwhelmed him with its sighs; at last his prick, swelled by the sensual tingling this ceremony produces in him, comes at last in my companion's hand and [he] rushes off, protesting he has never experienced such pleasure.

'Soon after, an even more extraordinary man demanded a certain something of me that does not deserve to be passed over in silence: Madame Guérin had me eat that day, almost by force, as copiously as I had seen my companion dine previously; she had taken care to serve me all the dishes she knew were my favourites, and, having warned me upon rising from the table of everything that was required with the old libertine she was to bring me, she had me swallow there and then three emetic granules in a glass of warm water. The lecher arrives, a brothel hound I had already seen at our place many times without bothering too much about what he was doing there: he kisses me, thrusting into my mouth his filthy, revolting tongue, the stench of which triggers the effects of the emetic; he sees my stomach heaving – he is in ecstasy. "Be brave, my little one," he cried, "be brave. I shall not spill a drop." Forewarned of everything that needed to be done, I sit him on the sofa, tip his head back over the side; his thighs are wide apart, I unbutton his breeches, grab a short and limp instrument that shows no sign of an erection, tug on it, and he opens his mouth. While I frig him, and while he fondles my buttocks with his shameless, wandering hands, I launch point-blank into his mouth the half-digested lunch disgorged by the emetic. Our man is in seventh heaven, he is in ecstasy, he swallows, he searches my lips for more of the foul ejaculation that so intoxicates him, he does not spill a drop, and when he thinks the operation is coming to an end he provokes its return with the tickling of his tongue, and his prick – this prick which I barely touch, so overwhelmed am I by my convulsions, this prick which no doubt only becomes inflamed through these abominations – swells, rises all by itself, and leaves between my fingers the indisputable proof of the impression this filth makes on him.'

'Oh, good God!' said Curval. 'Now there's a delicious passion, but it could be further refined.' 'And how?' asked Durcet, in a tone punctuated by lubricious sighs. 'How?' replied Curval. 'Oh, good God! By the choice of girl and of dishes.' 'Of girl . . . ? Ah,

I understand – you'd want a Fanchon in her place.' 'Oh, no doubt about it!' 'And the dishes?' added Durcet, as Adélaïde frigged him. 'The dishes?' continued the Président. 'Oh, God damn it! By forcing her to return to me what I would have just conveyed to her in the same manner.' 'Meaning,' replied the financier, whose imagination was starting to run riot, 'that you would puke into her mouth, that she would have to swallow and that she would then return it to you.' 'Precisely.' And with the two of them hurrying into their closets, the Président with Fanchon, Augustine and Zélamir, Durcet with Desgranges, Rosette and Bande-au-ciel, the others were obliged to wait almost half an hour for the resumption of Duclos's tales. They reappeared at last. 'You've been up to some filth,' the Duc said to Curval, who was the first to return. 'A little,' said the Président. 'It's what makes life worth living, and as for me I only value sensuality in its foulest and most revolting of guises.' 'But a little come must have been spilled at least?' 'Not another word!' said the Président. 'Do you think that we're all like you and that we all have come to spill every hour of the day as you do? I leave such exploits to you, and to vigorous champions like Durcet,' he continued, as he saw the latter return, barely able to stay upright from exhaustion. 'It's true,' said the financier, 'I couldn't resist – that Desgranges is so filthy both in what she says and does, she is so open to everything we desire . . .' 'Come, Duclos,' said the Duc, 'for if we don't cut him off the indiscreet little fellow will tell us everything he got up to, without thinking how dreadful it is to brag of the favours one has received from a pretty woman.' And so Madame Duclos, obeying, resumed her story thus.

'As these gentlemen like these capers so much,' said our story-teller, 'I am sorry they were unable to rein in their enthusiasm a moment longer, for the results would have been better placed after the tale I still have to tell you this evening: the thing that Mr. le Président claimed was needed to improve on the passion I have just described was to be found, to the letter, in the one that follows – I am sorry he did not allow me enough time to finish. The aged Président de Saclanges displays to the letter the very peculiarities that M. de Curval appears to desire: the doyenne of our chapter, a tall and fat 36-year-old girl – a florid, drunken, coarse and foul-mouthed fishwife though quite pretty for all that – had been chosen for him. The Président arrives, supper is served, they both get drunk, they both lose all sense of reason, they both vomit in each other's mouths, they both swallow and repay to the other what they have borrowed;[32] they collapse among the remnants of the supper, in the very filth they have just sprayed all over the floor; I am then sent in, as my companion has lost her wits as well as her strength. This was in fact the crucial moment for the libertine: I find him on the floor, his prick as straight and hard as a rod of iron; I grab the instrument, the Président babbles and swears, draws me to him, sucks on my mouth and comes like a bull, twisting this way and that as he continues to wallow in his own filth.

'Soon after, the same girl provided us with the spectacle of a fantasy that was at least as filthy as the last one: a fat monk, who paid her handsomely, straddled her belly; my companion's thighs were spread as wide as possible and tied to heavy furniture to stop her from budging; in this position a number of delicacies were placed without any dishes on her naked belly. The good fellow grabs the morsels in his hands, thrusts them into his Dulcinea's open cunt, turning them this way and that, and eats them only once he has completely drenched them in the salts yielded by her vagina.'

'Now that's a completely new way of dining,' said the Bishop. 'And one that would not be to your taste, is that not so, my Lord?' asked Duclos. 'No, by golly!' replied this servant of the Church. 'I don't like cunt enough for that.' 'Well,' resumed our storyteller, 'then listen to the tale with which I shall conclude my narrations for this evening – I am sure it will be more to your liking.

'I had been at Md. Guérin's for eight years. I had just turned 17 and throughout this time not a day had passed without me observing the arrival each morning of a certain farmer-general[33] who was held in high regard. He was at the time around 60 years of age, fat, short and resembling in many respects Mr. Durcet – he

had the same youthfulness and plumpness. He required a new
girl each day, and those of the house only served him as a last
resort or whenever an outsider failed to attend a rendezvous. Mr.
Dupont, as our financier was called, was as particular in his
choice of girls as he was in his tastes: he absolutely did not want
the girl to be a whore, unless there was no choice, as I have just
said; they had to be workers, shop-girls – dressmakers if possible.
Their age and the colour of their hair were also stipulated: they
had to be blonde, between the ages of 15 and 18, neither older
nor younger, and above all they had to have a sculpted arse of
such perfect complexion that the slightest spot near the hole was
grounds enough for their exclusion; when they were virgins he
paid double. On this particular day they had planned for him a
young lace-maker of 16 years of age, whose arse was a veritable
model of perfection, but he did not know this was the gift they
wanted to offer him, and as the young girl let it be known she
could not get away from her parents that morning and they
should therefore not wait for her, Madame Guérin – who knew
that Dupont had never seen me – ordered me immediately to
dress up as a respectable girl, to hire a carriage from the end of
the street and to return to her house in it a quarter of an hour
after Dupont's arrival, playing my part well and passing myself
off as a dressmaker's apprentice. But of all these requirements,
the most important was to fill my stomach there and then with
half a pound of aniseed, on top of which I swallowed a large
glass of a balsamic liquor[34] she gave me, the intended effect of
which you will hear about a little later. Everything goes perfectly
– we had fortunately had a few hours to ourselves to make sure
that no detail was neglected. I arrive with a callow look about
me; I am introduced to the financier who studies me attentively
at first, but, as I took the greatest care to keep myself in check,
he could discover nothing in me to contradict the story he had
been told. "Is she a virgin?" asked Dupont. "Not this way," said
Guérin, placing her hand on my belly, "but as for the other side,
I guarantee it!" . . . and she was lying quite brazenly; it did not
matter – our man was fooled and that was all that was required.
"Hitch them up, hitch them up!" said Dupont, and Madame
Guérin lifted my skirts up from behind, letting me lean against

her a little and thereby fully revealing to the libertine the temple
for his tribute. He studies it, touches my buttocks for a moment,
spreads them with his two hands, and, no doubt content with
his examination, he says my arse is fine and he will make do with
it; he then asks me a few questions about my age, about my job,
and, satisfied with my feigned innocence and the naive air I put
on, he has me go up to his rooms, as he had his own at Madame
Guérin's which no one but he could enter and which could not
be spied upon from anywhere else. As soon as we are inside, he
closes the door carefully and, having considered me further for
a moment, he asks me in a rather brutal tone and manner, one
that he would maintain throughout the scene to follow – he asks
me, as I say, if it is indeed true I have never been fucked in the
arse. As it was in keeping with my role to be ignorant of such an
expression, I had him repeat it, protesting that I did not understand it, and when he explained by gesturing what he meant in
a manner that left no room for confusion, I replied with apparent
horror and modesty that I would have been very sorry to have
ever lent myself to such abominations. He then told me to take
off just my skirts, and as soon as I obeyed him, he lifted my shift
(which I had kept down to hide my front) up over my backside
as high as he could beneath my stays, and, as his undressing me
had dislodged my neckerchief and my breasts were fully exposed,
he lost his temper. "The devil take your tits!" he yelled. "Who
asked you for tits? That's what annoys me about all these creatures – there's always that shameless mania for showing their
titties!" And hurriedly covering them up I approached him as if
to beg his forgiveness, but when he saw that the pose I was about
to strike would reveal my front, he became enraged once again
– "Oh, good God, stay as you were before!" he said grabbing my
hips and positioning me again so that he would see only my arse.
"Stay like that, damn it! Your cunt is no more welcome than your
tits – only your arse is needed here." At the same time he got up,
led me to the edge of the bed, upon which he positioned me lying
flat from the waist up, then, settling down on a very low seat
between my legs, it so happened his face was at exactly the same
height as my arse. He studies me again for a moment then, not
content with me in this pose, he gets up to place a cushion beneath

my belly, making my arse stick out even further; he sits down again, examines me, and does all this with the sangfroid, the composure, of the considered libertine. After a while, he grabs hold of my two buttocks, spreads them, places his open mouth over the hole, hermetically sealing it there, and, following both the orders I had received beforehand and my own extreme need, I immediately unleash into the back of his gullet the most booming fart he may ever have received in his life. He withdraws in a rage. "What on earth? You cheeky little minx!" he tells me. "You have the audacity to fart in my mouth?" And placing his mouth there again . . . "Yes, Monsieur," I tell him as I blow more smoke in his face, "this is how I treat anyone who kisses my arse." "Well then, fart! Fart, you little hussy, as you can't hold it in – fart as much as you like and as much as you can!" From this moment on, I contain myself no longer: the need to break wind – prompted by the drug I had swallowed – was indescribable, and our man blissfully receives my farts by turns in his mouth and nostrils. After a quarter of an hour of this routine, he lies down at last on a sofa, pulls me closer, his nose still between my buttocks, orders me to frig him in this position while continuing the routine that brings him such exquisite pleasure; I fart, I frig, I tug on a limp prick no longer or thicker than a finger. With these tugs and farts his instrument stiffens at last: the heightening of our man's pleasure, the very moment of his climax, is signalled by further iniquities on his part – it is his tongue no less that now provokes my farts, that darts deep into my anus to provoke more wind, and it is on his tongue that he wants me to force them out. He raves, I see he has lost his head, and his vile little tool mournfully sprays my fingers with seven or eight drops of clear, brownish sperm that restore his reason at last. But as his innate brutality both fomented and swiftly succeeded his delirium, he barely gave me time to straighten my clothes; he scolded, he grumbled, he revealed to me, in a word, the odious image of vice once its passion has been satisfied and that careless rudeness which seeks revenge, the moment the spell has broken, by insulting the idol usurped by the senses.'

'Now there's a man I like more than all the previous ones,' said the Bishop . . . 'and do you know if he had his little 16-year-old

novice the following day?' 'Yes, my Lord, he did, and the day
after that a 15-year-old maiden far prettier still – as few men
paid as much, few were as well served.' Because this passion had
inflamed minds so accustomed to disorders of this kind, and had
reminded them of a taste they all so venerated, they did not want
to wait any longer to put it to good use: each of them gleaned
what they could find and culled a little here, there and everywhere. Supper arrived and almost all the abominations they had
just heard were mixed in with it: the Duc got Thérèse drunk and
had her vomit into his mouth; Durcet had the whole harem fart
and received more than 60 that evening; as for Curval, whose
head was filled with all sorts of extravagant ideas, he said he
wanted to enjoy his orgies privately and shut himself away in
the far boudoir with Fanchon, Marie, Madame Desgranges, and
thirty bottles of champagne. All four had to be carried off after
they were found swimming in the floods of their own filth – the
Président asleep with his mouth sealed to that of Madame
Desgranges, who was still vomiting into it. The three others had
got up to just as much – along similar lines and different ones
as well: they too had spent their orgies drinking, getting their
catamites drunk, making them vomit, making the little girls fart,
getting up to who knows what; and without Madame Duclos
– who had kept her wits about her, had restored order, and sent
them to sleep – it is more than likely that rosy-fingered dawn,
upon opening the doors to the palace of Apollo, would have
found them wallowing in their own filth more like swine than
men. Needing nothing but rest, each slept alone to recover a
little strength for the following day in the arms of Morpheus.[35]

Seventh Day.

The friends no longer cared to spend an hour at Madame
Duclos's lessons each morning; wearied by the pleasures of the
night, fearing besides that this operation made them spill their
come too early in the morning, and judging moreover that this
ceremony left them jaded towards pleasures and objects it was
in their interest to keep in reserve, [they agreed] that each of the

fuckers in turn would take their place instead each morning. The inspections were carried out and they were only one young girl shy of having all 8 put down for correction: it was the beautiful and alluring Sophie, who was diligent in observing all her duties; however ridiculous these must have seemed to her, she nonetheless observed them, but Durcet, who had earlier briefed Louison, her warden, was so adept in luring her into his trap that she was declared to be at fault and thus put down in the fateful book. Sweet Aline, similarly subjected to close inspection, was also found guilty, and the list for that evening thereby comprised the 8 young girls, two wives and four young boys. These tasks complete, all thoughts now turned to the wedding that was to herald the festivities planned for the end of the first week: no permissions to relieve oneself in public at the chapel were granted that day; his Lordship dressed as a pontiff and they gathered at the altar – the Duc, who represented the girl's father, and Curval, who represented that of the young boy, led out Michette and Giton respectively. Both were exceptionally attired in their town clothes, but in reverse – that is to say the boy dressed as a girl, and the girl as a boy; because of the order we have set [ourselves] for these matters, we are unfortunately obliged to defer a little longer the pleasure the reader would doubtless have taken from the details of this religious ceremony, but the moment will doubtless come when these can be revealed to him. They went through to the drawing room, and it was while waiting for lunch to be ready that our four libertines shut themselves away with this charming couple in private, had them strip naked, and forced them to perform together all of the matrimonial ceremonies their age permitted, with the exception nonetheless of the virile member's introduction into the little girl's vagina, which could have taken place as the young boy was nice and hard but which was forbidden so that nothing would spoil a flower destined for other uses; this aside, they were allowed to touch and caress each other – young Michette fondled her little husband, and Giton, with the help of his masters, frigged his little wife very well. The two of them, however, were beginning to feel their own enslavement too keenly for sensuality – even of the kind their age allowed them to feel – to blossom in their little hearts. Lunch was served: the bride and groom were part of the festivities, but as they were inflaming the imaginations of the four friends over coffee they were stripped naked, along with Zélamir, Cupidon, Rosette and Colombe, who were serving the coffee that day; and as thigh-fucking was now in vogue at that time of day, Curval grabbed the groom, the Duc grabbed the bride, and they thigh-fucked the pair of them. The Bishop, who since coffee had been hounding Zélamir's charming arse, which he sucked and forced to fart, soon screwed him in the same manner while Durcet indulged in his own favourite little abominations with Cupidon's charming arse. Our two principal athletes did not come and soon after one of them grabbed Rosette and the other, Colombe: they screwed them from behind and between their thighs in the same manner as they had Michette and Giton, while ordering these two charming children to frig – with their pretty little hands as instructed – the monstrous heads of the pricks sticking out beyond their bellies; and meanwhile, the libertines freely fondled their little playthings' rosy and delectable arseholes. No come was spilled, however – they knew there was delightful work in store that evening, and they saved themselves for it. From this moment on, the rights of the young bride and groom vanished and their marriage, even though it had followed every convention, was no more than a charade; they each returned to the quadrilles reserved for them and everyone listened to Madame Duclos, who resumed her story thus.

'A man of more or less the same tastes as the financier with whom my tales concluded yesterday evening will, if you approve, Messieurs, open today's tales: he was a Master of Requests[36] of about 60 years of age and he combined the peculiarity of his fantasies with that of wanting only women older than himself. Madame Guérin provided him with an old bawd of her acquaintance, whose wrinkly buttocks had come to resemble that worn parchment used to keep tobacco moist. This was nevertheless the object to be used for our libertine's tributes: he kneels before this decrepit arse, kisses it lovingly, receives a fart in his face, is ecstatic, opens his mouth, receives more farts; his tongue enthusiastically goes in search of the moist wind unleashed for him. He cannot, however, resist the delirium to which such an operation leads; he pulls from his breeches a small member, as old, pale and wrinkly as the divinity to whom he pays tribute. "Oh, fart then! Fart then, my girl!" he yells as he frigs himself with all his strength. "Fart, my sweet – only your farts can break the spell cast on this rusty tool." The bawd redoubles her efforts, and the libertine, drunk with pleasure, spills between the legs of his goddess the two or three miserable drops of sperm to which he owed all his ecstasy.'

O the terrible effect of an example! Who would have thought it? At that very moment and as if they had given each other the word, our four libertines summon the duennas of their quadrilles, grab hold of their old and ghastly arses, solicit farts, receive them, and are on the verge of being as content as the Master of Requests – when their recollection of the pleasures awaiting them at the orgies holds them back; they remember these, however, and go no further, each dismissing his own Venus, and Duclos continues.

'I shall not labour the following, Messieurs,' said that lovable whore. 'I know that it has few devotees among you, but you ordered me to say everything and I do as I'm told. A very young man with a rather pretty face had a taste for gamahuching my cunt while I had my period: I lay on my back, my thighs spread; he kneeled before me and sucked, while supporting my loins with both hands to bring my cunt within easier reach; he swallowed both my come and my blood, for he did it so deftly and was so pretty that I did indeed come. He frigged himself; he was in 7th heaven – it seemed that nothing on earth could give him so much pleasure, and as he kept going the warmest and most fervent ejaculation soon arrived to persuade me that this was so. The following day he saw Aurore, then soon after my sister, and within a month we had all paraded before him, after which he no doubt went off to do the same in every other brothel in Paris.

'That fantasy, you will admit, Messieurs, is nevertheless no more peculiar than that of a former friend of Madame Guérin's, whom she had supplied for a long time, and whose sole pleasure consisted, so she assured us, of eating mooncalves[37] or miscarriages; he was always informed whenever there was a girl in this condition and would rush over and swallow the embryo as he swooned with pleasure.'

'I knew that man,' said Curval. 'There is not the slightest doubt about either his existence or his tastes.' 'That may be,' said the Bishop, 'but what I know just as well is that I shall not follow his example.' 'Why?' asked Curval. 'I am convinced that it can produce a climax, and if Constance is willing to let me – as she is said to be pregnant – I promise to draw out Monsieur her son before he is due and to crunch him like a sardine.' 'Oh, your hatred of pregnant women is well known,' replied Constance. 'Everyone knows well enough that you only got rid of Adélaïde's mother because she fell pregnant a second time, and if Julie were to take my advice she would do well to watch herself.' 'It is certainly true,' said the Président, 'that I have no love of progeny, and when the beast is burdened she provokes a furious disgust in me, but to imagine I killed my wife for that – that's where you may be mistaken. Understand, you slut, that I do not need a reason to kill a woman, and especially not a cow like you – one I would prevent from calving if she belonged to me.' Constance and Adélaïde began to cry, and this episode revealed something of the secret hatred the Président bore towards the Duc's charming wife; far from supporting her in this discussion, the Duc replied he had no more love of progeny than Curval, as the latter well knew, and added that although Constance was pregnant she was yet to give birth. At this point Constance's tears flowed all the more; she was on the sofa with Durcet, her father, whose idea of consolation was to tell her that if she did not shut up immediately, he would, despite her condition, kick her arse out the door. The poor wretch let the tears for which she had been reproached fall inwardly upon her broken heart and contented herself with saying, 'Alas, good God! I am indeed unfortunate, but this is my fate – I must submit to it.' Adélaïde, who burst into tears (and whom the Duc, on whose sofa she was sitting, fondled as roughly as he could to make her cry all the more), managed to dry her eyes as well, and as this rather tragic scene – albeit a very delightful one to our libertines' villainous souls – was now over, Duclos resumed in these terms.

'There was a room at Madame Guérin's that was very charmingly constructed and only ever used by one man: it had a double floor, and this very low kind of entresol, in which one had to be lying down, served to accommodate the peculiar libertine whose passion I served. He shut himself away with a girl in this kind of cubbyhole, and his head was positioned so it was directly beneath a hole opening on to the room above; the girl shut away with the man in question had no other task than to frig him, and I, positioned above him, was to do the same to another man. This very discreetly placed hole was left open as if by accident, and it was up to me, as if out of cleanliness and as if to avoid spoiling the floorboards, to manualize my man in such a way as to make him spill his come into the hole and thus on to the other man's face directly beneath it; everything had been constructed so skilfully that nothing showed and the operation succeeded perfectly: as soon as the recipient felt the come of the man frigging above him on his face he came as well and there was no more to be said.

'In the meantime the old woman I spoke of earlier returned, though she had to deal with a different champion: this one, a man of around 40 years of age, had her strip naked and then licked every orifice of her old cadaver – arse, cunt, mouth, nostril, armpit, ear, nothing was forgotten – and with each suck the rogue swallowed all he gleaned there. He did not stop at this: he had her chew on pastries which he would then suck into his own mouth as soon as she had ground them down; he had her hold great gulps of wine in her mouth for a long time, rinsing her mouth and gargling with them, and he would swallow these too, with such a prodigious erection throughout that his come seemed ready to escape without the need for any further provocation; at last he felt it was ready to let fly and, pouncing on the old woman again, he thrust his tongue a foot deep into her arsehole and came like a madman.'

'Oh, good God!' said Curval. 'Is there any need to be young and pretty to make come flow? Once again, in all carnal pleasures it is the dirty object that elicits come, and so the dirtier it is the more sensually come will be spilled.' 'There are salts,' said Durcet, 'emanating from the object serving our desires, that excite our animal spirits and set them in motion, and who can doubt that everything that is old, dirty or rank has a greater quantity of these salts and consequently a greater capacity to excite – and incite – our ejaculation?' They discussed both sides of this argument a while, and as there was much work to be done after supper, they were served a little earlier – and during the dessert, all the young girls condemned to penance returned to the chamber where they were to await punishment along with the similarly condemned four boys and two wives (making a total of fourteen victims, namely the 8 aforementioned girls, Adélaïde and Aline, and the four boys, Narcisse, Cupidon, Zélamir and Giton). Our friends, already drunk on the intense sensuality of the tastes that lay in store, excited their imaginations still further with a prodigious quantity of wine and liqueurs and left the table to go to the chamber – where the victims were waiting for them – in such a drunken, frenzied and lubricious state that absolutely no one would have wanted to be in the place of those unfortunate offenders. At the orgies that day only those found guilty and the four old women there for service were required: everyone was naked, everyone was trembling, everyone was crying, everyone was awaiting their fate when the Président settled into an armchair and asked Durcet for the name and offence of each subject. Durcet, as tipsy as his colleague, picked up the book and wanted to read from it, but as everything was a blur to him and he was unable to finish, the Bishop took his place and, though just as drunk as his fellow libertine, he held his drink better and read aloud, one after another, the name of the guilty parties and their offences – upon which the Président pronounced a penance in keeping with the constitution and age of the offender (but in each case very harsh nonetheless). Once this ceremony was over the sentences were carried out. We are mortified that the order of our plan prevents us from describing these lubricious punishments here, but let our readers not hold it against us: they sense as we do the impossibility of our satisfying them at this particular moment. They can be sure that they will lose nothing by it. The ceremony was very long – there were 14 subjects to punish and some very pleasant details were added; everything was delightful no doubt, as our four scoundrels all came and retired so weary, so drunk on wine and pleasure that, without the aid of the 4 fuckers who came to fetch them, they would never have made it back to their quarters, where – despite all they had just done – fresh depravities awaited them still. The Duc, who was to have Adélaïde in his bed that night, did not want her: she had been among those punished and he had punished her so well himself that, having spilled his come entirely in her honour, he wanted no more of her that evening; and, making her sleep on a mattress on the floor, he gave her place to Duclos, who was as secure as ever in his good graces.

8ᵗʰ Day.

As the examples of the day before had made a deep impression, they neither did nor could find fault with anyone the following day; the lessons continued upon the fuckers, and as no incident occurred before coffee, we shall pick up the day at that moment. It was served by Augustine, Zelmire, Narcisse and Zéphire: the thigh-fucking began again, Curval grabbed hold of Zelmire, and the Duc of Augustine, and once they had admired and kissed their pretty buttocks, which for some reason that escapes me had that day a grace, a charm, a vermilion that had not been observed before – once our libertines had, as I say, thoroughly kissed, thoroughly caressed these charming little arses, they demanded farts; the Bishop, who had hold of Narcisse, had already obtained some, those Zéphire released into Durcet's mouth could also be heard . . . why not follow their example? Zelmire had done so, but as much as Augustine tried, as much as she forced herself, as much as [the Duc] threatened her with a fate the following Saturday in keeping with those experienced the day before, nothing would come – and the poor little girl was already in tears by the time a silent one finally escaped, much to the Duc's satisfaction. He breathed it in and, content with this mark of docility from a pretty child he rather liked,

he planted his enormous tool between her thighs and, withdrawing it at the moment of climax, completely drenched both
her buttocks. Curval had done as much with Zelmire, but the
Bishop and Durcet contented themselves with what is known
as *goosing around*,[38] and after a nap they went through to the
chamber, where the beautiful Duclos – dressed that day in so
many fineries her age was forgotten – appeared truly beautiful
in the candlelight, and so much so that our libertines, inflamed
by the sight of her, would not allow her to continue until she
had from the height of her rostrum shown off her buttocks to
those assembled. 'She really does have a fine arse,' said Curval.
'Indeed, my friend,' said Durcet, 'I swear I've seen few finer.'
And after these compliments, our heroine lowered her skirts,
sat down and took up the thread of her story in a manner that
the reader will discover if he makes the effort to continue, which
we advise him to do in the interest of his own pleasures.

'A reflection and an event were the reasons, Messieurs, that the
stories I have still to share with you will now take place on a
different battlefield. The reflection is quite simple – it was the
wretched state of my purse that gave rise to it. In the 9 years I
had stayed at Md. Guérin's, though I spent very little, I never had
so much as a hundred *louis* to hand; this extremely artful woman,
with a perfect understanding of her own interests, always
managed to keep for herself two thirds of the house receipts and
retained a great deal of the other third as well. This merry-go-
round rankled with me and, keenly solicited by another bawd
named Fournier to go and live with her, and knowing that this
Fournier entertained old lechers of much better and richer stock
at her house than did Madame Guérin, I resolved to take leave
of the latter and join the former. As for the event that lent weight
to my reflection, that was the loss of my sister: I was deeply
attached to her, and could not remain in a house where I was
reminded of her everywhere but could find her nowhere. Over
the last 6 months this dear sister had been visited by a tall man,
wizened and dark, whose physiognomy I found extremely
unpleasant; they would shut themselves away together, but I don't
know what they would get up to as my sister never wanted to

tell me – and they never went to the room where I might have watched them. Whatever the case may have been, one fine morning she comes into my room, embraces me, and tells me she has made her fortune, that she is being kept by this tall man I disliked – and all I could gather was she owed her future prosperity to the beauty of her buttocks. And with that she gave me her address, settled her accounts with Madame Guérin, embraced us all and left. I did not fail, as you can well imagine, to visit this address two days later, but no one there understood a word I was saying; I saw only too well that my sister had herself been tricked, as I could not conceive she would willingly have deprived me of the pleasure of seeing her. When I complained to Madame Guérin about what had happened, I saw her give a malicious smile and she refused to say any more about it; I thus concluded she was in on the mystery of this deal, but that I was not meant to uncover the truth. All of this affected me greatly and made my mind up once and for all – and as I shall no longer have occasion to speak to you of this dear sister, I shall tell you, Messieurs, that for all my searching, for all my efforts to find her, I found it utterly impossible to discover what had become of her.'

'I can well believe it,' said Madame Desgranges, 'for she was dead within 24 hours of leaving you. She did not deceive you, she was tricked herself – but Madame Guérin knew what was afoot.' 'Heavens above, what are you telling me?' asked Madame Duclos. 'Alas! Though deprived of seeing her I still had hopes she was alive!' 'Quite wrongly,' replied Madame Desgranges, 'but Guérin had not lied to you – it was the beauty of her buttocks, the stunning superiority of her arse that earned her the deal she hoped would make her fortune, but which led only to her death.' 'And the tall, wizened man?' asked Duclos. 'He was only the broker for the deal – he was not working on his own behalf.' 'But,' said Duclos, 'he nevertheless visited her assidu-ously for 6 months.' 'To trick her,' replied Desgranges. 'But continue your tale – such revelations may prove tedious to these gentlemen, and as this anecdote concerns me, I shall give them a thorough account of it in due course.' 'Spare us this sudden tenderness, Duclos,' the Duc told her drily, seeing she was struggling to hold back a few involuntary tears. 'We do not recognize such regrets here, and the whole of nature could fall to ruin without us breathing so much as a sigh – leave tears for imbeciles and children, and may they never again sully the cheek of a reasonable woman we hold in high esteem.' At these words our heroine composed herself and promptly resumed her tale.

'So, because of the two reasons I have just explained, I made up my mind, Messieurs, and as Madame Fournier offered me better lodgings, a table with far better fare, trysts that were much better paid if more arduous – but always an equal share and no deductions – I came to a decision there and then. Md. Fournier occupied a whole house, and five young and pretty whores comprised her harem; I was the 6th. If it pleases you I shall do here as I did with Md. Guérin, that is to say I shall describe my companions only when they have a role to play. From the day after my arrival I was kept busy, as the clients never stopped coming at Madame Fournier's, and each of us often had five or 6 a day, but I shall share with you, as I have done up until now, only those that may excite your attention by their piquancy or peculiarity. The first man I saw in my new home was a public treasurer,[39] a man of about 50 years of age: he had me kneel on the floor, my head resting upon the bed, and, kneeling down himself on the bed, he frigged himself with his prick in my mouth, ordering me to open wide; I did not spill a drop, and the lecher took prodigious pleasure in the contortions and retching this disgusting mouthwash prompted in me.

'You would wish me, Messieurs,' continued [Madame Duclos], 'to follow this up immediately with the four adventures of the same kind I encountered at Md. Fournier's, even though these occurred at different times. These tales will not displease M. Durcet, I know, and he will doubtless be grateful to be entertained for the rest of the evening with a taste he appreciates, and which procured me the honour of meeting him for the first time.'

'What?' asked Durcet. 'You're going to have me play a role in your story?' 'If it pleases you, Monsieur,' replied Madame Duclos, 'with the sole precaution of warning these gentlemen when I reach your particular case.' 'And my modesty? . . . What's this? Before all these young girls, you will reveal all my depravities just like that?' And when everyone had laughed at the financier's amusing concern, Duclos resumed thus.

'Another libertine, far older and far more revolting than the one I have just cited, provided me with the second performance of this mania: he had me lie down completely naked on a bed, then stretched himself over me the other way round, put his prick in my mouth and his tongue in my cunt, and in this position demanded I return in kind the sensual stimulation he claimed his tongue was offering me; I sucked as best I could. For him it was my virginity: he licked, dabbled, and doubtless worked far harder for himself in all his manoeuvring than for me. In any case I remained unmoved, though quite content not to be utterly revolted, and the libertine came: an operation that, according to the request of Madame Fournier, who had warned me of everything – an operation that, as I say, I made as lubricious as possible for him by squeezing with my lips, by sucking, by pumping into my mouth the juice that escaped him, and by stroking his arse with my hands to tickle his anus, an accompaniment he indicated I should provide by doing the same himself as best he could . . . Once it was over, our man made himself scarce, assuring Madame Fournier he had never been supplied with a whore who could satisfy him better than me.

'Soon after this adventure, curious to know what an old witch of over 70 years of age was doing at the house, as she seemed to be waiting for work, I was told she was indeed going to get some. Extremely curious to see the use to which such an old crone was to be put, I asked my companions whether they had in their house a room where we could watch, like at Madame Guérin's. One of them said yes, led me there, and as there was room enough for two, we got into position and this is what we saw and what we heard – as the two rooms were separated only by a partition it was very easy to hear every word. The old woman entered first and, having looked at herself in the mirror, she fixed herself up as if she believed her charms would still have some effect: a few minutes later we saw the Daphnis to this

Chloe[40] arrive, and this one was 60 years old at most; he was a
public treasurer, a gentleman who was very comfortably off and
who preferred to spend his money on cast-off tarts than pretty
whores, because of that peculiarity in his tastes that you understand, as you say, Messieurs, and that you explain so well. He
steps forward, looks his Dulcinea up and down as she gives him
a low curtsey. "Spare me the ceremony, you old slut!" says the
lecher. "And strip naked . . . but first let's see – do you have any
teeth?" "No, Monsieur, I don't have a single one left," says the
old woman as she opened her rotten mouth . . . "Have a look
yourself." So our man approaches and, taking her head in his
hands, plants on her lips one of the most ardent kisses I have
ever seen given in my life. He not only kissed, but he sucked, he
devoured – he lovingly darted his tongue deep into her putrefied
gullet, and the old dear, who had not been treated to such a good
time for many years, returned all this with such tenderness . . .
that it would be difficult for me to describe. "Come!' said the
financier, "strip naked!" And meanwhile, he undoes his breeches
and airs a black and wrinkly member which did not look like
growing any time soon. The old woman is now naked, and
brazenly comes over to offer her lover an aged body, sallow and
wrinkly, withered, sagging and gaunt, the description of which
– no matter how far your fantasies of such things may take you
– would revolt you too much for me to wish to undertake it;
but far from being disgusted by it, our libertine is in ecstasy – he
grabs her, pulls her closer to the armchair in which [he] had been
manualizing himself while waiting for her to undress, darts his
tongue once again into her mouth and, turning her the other
way, promptly offers his tribute to the other side of the coin. I
distinctly saw him fondle her buttocks – did I say buttocks? – the
two withered rags that hung down from her hips and rippled
over her thighs; whatever they were, he spread them, sealed his
lips sensually over the foul cloaca they enclosed, thrust his tongue
in several times, and all this while the old woman strove to give
a little firmness to the lifeless member on which she was tugging.
"Let's cut to the chase," said her Céladon. "Without my favourite little accompaniment, all your efforts will be useless, as you
have been warned." "Yes, Monsieur." "And you do know you

have to swallow?" "Yes, my little doggy-woggy! Yes my little chicky! I'll swallow – I'll devour every drop." And at that very moment, the libertine plants her on the bed with her head hanging down: in this position he puts his limp tool in her beak, thrusts it in up to his balls, shifts to take hold of his plaything's legs, sticks them over his shoulders, and by this means his snout is absolutely buried in the duenna's buttocks; his tongue finds the depths of this delicious hole again – the bee drawing out the nectar of the rose does not suck more sensually; meanwhile, the old woman sucks, our man stirs. "Oh, fuck!" he cries after a quarter of an hour of this libidinous exercise. "Suck, suck, bitch! Suck and swallow! It's flowing, God damn it! It's flowing – can't you feel it?" And then, kissing everything that is offered him – thighs, vagina, buttocks, anus – everything is licked, everything is sucked, the old woman swallows and the poor old wreck, who withdraws as limp as he entered, and who apparently came without an erection, rushes off quite ashamed of his waywardness and makes for the door as quickly as he can to avoid seeing with a cool head the hideous object which has just seduced him.'

'And the old woman?' asked the Duc.

'The old woman coughed, spat, blew her nose, got dressed as quickly as she could and left.

   'A few days later, it was the turn of the same companion who had provided me with the pleasure of this scene – a girl of about 16 years of age, blonde, with the most alluring physiognomy in the world; I leapt at the chance to see her at work. The man for whom she was summoned was at least as old as the public treasurer: he had her kneel between his legs, held her head in position by grabbing hold of her ears, and stuck in her mouth a prick that seemed to me dirtier and more revolting than a rag dragged through a sewer; my poor companion, seeing this disgusting morsel approaching her rosy lips, tried to throw herself backwards, but it was not for nothing that our man held her by the ears like a barbet.[41] "Come on then, you slut!" he said to her. "Stop being difficult." And, threatening to send for Madame Fournier, who had doubtless advised her to be very accommodating, he managed to overcome her resistance. She parts her lips, recoils, opens them again and finally devours, gagging, that foul relic in the sweetest of mouths. From that moment on the scoundrel offered nothing but vile insults: "Oh, you hussy!" he said in a fury. "You're kicking up quite a fuss about sucking the most handsome prick in France – do you really think everyone's going to wash in a bidet every day just for you? Go on, suck, bitch! Suck the sweetmeat!" And becoming inflamed with these sarcastic barbs and with the disgust he inspires in my companion – so true it is, Messieurs, that the very disgust you inspire in us spurs on your pleasure – the libertine is in ecstasy and leaves in this poor girl's mouth the unequivocal proofs of his virility. Less accommodating than the old woman, and far more revolted, she swallowed none of it, vomiting in a moment everything she had in her stomach, and our libertine, tidying himself up without paying her very much attention, quietly sniggered at the cruel effects of his libertinage.

'It was my turn, but more fortunate than the two before me, it was for Cupid himself that I was destined, and once I had satisfied him I was left with only the astonishment of finding such strange tastes in a young man so beautifully formed to please. He arrives, has me strip naked, lies down on a bed, orders me to squat on his face and to coax to a climax with my mouth a very modest prick, which he nonetheless commends to me, and whose come he implores me to swallow the moment I feel it flow. "But do not remain idle in the meantime," added the little libertine. "Let your cunt flood my mouth with urine which I promise to swallow just as you will swallow my come, and let this fine arse fart in my face." I get down to work, and carry out my three tasks with such skill that the little sprat soon spews all its fury into my mouth while I swallow, and while my Adonis does as much to the urine with which I flood him; and all this as he breathes in the farts with which, one after another, I perfume him.'

'In truth, Mademoiselle,' said Durcet, 'you might well have dispensed with such revelations of the childish trifles of my youth.' 'Aha!' said the Duc, laughing. 'Eh? What? You – who barely dares look at a cunt today – you used to make them piss in those days?' 'It's true,' said Durcet. 'It makes me blush – it's dreadful to have to reproach oneself for depravities of this sort. At this very moment, my friend, I feel the full weight of my shame ... Delectable arses!' he yelled in his enthusiasm as he kissed Sophie's backside, which he pulled closer to fondle for a moment. 'Divine arses! How I reproach myself for the tributes I stole from you. O delectable arses! I promise you an expiatory sacrifice – I swear on your altars never to stray again for the rest of my life.' And as this fine backside had inflamed him somewhat, the libertine placed the novice in a highly indecent position, but one that allowed him, as we have seen above, to have his little sprat suckled while he sucked on the rosiest and most sensual anus. But Durcet, too inured to this particular pleasure, only very rarely recovered his vigour by it: no matter how much he was sucked, or how much he reciprocated, he was obliged to withdraw in the same feeble state and, as he cursed and swore at the young girl, to defer to some happier occasion the pleasures Nature was refusing him at that moment. Not everyone was so unfortunate: the Duc, who had gone into his closet with Colombe, Zélamir, Brise-cul and Thérèse, let out great roars that made his delight clear, and Colombe, spluttering violently as she returned, left no doubt as to the temple where he had paid tribute. As for the Bishop, lying quite comfortably on his sofa with Adélaïde's buttocks over his face and with his prick in her mouth, he swooned as he made the young woman fart, while Curval, standing up and sticking his enormous trumpet into Hébé's mouth, spilled his come while his hands strayed elsewhere.

They were served, and the Duc wished to contend over supper that if happiness consisted in the complete satisfaction of all the pleasures of the senses, it was difficult to be happier than they were. 'That is not the remark of a libertine,' said Durcet, 'and how can you be happy when you can find satisfaction at any moment? It is not in pleasure that happiness consists, it is in desire – it is in breaking the chains that hold back this desire; now, can all that be found here, where I have only to wish in order to have? I swear,' he said, 'that since our arrival my come has not flowed once for the objects that are here – it has been spilled only for those that are not – and besides,' added the financier, 'as I see it, one thing that is essential to our happiness is missing. It is the pleasure of comparison, a pleasure that can arise only from the spectacle of the unfortunate, and we do not see any of those here; it is from seeing someone who does not have what I have, and who suffers for it, that the pleasure of being able to say to oneself, *So I am happier than he*, arises. Wherever men shall be equal and where differences shall cease to exist, happiness too shall cease to exist – it is the tale of a man who does not truly know the value of good health until he has fallen ill.' 'In that case,' said the Bishop, 'you would contend there is a genuine pleasure in contemplating the tears of those in the grip of penury.' 'Absolutely,' said Durcet. 'There is no pleasure in the world more sensual than the one you describe.' 'What? Without coming to their aid?' asked the Bishop, who was delighted to have Durcet elaborate on a subject so much to everyone's taste and one that he was so capable of addressing in depth. 'What do you mean by *coming to their aid*?' asked Durcet. 'The pleasure that arises for me from that sweet comparison between their state and mine would no longer exist if I came to their aid, for by rescuing them from their state of penury I would be giving them a momentary taste of pleasure that, by making them like me, would deprive me of all pleasure of comparison.' 'Well in that case,' said the Duc, 'it would be necessary, in order to reinforce in some way this contrast that is essential to happiness – it would be necessary, as I say, to aggravate their plight.' 'There is no doubt about it,' said Durcet, 'and this is what explains the abominations for which I have been reproached on this score my whole life – those who were unaware of my motives called me harsh, ferocious and barbaric, but not caring a fig for all the names I was called, I carried on regardless. I committed, I admit, acts that fools call atrocities, but I discovered pleasures of comparison that were delectable, and I was happy.' 'Confess the truth,' the Duc said to him. 'Admit that you have more than twenty times happened to bring ruin on unfortunates simply to serve the perverted tastes you are confessing here.' 'More than twenty times?' said Durcet. 'More than two hundred, my friend, and I could without exaggeration cite more than 400 families reduced to begging by me alone.' 'Did you profit by this at least?' asked Curval. 'Almost always, but often I did it purely out of this peculiar wickedness that nearly always awakens in me the organs of lubricity. Evil acts make me hard – I find in evil a charm piquant enough to awaken every sensation of pleasure in me, and I give myself to evil for evil alone, and without any other interest than evil alone.' 'There's nothing like this particular taste,' said Curval. 'When I was at the Courts of Justice I voted a hundred times for the hanging of wretches I knew full well to be innocent, and I never indulged in that petty injustice without feeling deep within myself a sensual tingling where the organs of pleasure in my balls would immediately become inflamed – imagine what I felt when I did worse than this!' 'There is no doubt,' said the Duc, whose brain was beginning to smoulder as he fondled Zéphire, 'that only crime has enough charm to inflame all the senses by itself, without one needing recourse to any other expedient, and no one knows better than I that even crimes far removed from those of libertinage can make one as hard as those that belong to it. As for me, speaking to you now, I got hard stealing, murdering, committing arson, and I am perfectly sure it is not the object of libertinage that drives us, but the idea of evil; that consequently it is for evil alone that we get hard and not for the object, so that if this object were stripped of the power to harm us, it would no longer make us hard.' 'Nothing is more certain,' said the Bishop, 'and from this arises the certitude of the greatest pleasure from the greatest infamy, and the system from which we must not stray, which is that the more pleasure one wishes to gain from crime, the more dreadful this crime will need to be. And as for me, Messieurs,' he added, 'if I am permitted to cite myself, I confess I am at the point of no longer feeling that sensation of which you speak – of no longer feeling it, as I say, for small crimes, and if the one I do commit does not combine as much darkness, as much depravity, as much deceit and betrayal as possible, the sensation no longer arises.' 'So,' said Durcet, 'is it possible to commit crimes as we conceive them and as you describe them? As for me, I confess that my imagination has always been in this respect beyond my means, I have always conceived a thousand times more than I have carried out[42] and have always railed against Nature, who, in giving me the desire to offend her, always robbed me of the means to do so.' 'There are no more than two or three crimes to commit in the world,' said Curval. 'Once those are done there is no more to be said – what remains is inferior and one no longer feels a thing. How many times, good God, have I not wished it were possible to attack the sun, to deprive the universe of it, or to use it to set the world ablaze – those would be crimes indeed, and not the little excesses in which we indulge, which do no more than metamorphose, in the course of a year, a dozen creatures into clods of earth.' And thereupon, with minds becoming inflamed, as two or three young girls had already found out, and with pricks beginning to rise, they left the table to pour into some pretty mouths the floods of that liqueur, whose unbearably acute tingling was prompting so many profanities. They limited themselves to pleasures of the mouth that evening, but conceived a hundred ways to vary these, and, when they had had their fill, they tried to find in a few hours' rest the strength required to begin again.

Ninth Day.

Duclos warned that morning that she thought it prudent either to offer the young girls other dupes for the masturbation exercises than the fuckers thus employed or to put an end to their lessons, as she believed them sufficiently trained. She said, very reasonably and plausibly, that using these young people known by the name of fuckers could lead to liaisons it would be wise to avoid, and that in any case these young people were useless for this exercise as they came straight away – and that this took away from the pleasures expected by these gentlemen's arses. It was therefore decided the lessons would come to an end, especially as there were already among the girls some who frigged splendidly. Augustine, Sophie and Colombe could have vied, for deftness and lightness of wrist, with the most celebrated mastur-batrix of the capital. Zelmire was the least proficient of all the girls, not for any lack of agility or skill in all that she did, but because her tender and melancholic character prevented her from forgetting her sorrows and she was always sad and preoccupied. At the breakfast inspection that morning, her duenna accused her of having been caught the previous evening praying to God before going to bed: she was summoned, questioned and asked what the subject of her prayers was; at first she refused to say, but once threatened, she confessed in tears that she had prayed to God to deliver her from the dangers that surrounded her and to do so above all before any attempt had been made on her virginity. The Duc thereupon declared that she deserved to die and had her read the explicit clause of the statutes. 'Well then,' she said, 'kill me. God, whom I invoke, shall at least take pity on me. Kill me before dishonouring me and this soul I devote to Him shall at least fly pure to His breast. I will be released from the torment of seeing and hearing so many horrors each day.' An answer in which such virtue, such candour and such sweetness prevailed made our libertines prodigiously hard. There were those who were in favour of deflowering her on the spot but the Duc, reminding them of the inviolable commitments they had made, contented himself with condemning her unanimously, along with his friends, to a violent punishment the following Saturday, and, in the meantime, to getting down on her knees and sucking the pricks of each of the friends for a quarter of an hour – having duly warned her that should she fail to do so she would unquestionably lose her life and be judged with the full rigour of the law. The poor child came over to fulfil the first part of her penance but the Duc, whom the proceedings had inflamed, and who had groped her arse extravagantly after the sentence had been pronounced, spurted his seed like a rogue into that pretty little mouth, threatening to strangle her if she spilled a drop, and the poor little wretch swallowed it all, but not without violent revulsion. The three others were sucked in turn, but did not spill a drop, and, after the usual ceremony of the inspections of the boys' quarters and the chapel, which did not produce anything that morning as almost everyone had been refused permission, they had lunch and went through for coffee; it was served by Fanny, Sophie, Hyacinthe and Zélamir. Curval dreamt up the idea of thigh-fucking Hyacinthe and making

Sophie kneel between Hyacinthe's thighs to suck the part of the prick that protruded. The scene was entertaining and sensual: he frigged and made the little fellow come in the little girl's face, and the Duc, who, because of the length of his prick, was the only one who could imitate this scene, positioned himself in the same manner with Zélamir and Fanny, but the boy was still too young to come and so the Duc was deprived of the very pleasant episode Curval had so enjoyed. After these two, Durcet and the Bishop rearranged the four children and had themselves sucked as well, but no one came and after a short nap they went through to the chamber of stories, where, once they had all taken their places, Madame Duclos took up the thread of her narrations.

'With anyone but yourselves, Messieurs,' said that lovable whore, 'I should dread to broach the subject of the tales which will occupy us for the whole of this week, but as depraved as it may be, I know your tastes too well to fear offending you and am on the contrary very sure you will be pleased with me. You will, I warn you, hear of filthy abominations, but your ears were made for them, your hearts love and desire them, and without further ado I shall make a start. We had an old client at Md. Fournier's whom we called the Chevalier (I do not know how or why he came by the name) and who would visit the house regularly each evening for a ceremony as simple as it was bizarre: he would unbutton his breeches, and every one of us in turn would have to drop a stool in them; he would promptly button them back up and leave quickly, carrying this package with him; while we were providing him with it he would frig himself for a moment, but we would never see him come, nor did we know where he would go with his turd in his breeches.'

'Oh, by God!' said Curval, who never heard anything without wanting to do it himself. 'I want someone to shit in my breeches and to keep it there all evening.' And ordering Louison to come and do him this service, the old libertine offered those assembled an actual demonstration of the taste they had just heard described. 'Go on then, continue,' he said calmly to Duclos, planting himself on the sofa. 'As far as I can see, only the beautiful Aline, my charming companion for the evening, could possibly be discomfited by this business here – as for me, I'm very happy with it.' And Duclos resumed in these terms.

'Forewarned,' she said, 'of everything that was to take place at the libertine's house where I had been sent, I dressed up as a boy and, as I was only twenty years of age, with beautiful hair and a pretty face, these clothes suited me splendidly. I take care before I leave to do in my breeches what M. le Président has just had done in his. My man was waiting for me in bed: I approach, he kisses me two or three times very lubriciously on the mouth, he tells me I am the prettiest little boy he has ever seen, and as he praises me he looks to unbutton my breeches; I defend myself a little, but with the sole intention of further inflaming his desires. He forces himself on me, he succeeds, but how to describe the ecstasy that takes hold of him as soon as he notices the little package I am carrying, and the mess it has made on both my buttocks? "What's this, you little rascal?" he said to me. "You've shat in your breeches . . . But how can one make such a mess?" And that moment, holding me still with my back to him and my breeches down, he frigs, fondles, and rubs himself against my back and spurts his come over the package as he thrusts his tongue into my mouth.'

'What's that?' said the Duc. 'He didn't touch anything? He didn't grab any you know what?' 'No, my Lord,' said Madame Duclos. 'I am telling you everything and hiding none of the circumstances – but a little more patience and we shall arrive by degrees at the very thing you mean.

'"Let's go see one who's very amusing," one of my companions tells me. "This one has no need for a girl – he has a good time all by himself." We go to the hole, informed that in the neighbouring room, where he was to appear, there was a pot from a close stool that we had been ordered to fill for the last four days, and there must have been more than a dozen turds at least; our man arrives, an old tax-collector[43] of about 70 years of age. He shuts himself away, goes straight to the pot, which he knows holds the scents reserved for his enjoyment. He picks it up and, sitting in an armchair, lovingly examines for an hour all the riches in his possession: he breathes in, he touches, he squeezes – seems to take all of them out, one by one, to have the pleasure of inspecting them more closely; in ecstasy at last, he pulls from his fly an old black rag that he tugs on with all his might. One hand frigs, the other reaches into the pot, brings out for that tool we worship a dish capable of inflaming his desires, but it rises no further; there are times when Nature is so stubborn that even those excesses that delight us the most are unable to over-come it. Try as he might, nothing would rise, but, by dint of tugging away with the same hand he had just dipped in excre-ment, he manages to ejaculate – he stiffens, falls over backwards, sniffs, breathes in, rubs his prick and comes over the pile of shit which has so delighted him.

'Another supped privately with me, and wanted twelve plates full of the same fare on the table, alongside those for supper: he smelled them, breathed them in one by one, and ordered me to frig him after the meal over the one that seemed to him the finest.

'A young Master of Requests paid for as many enemas as one was willing to receive; when I went with him I had seven – all seven of which he administered by his own hand. As soon as I had held one in for a few minutes, I had to climb a stepladder; he placed himself below it, and I unleashed over the prick he frigged the solution with which he had just swamped my guts.'

One may well imagine the whole evening was spent on more or less the kind of filth that had just been heard, and one may believe this all the more as all our four friends shared this taste – and though Curval was the one who took it furthest, the three others were no less smitten with it. The little girls' 8 turds were placed among the supper dishes, and at the orgies they doubtless raised the stakes further with the little boys, and so ended this 9th day, the end of which was greeted with all the more pleasure as it was hoped that the following day would offer more detailed stories about that object they cherished so much.

Tenth Day

Remember to conceal better in the beginning the matters you will shed light on here

The further we advance, the better we can enlighten our reader regarding certain facts we were obliged to keep concealed from him in the beginning; now, for example, we can tell him the purpose of the morning inspections of the children's bedrooms, the grounds for punishment when some offenders were discovered during these inspections, and what pleasures were tasted at the chapel. It was expressly forbidden for subjects of either sex to relieve themselves without express permission, so that these needs – thus contained – might instead serve the needs of those who desired them. The inspection allowed for a thorough examination to ensure no one had infringed this order: the friend of the month would carefully inspect all the chamber pots, and if one of them were full, the subject would promptly be put down in the book of punishments. Provision was nevertheless made for those who could not hold it in, and this was to go shortly before lunch to the chapel, which had been transformed into a latrine designed for our libertines to enjoy all the delights the satisfaction of this need could offer them; and the rest who were able to hold in their package would drop it in the course of the day in the manner that best pleased the friends – and always most assuredly in one of those ways we shall soon hear described (for these descriptions will cover all the different ways of abandoning oneself to this form of sensuality). There was also another reason for punishment and it was this. What is known as the ceremony of the bidet did not exactly please our four friends: Curval, for example, could not bear to deal with subjects who washed themselves; Durcet was the same, and so both of them would warn the duenna of the subjects they intended to have their way with the following day, and these subjects would be forbidden from any washing or wiping whatsoever; the two others (who were not dead against this, even though it was not essential to them as it was to the first two) would join in the execution of this episode, and if any of the subjects took it upon themselves to wash after having been warned to be unclean, they would instantly be put down on the list of punishments. This was the case of Colombe and Hébé that very morning: they had shat the previous evening at the orgies and, knowing they had to serve the coffee the next day, Curval, who had planned to have his way with the two of them and had even warned he would make them fart, had insisted that matters should be left in the state they were in when the children went to bed. At the morning inspection, they did not do any business; informed of this, Durcet was very surprised to find them in the cleanest possible state; they apologized, saying they had forgotten, and were put down in the book of punishments regardless. No chapel permissions were granted that morning (the reader would do well in future to remember what is understood by this) as the friends were far too aware of the need they would have for these matters at the storytelling that evening not to keep them all in reserve until that time. They also put an end on this day to the masturbation lessons for the boys: these had become useless as they all frigged like the most skilled Parisian whores. Zéphire and Adonis had the upper hand over all the others by their dexterity and deftness above all, and there are few pricks that would not have ejaculated till they bled in such nimble and delectable little hands. Nothing happened before coffee; it was served by Giton, Adonis, Colombe and Hébé. These four children, as instructed, were stuffed full of all those drugs that may best provoke wind, and Curval, who offered to make them fart, received a great many wafts; the Duc had himself sucked by Giton, whose little mouth could not quite wrap itself around the enormous prick put before him, Durcet got up to some choice little abominations with Hébé, and the Bishop thigh-fucked Colombe. 6 o'clock sounded, they went through to the chamber, where, as everything was ready, Madame Duclos began the story we are about to read.

'A new companion had just arrived at Md. Fournier's, who, because of the role she will play in our account of the following passion, merits at least a rough sketch. She was a young

dressmaker, debauched by the seducer I mentioned at Madame
Guérin's, who also worked for Madame Fournier: she was 14
years of age with brown hair, brown, sparkling eyes, a small face
as sensual as one could ever hope to find, skin white as a lily
and soft as satin, a shapely figure, but a little fleshy nevertheless
– a slight shortcoming that made for an arse as sweet and pretty,
as plump and white as there was perhaps in all of Paris. The
man I saw her with through the hole was to break her in, as she
was still a virgin – and in every way at that. Such goods are
moreover only offered to a true friend of the house: this was the
old Abbé de Fierville, as well known for his wealth as for his
debauchery, and gouty to the tips of his fingers; he arrives, his
head wrapped up in a bonnet, makes himself comfortable in the
room, inspects all the instruments he will require, prepares
everything, and the little girl arrives – she was called Eugénie.
A little frightened by the grotesque face of her first lover, she
lowers her eyes and blushes. "Come here, come here," the libertine tells her, "and show me your buttocks!" "Monsieur," says
the child, taken aback. "Come on then, come on then!" says the
old libertine. "There is nothing worse than all these little novices
– they never understand it's arses we want to see. Come on, hitch
them up then, hitch them up!" And the little girl, approaching
at last for fear of displeasing Madame Fournier, whom she had
promised she would be obliging, hitches her skirts up halfway
at the back. "Higher, higher!" said the old lecher. "Do you think
I can be bothered to do it myself?" And at last her fine arse is
fully revealed. The Abbé ogles it, has her stand straight, bend
over, clamp her legs together, spread them apart and, pushing
her against the bed, he crudely rubs all his parts, which he has
given an airing, against Eugénie's pretty arse for a moment as if
to electrify himself,[44] as if to draw some of the heat of this pretty
child to himself; from there he moves on to kisses, kneeling to
do so more comfortably and spreading those beautiful buttocks
as wide as possible with his two hands, his tongue and mouth
foraging between them for treasure. "They weren't lying," he
said, "you have quite a nice arse. Has it been long since you last
shat?" "A moment ago, Monsieur," said the little girl. "Madame
had me take that precaution before coming up." "Aha! . . . So

there's nothing left in your bowels?" asked the lecher. "Well, we shall see." And so, grabbing hold of the syringe, he fills it with milk, returns to the object of his affections, aims the cannula and injects the enema; Eugénie, forewarned, submits to all this, but the remedy is no sooner in her belly than, lying down flat on the sofa, he orders her to come over and straddle him and to do all her little business into his mouth. The shy creature places herself as she is told, she pushes, the libertine frigs himself; his mouth, hermetically sealed over her hole, does not let spill a drop of the precious liqueur that pours from it. He swallows it all with the greatest care, and is no sooner on his last mouthful than his come escapes and plunges him into delirium. But what exactly is that mood, that disgust which for almost all true libertines follows the breaking of the spell? The Abbé, brutally pushing the little girl away from him as soon as he has finished, straightens his clothes, says that they were lying when they said they would have the child shit beforehand, and that he had swallowed half her turd. [It is] worth observing that M. l'Abbé wanted only milk. He grumbles, he swears, he curses, says that he will not pay, that he will not come back, that snotty little girls like these are hardly worth the effort of a visit, and leaves, adding to this a thousand other insults I shall have occasion to describe in another passion where these are the principal element, whereas here they would be only very incidental considerations.'

'My word,' said Curval. 'This is a very fussy man indeed, to lose his temper just because he has received a little shit – what about those that eat it?' 'Patience, patience, my Lord,' said Duclos. 'Let my tale follow the order you yourself have demanded and you'll see that we'll come to the turn of the singular libertines you have just mentioned.'

This strip was written in 20 evenings from 7 to 10 o'clock and is finished this 12th 9ber 1785.

Read the rest on the reverse of this strip.[45] What follows forms the continuation of the end of the reverse.

*

'Two days later it was my turn: I had been forewarned and had been holding it in for the last 36 hours. My hero was a king's almoner, old and crippled with gout like the one before. One could only approach him naked, but the greatest care had to be taken to cover one's front and breasts – this condition had been impressed upon me with absolute precision and I was warned that if by some misfortune he were to catch the slightest glimpse of those parts, I would never be able to make him come. I approach, he examines my backside attentively, asks my age, whether it is true I have an urgent need to shit, what kind of shit I produce – whether it is soft, whether it is hard – and a thousand other questions that seemed to excite him, for little by little as he talked his prick rose, and he showed it to me. This prick of roughly 4 inches in length by two or three inches in circumference had for all its lustre such a humble and pitiful appearance one almost needed spectacles to be sure of its existence; I took hold of it nonetheless at the man's request, and, seeing that my tugs excited his desires pretty well, he readied himself to consume the sacrifice. "But is it absolutely genuine," he asked me, "this need to shit you're claiming? For I don't like to be deceived. Let's see – let's see if you really have shit in your arse." And as he said this, he thrust the middle finger of his right hand straight up my fundament, while with his left hand he kept up the erection I had teased from his prick. This probing finger did not have to go far to persuade itself of the very real need I had impressed upon him – he had no sooner touched it than he was in ecstasy: "Oh, golly!" he said. "She's not lying – the hen is about to lay, and I have just felt the egg!" The lecher, quite enchanted, kisses my arse for a moment, and, seeing that I'm squeezing it tight and can barely hold it in any more, has me climb on to a kind of contraption – rather like the one you have here, Messieurs, in your chapel: there my backside, perfectly exposed to his gaze, could make its deposit into a chamber pot placed just beneath it, two or three inches from his nose. This contraption had been made for him, and he made frequent use of it, for a day never went by without him coming to Madame Fournier's for such exploits, either with strangers or with girls of the house. An armchair placed beneath the ring supporting my arse served as this character's throne; as soon as he sees me in position he takes his place, and orders me to begin. A few farts serve as a prelude; he breathes them in. At last the turd appears – he swoons: "Shit, my little one! Shit, my angel!" he exclaims, all ablaze. "Let me have a good look at the turd as it drops from your fine arse." And he helped it along: his fingers squeezing my anus expedited the explosion; he frigged, he observed, he became giddy with delight, and, quite beside himself with this surfeit of pleasure, his cries, his sighs, his caresses all convince me he is approaching the final moment of pleasure, and I am all the more certain of this when I turn my head to see his minute tool disgorging a few drops of sperm into the same pot I had just filled. This one left without ill-humour – he even assured me he would do me the honour of seeing me again, though I was sure of the contrary, knowing full well he never saw the same girl twice.'

'But this I understand,' said the Président, who was kissing the arse of his sofa companion, Aline. 'One has to be where we find ourselves now – one has to be reduced to the scarcity that assails us to have an arse shit more than once.' 'Monsieur le Président,' said the Bishop, 'there is a somewhat halting tone to your voice that tells me you are hard.' 'Oh, not a bit!' replied Curval, 'I am kissing the arse of Milli[46] your daughter, who won't even do me the kindness of letting fly one measly fart.' 'I am more fortunate than you then,' said the Bishop, 'for here is Md. your wife, who has just done me the finest and most abundant turd . . .' 'Come now – silence, Messieurs, silence!' said the Duc, whose voice seemed to be stifled by something covering his head. 'Silence, damn it! We are here to listen and not to act.' 'Meaning that you're not up to anything, then,' the Bishop said to him, 'and that it's in order to listen that you're sprawled under three or four arses?' 'Come, come – he's right. Continue, Duclos, it would be wiser for us to listen to follies than to commit them.' And Duclos was about to resume when they heard the usual roars and customary blasphemies of one of the Duc's climaxes as, surrounded by his quadrille, he was lubriciously spilling his come – frigged by Augustine (who, he said, was fondling him delight-fully) and indulging in all sorts of mischief with Sophie, Zéphire and Giton along the very same lines as that which had been described. 'Oh! Good God!' said Curval. 'I cannot bear these wicked examples: I don't know of anything that makes one come more than come itself – and there is that little whore,' he said, speaking of Aline, 'who couldn't do any before, but who's now doing as much as anyone wants ... Never mind, I shall hold on. Oh! You can shit all you want, you slut, shit all you want – I will not come!' 'I can see, Messieurs,' said Duclos, 'that having perverted you it is now down to me to restore your reason, and to do this I shall resume my tale without waiting for your orders.' 'Oh, no! No!' said the Bishop. 'I do not have M. le Président's self-restraint: my come is prickling me and it has to let fly.' And as he said this, he was seen in front of everyone doing things that the order we have set ourselves still prevents us from revealing, but the sensuality of which very soon made the sperm, whose prickling was beginning to discomfort his balls, flow freely. As for Durcet, absorbed in Thérèse's arse, he could not be heard, and in all likelihood Nature had refused him what she had granted the two others, for he was not usually mute when she granted him her favours. Madame Duclos, seeing that all was now calm, resumed her lubricious adventures thus.

'A month later I saw a man one almost had to rape for an operation rather similar to the one I have just described: I shit upon a plate and thrust it under his nose, while he is sitting in an armchair reading without appearing to take any notice of me; he insults me, asks me how I could be so insolent as to do such a thing in front of him, but for all that he smells the turd, looks at it and handles it; I beg his forgiveness for the liberty I have taken; he continues to talk nonsense and comes, the turd under his nose, telling me he will track me down again and that one day I shall have to answer to him.

'A fourth only employed women of 70 years of age or over for such festivities – I saw him at it with one who was at least 80: he was lying on a sofa; the matron, straddling him, made her decayed deposit on his belly as she frigged a wrinkly old prick that barely came.

'There was at Madame Fournier's another rather peculiar

piece of furniture: it was a kind of close stool into which a man could introduce himself such that his body would protrude into another bedroom while his head took the place of the pot; I would be next to his body and, kneeling between his legs, would suck his prick as best I could during the operation. Now this peculiar ceremony consisted of a commoner – hired for this without ever knowing or getting to the bottom of what he was doing there – entering the room with the close stool, sitting on it and producing a turd, which, by this means, landed flat on the face of the recipient whom I was expediting; but this commoner absolutely had to be a peasant and plucked from the most ghastly dregs of society; he also had to be old and ugly. He was paraded in front of the other man beforehand and without all these qualities the latter was not interested. I could not see anything, but I did hear: the moment of impact was that of my man's climax – his come spurted into my gullet as the turd covered his face, and I saw him leave in a state that showed me he had been well served. Some time after this operation, chance led to an encounter with the gentleman who had just been of service: he was a good and decent man from Auvergne who worked as a builder's labourer – utterly delighted to earn a humble *écu* from a ceremony that, by simply relieving him of the surfeit in his bowels, became for him much more pleasant and agreeable than carrying his hod.[47] His ugliness made him an appalling sight and he looked over 40 years of age.'

'God be damned!' said Durcet. 'That's how it should be done.' And, heading into his closet with the oldest of the fuckers, Thérèse and Madame Desgranges, he could be heard bellowing a few minutes later, though he did not wish to share with the company upon his return the excesses to which he had just lent himself. Supper was served, was quite as libertine as usual, and the friends indulged the fantasy of shutting themselves away each in their own closets afterwards, rather than taking their pleasure all together as they usually did at this time of day: the Duc took the far boudoir with Hercule, Madame Martaine, his daughter Julie, Zelmire, Hébé, Zélamir, Cupidon and Marie;

Curval laid claim to the chamber of stories with Constance (who still trembled whenever she had to be with him, and whom he did nothing to reassure), with Fanchon, Madame Desgranges, Brisecul, Augustine, Fanny, Narcisse and Zéphire; the Bishop went through to the assembly room[48] with Madame Duclos (who was unfaithful to the Duc that evening in revenge for his own infidelity in going off with Martaine), with Aline, Bande-au-ciel, Thérèse, Sophie, charming little Colombe, Céladon and Adonis; as for Durcet, he stayed in the dining room, which was cleared away and had rugs and cushions strewn on the floor – he shut himself away, as I say, with Adélaïde his dear wife, Antinoüs, Louison, Champville,[49] Michette, Rosette, Hyacinthe and Giton. A redoubling of lubricity rather than any other reason had no doubt determined this arrangement, for their minds were so inflamed that evening that they unanimously agreed not to go to bed – though what they got up to in terms of obscenities and abominations in each room is unimaginable. As the break of dawn approached they decided to sit down to eat once again, even though they had drunk a great deal during the night; everyone sat pell-mell and the cooks, who were woken up, sent in scrambled eggs, *chincara*,[50] onion soup and omelettes. They drank some more, but Constance was in a state of despair that nothing could assuage. Curval's hatred swelled at the same rate as her poor belly: she had suffered this throughout that night's orgies, with the exception of any violent blows, as they had agreed to leave the pear to ripen – she had suffered with this exception, as I say, all that one can imagine in the way of ill-treatment. She tried to complain to Durcet and the Duc, her father and her husband, both of whom said to the devil with her, adding that there must be something wrong with her that they could not see for her to so offend the most virtuous and decent of human beings; that was all she got out of them. And everyone went to bed.

11th Day.

Everyone rose very late and, dispensing entirely for this day with the usual ceremonies, went straight from their beds to the lunch table. Coffee, served by Giton, Hyacinthe, Augustine and Fanny was quite calm, although Durcet absolutely insisted on making Augustine fart, and the Duc on sticking his prick in Fanny's mouth. Now as there was never more than a single step from desire to effect with minds such as these, they all had their way; fortunately Augustine was prepared for this – she farted almost a dozen times into the little financier's mouth, and this was almost enough to make him hard. As for Curval and the Bishop, they contented themselves with fondling the buttocks of the two little boys, before they all went through to the chamber of stories.

'One day little Eugénie, who was beginning to get to know us, and whom 6 months in the brothel had only made prettier, said "Come and look" to me. "Look, Duclos," she said, hitching up her skirts, "see how Md. Fournier wants me to have my arse all day." And as she said this she showed me a layer of shit an inch thick that completely covered her pretty little arsehole. "And what does she want you to do with that?" I asked. "It's for an old gentleman who's coming this evening," she said, "and who wants me with shit on my arse." "Well then," I said, "he'll be happy – for it would be impossible to have any more than that." And she told me that once she had shat, Madame Fournier had smeared her like that on purpose. Curious to see such a scene, as soon as this pretty little creature was summoned I flew to the hole: he was a monk, but one of those known as *bigwigs*; he was of the Cistercian order, fat, tall, vigorous and approaching sixty years of age. He strokes the child, kisses her on the mouth and, having asked if she was truly clean, hitches up her skirts to see for himself the state of hygiene which Eugénie was claiming – she had been told to speak this way, even though she knew full well the opposite to be true. "What? You little hussy!" the monk said to her, seeing this state of affairs. "How dare you tell me you're clean with an arse that filthy? It must have been more than a fortnight since you last wiped your arse. See the trouble you put me to? I want to see it clean after all, and now I'll have to take care of it myself." And while he was saying this he had pushed the girl against the bed and kneeled beneath her buttocks, spreading them apart with both hands. At first it looks as if he's simply observing the situation, which seems to surprise him, then little by little he gets used to it, he approaches with his tongue, which dislodges the morsels, his senses become inflamed, his prick rises, his nose, mouth and tongue all appear to work in tandem. His ecstasy seems so delectable he can barely speak, his come rises at last, he grabs his prick, frigs it, and ejaculates just as he finishes cleaning that anus so thoroughly one would never have imagined it had ever been dirty. But the libertine did not stop there and this sensual mania was for him nothing but a preliminary: he gets up, kisses the little girl once again, shows her a fat, ugly and dirty arse which he orders her to fondle and socratize.[51] This operation makes him hard again: he grabs hold of my companion's arse once more, smothers it with more kisses and, as what he did next is neither within my purview nor to be placed in these preliminary stories, you will allow me to leave it to Madame Martaine to tell you about the misbehaviour of a scoundrel she herself knew only too well – and to avoid any questions on your part, Messieurs, which I would not be permitted by your very own laws to answer, I shall move on to another case.'

'Just one word, Duclos,' said the Duc. 'I shall speak in veiled terms so that your replies don't break our laws: did the monk have a big one, and was it the first time that Eugénie . . . ?' 'Yes, my Lord, it was the first time and the monk had one almost as big as yours.' 'Oh fuck!' said Durcet. 'What a lovely scene and how I would like to have seen it!'

'Perhaps you would have shown the same curiosity,' said Duclos, continuing, 'for the character who fell into my hands a few days later. Armed with a chamber pot containing 8 to 10 turds taken from all around, and whose authors it would have irked him to know, I had to rub this fragrant pomade all over him with my hands: no part of him was spared, not even his face, and when I got to his prick, which I was frigging all the while, the vile pig left in my hand the proofs of his pitiful virility as he admired himself in a mirror.

'Here we are at last, Messieurs – at last we shall pay tribute at the true temple. I had been told to be ready: I had contained myself for two days; he was a Commander of the Order of Malta who saw a new girl each morning for operations of this kind; it was at his home that the scene took place. "Such fine buttocks!" he said to me as he kissed my backside. "But having a fine arse is not everything – that fine arse also has to shit – do you need to?" "I am dying to, Monsieur," I replied. "Oh, by God! That's delightful!" said the Commander. "That's what we call keeping the customers happy – but would [you] be so good as to shit into the chamber pot I'm going to give you?" "My word, Monsieur," I replied, "my need is so great I would shit anywhere, even in your mouth . . ." "Oh! In my mouth? She is delightful! Well, that indeed is the only pot I have to offer you." "Well then give it to me, Monsieur, give it to me right now!" I replied. "For I can't stand it any longer!" He takes up his position: I straddle him, frigging him as I proceed; he supports my hips with his hands and first receives then spits out, bit by bit, all that I deposit in his beak; as he does so he is in ecstasy; my wrist is barely strong enough to squirt out the floods of semen he spills; I frig him, I finish shitting, our man is in ecstasy and I leave him quite enchanted with me, at least according to what he was good enough to pass on to Madame [Fournier] as he requested another girl for the following day.

'The next one with more or less the same details added that of keeping the morsels in his mouth for a good while longer: he reduced them to liquid, rinsed his mouth with them for a good while, and only spat them out when they were watery.

'A fifth one had a fantasy that was even more bizarre, if that's possible. He wanted to find four turds without a single drop of urine in the pot of a close stool; he would be shut away by himself in a room where this treasure was waiting for him; he never took a girl in with him, and the greatest care had to be taken for everything to be properly closed, so he could be neither watched nor glimpsed from any side; then he would begin, but it would be impossible for me to tell you what he did, for no one ever saw him – all that we know is that when we returned to the room after he had left, the pot was quite empty and extremely clean, but what he did with the 4 turds I think the devil himself would struggle to tell you. He had the opportunity to throw them into the latrine, but perhaps he did something else; one reason for believing he did not do that other something you might imagine is that he would leave it to Madame Fournier to provide the 4 turds without asking who they came from and without once offering the slightest compliment on them. One day, to see if what we were about to tell him would alarm him – an alarm that might have given us some hint as to the fate of these turds – we told him that the ones we had given him that day were from various people in poor health and stricken with the pox. He laughed it off without losing his temper, which he would in all likelihood have done had he used these turds for something other than simply throwing them away. When on occasion we tried to press further with our questions he told us to be quiet and we never discovered any more about it.

'That is all I have to say for this evening,' said Duclos, 'as I pause before entering into a new state of affairs tomorrow – at least as far as my own life is concerned. As for all that relates to the charming taste you idolize, I still have the honour of speaking on this for at least two or three days, Messieurs.'

Opinions were divided over the fate of the turds belonging to the man she had just mentioned and while this was debated a few more were produced; and the Duc, who wanted everyone to see the taste he had developed for Madame Duclos, showed the whole company the libertine manner in which he liked to have his way with her – and the ease, skill, readiness and pretty words which she used so exquisitely to satisfy him. The supper and the orgies were quite calm and, as nothing of consequence happened until the following evening, we shall begin the story of the 12th day with Duclos's jolly tales.

Twelfth Day.

'The new post I am about to take up obliges me,' said Madame Duclos, 'to bring you back for a moment, Messieurs, to the details of my appearance – it is easier to imagine the pleasures being described when one is acquainted with the object providing them. I had just turned twenty-one: I had brown hair but skin of a most pleasant whiteness nonetheless; my luxuriant head of hair fell in flowing, natural curls down to my knees; I had the eyes you can see for yourself and which have always been held to be beautiful; my figure was a little full though tall, supple and slender. As for my backside, that part of such interest to the libertines of the day, it was by common consent superior to the most sublime that had ever been seen of its kind, and there were few women in Paris with one as delightfully sculpted: it was full, round, very fleshy and decidedly plump, without this portliness detracting from its elegance; the slightest movement immediately revealed that little rose you so cherish, Messieurs, and which, I believe just as you do, is the most delightful of a woman's charms. Although I had been steeped in libertinage for a very long time, I could not have been more youthful, as much because of the strong constitution Nature had given me as because of my supreme prudence concerning any pleasures that risked spoiling my youthfulness or ruining my constitution. I cared very little for men and had only ever had feelings for one; there was barely anything libertine about me other than my mind, but this was extraordinarily so, and, as I have described my charms, it is only fair that I tell you a little about my vices. I have loved women, Messieurs, I do not hide it. Not, however, to the same degree as my dear companion, Md. Champville, who will no doubt tell you they were her downfall, but I have always preferred them to men in my pleasures, and these pleasures they have given me have always had a greater hold on my senses than masculine delights. This aside, I have always had a weakness for theft – it is unbelievable how far I have taken this mania: utterly convinced that all the goods in the world should be shared out equally and that it is only force and violence that oppose this equality – the first law of Nature – I have striven to correct Fate and to restore the balance as best I can. And without this accursed mania perhaps I would still be with the benevolent mortal of whom I shall now speak.'

'And have you stolen a lot in your life?' Durcet asked her. 'Astonishingly so, Monsieur. If I had not always spent what I had stolen

I would be very rich today.' 'But did you add any aggravating
details?' continued Durcet. 'Was there any breaking and entering,
abuse of trust, blatant deceit?' 'There was everything there could
possibly be,' said Duclos. 'I did not think I should dwell on such
matters for fear of disrupting the order of my storytelling, but
as I see that you may find them amusing, I shall remember in
future to tell you about them. To this weakness I have always
been reproached for adding another – that of a very hard heart.
But is it my fault? Is it not from Nature that we receive our vices
or our qualities, and can I soften this heart which she made
insensible? I do not know if I have ever in all my life cried over
my misfortunes, let alone the misfortunes of others; I loved my
sister and lost her without the slightest pain – you have witnessed
yourselves the indifference with which I have just learned of her
demise. I would, thank God, watch the universe perish without
shedding a tear.' 'This is how it should be,' said the Duc. 'Compassion is the virtue of fools, and, when we look within ourselves
we see that it is that alone which takes away from our pleasures.
But with this failing you must have committed crimes, for that
is where insensibility directly leads?' 'My Lord,' said Duclos, 'the
rules you have prescribed for our tales forbid me to tell of a
great many things – you have left this task to my companions
– but I have just one word to say: when they come to paint
themselves as villains in your eyes, be perfectly clear that I was
never any better than they.' 'Now that's what I call doing yourself justice!' said the Duc. 'Go on, continue – we must make do
with what you have to say as we placed these limits on you
ourselves, but remember that in our tête-à-têtes I shall not let
you pass over your own little misdemeanours.' 'I shall hide nothing from you, my Lord – may you not come to regret, once you
have listened to me, granting a little kindness to such a bad sort.

'And so I begin: despite all these failings and, above all, that of
remaining entirely ignorant of the humiliating sentiment of gratitude (which I regarded as no more than an insulting burden
upon humanity and one that utterly demeans the pride that
Nature has instilled in us) – despite all these failings, as I say,
my companions were fond of me, and of all of them I was the

most sought after by men. This was the situation when a farmer-general named d'Aucourt came for a tryst at Madame Fournier's: as he was one of her regular clients, if more often for girls from outside rather than those of the house, he was treated with great consideration and Madame, who wanted absolutely to introduce us, warned me two days before to save you know what for him – which he adored more than any of the men I had encountered before, as you will soon see from my description. D'Aucourt arrives and, having looked me up and down, scolds Md. Fournier for not having procured him this pretty creature before; I thank him for his gallantry and we head upstairs. D'Aucourt was a man of about 50 years of age, large, plump, but with a pleasant face, great wit and – what I liked most about him – a sweetness and decency of character that enchanted me from the very first moment. "You must have the finest arse in the world!" said d'Aucourt as he pulled me closer, shoving his hand up my skirts and aiming straight for my backside – "I am a connoisseur and girls of your bearing almost always have a fine arse. Well, well! Didn't I say so?" he continued as soon as he felt it for a moment. "How sweet it is, how round!" And as he deftly turned me around, raising my skirts up over my loins with one hand and feeling them with the other, he set about examining the altar to which his desires were drawn. "By God!" he cried. "It really is one of the finest arses I've seen in my life, and I've seen a great many . . . Spread them . . . Let's see that strawberry . . . let me suck it . . . let me devour it . . . It really is a very fine arse indeed, this one . . . Oh, tell me, my little one – did they warn you?" "Yes, Monsieur." "Did they tell you that I made girls shit?" "Yes, Monsieur." "But what about your health?" the financier asked. "Oh! Monsieur, it is beyond doubt." "It's just that I push matters a little far," he continued, "and if you are not in perfect health, I would be at risk." "Monsieur," I told him, "you can do absolutely whatever you like: I vouch for myself as I would for a newborn child – it is safe for you to proceed." After this preamble d'Aucourt had me lean towards him, still holding my buttocks apart, and, sealing his mouth to mine, sucked my saliva for a quarter of an hour – pausing to blurt out a *fuck* or two and immediately resuming his amorous sucking. "Spit! Spit into my mouth!" he told me from time to time. "Fill it with saliva!" And so I felt his tongue circling my gums, thrusting itself as far forward as it could go and seeming to draw in everything it touched. "Come!" he said. "I'm hard – let's get to work." So he went back to contemplating my buttocks as he ordered me to free up his prick: I pulled out a tool as thick as three fingers clamped together and almost 5 inches long – very stiff and very rampant. "Take your skirts off," d'Aucourt told me. "I shall remove my breeches – both your buttocks and mine must be unencumbered for the ceremony we are to carry out." Then, as soon as he saw I had obeyed: "Lift your shift up high," he continued, "up to your stays and leave your backside completely bare . . . Lie down flat on the bed." And so he sat on a chair and went back to caressing my buttocks, the view of which seemed to intoxicate him; he spread them for a moment and I felt his tongue penetrate deep inside in order to check, so he said, beyond all doubt whether it was indeed true that the hen was ready to lay – I am using his own expressions here. In the meantime, I did not touch him – he gently roused by himself the withered little member I had just laid bare. "Come, my child," he said, "let's get to work. The turd is ready – I have felt it. Remember to shit little by little and always to wait until I've devoured one morsel before pushing out the next one. My routine takes a long time, but do not rush it – a little slap on your bottom will let you know you when to push, but it should always be piecemeal." Having positioned himself as comfortably as possible relative to the object of his devotion, he seals his mouth to it and I almost immediately deposit a lump of shit as large as a small egg: he sucks it, turns it over and over a thousand times in his mouth, chews it, savours it and, after two or three minutes, I clearly see him swallow it; I push again – the same ceremony, and as my need was great, his mouth fills and empties ten times in a row without him ever seeming satisfied. "It's done, Monsieur," I told him in the end. "I would be pushing in vain, now." "Yes, my little one," he said. "Is it done? So then, I must come. Yes, I must come while wiping this fine arse. Oh! Good God! What pleasure you're giving me! I've never eaten more delicious shit! I would swear it before the whole world! Give it to me, my angel, give me this

fine arse so I can suck on it, so I can devour it again!" And
thrusting his tongue in a foot deep as he manualizes himself, the
libertine sprays his come over my legs, not without a multitude
of vile words and curses – necessary, so it seemed to me, to
complete his ecstasy.

'When he was done, he sat down, had me come close to him
and, looking at me with interest, he asked me whether I was not
weary of brothel life and whether I would be pleased to find
someone who would agree to take me away from it. Seeing he
was taken with me, I played hard to get and, to spare you details
that would be of no interest to you, after an hour's debate I let
myself be persuaded, and it was decided that I would go live
with him the following day for 20 *louis* a month, including
board; that, as he was a widower, I could move into the entresol
of his mansion without any trouble; that I would have a girl to
serve me there and the company of three of his friends and their
mistresses, with whom he met up for libertine suppers four times
a week at one or another of their homes; that my sole occupation
would be to eat a great deal, but always meals he would have
prepared for me, because doing what he did it was essential he
fed me in his own fashion – to eat well, as I say, to sleep well to
aid my digestion, to purge myself regularly each month, and to
shit twice a day in his mouth; that this number should not daunt
me, because by swelling me with food as he was going to I might
well need to go 3 times rather than twice. To seal the deal, the
financier gave me a very pretty diamond, embraced me, told me
to make all my arrangements with Madame Fournier and to be
ready the following morning, at which time he would come fetch
me himself. My goodbyes were soon said: my heart had no
regrets, for it did not know the art of forming attachments,
though my pleasures pined for Eugénie – to whom I had been
very intimately attached for the last 6 months – and I left. D'Aucourt made me marvellously welcome and set me up himself in
the very fine apartment that was to be my home, and I was soon
perfectly settled in. I was condemned to eat four meals a day,
from which countless things were excluded that I would have
enjoyed very much indeed, such as fish, oysters, salted meats,
eggs and every kind of dairy food; but I was on the other hand

so well compensated for this that in truth it would have been churlish of me to complain. The staple of my everyday fare was an abundance of chicken breasts and boned game prepared in all sorts of ways, not much red meat, no fat of any kind, very little bread or fruit. I had to eat this kind of meat even in the morning at breakfast and in the evening at tea;[52] at these hours they were served without bread, and d'Aucourt, little by little, asked me to abstain from bread completely, to the point where I eventually ate none at all, no more than I did soup. From this regimen, as he had anticipated, there resulted two stools a day, greatly softened, very velvety and with a most exquisite taste, or so he claimed, that would not have been the case with an ordinary diet – and he had to be believed on this as he was a connoisseur. Our routines were carried out when he rose and when he retired. The details were more or less the same as those I have described: he always began with very prolonged sucking of my mouth, which I was always to present to him in its natural state and without ever washing it out; I was only allowed to rinse it afterwards; he would not, by the way, come every time. Our arrangement demanded no fidelity on his part: d'Aucourt kept me at his home as his main course – as his meat and drink – but still went out every morning to entertain himself elsewhere too. Two days after my arrival, his companions in debauchery came to his house for supper, and, as each of the three demonstrated, in terms of the taste we are analysing, a type of passion that was distinct but fundamentally the same, you will deem it fitting, Messieurs, as we have to make up the numbers in our collection, if I draw from the fantasies they indulged. The guests arrived.[53] The first was an old judge at the Courts of Justice of around 60 years of age, who was called d'Erville:[54] he had as his mistress a woman of forty years of age, very beautiful, with no other failing than a little too much plumpness – she was named Md. du Cange. The second was a retired military man of 45 to 50 years of age who was called Desprès: his mistress was a very pretty woman of 26 years of age, blonde, with the prettiest body one could ever hope to see – she was called Marianne. The third was an old Abbé of 60 years of age who was named Du Coudrais and whose mistress was a young boy of 16 years of age – radiant as the sun and whom he passed off as his nephew. Supper was served in the entresol, where my quarters were; the meal was as jolly as it was refined and I noticed the lady and the young boy were following more or less the same regimen as me. Their personalities emerged during the supper: it was impossible to be more libertine than d'Erville; his eyes, his words, his gestures – everything suggested debauchery, everything conveyed libertinage. Després seemed to have more composure, but lechery was just as much the soul of his existence; as for the Abbé, he was the boldest atheist one could ever hope to meet – blasphemies flew from his lips with almost every word he spoke. When it came to the ladies, they emulated their lovers – they were chatterboxes, but in quite a pleasant vein nonetheless; as for the young man, he seemed to me as dumb as he was pretty and barely appeared to notice the tender looks cast in his direction from time to time by Madame du Cange, who seemed a little smitten with him. All decorum was abandoned during dessert and the conversation turned as filthy as the acts themselves: d'Erville congratulated d'Aucourt on his new acquisition and asked him if I had a nice arse and if I shat well. "By God!" my financier told him. "It's up to you to find out – you know that between us all goods are to be shared and that we lend our mistresses as willingly as our wallets." "By God!" said d'Erville. "I accept!" And, taking me immediately by the hand, he proposed that I accompany him to a closet; as I was hesitating, Madame du Cange said to me brazenly, "Come, come, Mademoiselle! We put on no airs and graces here – I shall look after your lover while you are gone." And when d'Aucourt, whose eyes I consulted, indicated his approval, I followed the old judge – it is he, Messieurs, who will offer you (along with the two that follow) the three episodes of the taste we are addressing and which should take up the best part of my storytelling this evening.

'As soon as I was shut away with d'Erville, who was quite inflamed by the fumes of Bacchus, he kissed me on the mouth with the greatest fervour and vented three or four belches of Vin d'Aï[55] intended to elicit from my mouth the very thing he soon seemed keen to see escaping from elsewhere. He hitched up my skirts, examined my backside with all the lubricity of a consummate libertine, then told me that d'Aucourt's choice did not surprise him as I had one of the finest arses in Paris; he invited me to begin with a few farts and, when he had received half a dozen, he began to kiss me on the mouth again, groping me and firmly spreading my buttocks. "Do you feel the urge?" he asked me. "It's just coming," I said to him. "Well then, sweet child," he said to me, "shit on this plate." And to this end he had brought with him one made of white porcelain that he held as I pushed, and examined meticulously as the turd emerged from my backside – a delicious spectacle that, so he said, left him giddy with pleasure. As soon as I was done he picked up the plate once more, breathed in delightedly the sensual dish it contained, touched, kissed, smelled the turd, then, telling me he could bear it no longer and that lust was making him giddy at the sight of a turd more delicious than any he had ever seen in his life, he bade me suck his prick. Although there was nothing pleasant about this task, the fear of vexing d'Aucourt by failing his friend made me go along with it: he sat in an armchair, the plate beside him on a table over which he inclined the upper half of his body, his nose over the shit; he spread his legs, I sat on a lower chair near him and, having pulled from his fly the merest hint of a very limp prick rather than a real member, I set about sucking on that fine relic, despite my revulsion, hoping that it would become a little firmer in my mouth; I was mistaken. As soon as I had gathered him in, the libertine began his routine. He devoured rather than ate the pretty little egg I had freshly laid for him; this took three minutes during which his stretches, his movements, his contortions revealed the most ardent and animated of sensual pleasures. But try as he might, nothing would rise, and the ugly little tool, having wept out of spite in my mouth, withdrew more ashamed than ever and left its master in that state of exhaustion, of neglect – the sombre aftermath of sensual pleasures.

'We returned. "Oh! God be damned!" said the judge. "I've never seen anyone shit like that!" Only the Abbé and his nephew were there when we came back, and as they were hard at work, I can describe this to you right now. However often mistresses were changed in this company, Du Coudrais, always content, never took another and never gave up his own; it would have been impossible for him, I was told, to enjoy himself with a woman – this was the only difference between d'Aucourt and him. Indeed, as far as these ceremonies were concerned, he went about things the same way, and when we appeared the young man was leaning on the bed displaying his arse to his dear uncle, who, kneeling before him, lovingly received its contents in his mouth and swallowed as he did so – and all this as he frigged a very small prick we saw hanging between his thighs. The Abbé came, despite our presence, swearing that this child shat better and better each day.

'Marianne and d'Aucourt, who were enjoying themselves together, reappeared soon after and were followed by Desprès and du Cange, who had, so they said, only played around while waiting for me – "Because," says Desprès, "she and I are old acquaintances, whereas you, my beautiful queen, whom I'm seeing for the 1st time, inspire in me the most ardent desire to have my wicked way with you." "But, Monsieur," I say to him, "his Honour has taken it all, I have nothing left to offer you." "Well then," he replies, laughing, "I shall not ask anything of you, it is I who shall provide everything – I need only your fingers." Curious to see what was meant by this enigma, I follow him and, as soon as we are shut away, he asks to kiss my arse for just a minute; I offer it to him, and after two or three sucks of the hole, he unbuttons his breeches and begs me return the favour he has just done me. The position he had assumed was arousing my suspicions a little: he was straddling a chair, leaning against its back, with a chamber pot ready to be filled beneath him; for this reason, seeing him ready to carry out the operation himself, I asked him what necessity there was for me to kiss his arse. "The greatest, my dear," he replied, "for my arse, the most capricious of all arses, only shits when it is being kissed." I obey, but without taking any chances, and as he realizes this – "Closer, damn it! Closer, Milli!" he tells me imperiously. "Are you really afraid of a little shit?" Finally, to be obliging, I brought my lips close to the hole, but he had no sooner sensed this than he opened the floodgates, and the eruption was so violent that one of my cheeks was quite splattered – it took only one shot to fill the dish. In all my life I had never seen such a turd – it filled a very deep salad bowl all by itself; our man grabs it, lies down on the edge of the bed with it, shows me his shitty arse and orders me to fondle it vigorously while he immediately goes about filling his guts again with all he has just disgorged. As filthy as this backside was, I had to obey: "No doubt his mistress does this," I said to myself, "I cannot be fussier than she" – I thrust three fingers into the mucky hole in front of me. Our man is in seventh heaven: he dives into his own excrement, dabbles, feasts on it; one of his hands holds the plate, the other tugs on a prick that rises very majestically between his thighs; meanwhile I redouble my efforts and they are rewarded – I see by the tightening of his anus that the erectile muscles are ready to spurt out the semen; I carry on regardless, the plate is emptied and my man comes.

'On our return to the drawing room, I found my unfaithful d'Aucourt with the beautiful Marianne: the rogue had already had his way with both women. Only the pageboy was left and I think he would happily have come to an arrangement with him too, had the jealous Abbé agreed to relinquish him. When everyone had returned, it was decided we should all strip naked and carry out a few extravagances in front of each other. I was delighted at the prospect as it would allow me to see Marianne's body, which I had a pressing desire to examine: it was delectable – firm, white, pert – and her arse, which I playfully fondled two or three times, seemed to me a veritable work of art. "What good is such a pretty girl to you," I asked Després, "in the pleasure you seem to hold so dear?" "Oh!" he replied. "You do not know all our mysteries." It was impossible for me to find out any more, and even though I lived for more than a year with them, neither one nor the other ever wished to enlighten me, and I always remained ignorant of the rest of their secret dealings – which, whatever they may have been, do not prevent the taste her lover satisfied with me from being a passion in its own right and worthy in all respects of a place in this collection. Whatever it may have been could in any case only have been incidental, and doubtless either has been or will be described on another evening. After a few rather indecent libertine trifles, a few farts, a few more little leftovers of turds, plenty of talk and outrageous blasphemies on the part of the Abbé, who seemed to take the greatest delight in uttering these, everyone got dressed again and went to bed. The following morning I appeared as usual as d'Aucourt rose, without any reproaches on either side for our little infidelities of the previous evening; he said that aside from me, he knew of no girl who shat better than Marianne. I asked him a few questions about what she was doing with a lover who seemed so perfectly self-sufficient, but he told me it was a secret neither one nor the other had ever wished to reveal. And so we resumed, my lover and I, our daily life. I was not so confined to d'Aucourt's house as to be refused permission to go out from time to time: he relied entirely, so he said, on my honesty – I could see the danger to which I would expose him if I were to damage my health, and so he left me mistress of everything else. I therefore pledged my faith and allegiance for anything relating to that state of health in which he took such an egotistical inter- est, but, as for everything else, I considered myself free to do just about anything that would make me money; and consequently, keenly solicited by Madame Fournier to turn some tricks at her house, I went whenever she could promise me an honest profit. I was not one of her whores any more – I was a farmer-general's kept lady, who, just to please her, was willing to come and spend an hour at her house . . . you may be the judge of how well it paid. It was in the course of these fleeting infidelities that I encountered the new devotee of shit I shall describe for you now.'

'One moment,' said the Bishop. 'I didn't want to interrupt you before you reached a natural lull but now you have done so, pray enlighten us regarding two or three matters essential to this last part: when you participated in the orgies after the private tête-à-têtes, was the Abbé, who had up to that point caressed only his catamite, then unfaithful to him? And did he touch you? And were the others unfaithful to their women in caressing the young man?' 'My Lord,' said Duclos, 'the Abbé never left the side of his young boy – he barely even looked in our direction, even though we were naked and right next to him, but he played with the arses of d'Aucourt, Desprès and d'Erville: he kissed them, he gamahuched them, d'Aucourt and d'Erville shat in his mouth, and he swallowed more than half of each of these two turds, but as for the women, he did not touch them; this was not true of the other three friends in relation to his young catamite – they kissed him, they licked his arsehole, and Desprès shut himself away with him for I don't know what operation.'

'Well,' said the Bishop, 'so you see, you did not say everything, and this last one, which you did not mention before, forms yet another passion, as it describes the taste of a man who has other men shit in his mouth despite their advanced years.' 'That's true, my Lord,' said Duclos. 'You show me the error of my ways more clearly than ever, but I have no regrets as it means my storytelling this evening is now done, and it was already overlong. A certain bell we're about to hear would have convinced me there was no time to conclude our evening with the story I was about to begin, and so, if it pleases you, we shall defer it until tomorrow.'

The bell indeed rang and, as no one had come that evening and all the pricks were still very much aloft, supper was taken with the promise of making up for this at the orgies, but the Duc could not make it that far and, ordering Sophie to show him her buttocks, he had this girl shit and then swallowed the turd for his dessert. Durcet, the Bishop and Curval, all equally occupied, had the same operation carried out – the first on Hyacinthe, the second on Céladon and the third on Adonis; the last of these, unable to provide satisfaction, was put down in the fateful book of punishment and Curval, swearing like a scoundrel, took his revenge on Thérèse's arse, which unleashed point-blank the most perfectly complete turd one could ever hope to see. The orgies were libertine and Durcet, spurning the turds of the young, said that for this evening he wanted only those of his three old friends; he had his wish and the little libertine came like a stallion as he devoured Curval's shit. Night came to bring a little calm to all this intemperance, and to restore our libertines' desires and strength.

Thirteenth Day.

The Président, who went to bed that night with his daughter Adélaïde, enjoyed himself with her until the moment he fell asleep, then relegated her to a mattress on the floor near his bed in order to give her place to Fanchon, whom he always wanted by his side when lust roused him – as it did almost every night. Around three in the morning, he awoke with a start, swearing and blaspheming like a scoundrel – a kind of lubricious frenzy had possessed him that could, on certain occasions, take a dangerous turn. This is why he liked to have old Fanchon by his side at such moments, for she had perfected the art of calming him, either by offering herself or by immediately showing him one of the objects sleeping in his room. That night the Président, who suddenly remembered some abominations he had inflicted on his daughter as he first fell asleep, summoned her immediately to begin them again, but she was not there. Imagine the commotion and clamour sparked by such an event: Curval gets up in a frenzy, demands his daughter, they light candles, they search, they look everywhere, but find nothing; their first impulse was to look in the girls' quarters, they check all the beds and the alluring Adélaïde is found at last, sitting up in her nightdress by Sophie's bed. These two charming girls, sharing the same sweetness of character, with absolutely the same devoutness, virtuous sentiments, candour and amiability, had been taken with the most exquisite reciprocal tenderness and were consoling each other for the dreadful fate that assailed them. Nothing had been suspected until then, but it later transpired this was not the first time this had happened, and they realized the older of the two had been instilling the noblest of sentiments in the other and urging her above all not to stray from religion or from her duties towards a God who would one day console them for all their woes. I leave it for the reader to judge Curval's fury and fits of temper upon discovering the beautiful missionary in their midst: he grabbed her by the hair and, showering her with insults, dragged her into his room, where he tied her to the bedpost and left her until the following morning to reflect on her folly. As all the friends had raced to this scene, one can easily imagine the eagerness with which Curval had the two offenders put down in the book of corrections; the Duc was minded to carry out an immediate punishment, and the one he proposed was not a gentle one, but as the Bishop raised a very reasonable objection against what he wanted to do, Durcet contented himself with putting down their names. There was no way the old women could be blamed – Messieurs had that evening sent them all to sleep in their bedroom; this incident therefore brought to light an administrative failing, and so it was agreed that in future there would always and without exception be at least one old woman in the girls' quarters and one in the boys' quarters. Everyone went back to bed and Curval, whose anger had only made him even more cruelly indecent, did things to his daughter we cannot yet describe, but which, by prompting him to come, at least made him fall quietly back to sleep. The following day all the hens were so terrified that no offenders were found and among the boys there was only little Narcisse, who had been forbidden from wiping his own arse since the previous evening as Curval wanted it to be shitty at the coffee the child was due to serve that day, but who had unfortunately forgotten this order and cleaned his anus with the greatest care. However much he insisted his offence was reparable, as he still needed to shit, he was told to keep it in and that he would be put down in the fateful book regardless, a ceremony the formidable Durcet carried out there and then before his very eyes, driving home the enormity of his offence – one that might by itself have been enough to prevent M. le Président from coming. Constance, who was no longer harassed on this score because of her condition, Madame Desgranges and Brise-cul were the only ones to obtain chapel permissions, and all the others were under orders to save themselves for the evening. The night's events provided the conversation over lunch: the Président was mocked for letting the birds fly from his cage, the champagne restored his good humour, and they went through for coffee; Narcisse and Céladon, Zelmire and Sophie served it. The last of these was very ashamed of herself: she was asked how often this had happened – she replied that it was only the second time and that Madame

de Durcet gave her such good counsel that it was in truth quite
unjust to punish the two of them for that. The Président assured
her that what she called good counsel was actually very poor in
her situation and that the piety with which Madame de Durcet
was filling her head would serve only to get her punished each
day; that she should not have in this place any other masters or
any other gods than his three friends and himself, nor any religion other than that of serving and obeying them blindly in all
things. And as he was delivering this sermon, he had her kneel
between his legs and ordered her to suck his prick, which the
poor little wretch did, trembling all the while. The Duc, still
partial to thigh-fucking for want of anything better, screwed
Zelmire in this manner, making her shit in his hand and wolfing
it down as he received it – and all this while Durcet had Céladon
come in his mouth and the Bishop had Narcisse shit. They
allowed themselves a few minutes nap and, having settled down
in the chamber of stories, Duclos took up the thread of her story
thus.

'The gallant octogenarian Madame Fournier had arranged for
me was, Messieurs, a Master of Accounts[56] – short, portly, with
a very unpleasant face. He set a chamber pot down between the
two of us; we positioned ourselves back to back; we shat at the
same time; he grabs the pot, blends the two turds together with
his fingers and swallows the two of them, while I make him
come in my mouth. He barely looked at my backside – he did
not kiss it, but his ecstasy was no less intense; he stamped his
feet, swearing as he wolfed it down and as he came – and withdrew, giving me four *louis* for this bizarre ceremony.

'Meanwhile, my financier's feelings of trust and friendship
for me grew with each passing day and this trust, which I lost
no time in abusing, soon became the cause of our eternal separ-
ation. One day, when he had left me alone in his closet, I noticed
that he replenished his wallet, before going out, from a very large
drawer entirely filled with gold. "Oh! What a haul!" I said to
myself and, struck from that very moment with the idea of
grabbing hold of that stash, I paid the greatest attention to
everything that might help me make it mine. D'Aucourt did not

close this drawer but he did take the key to his closet with him, and, having seen that this door and its lock were very flimsy, I didn't think it would take much to break them open. With this plan in mind I had no other thought than to seize the moment as soon as d'Aucourt absented himself for the whole day – as he did twice a week, on the days of his private bacchanalia, when he would meet with Després and the Abbé for matters that Md. Desgranges may perhaps describe to you but that do not fall within my remit. The opportune moment soon presented itself: the valets – as libertine as their master – never failed to attend their own parties on such days so I had the house almost to myself; bursting with impatience to carry out my plan, I head straight to the closet, force it in with a single blow, fly to the drawer, find the key inside – I knew it! I pull out everything I can find – there was no less than three thousand *louis*; I fill my pockets, rummage through the other drawers – a very lavish casket offers itself to me, I grab hold of it, but what else did I find in the other drawers of this fabulous cabinet? Lucky d'Aucourt! How fortunate for you that your imprudence was only discovered by me! There was enough there to have him broken on the wheel, Messieurs, that's all I can tell you. Aside from the clear and explicit notes that Després and the Abbé had sent him about their secret bacchanalia, there were all the implements that could be used at such abominations . . . but I shall stop there – the limits you have set me prevent me from saying any more, and Madame Desgranges will explain all of this. As for me, my theft accomplished, I made myself scarce, trembling inside from all the risks I had perhaps run by keeping company with such scoundrels: I headed to London and, as my stay in that city, where I lived the high life for six months, would offer you, Messieurs, none of those details of interest to you alone, you will allow me to skip over that part of my life's adventures. I had kept in touch with no one in Paris other than Madame Fournier, and as she informed me of all the fuss the financier had kicked up over that paltry theft, I decided in the end to shut him up by writing curtly to him that the person who had found his money had also found other things, and that if he was determined to continue his proceedings against me I had no objection, but that if I were to hand in the contents of the small drawers to a judge, I would at the same time hand in the contents of the larger drawers too. Our man fell silent and as the debauchery of those three came to light 6 months later and they too headed for foreign climes, I returned to Paris with nothing left to fear and – must I confess my sins, Messieurs? – I returned there as poor as I had left it, so much so that I was obliged to move back to Madame Fournier's house. As I was only 23 years old I was not short of action – I shall leave aside those exploits that fall outside our purview and shall resume, if it pleases you, Messieurs, the only ones I know are of some interest to you at present.

'A week after my return, a barrel full of shit was placed in the room intended for pleasures; my Adonis arrives – he's a saintly churchman but so utterly inured to these pleasures that he was no longer capable of being moved other than by the excess I shall describe. He enters: I was naked; he looks[57] at my buttocks for a moment, then, having touched them quite brutally, he tells me to undress him and [help] him climb into the barrel. I strip him naked, I bear his weight, the old pig lands in his element; after a moment he sticks his nearly hard prick through a hole made earlier and orders me to frig it, despite the filth and foulness with which it is covered. I do so – he plunges his head into the barrel, he wallows, swallows, roars, comes, and leaps from there into a bathtub where I leave him in the hands of two servants of the house, who washed him for a quarter of an hour.

'Another one appeared soon after: a week earlier I had shat and pissed into a chamber pot carefully kept for that purpose – this interval was necessary for the turd to be in the condition the libertine wanted. He was a man of around 35 years of age whom I suspected was a financier. He asks me as he enters where the pot is, I present it to him, he breathes it in – "Is there absolutely no doubt," he asks me, "that it was done a week ago?" "I can guarantee it, Monsieur," I tell him, "and you can see it's already beginning to go mouldy." "Oh! That's what I need!" he tells me. "It can never be too mouldy for me – let me see, I beg you," he continued, "the fine arse that shat this." I show it to him. "Come," he said, "stick it right in front of me, so I can keep it in view as I devour the fruit of its labours." We assume our positions, he takes a taste, he is in ecstasy, he throws himself into his task and devours this delicious dish in a minute, pausing only to look at my buttocks, but without any other kind of accompaniment, for he did not even pull his prick from his breeches.

'The libertine who showed up one month later wanted to be entertained only by Madame Fournier herself – and what a choice, good God! She was 68 years old at the time, erysipelas was devouring all her skin and the 8 rotten teeth which adorned her mouth gave off such a fetid stench it was becoming almost impossible to speak to her up close, but it was these very failings that so enchanted the lover she was to entertain. Curious about such a scene, I fly to the hole: the Adonis was an old doctor, but younger than she nonetheless; as soon as he has her in his arms he kisses her on the mouth for a quarter of an hour, then, having her reveal a wrinkly old bottom resembling the udder of an old cow, he kisses and sucks it avidly; a syringe and 3 half-bottles of liqueurs are brought to him. This disciple of Aesculapius[58] plunges the anodyne drink, by means of the syringe, into the bowels of his Iris;[59] she receives it, she keeps it in; meanwhile, the doctor keeps kissing and licking her all over her body. "Oh! My friend," says our old Mother at last, "I can't hold it in any longer, I can't hold it in any longer – get ready, my friend, I have to let it out." The student of Salerno[60] kneels down, pulls from his pants a black and wrinkly rag which he tugs on vigorously; Madame Fournier settles her fat ugly bottom on his mouth; she pushes, the doctor drinks, some turd doubtless mixes with the liquid, it all goes down, the libertine comes and falls flat on his back, dead drunk. So it was that this debauchery satisfied two passions at once – his drunkenness and his lubricity.'

'One moment,' says Durcet. 'These excesses always make me hard. Desgranges,' he continues, 'I imagine your arse perfectly resembles the one Duclos has just described – come lay it on my face.' The old bawd obeys. 'Let it go! Let it go!' says Durcet, whose voice sounds stifled beneath this duplicate pair of dreadful buttocks. 'Let it go, bitch! If it's not liquid it will be solid, and I'll swallow it regardless!' And the operation comes to an end, while the Bishop does likewise with Antinoüs, Curval with Fanchon, and the Duc with Louison. But our four athletes, well drilled in all these excesses, indulged in them with their usual composure and the four turds were wolfed down without a single drop of come being spilled by anyone.

'Come – finish now, Duclos,' says the Duc. 'If we are no calmer, at least we are less impatient and more prepared to listen.'

'Alas! Messieurs,' said our heroine. 'The one that remains for me to tell you this evening is, I think, far too straightforward for the state I find you in. Never mind: its turn has come – it must keep its place. The hero of this adventure was an old brigadier in the King's armies: he had to be stripped bare then swaddled like a baby; in this state I was to shit in front of him into a dish and feed him my turd with the tips of my fingers as if it were pap; all this was done – our libertine swallows everything and comes in his swaddling, while mimicking the cries of a baby.'

'Let us then make use of the children,' says the Duc, 'as you have ended on a children's story. Fanny,' continues the Duc, 'come shit in my mouth and remember to suck my prick while you're at it, as I have to come again.' 'Granted!' says the Bishop. 'Come over here then, Rosette, you heard the order given to Fanny – do the same.' 'Let the same order apply to you,' says Durcet to Hébé, who also steps forward. 'So we have to keep up with the times,' says Curval. 'Augustine, copy your companions and do it, my child – make my come flow into your gullet and your shit into my mouth at the same time.' All this was done, and this time everything came off – shitty farts and climaxes were heard on all sides; and, their lust sated, the friends went off to satisfy their appetite. But at the orgies they refined their pleasures, and the children were all sent to bed: these delightful hours were spent with just the four senior fuckers, the 4 servants, and the 4 storytellers; they got completely drunk and committed abominations of such utter filth I could not describe them without doing an injustice to the milder scenes of libertinage I still have to share

with our readers. Curval and Durcet were carried off unconscious, but the Duc and the Bishop, as composed as if they had
done nothing at all, nevertheless went off to indulge their usual
pleasures for the rest of the night.

Fourteenth Day.

It appeared that day that the weather had again come to the aid
of our libertines' vile plans and concealed them better even than
their own preparations from the eyes of the entire universe: a
dreadful amount of snow had fallen which, filling the surrounding valley, seemed to render our four scoundrels' retreat
inaccessible even to wild beasts; as for human beings, there could
not have been one alive who would have dared try to reach them.
One cannot imagine how well sensuality is served by these measures, and the things one undertakes when one can say to oneself,
'I am alone here, I am at the end of the earth, hidden from all
eyes, and with no creature able to reach me – no more constraints,
no more limits.' From that moment, desires soar forth with a
recklessness that knows no bounds, emboldened by an impunity
that heightens this giddiness most delectably; there, one has
nothing but God and one's conscience – and how strong can
that 1st constraint be in the eyes of a committed and considered
atheist? And what hold can conscience have over someone so
accustomed to vanquishing remorse that it has almost become
a thrill of its own for him? O wretched flock! Abandoned to the
murderous teeth of such scoundrels, how you would have trembled had the experience you lacked allowed such reflections!
This was the day of the second week's festivities – these celebrations were their only concern: the wedding to be held was that
of Narcisse and Hébé, but, rather cruelly, both the bride and
groom were due to be punished that same evening; and so, from
the bosom of nuptial pleasures, they had to proceed to the bitterness of the classroom – what agony! Young Narcisse, who was
no fool, realized this, but they conducted the usual ceremonies
regardless. The Bishop officiated, the bride and groom were
married and permitted to do whatever they wanted as they faced

each other in full view of the whole assembly – but who would have believed it? The order was too liberal and the little fellow – a quick learner – utterly enchanted by his young wife's appearance and unable to have his way with her was nonetheless about to deflower her with his fingers had they let him; they stopped him in time and the Duc, grabbing hold of her, promptly thigh-fucked her while the Bishop did the same to the groom. Lunch was served, they were admitted to the feast, and, as they were made to eat a huge amount, both of them, as they left the table, shat to the satisfaction of Durcet and Curval, who gleefully swallowed this youthful excrement. Coffee was served by Augustine, Fanny, Céladon and Zéphire; the Duc ordered Augustine to frig Zéphire and the latter to shit in his mouth as he came; the operation was a marvellous success, so much so that the Bishop wanted to do the same to Céladon – Fanny frigged him, and the little fellow was ordered to shit in his Lordship's mouth the moment he felt his come flow. But this time the result was not as dazzling a success as last time – the child never managed to shit and come at the same time, and as this was only a test and the regulations made no mention of it, no punishment was inflicted on him. Durcet made Augustine shit, and the Bishop, who was firmly erect, had himself sucked by Fanny as she shat in his mouth; he came and, as his climax had been violent, he brutalized Fanny somewhat and was unfortunately unable to have her punished, however much he seemed to want to do so. There was no one as spiteful as the Bishop: they all knew that the moment he came he would happily see the object of his pleasures go to hell, and there was nothing the young girls, wives and young boys feared more than making him spill his come. After their nap, they went through to the chamber, where, once everyone had taken their place, Duclos took up the thread of her narration thus.

'I sometimes used to turn tricks in town, and as these were generally more lucrative, Madame Fournier tried to find as many of these as she could. One day she sent me to an old Knight of Malta, who showed me a kind of wardrobe full of compartments, each with a porcelain pot containing a turd; this old lecher had come to an agreement with a sister of his, who was the abbess of one of the grandest convents in Paris. This little lady would, as he requested, send him each morning boxes full of the turds of her prettiest boarders; he arranged them all in order, and when I arrived he told me to take such and such a number, which he would read out and which would be the oldest; I then presented this to him. "Ah!" he said. "This is from a 16-year-old girl as pretty as the day – frig me while I eat it." The entire ceremony consisted of me tugging away on him and showing him my buttocks while he devoured it, then leaving on the same dish a turd of my own in place of the one he had just gobbled down; he watched me do this, wiped my arse clean with his tongue and came as he sucked my anus. Next, the drawers were shut again, I was paid, and our man, whom I had visited fairly early in the morning, went back to sleep as if nothing had happened.

'Another one, who was in my view even more extraordinary (an old monk) comes in, requests 8 to 10 turds from the first to arrive – girls or boys, it's all the same to him. He mixes them together, kneads them, bites into the middle and comes as he devours at least half of it while I suck him.

'A third one, and this is undoubtedly the one who disgusted me more than any other in my whole life: he orders me to open wide; I am naked, lying on a mattress on the floor as he straddles me; he makes his deposit into my gullet and the rogue then bends down to eat it out of my mouth as he showers my breasts with his come.'

'Ha, ha! He's a funny one, that fellow,' said Curval. 'By God! It just so happens I need a shit – I must try this out. Who shall I take, Mr. le Duc?' 'Who?' replied Blangis. 'My word, I suggest my daughter Julie – there she is, close at hand. You like her mouth – use it!' 'Thanks for that suggestion,' grumbled Julie. 'What did I do to you to make you say such a thing?' 'Well then, since that has vexed her,' said the Duc, 'and since she's a good girl, take Milli Sophie – she's fresh, pretty and only 14 years old.' 'Fine – Sophie it is,' said Curval, whose rampant prick was beginning to gesticulate. Fanchon approaches the victim – the poor little wretch's stomach is already turning. Curval scoffs at her

– he brings his fat, revolting, filthy bottom up close to that delightful little face and seems to us like a toad about to wither a rose; he is frigged, the bomb explodes; Sophie does not spill a single morsel, and the swine then sucks up what he let out and swallows it all in 4 mouthfuls, as his prick is tugged over the belly of the poor little wretch, who, once the operation is over, vomits her guts up and into Durcet's face; he receives it with all due pomp and frigs as he drenches himself in it. 'Come, Duclos! Continue,' said Curval, 'and rejoice in the power of your words – you see the effect they have.' So Duclos resumed in these terms, utterly enchanted deep in her soul to be succeeding so well in her tales.

'The man I saw after the one whose example has just seduced you,' said Duclos, 'insisted the woman presented to him should have indigestion; consequently, Madame Fournier, who had not given me the least warning, had me swallow a certain drug over lunch that softened my stool and made it runny, as if I had taken a laxative. Our man arrives and, after some preliminary kisses offered to the object of his cult, which I could not allow him to prolong because of the colic that was beginning to torment me, he lets me proceed: it squirts out; I was holding his prick; he swoons, he swallows it all, asks me for more; I unleash a second broadside, followed swiftly by a third, and the libertine sprat finally leaves between my fingers the unequivocal proof of the sensations it received.

'The following day I dealt with a character whose baroque mania will perhaps find some disciples among you, Messieurs: first of all he was left alone in the room next to the one in which we normally performed our duties and where that hole was so conveniently placed for our observations; he made himself comfortable there; another actor was waiting for me in the adjoining room – he was a coachman chosen at random and forewarned about the whole plan. As I had also been forewarned, we performed our roles admirably. The Phaeton[61] was to shit directly before the hole, so that the hidden libertine should miss nothing of the operation: I receive the turd in a dish, help to coax it all out, spread the buttocks, squeeze the anus – I do everything I can think of to make shitting more commodious; as soon as my man has finished I grab his prick and make him come over his shit, and all of this in full view of our observer; at last, with the package ready, I rush into the other room. "Here, gobble it down quickly, Monsieur," I cried, "it's nice and warm!" He does not need telling twice: he snatches the dish, offers me his prick to frig, and the rascal swallows everything that I have presented, while his come flows under the supple movements of my diligent hand.'

'And how old was the coachman?' said Curval. 'About thirty,' said Duclos. 'Oh, that's nothing,' replied Curval. 'Durcet will tell you, whenever you like, about a man we knew who did the same thing and in exactly the same circumstances, but with a man of 60 or 70, who had to be found among the most depraved dregs of society.' 'But that's the only pretty way to do it,' said Durcet, whose little tool was beginning to raise its head after Sophie's aspersion. 'I wager, whenever you so wish, that I could do it with the most ancient of invalids.' 'You're hard, Durcet,' said the Duc. 'I know you – when you start getting filthy it's because your little come is bubbling up. Look – I am not the most ancient of invalids, but to satisfy your intemperance I offer you what is in my bowels and I think it will be plentiful.' 'By golly!' cried Durcet. 'What a stroke of luck that is, my dear Duc.' As the Duc steps forth to play his part, Durcet kneels beneath those buttocks that will fill him with joy; the Duc pushes, the financier swallows, and the libertine, transported by this excess of depravity, comes as he swears he has never felt such pleasure. 'Duclos,' says the Duc, 'come and do for me what I've done for Durcet.' 'My Lord,' our storyteller replied, 'you know I did so this morning and you even swallowed it yourself.' 'Oh, that's true,' said the Duc. 'Well then, Martaine, I must therefore turn to you, for I don't want a child's arse – I sense my come wants to let fly, but that it will only escape with difficulty, so I want something unusual.' But Martaine was in the same situation as Duclos – Curval had made her shit that morning. 'What's this, God damn it?' asked the Duc. 'Shall I not find a turd this evening?' And thereupon Thérèse stepped forward and offered the foulest, largest and smelliest

arse it was possible to see. 'Ah! That'll do,' said the Duc as he
moved into position, 'and if in my current state this foul arse
has no effect, then I don't know what I'll do!' Thérèse pushes,
the Duc receives; the tribute was just as ghastly as the temple
from which it emerged, but when one is as hard as the Duc, an
excess of filth is never a cause for complaint. Giddy with pleasure, the scoundrel swallows it all and blasts the most
incontrovertible proof of his male vigour into Duclos's face as
she frigs him. They sat down to eat. The orgies were devoted to
the penances – there were 7 offenders that week: Zélmire,
Colombe, Hébé, Adonis, Adélaïde, Sophie and Narcisse; the
tender Adélaïde was not spared; Zélmire and Sophie also left
bearing the marks of the treatment they suffered, and, without
going into further details, as these circumstances do not yet allow
us to provide them, everyone went to bed to find in the arms of
Morpheus the strength needed to make further sacrifices to
Venus.

15th Day.

Rarely did the day following the punishments yield any offenders; there were none that day, but the friends were as strict as
ever regarding the permissions to shit in the morning, granting
this favour only to Hercule, Michette, Sophie and Madame
Desgranges, and Curval thought he would come as he watched
the last of these doing her business. They did not get up to much
at coffee – they contented themselves with fondling buttocks
and sucking some arseholes, and when the clock chimed they
promptly took their places in the chamber of stories, where
Duclos resumed in these terms.

'A young girl of about 12 or 13 years of age had just arrived at
Madame Fournier's, once again the fruit of the seductions of
that peculiar man of whom I have already spoken, but I doubt
he had debauched anything as sweet, fresh and pretty for a very
long time: she was blonde, tall for her age, pretty as a picture,
with a tender and sensual physiognomy, the most beautiful eyes

one could ever hope to see, and a charming figure of delicate
and alluring graces that made her quite captivating. But what
degradation were all these charms to suffer and what shameful
initiation was in store for them? She was the daughter of a draper
to the law courts, very comfortably off and most certainly
destined for a more auspicious fate than that of a whore, but
the more our man deprived his victims of happiness through his
perfidious seductions, the greater his pleasure. From the moment
she arrived, little Lucile was destined to satisfy the foul and
disgusting whims of a man who was not content with the most
depraved of tastes, but wanted to inflict these upon a young
maiden. He arrives: he's an old notary, rolling in money, and
whose wealth was accompanied by all the brutality that avarice
and lust combine to foment in an old soul. He is shown the child:
as pretty as she is, his first response is disdain; he grumbles – he
swears under his breath that it is impossible to find a pretty girl
in Paris these days. At last he asks if she is most definitely a
maiden; he is assured she is indeed, and offered a closer look.
"Me – look at a cunt, Md. Fournier? Me – look at a cunt? You
can't be serious – have you often seen me contemplating them
in my previous visits to your house? I make use of them, it's true,
but in such a manner, I believe, that proves no great attachment
to them." "Well then, Monsieur," says Madame Fournier, "in
that case, you may rely on us – I swear to you she is as much a
virgin as a newborn child." They go upstairs and, curious to see
such a tête-à-tête as you may well imagine, I take up my position
at the hole. Poor little Lucile felt a shame that can only be
described in the same superlative terms required to describe the
impudence, brutality and ill-humour of her sexagenarian lover.
"Well then? What are you doing, standing there like a dumb
animal?" he asked her brusquely. "Do I have to tell you to hitch
up your skirts? Shouldn't I have seen your arse 2 hours ago? . . .
Well then, let's get on with it!" "But, Monsieur, what am I to
do?" "Oh, good God! Do you really have to ask? . . . What are
you to do? You are to hitch up your skirts and show me your
buttocks." Lucile obeys, trembling, and reveals a small arse as
pretty and white as that of Venus herself. "Hmm, what a pretty
prize!" says the brute. "Come closer." Then, roughly grabbing

her buttocks and spreading them apart – "Are you quite sure no one has ever done anything to you here?" "Oh, Monsieur! No one has ever laid a finger on me!" "Right then – now fart." "But, Monsieur, I cannot." "Well then – force yourself." She obeys – a little wind escapes, echoing in the poisoned mouth of the old libertine, who murmurs in delight. "Do you need to shit?" the libertine continues. "No, Monsieur." "Oh well, I do – and my need is abundant, let me tell you – so prepare yourself to satisfy it . . . take those skirts off." These fly off. "Get on this sofa, your thighs up high and your head down low." Lucile settles herself down; the old notary arranges and positions her with her legs spread apart, leaving her pretty little cunt as wide open as possible and so perfectly level with our gentleman's bottom that he can use it as a chamber pot; this was his heavenly intention, and to make the vessel more commodious, he begins by stretching it apart with all the strength his two hands can muster. He gets into position, pushes, a turd emerges and drops into the sanctuary where Cupid himself would not have scorned a temple; he turns around and, with his fingers, thrusts as much as he can of the filthy excrement he has just deposited into her gaping vagina. He gets back into position, pushes out another one, then a third, and on each occasion with the same ceremony of introduction; in the end, with the final one, he shoves it in so brutally the little girl cried out and may even have lost by this disgusting operation the precious flower Nature only bestowed for her to share in marriage. This was the moment of our libertine's climax: having filled that young and pretty little cunt with shit, his supreme delight was to thrust it in there again and again; he pulls out a sorry excuse for a prick from his fly, rousing it as he does so; as soft as it is, he tugs away on it and manages, as he busies himself with his disgusting handi-work, to speckle the floor with a few rare drops of discoloured sperm, the loss of which should have been a cause of regret as it only came from such abominations. Once he is done, he makes himself scarce. Lucile washes herself and there is no more to be said.

'Another man was let loose on me some time after, whose mania struck me as even more disgusting – he was an old judge at the Supreme Court; I had not only to watch him shit, but to help him, to ease the disgorging of this matter with my fingers by pressing, opening, squeezing the anus at the right moment, and once this operation was over, to lick clean with the greatest care every inch that had just been soiled.'

'Oh, by God! That is indeed a most exhausting chore,' said the Bishop. 'Don't the four ladies you see here – and these are our wives, daughters or nieces no less – carry out that duty each day? And, I ask you, what the devil is a woman's tongue for if not to wipe arses? As for me, I know of no other use for it. Constance,' continued the Bishop, addressing the Duc's beautiful wife, who was on his sofa, 'give Duclos a little demonstration of your skill in this regard. Look! Here's my filthy arse: it has not been wiped since this morning – I was keeping it for you . . . Go on, show us your talents.' And the wretch, all too accustomed to these horrors, carries them out as the consummate wife she was. See, good God, where fear and servitude can lead! 'Oh, by God!' said Curval as he presented his vile, mucky arsehole to the charming Aline. 'You won't be the only one here to set an example. Come on, you little whore!' he said to this beautiful and virtuous girl. 'Outshine your companion.' And they take their turn. 'Go on, continue, Duclos,' said the Bishop. 'We simply wanted to show you there was nothing very peculiar about your man's demands, and that a woman's tongue is only fit for wiping an arse.' The lovable Duclos laughed and continued with the story you are about to read.

'Allow me, Messieurs,' she said, 'to interrupt for a moment this tale of the passions to share with you an event that has nothing to do with them; it concerns me alone, but as you have ordered me to trace the interesting events of my life, even when they are not related to this tale of many tastes, I thought this was of a kind that should not be passed over in silence. I had been at Md. Fournier's for a very long time, and was now the most senior whore in her harem and the one she trusted the most; more often than not I would be the one to arrange the trysts and receive payment for them. This woman had become like a mother to me: she had helped me in times of need, had loyally written to me in England, had generously opened her house to me on my return when my troubles led me to seek sanctuary. She had lent me money on more than a dozen occasions and often without demanding repayment; the moment came to show her my gratitude and to live up to her absolute trust in me, and you will judge, Messieurs, how my soul embraced virtue and how easily it came by it. Madame Fournier falls ill and the first thing she does is send for me – "Duclos, my child, I love you," she tells me. "You know this and I'll prove it to you by the absolute trust I'm going to place in you at this very moment. For all your wicked ways, I believe you are incapable of betraying a friend; I'm now very ill, I'm old, and so I don't know what will come of this. I have some relatives who will pounce on my estate – I want at least to deprive them of the hundred thousand *francs* I have in gold in this little coffer. Look, my child," she says, "here it is – I am placing it in your hands on condition that you dispose of it in accordance with my instructions." "Oh, my dear mother," I say, reaching out to her, "these measures fill me with sadness – they will doubtless be unnecessary, but if by some misfortune they are needed, I give you my word I shall fulfil your intentions to the letter." "I believe you, my child," she tells me, "and this is why I turned to you. So then, this little coffer contains a hundred thousand *francs* in gold; I have some scruples, my dear friend, some pangs of remorse about the life I've led, about the number of girls I've driven to crime and snatched from God. So I want to try two means of making the divinity less severe towards me – alms and prayer. The first two parts of this sum, each of which you will allocate fifteen thousand *francs*, are to be delivered to the Capuchin monks on the Rue St. Honoré,[62] so that these good fathers may say Mass in perpetuity for the salvation of my soul, and, as soon as my eyes have closed, to the parish priest, so that he can distribute alms to the poor of this district. Alms are a wonderful thing, my child – there is nothing like them, in God's eyes, to redress the sins we have committed on this earth. The poor are His children and He cherishes all who bring them succour; nothing pleases Him more than when we give alms – it's the true way to reach heaven, my child. For the third part you will set aside 60 thousand *livres*, which you will deliver, straight after my death, to a certain Petitgnon, a cobbler's apprentice, on the Rue du Bouloir.[63] Unbeknownst to him, this poor wretch is my son – an illegitimate bastard; upon my death I want to give this wretched orphan some tokens of my affection. As for the remaining 10 thousand *livres*, my dear Duclos, I beg you to keep them as a humble token of my attachment to you and to recompense you for the trouble that distributing the rest will cause you. May this humble sum help you find a good match and leave this shameful trade of ours, in which there is no salvation nor any hope of finding it." Inwardly delighted to be in possession of such a fine sum and quite decided to take it all for myself for fear I might get in a muddle doling it out, I wept crocodile tears as I threw myself into the arms of this old matron – repeating my pledges of loyalty – and concerned myself only with finding ways to ensure a cruel return to health did not change her resolve. This way presented itself the very next day: the doctor ordered an emetic, and, as I was looking after her, he entrusted me with the package, warning me there were two doses, to take great care to space them apart – for she would croak if I gave it all at once – and only to administer the second dose should the first have little effect. I promised this Esculapius to take every possible care and, as soon as his back was turned, banishing from my heart all those futile feelings of gratitude that would have stopped a feeble soul, dismissing all repentance and all weakness and with no other thought than my gold, the sweet enchantment of possessing it and the delightful tingling one feels whenever one plans a wicked deed (a sure sign of the pleasure it will bring) – giving in to all of this, as I say, I promptly dropped the two doses into a glass of water and handed the drink to my dear friend, who, swallowing it without a qualm, soon found therein the death I had sought for her. I cannot convey what I felt when I saw the fruits of my labour. Every retch with which she breathed out her life produced a truly delectable sensation in my whole body; I listened to her, I watched her, I was utterly intoxicated. She reached out to me, bade me a final farewell, and I was in raptures – and I was already making a thousand plans for this gold I was about to get my hands on. It did not take long: Fournier croaked that very evening and I was now mistress of the stash.'

'Duclos,' said the Duc, 'tell the truth – did you frig yourself? Did the delicate and voluptuous sensation of the crime reach your organ of sensuality?' 'Yes, my Lord, I confess it did – and it made me come 5 times in a row that same evening.' 'So it's true!' exclaimed the Duc. 'So it's true that crime in itself has such powers of attraction that, independently of any sensual pleasure, it can on its own inflame the passions and bring on the same delirium as actual acts of lubricity! And so? . . .' 'And so, Mr. le Duc, I had my mistress honourably buried, inherited the bastard Petit-gnon's share, made a point of having no Masses said and above all to distribute no alms – the kind of act I have always despised, whatever Madame Fournier had to say about it. I maintain that it is necessary for there to be unfortunate people in this world, that Nature wills this, that she demands it and that to try to restore equilibrium is to go against her laws if what she had wanted was disorder.' 'Indeed, Duclos,' said Durcet, 'so you do have principles! I am delighted to see you do on this matter – all succour given to misfortune is a real crime against Nature's order. The inequality she has instilled in us as individuals proves that this discord pleases her, since she established it and wills it in our fortunes as well as in our bodies, and just as the weak are free to correct this inequality by stealing, so the strong are free to restore it by refusing succour. The universe would not survive for a second if all creatures were exactly alike; it is from this very dissimilarity that the order that sustains and drives everything arises – one must therefore be careful not to erode it. Besides, while I may believe I am doing some good for this class of unfortunates, I am also doing a great deal of harm to another, for misfortune is the breeding ground where the rich man will seek out the objects of his lust or cruelty; I am depriving him of this form of pleasure whenever my helping hand prevents this class from succumbing to him. By these alms I have thus only mildly obliged one part of the human race, and prodigiously harmed another; I therefore regard the giving of alms not just as a bad thing in itself, but consider it a real crime against Nature, which, in showing us our differences, never intended us to erode them. And so, far from helping the pauper, consoling the widow and relieving the orphan, if I am to act in accordance with Nature's true intentions, I shall not only leave them in the state in which Nature left them, but shall even serve her designs by prolonging this state and vigorously opposing any of their attempts to change it – and I shall always believe any means to this end are justified.' 'What?' said the Duc. 'Even robbing them and bringing ruin upon them?' 'Absolutely!' said the financier. 'Even adding to their numbers, as their class serves another – and if I make matters worse by prompting one to proliferate, I shall be doing a great deal of good to the other.' 'What a harsh system that is, my friends,' said Curval. 'It is, however, so delightful – or so they say – to help the unfortunate.' 'What a fallacy!' Durcet replied. 'That pleasure cannot compare to the other: the former is illusory, the latter is real; the former derives from prejudice, the latter is founded on reason. The one, speaking to our pride, the most false of all our sensations, may tickle the heart for a moment; the other is a veritable ecstasy of the mind and one that inflames all the passions precisely because it defies received opinion. In a word, one makes me hard,' said Durcet, 'and the other leaves me cold.' 'But must we always relate everything to the senses?' asked the Bishop. 'Everything, my friend,' said Durcet. 'They alone must guide us in all our actions in life, because their voice alone is truly imperious.' 'But thousands upon thousands of crimes might arise from this system,' said the Bishop. 'Oh, what does crime matter to me,' replied Durcet, 'as long as I am satisfied? Crime is one of Nature's means, a way in which she drives man on – why not let myself be driven in this direction rather than towards virtue? She needs both one and the other, and I serve her just as well in one as in the other. But here we are embarking on a discussion that could go on and on – it will soon be time for supper, and Duclos is far from having completed her task. Continue, my charming girl, continue, and rest assured you have just confessed to an act and to a system for which you will for ever deserve our esteem, as well as that of all philosophers.'

'As soon as my dear mistress had been buried, my first thought was to take over her house myself and keep it on the same footing. I revealed this plan to my companions, all of whom – and especially Eugénie, who was still my little darling – promised to consider me their Mother. I was not too young to aspire to such a title: I was almost thirty years old with all the wit necessary to run our convent – and so, Messieurs, it is no longer as a common whore that I shall finish the tale of my adventures, but as an abbess, young enough and pretty enough to turn a trick myself, as I often did and as I shall be sure to describe whenever this should be the case. All of Madame Fournier's clients stayed with me and I had the knack of attracting new ones as well, as much by the cleanliness of my rooms as by my girls' extreme submission to the libertines' every whim, and by my delightful selection of ladies. The first of the regulars to pay me a visit was an old Treasurer of France,[64] a former friend of Madame Fournier: I handed him over to young Lucile, about whom he seemed most enthusiastic; his usual mania, as filthy as it was unpleasant for the girl, involved shitting on the very face of his Dulcinea, smearing his turd all over it, and then kissing and sucking her in this state; Lucile, out of friendship for me, let the old satyr do everything he pleased, and he came over her belly while kissing his revolting handiwork over and over.

'Soon after another one arrived, whom Eugénie received: he had a barrel full of shit brought in, plunged the naked girl into it and licked every part of her body, swallowing as he went, until he left her as clean as he had found her. This one was a famous lawyer, a rich and very well-known man who, endowed with few of the qualities needed to enjoy women, made up for this by a form of libertinage he had loved all his life.

'The Marquis de . . . , one of Madame Fournier's old clients, visited shortly after her death to assure me of his goodwill; he assured me he would continue to visit the house and, to convince me of this, he saw Eugénie that same evening. This old libertine's passion consisted firstly of extravagantly kissing the girl's mouth; he swallowed as much of her saliva as he could, then kissed her buttocks for a quarter of an hour, made her fart and was finally ready for more serious business. As soon as this had been done, he kept the turd in his mouth and had the girl lean over him – gripping him with one hand and frigging him with the other;

while he enjoyed this masturbation and tickled her shitty hole, the young lady had to eat the turd she had just deposited in his mouth. Although he paid handsomely for this taste, he could find very few girls willing to submit to it; that's why the Marquis had come to pay his respects to me – he was as keen to retain my services as I was to provide them.'

At that moment the inflamed Duc said that even if the bell for supper were to ring he wanted to enact that fantasy before sitting down to eat, and this is how he went about it: he called Sophie over, received her turd in his mouth, then forced Zélamir to come eat Sophie's turd. For anyone other than a child like Zélamir, this mania could have become a great thrill; not mature enough to appreciate quite how delicious it was, he could view it only with revulsion, and started to kick up a fuss – but with the Duc threatening him with the full force of his anger were he to demur a moment longer, he did as he was told. This fancy was held to be so delightful that each of them followed his example more or less, for Durcet claimed such favours had to be shared equally and that it was not fair for the little boys to eat the girls' shit while the girls were left with nothing; and as a result he had Zéphire shit in his mouth and ordered Augustine to come eat the marmalade, which this beautiful and alluring girl did until she vomited blood. Curval followed the example of this reversal and received his darling Adonis's turd, which Michette ate – not without sharing Augustine's revulsion; as for the Bishop, he followed his brother's example and had the exquisite Zelmire shit, while forcing Céladon to come swallow the jam. There were some revolting details of great interest to libertines who see the torments they inflict as great thrills. The Bishop and the Duc came, the two others either could not or would not, and they all went for supper. Duclos's actions were praised to the skies. 'She had the wit to sense,' said the Duc, who protected her to an extraordinary degree, 'that gratitude is a delusion, and that its bonds should never stop or even delay the effects of crime, because the object that has served us has no claim upon our hearts; it has only looked after its own interests – its presence alone is humiliating to the brave of heart, and it must be despised

or dismissed.' 'That's so true,' said Durcet. 'You will never see
an intelligent man looking for gratitude. All too sure of making
enemies for himself, he will never strive to that end.' 'The aim
of the person who serves you is not to make you happy,' interrupted the Bishop, 'it is to raise himself above you through his
good deeds. I must ask, therefore, what do such plans deserve?
In serving us he does not say, "I am serving you because I want
to do you some good" – he says only, "I am obliging you only
in order to put you down and raise myself above you."' 'These
reflections,' said Durcet, 'thus prove the fallacy of helping others
and show how absurd good deeds are. But, so they say, it is for
its own sake: so be it for those whose frailty of spirit lends itself
to such trifling pleasures, but those who are revolted by them
– as we are – would, by God, be utter fools to indulge in them.'
Their minds inflamed by this theory, they drank a great deal and
went to celebrate the orgies, concerning which our fickle libertines decided to send the children to bed and spend part of the
night drinking with just the 4 old women and the 4 storytellers
– and to outdo each other in venting obscenities and abominations. As there was not one among these 12 interesting
characters who would not have merited the noose or the wheel
several times over, I leave it to the reader to reflect and imagine
what was said there. Words gave way to deeds, the Duc became
inflamed, and I do not know how or why, but it was claimed
that Thérèse bore the scars for some time. Whatever the case
may be, let us leave our actors to head from these bacchanalia
to their wives' chaste beds, which had been specially prepared
for them all that evening, and see what happened the following
day.

16ᵗʰ day.

All our heroes rose as sprightly as if they had just come from
confession, except for the Duc, who was beginning to wear
himself out a little. Duclos was blamed for this: there was no
doubt this girl had thoroughly mastered the art of gratifying
his senses and he confessed it was only with her that he came

lubriciously. So true it is that in such things everything hinges
on a whim – that age, beauty, virtue, all this makes no difference,
that it is simply a matter of a certain delicacy grasped more
often by beauties in the autumn of their lives than by those
lacking in experience whom spring still crowns with all its gifts.
There was also another creature among their company who
was beginning to make herself most delightful and to become
most alluring: this was Julie. She was already showing signs of
imagination, debauchery and libertinage; politic enough to sense
she needed protection, false enough to cosy up even to those
for whom deep down she perhaps cared little, she made friends
with Madame Duclos in an attempt to remain on good terms
with her father, whose influence among the company she recognized. Whenever it was her turn to sleep with the Duc, she joined
forces so effectively with Madame Duclos, she showed such
skill and such acquiescence, that the Duc was always sure to
come delectably whenever these two creatures set about the
task. Nonetheless he was utterly jaded when it came to his
daughter and, without the help of Madame Duclos, who used
all her influence to support her, she would perhaps never have
succeeded in her designs; her husband, Curval, felt more or less
the same way about her, and though she could still make him
come on occasion with her mouth and her impure kisses, his
sense of disgust was never far away – it seemed to spring from
the very flames of her shameless kisses. Durcet held her in rather
low esteem and she had barely managed to make him come
twice since their arrival; so that left only the Bishop, who adored
her libertine turn of phrase and thought she had the finest arse
in the world – there was no doubt she had one as shapely as
Venus herself. She thus fought a rearguard campaign, for she
was keen to please, whatever the price; because she realized she
was in desperate need of protection, she wanted this badly. Only
Hébé, Constance and Madame Martaine appeared at the chapel
that day, and no one had been found to be at fault that morning;
after the 3 subjects had made their deposits, Durcet wanted to
do the same – the Duc, who had been flitting around his backside all morning, seized this moment to satisfy himself, and they
both shut themselves away in the chapel with only Constance

in attendance. The Duc satisfied himself, as the little financier completely filled his mouth with shit; these gentlemen did not stop at this, and Constance later told the Bishop the two of them had continued their abominations together for another half an hour. As I said earlier . . . they had been childhood friends, and had revisited their schoolboy pleasures endlessly ever since. As for Constance, she played no great part in this tête-à-tête: she wiped arses, sucked and frigged pricks, but no more; they went through to the drawing room, where, after a little conversation between the 4 friends, lunch was announced. It was as splendid and libertine as ever, and after some libertine fondling and kissing and several scandalous exchanges that added spice to the meal, they returned to the drawing room, where they found Zéphire and Hyacinthe, Michette and Colombe serving coffee. The Duc thigh-fucked Michette, and Curval did the same to Hyacinthe; Durcet made Colombe shit and the Bishop put him in Zéphire's mouth. Curval, remembering one of the passions Duclos had described the previous evening, wanted to shit in Colombe's cunt; the venerable Thérèse, who was there at the coffee, placed her in position and Curval began – but as his stools were prodigious, and proportionate to the immense quantity of food with which he stuffed himself each day, almost all of it spilled on to the floor and it was only, so to speak, superficially that he beshat that pretty little virgin cunt, which did not seem to have been in any way intended by Nature for such foul pleasures. Frigged delectably by Zéphire, the Bishop spilled his come philosophically, combining the pleasure he felt with that of the delightful spectacle he had been given to admire. He was furious: he scolded Zéphire, he scolded Curval, he lashed out against everyone; he was made to swallow a large glass of elixir to recover his strength; Michette and Colombe laid him down on a sofa for his nap and did not leave his side. He awoke fully revived and, to restore his strength further still, Colombe sucked him for a moment: his tool raised its head again and they went through to the chamber of stories. That day he had Julie on his sofa – as he was rather fond of her, this sight restored some of his good humour; the Duc had Aline, Durcet had Constance, and the Président, his daughter.

With everything ready, the beautiful Duclos took to her throne
and began as follows.

'It is utterly false to say that money acquired through crime
brings no happiness: no theory could be more wrong – I guarantee it. My house was prospering in every way – Madame
Fournier had never seen as many clients; it was then that I hit
on an idea, a rather cruel one, I admit, but one that I dare say
will not be entirely displeasing to you, Messieurs. It seemed to
me that when one had not done someone the good turn one
ought to have done, there was a certain malicious thrill in doing
him harm, and my perfidious imagination inspired me to commit
the following libertine spitefulness against that same Petitgnon,
my benefactress's son, to whom I had been supposed to pay out
a fortune that would certainly have been most welcome to that
wretch, and that I was already beginning to squander on frivol-
ities. This is how the opportunity arose: this unfortunate cobbler's
apprentice had married a poor girl of his own rank, and the sole
fruit of that wretched union was a young girl of about 12 years
of age, who I had been told combined childlike features with all
the graces of the most refined beauty; this child, raised in poverty
but with all the care her parents' indigence allowed, was their
pride and joy and seemed to me an excellent catch. Petitgnon
never frequented my house – he did not suspect his rights to it
– but as soon as Madame Fournier told me about him, the first
thing I did was make enquiries about him and those close to
him, and this is how I discovered the treasure he kept at home.
Meanwhile, the Comte de Mesanges, the famous and avowed
libertine of whom Madame Desgranges will no doubt have cause
to speak on more than one occasion, had approached me, looking for a maiden not yet 13 years old, no matter the price. I have
no idea what he wanted to do with her, as he was not known
for being particularly exacting on this score, but he made it a
condition that, once her virginity had been confirmed by experts,
he would buy her from me for a fixed sum and thereafter would
have no further dealings with anyone at all, given that, as he
said, the child would be sent abroad and might perhaps never
return to France. As the Marquis[65] was one of my regular clients

(and you will soon see him enter upon the stage) I did everything I could to satisfy him, and the little Petitgnon girl seemed to me exactly what he was after – but how to get her out of the country? The child never left the house – she was even schooled at home, and guarded so wisely and circumspectly I was left with no hope; I was unable at the time to employ the famous debaucher of girls I have mentioned – he was away in the country at the time, and the Marquis was hounding me. I found just one way and this served to perfection the secret little wickedness that drove me to commit this crime, for it only compounded it. I decided to cause trouble for the husband and wife – to try to have them both locked away – and, with their young daughter less closely watched or with friends, I should thus find it easy to lure her into my trap. I set a prosecutor on them: he was a friend of mine, capable of all sorts, and whose skill I could count on entirely; he makes enquiries, unearths creditors, goads them, lends them his support – in short, within a week both husband and wife are in prison. From that moment on everything went smoothly for me. An accomplished walker soon accosted the little girl, who had been abandoned to the care of impoverished neighbours. She was sent to my house: she lived up to her outward appearance in every way – the softest, whitest skin, the most rounded, the most shapely charms . . . It was, in short, difficult to find a prettier child. As she cost me around twenty *louis*, all expenses paid, and the Marquis wished to buy her for a fixed sum (he maintained he would neither speak nor deal with anyone once payment had been made) I let him have her for one hundred *louis*,[66] and as it had become essential for me that no one should ever catch wind of my scheming, I contented myself with earning 60 *louis* from this deal and handed over another 20 to my prosecutor to muddy the waters, which he did so well that the young girl's father and mother were unable to discover any news of their child for quite some time. But learn they did: it was impossible to conceal her disappearance; the neighbours, guilty of negligence, excused themselves as best they could, and as for the dear cobbler and his wife, my prosecutor was so effective that they were never able to remedy this misfortune, for they both died in prison after almost eleven years behind bars. I profited twice over from this little mishap, for it assured me both of the absolute ownership of the girl I was to sell and of the 60 thousand *francs* I had been left for her father. As for the little girl, the Marquis had told me the truth – I never heard word of her again, and it will in all likelihood be for Md. Desgranges to tell you the end of her story. It is time to return to mine and to those daily events that may provide you with the sensual descriptions we have set about listing.'

'Oh, by God!' said Curval, 'I adore your prudence to distraction. There is a considered wickedness about it, an order that pleases me more than words can say – and the spitefulness, besides, of delivering the final blow to a victim whom you had as yet only grazed by chance, strikes me as a refinement of infamy that ranks alongside our own masterpieces.' 'I myself would have done worse, perhaps,' said Durcet, 'for those people could have been released after all. There are so many fools in the world whose only concern is to help such people – you must have been anxious while they were still alive.' 'Monsieur,' replied Madame Duclos, 'when one does not have the kind of influence you enjoy in society and when one is obliged to employ subordinates for one's peccadilloes, circumspection is often required, and so one dares not do all one would like.' 'That's true, that's true,' said the Duc, 'she could have done no more.' And this lovely creature resumed her narration as follows.

'It is dreadful, Messieurs,' said this beautiful whore, 'to have to speak to you again of depravities such as those I've now been describing for several days, but [you] insisted [I] bring together everything that might bear some relation to them and so I'm leaving no stone unturned. Here are three more examples of these foul abominations and then we shall turn to other fantasies. The first I shall cite is that of an old director of the royal estates of about 66 years of age. He would make the woman strip entirely naked and, having briefly caressed her buttocks with more brutality than delicacy, would make her shit in front of him, on the floor, in the middle of the room; once he had enjoyed this view, he would take his turn to make his deposit on the same spot; then, mixing both turds together in his hands, he would make the girl crawl forward on all fours and eat this stew, all the while exposing her backside, which she had to be sure to leave thoroughly smeared with shit. He would manualize himself during this ceremony and come when everything had been eaten. As you may imagine, Messieurs, few girls agreed to submit to such filth, but he needed them young and fresh nonetheless . . . I found them, because in Paris everything can be found, but I made him pay for the privilege.

'The second of the three examples of this kind I have to cite also demanded tremendous docility as far as the girl was concerned, but as the libertine wanted her to be extremely young it was easier for me to find children willing to engage in such things than more experienced girls. I handed over a very pretty little flower girl of 13 to 14 years of age to the man whom I shall cite here: he arrives, makes the girl remove only what is covering her from the waist down; he fondled her backside for a moment, made her fart, then gave himself four or five enemas that he made the girl receive in her mouth and swallow as they streamed into her throat. Meanwhile, as he was straddling her bosom, he frigged quite a large prick with one hand and manhandled her crotch with the other, and, because of this, [it] had to be entirely hairless. This man I am describing was ready to begin again after 6 of these, as he still hadn't come; the little girl, who was vomiting all the while, begged for mercy, but he laughed in her face and carried on regardless, and it was only on the 6th occasion I saw his come flow.

'Finally, an old banker will provide us with the last example in which such filth plays a key role, though I should warn you we shall often see it play an incidental part in future. He required a beautiful woman, but one of 40 to 45 years of age and with a heavily sagging bust; as soon as he was alone with her, he would have her strip from the waist up and, having brutally groped her breasts, would yell, "What fine udders! What's tripe like this good for, if not for wiping my arse?" He would then squeeze them, twist them around each other, tug on them, knead them, spit on them and sometimes stick his muddy foot on them, saying all the while how abominable breasts were and how he could not conceive what Nature had intended those hides for or why she had spoiled and dishonoured women's bodies with them. After all these preposterous remarks, he stripped stark naked. But – Heavens! What a body! How can I begin to describe it to you, Messieurs? It was little more than an ulcer, puss seeping endlessly from head to toe with a rank stench that could be smelled even from the adjoining room where I was watching – this was nevertheless the fine relic that had to be sucked.' 'Sucked?' said the Duc. 'Yes, Messieurs,' said Duclos, 'sucked from head to toe without leaving any spot larger than a gold *louis* unlicked. As much as I had forewarned the girl I had given him, as soon as she saw this walking cadaver, she recoiled in horror. "What's this, you slut?" he said. "You may find me disgusting, but you must suck me nonetheless – your tongue must lick absolutely every part of my body. Oh, don't act all disgusted – others have done it before you! Come, come – no more airs and graces!" It is true to say that people would do anything for money: the hapless wretch I'd given him was in the most extreme penury, and there were two *louis* to be earned – she did everything he wanted, and the old swine, thrilled to feel a tongue wandering over his hideous body and soothing the stinging that devoured him, frigged himself sensually throughout the operation. Once this was done – and, as you may well imagine, it was not without utter revulsion on this unfortunate woman's part – once this was done, as I say, he made her lie down on her back, straddled her, shat on her breasts and then, squeezing them one after the other, wiped his backside with them. But as for whether he came or not, I saw no sign of it and discovered some time after that he required several similar operations to make it that far; and as he was a man who hardly ever returned to the same place twice, I never saw him again and was in truth most grateful for this.'

'My word,' said the Duc, 'I find the conclusion of that man's routine to be most reasonable, and I've never understood how tits could really serve any other purpose than wiping arses.' 'There's no doubt,' said Curval, who was rather brutally groping the breasts of the tender and delicate Aline, 'there's no doubt indeed that tits are utterly vile. I can never see them without flying into a rage . . . I feel a certain disgust, a certain revulsion when I see them – only the cunt revolts me more intensely.' And at that moment he rushed into his closet, dragging Aline along by her breast, with Sophie and Zelmire, the two girls from his harem, and Fanchon obliged to follow; we are not too sure what he did in there, but we heard a woman's piercing scream and, shortly after, the roars of his climax. He returned; Aline was crying as she held a handkerchief to her breast, and because none of these incidents ever caused a stir – other than a burst of laughter at most – Duclos promptly took up the thread of her story.

'A few days later,' she said, 'I myself dealt with an old monk whose mania, though most tiring for the hand, was, however, less revolting to the stomach. He presented me with a fat ugly bottom with skin like parchment: I had to pummel his arse, grope it, squeeze it with all my strength, but when it came to its hole, nothing seemed violent enough for him – I had to grab its skin, rub it, pinch it, wiggle it vigorously between my fingers, and it was only the forcefulness of this operation that led him to spill his come. In addition, he frigged himself throughout this operation and did not so much as hitch up my skirts. But this man must have been fiercely attached to all this manual labour, as his backside, though flabby and pendulous, was nevertheless covered in skin as thick as leather.

'The next day, having no doubt praised my handiwork back at his monastery, he brought me one of his fellow monks, whose arse I had to smack with all my strength; but this one, more libertine and more exacting, would carefully inspect a woman's buttocks first, and my arse was kissed and tongued ten to twelve times in a row, with some smacks administered to his arse in between. Once his skin had turned scarlet his prick sprang up and I can confirm it was one of the finest tools I had yet handled; he then placed it in my hands, ordering me to frig him with one while continuing to smack him with the other.'

'Either I am mistaken,' said the Bishop, 'or we have arrived at the chapter on passive fustigation.' 'Yes, my Lord,' said Madame

Duclos, 'and since my task for today is done, you will allow me to wait until tomorrow before embarking on tastes of a kind that will occupy us for several evenings to come.' As there was still almost half an hour before supper, Durcet said he wished to have a few enemas to whet his appetite; this came as no surprise, and all the women trembled, but the judgement had been delivered and there was no going back. Thérèse, who was attending to him that day, assured him she gave these marvellously well; the proof was in the pudding and, as soon as the little financier had his bowels filled, he beckoned Rosette to come over and open wide. There was some baulking, some demurring, yet there was no choice but to obey and the poor little girl had to swallow two loads, even if it meant vomiting them up afterwards – which, as you may well imagine, did not take long. Fortunately it was time for supper, for he was doubtless about to begin again, but as this news distracted them all, they turned to other pleasures. At the orgies a few stools were dropped on to breasts and arses were made to shit a great deal; the Duc ate Madame Duclos's turd in front of everyone while this lovely whore sucked him, and the lecher's hands strayed here and there – his come let fly in abundance and, once Curval had followed his example with Madame Champville, they at last spoke of going to bed.

17th day.

The Président's terrible antipathy towards Constance boiled over each day; he had spent the night with her by private agreement with Durcet, to whom she answered, and the next day he complained about her in the bitterest terms. 'Since we do not, given her condition,' he said, 'want to submit her to the usual punishments in case she gives birth before we are ready to receive that fruit,' he said,[67] 'we must at the very least, by God, find a way to punish this whore when she behaves so foolishly.' But let us examine for a moment the accursed mind of a libertine: when we come to analyse this colossal mistake, O reader, guess what it was – she had unfortunately presented her front when they had asked for her rear, and such mistakes were not forgiven.

But, even worse than this, she denied doing so: she claimed . . . with some justification that this was slander on the part of the Président, who sought only to bring about her ruin, and that she could not spend a night with him without him making up such lies. But as the laws were clear on this point, and as the women were never believed, it was simply a matter of determining how they would punish this woman in future without running the risk of spoiling her fruit. It was decided that for each offence committed, she would be forced to eat a turd, and so Curval demanded she start at once. This was approved: breakfast was being served at the time in the girls' quarters – she was summoned there; the Président shat in the middle of the room, and she was ordered to get on all fours and devour what that cruel man had just done. She fell to her knees, she begged forgiveness, nothing moved them – Nature had placed bronze instead of a heart in their breasts; there was nothing more amusing than all the airs and graces the poor little woman put on before she complied, and God knows they enjoyed it. In the end she had to accept her fate: though her stomach heaved halfway through the deed, she had to see it through nonetheless, and it all went down in the end. Excited by this scene, each of our scoundrels had a little girl frig him as he watched, and Curval, particularly excited by this operation and frigged marvellously well by Augustine, felt ready to burst and summoned Constance, who had barely finished her miserable meal: 'Come here, whore,' he told her. 'When you've gobbled the fish, you need to add a little sauce: this one's white – come and have some.' Augustine had to get through this as well, and Curval, who made her shit as he put her to work, opened the floodgates into the mouth of the Duc's wretched wife as he swallowed that alluring Augustine's fresh and delicate little stool. The inspections were carried out: Durcet found shit in Sophie's chamber pot – the young girl apologized, saying she had been feeling indisposed. 'No,' said Durcet as he handled the turd, 'that's not true – indigestion causes runny stools, and this turd is perfectly healthy.' And promptly taking out his fateful book, he put down the name of this charming creature, who went off to hide her tears and bemoan her plight. Everything else was in order, but in the boy's bedroom Zélamir, who had shat at the previous evening's orgies and who had been told not to wipe his arse, had cleaned it without permission – this was a capital offence: Zélamir's name was put down. Despite this, Durcet kissed his arse and had himself sucked by him for a moment, then everyone headed to the chapel, where they watched two subaltern fuckers, Aline, Fanny, Thérèse and Madame Champville all shit. The Duc received Fanny's turd in his mouth and ate it, the Bishop those of the two fuckers – one of which he gobbled down, Durcet that of Champville, and the Président that of Aline, which ended up alongside Augustine's even though he had already come. The scene with Constance had inflamed their minds, for it had been a long time since they had allowed themselves such follies in the morning. They discussed morality over lunch: the Duc said he could not imagine why, in France, the laws cracked down on libertinage, since libertinage, by keeping the citizens busy, distracted them from plots and revolutions; the Bishop said the laws did not crack down on libertinage as such but rather its excesses; these excesses were therefore analysed, and the Duc proved that not one of them was dangerous, not one posed a threat to the government, and consequently that it was not only cruel but indeed absurd to try to conspire against such trifles. Words gave way to actions: the Duc, half-drunk, lost himself in Zéphire's arms and sucked this lovely child's mouth for an hour while Hercule, taking advantage of the situation, thrust his enormous tool into the Duc's anus. Blangis let him have his way and, moving and stirring only to kiss, he changed sex without noticing; his companions for their part indulged in other abominations, and coffee was served. As they had just made much mischief, this coffee was relatively quiet, and may have been the only one of the whole expedition with no come spilt; Duclos, already on her rostrum, awaited the company and, once everyone had taken their places, she spoke in the following manner.

'I had just suffered a loss from my house that had affected me in all sorts of ways: Eugénie, whom I loved with a passion and who was particularly useful to me because of her extraordinary acquiescence when it came to anything that could bring me money

– Eugénie, as I say, had just been snatched from me in the most peculiar manner. Having paid the agreed amount, a servant had come to collect her, so he said, for a supper in the country that might bring her seven or eight *louis* perhaps. I wasn't at home when this had happened, for I would never have let her leave with a stranger like that, but he talked to her and her alone, and she accepted . . . I have not seen her since in all my days.'

'Nor shall you,' said Desgranges. 'The tryst she was offered was the last of her life and it will be for me to conclude the story of this beautiful girl.'[68] 'Oh, good God!' said Duclos. 'Such a beautiful girl – at 20 years old the most delicate and appealing face!' 'And add to that,' said Desgranges, 'the finest body in Paris. All those charms turned out to be fatal for her, but continue, and let us not encroach upon the circumstances.'

'It was Lucile,' said Madame Duclos, 'who replaced her both in my heart and in my bed, if not in the work of the house, for she was far from being as submissive or as obliging. In any case it was in her hands that shortly thereafter I placed the Benedictine prior who came from time to time to pay me a visit and who usually took his pleasure with Eugénie: after this good Father had tickled her cunt with his tongue and given her mouth a good sucking, he had to be lightly flogged with a birch, but only on his prick and balls, and he would come (without getting hard) from the friction alone, simply from the blows from the birch to those parts; his greatest pleasure consisted in seeing the girl flick the drops of come from his prick into the air with the tips of the birch.

'The following day I dealt with one myself whose backside I had to thrash exactly one hundred times with the birch; beforehand he would kiss my backside and, while he was being flogged, he frigged himself.

'A third required my services some time later, but he was in every respect far more particular. I was notified a week in advance and, during all that time, I was not to wash any part of my body, and especially not my cunt, arse or mouth; and as soon as that notice was given, I was to leave at least three birches to soak in a pot full of piss and shit. At long last he arrived: he was an old salt-tax-collector,[69] very comfortably off, a childless widower who often engaged in such trysts; the first thing he asked was if I had been scrupulous in abstaining from ablutions, as he had prescribed; I assured him I had indeed, and to see for himself he began by planting a kiss on my lips that no doubt satisfied him, for we headed upstairs. I knew that if he had sensed from that kiss – given for my part on an empty stomach – that I had freshened myself up in some way, he would not have wanted to consummate our tryst. So we head upstairs: he eyes the birches in the pot where I had placed them, then, ordering me to undress, he approaches and carefully sniffs all those parts of my body he had expressly forbidden me to wash; as I had been very scrupulous, he doubtless found there the scent he desired, for I saw him get all hot and bothered and exclaim, "Oh, fuck! That's it, that's just what I want!" Then it was my turn to grope his backside – it was just like boiled leather, as much in its colour as in the toughness of its hide. After briefly stroking, groping and spreading those gnarled buttocks, I grab hold of my birches and, without wiping them, I start by flaying him ten times with all my might; but not only did he not flinch in the slightest, my blows did not even seem to graze that inviolable citadel. After this first round, I thrust three fingers into his anus and began to wiggle them about in there with all my strength, but our man was equally insensitive all over – he did not so much as flinch. Once these 1st two ceremonies were over, it was his turn to act: I bent over with my belly across the bed; he kneeled down, spread my buttocks, and his tongue roamed in turn from one hole to the other – neither of which, given his orders, could have been too fragrant; once he has had a good suck, I flog him a second time and socratize him; he kneels down again and licks me, and so on for at least fifteen rounds. At long last, understanding my role and attuning my actions to the state of his prick, which I observed without touching, I let drop a turd on his face with the utmost care while he is genuflecting; he falls over, calls me insolent, and comes as he frigs himself, yelling so loudly he would have been heard from the street had I not taken the precaution of preventing his cries from reaching that far. But the turd dropped to the floor: he did no more than look and sniff at it, but didn't take it into his mouth and didn't touch it; he had received at least two hundred lashes and, may I say . . . without any trace of having done so, without his backside – leathery from this long-standing habit – bearing even the slightest mark.'

'Oh, by God!' said the Duc. 'There's an arse, Président, that can outshine yours.' 'It's quite clear,' said Curval, stammering because Aline was frigging him, 'it's quite clear that this man we're talking about has absolutely the same buttocks and tastes I do, for I thoroughly approve of going without a bidet, but I'd prefer the girl to go without one for longer – I'd prefer her to stay away from water for at least three months.' 'Président, you are hard,' said the Duc. 'Do you think so?' said Curval. 'My word, ask Aline – she'll tell you what's up; as for me, I'm so used to this state that I never notice when it ends or when it begins. All I can tell you for certain is that at this very moment I'm speaking to you I could do with a really foul whore – I'd like her fresh from the seat of a close stool, her arse reeking of shit, and her cunt smelling of fish. Ho there, Thérèse! You whose filthiness dates back to the Flood, you who haven't wiped your arse since you were baptized and you whose vile cunt stinks for ten miles around, bring all that over here, I beg you, and add a turd, too, if you like.' Thérèse approaches: she rubs her foul, revolting and withered charms in the Président's face; she also leaves the requested turd there; Aline frigs the libertine, he comes, and Duclos resumes her narration as follows.

'An old boy, who used to receive a new girl each day for the operation I shall describe, had one of my friends ask me to pay him a visit, and I was forewarned at the time about this inveterate lecher's customary ritual. I arrive, he examines me with that phlegmatic glance that comes from inveterate libertinage – an assured glance that sizes up the object on offer in a moment. "I was told you have a fine arse," he says to me, "and as I have for almost 60 years had a decided weakness for pretty buttocks, I wanted to see if you deserved your reputation . . . Hitch up

your skirts." These forceful words were order enough; I not only
offer this professed libertine the prize he seeks, but bring it as
close as I can to his face. At first I stand up straight; little by
little I bend over and show him the object of his worship in all
the poses that might best please him. With every movement I
felt the lecher's hands roaming over the surface of my buttocks,
perfecting their appearance, either by squeezing them together
or by arranging them as he pleased. "The hole is rather large,"
he tells me, "you must have prostituted yourself sodomitically
with reckless abandon in your time." "Alas, Monsieur," I say to
him, "we live in an age where men are so capricious that in order
to please them we have to submit to a little of everything." I then
feel his mouth hermetically seal itself to my arsehole, and his
tongue try to penetrate the orifice. I deftly seize my chance, as I
had been counselled, and let the most succulent and moist vapour
slip out on to his tongue. This operation does not displease him
in the slightest, but neither does it spur him on; at last, after half
a dozen of these, he gets up, leads me to his bedside, where he
shows me a china pot in which four birches had been left to
soak; above the pot, hanging from some golden hooks, were
several cat-o'-nine-tails. "Arm yourself," said the lecher, "with
these two weapons. Here's my arse. As you see, it's withered,
scrawny and very tough – touch it." And when I had obeyed, he
continued: "As you can see, it's a piece of old leather, inured to
blows and inflamed now only by the most incredible excesses.
I shall take up this position," he said, stretching over the foot of
the bed, resting on his belly with his legs on the floor. "Use these
two instruments in turn – first the birch, then the cat-o'-nine-
tails. It will take an age, but you will know without question
when the denouement is approaching; as soon as you see something extraordinary happening to this arse, get ready to follow
its example. We shall change places – I shall kneel before your
beautiful buttocks, you will do what you will have seen me do,
and I shall come. But do not lose patience, above all, for I warn
you again we shall be here for a very long time." I begin, I switch
instruments as he recommended. But, good God! How imper-
turbable he was! I was drenched in sweat; he had me bare my
arms to the shoulder so I might strike him with greater ease. I

had been roundly thrashing him for more than three quarters of an hour, at times with the birch and at times with the cat-o'-nine-tails, but for all that I could not see any sign of progress. Stock-still, our lecher stirred no more than if he were dead – it looked as if he were silently savouring the internal movements of pleasure he received from this operation, but there was not the slightest outward trace, nor any sign it had made the least impression on his skin. Finally, the clock struck two and I had been hard at work since eleven o'clock – suddenly I see him raise his loins; he spreads his buttocks; from time to time I use the birch, flogging him all the while with the cat-o'-nine-tails; a turd appears; I flog him – my blows [make] the shit fly all over the floor. "Come on, chin up!" I tell him. "We're almost home and dry." Our man then gets up in a frenzy; his hard, rampant prick was glued to his belly. "Do as I did," he tells me, "do as I did – I just need some shit before I give you my come." I promptly take his place and bend over, he kneels down as he said he would, and I lay in his mouth an egg I'd been keeping to this end for nearly three days. As he receives it, his come lets fly, and he throws himself backwards, roaring with pleasure, but without swallowing or even keeping for a second the turd I had just deposited in his mouth. Moreover, other than you, Messieurs, who are without doubt the epitomes of this type, I have seen few men experience such acute paroxysms; he almost fainted as he sprayed his come. The session earned me two *louis*.

'But no sooner had I returned home than I found Lucile grappling with another old man, who, without any preliminary caresses, was simply having himself flogged from the top of his loins down to his calves with birches soaked in vinegar, and – with these blows raining down for as long as she still had strength in her arm – he concluded the operation by having himself sucked off. The girl fell to her knees before him as soon as he gave the signal and, letting his old, withered balls dangle over her breasts, she took the floppy tool into her mouth where the reformed sinner did not take long to weep for his crimes.'

And as Duclos had finished what she had to say for that evening and it was not yet time for supper, they horsed around while they waited. 'You must be spent, Président,' the Duc said to Curval. 'That's twice today I've seen you come, and you are hardly used to spilling so much in a single day.' 'Let's wager on three in a row,' said Curval, who was pawing Madame Duclos's buttocks. 'Oh, whatever you like,' said the Duc. 'But I have one condition,' said Curval, 'and that is to be allowed to do whatever I please.' 'Oh, no!' replied the Duc. 'You know full well there are certain things we've promised not to do until the time has come for them to be described. Getting fucked was one of these: before we could do that we had to wait for an example of that passion to be cited in the agreed order – and yet, following all of your representations, Messieurs, we have let this go. There are also many private pleasures we ought to have forbidden until the moment of their narration and that we tolerate as long as they take place either in our bedrooms or in our closets. Just a short while ago you yourself indulged in such delights with Aline – was it over nothing she uttered a piercing scream and now has a handkerchief over her breasts? Well then, go ahead and take your pick – either from those mysterious pleasures or from those we allow ourselves in public – and may your third one come from this sort of thing alone. I wager one hundred *louis* that you don't manage it.' So the Président asked if he could go to the far boudoir, along with any subjects of his choosing; this request was granted with the sole condition that Duclos should be present and that only her word on the outcome would be trusted. 'Very well,' said the Président, 'I accept.' And to begin with, he first had Madame Duclos give him five hundred lashes of the whip in front of everyone; once that was done, he took with him his dear and faithful friend Constance, whom he was nevertheless begged not to touch in any way that might endanger her pregnancy; he also took with him his daughter Adélaïde, Augustine, Zelmire, Céladon, Zéphire, Thérèse, Fanchon, Madame Champville, Madame Desgranges and Madame Duclos, along with three fuckers. 'Oh, for fuck's sake!' said the Duc. 'We never agreed you could use so many subjects.' But the Bishop and Durcet, taking the Président's side, maintained it had never been a matter of numbers. The Président – with his troop – went and shut himself away and after half an hour, which the Bishop,

Durcet and Curval,[70] along with the remaining subjects, did not spend in prayer – after half an hour, as I say, Constance and Zelmire returned in tears and the Président followed behind soon after with the rest of his troop, propped up by Madame Duclos, who testified to his vigour and confirmed that in all fairness he deserved a crown of myrtle leaves.[71] The reader will understand if we do not reveal to him what the Président had done; circumstances do not yet allow us to do so; but he had won his wager and that was the important thing. 'These one hundred *louis* here,' he said upon receiving them, 'will allow me to settle a fine I fear I'll soon be ordered to pay.' Here is yet another matter which we beg the reader's indulgence to explain only when the moment comes, but he should for the time being observe how this scoundrel foresaw his own offences, and how he resigned himself to the punishment they would bring upon him without bothering in the slightest to prevent or avoid them. As nothing out of the ordinary happened from this moment until the storytelling began the following day, we shall usher our reader there at once.

18th day.

Duclos, beautiful in all her finery and more resplendent than ever, began the tales of her 18th evening as follows.

'I had just acquired a tall, fat creature named Justine: she was 25 years old, 5 feet 6 inches, as strong as a barmaid and with beautiful features, a fine complexion and the loveliest figure in the world. As my house was full of the kind of old lechers who find some quiver of pleasure only in the torments they choose to suffer, I thought a boarder such as this could only be a great help to me; the day after she arrived, in order to put her fustigatory talents to the test (as these had been so fulsomely vaunted to me) I sent her to do battle with an old district commissioner,[72] who had to be roundly flogged from his lower chest down to his knees and from halfway down his back to his calves, until blood was dripping from everywhere. Once this operation was over, the libertine simply hitched up the wench's skirts and dumped his load on her buttocks. Justine conducted herself like a veritable heroine of Cythera, and our lecher came to tell me I had a real gem there and that in all his days he had never been fustigated as well as he had by that hussy.

'To show her how highly I thought of her, I put her with an old veteran of Cythera a few days later who liked to receive over a thousand lashes of the whip over his body, and when he was covered in blood, the girl would have to piss in her own hand and rub her urine into all the most badly mauled parts of his body; once this lotion had been applied, they would set to work again, then he would come, the girl would carefully collect his come in her hand, and would rub him down a second time with this fresh balm. My new acquisition enjoyed these and other successes, and to greater acclaim each day, but it was not possible to use her for the champion who made an appearance on this occasion.

'The only feminine thing this peculiar man wanted was the outfit, but in fact it was a man he required, for, to make myself clearer, the lecher wanted to be spanked by a man dressed as a woman. And you should have seen the weapon that was used! Don't imagine for one moment it was a birch – it was a bunch of willow switches that would barbarously tear his buttocks to shreds. In fact, as this business had a whiff of sodomy about it, I should not have got too involved; however, as he was a former client of Madame Fournier's, a man genuinely attached to our house since time immemorial and who – because of his position – could be of some service to us, I didn't make a fuss, and, having prettily disguised a young boy of 18 years of age who sometimes ran errands for us and who had a very sweet face, I introduced him to the client armed with the bunch of willow switches. There was nothing more amusing than this ceremony, and you can well imagine I wanted to see it. He began by closely examining his supposed maiden, and, having doubtless found her to his taste, he opened with five or six kisses on the mouth with a whiff of burning faggots[73] about them that could be smelled three miles away; next, he bared his buttocks and, still seeming from the way he spoke to take the young man for a girl, he told him to grope and knead them quite roughly. I had thoroughly briefed the young boy and he did everything that was asked of him. "Come on, then," said the lecher, "flog me and, above all, show me no mercy." The young boy grabs hold of a switch and immediately rains down fifty vigorous blows on the buttocks offered him; the libertine, already vigorously marked by the lashes of these willow switches, flings himself upon his male flagellatrix, hitches up her skirts, checking her sex with one hand, avidly grabbing her two buttocks with the other. He does not know which temple to worship at first – the arse prevails in the end, and he ardently seals his mouth to it. Oh! What a difference there is between the worship decreed by Nature and that which is said to outrage her. O good God! If this outrage were genuine, would the tribute be so ardent? Never has a woman's arse been kissed as that young boy's was – the lecher's tongue completely disappeared into his anus three or four times. Finally, assuming his position again, he cried, "O dear child! Proceed." He is flogged again, but as he was more animated, he withstands this second assault with far greater fortitude. He is flogged bloody: at that moment his prick springs up and he urges the young object of his bliss to grasp it. As the latter strokes it, the former wants to return the favour: he hitches up the other's skirts again, but it is the prick he is after this time: he touches it, fondles it, tugs on it, and soon introduces it into his mouth. After these preliminary caresses, he presents himself for a 3rd round of blows. This final scene leaves him in an absolute frenzy: he flings his Adonis on to the bed, stretches over him, presses their pricks together, seals his mouth to the lips of this beautiful boy and, having managed to inflame him with his caresses, sends him into divine raptures at the very moment he tastes them himself; they both come at the same time. Delighted by this episode, our libertine strove to overcome my scruples, and made me promise to keep providing the same pleasures for him either with that boy or with others; I wanted to try to convert him – I assured him I had charming girls who would flog him just as well; he would not even look at them.'

'I can well believe it,' said the Bishop. 'When one has a decided taste for men, one does [not] change: the distance is so extreme one is not even tempted to try.' 'My Lord,' said the Président, 'you are embarking upon a thesis that would merit two hours of discussion.' 'And that would always conclude in support of my assertion,' said the Bishop, 'because there is no doubt a boy is preferable to a girl.' 'No doubt,' replied Curval, 'but one could nevertheless raise some objections to this theory and argue that, for pleasures of a certain kind – such as those, for example, that Martaine and Desgranges will describe – a girl is preferable to a boy.' 'I refute that,' said the Bishop, 'and even for those you mean, a boy is preferable to a girl. Consider this in relation to evil, which is almost always the true attraction of pleasure – the crime will strike you as greater when you are with someone of your own kind than with someone who is not, and so the pleasure is immediately doubled.' 'Yes,' said Curval, 'but that despotism, that hold, that delight which comes from abusing one's power over the weak?' 'It is there all the same,' retorted the Bishop. 'If the victim is yours alone, that hold which you believe is more firmly established over a woman than a man in such cases has come only from prejudice, has come only from the custom which more commonly submits that sex to your whims rather than the other. But renounce for a moment those prejudiced opinions and imagine that other person utterly bound by your chains – enjoying the same authority, you will uncover the possibility of a greater crime and your lubricity will inevitably double.' 'I agree with the Bishop,' said Durcet, 'and once it is clear that this hold has been firmly established, I believe the abuse of power to be even more delectable when committed against one's own kind than against a woman.' 'Messieurs,' said the Duc, 'I should very much like you to defer your discussions until it is time to eat, and not to spend these hours, set aside for us to listen to the narrations, exchanging sophistries.' 'He's right,' said Curval. 'Go on, Duclos, continue.' And the loveable mistress of Cythera's pleasures resumed in the following terms.

'An old registrar[74] at the Courts of Justice,' she said, 'comes to visit me one morning, and as he had been accustomed to dealing only with me since the days of Madame Fournier, he had no desire to change his routine. While frigging him, I had to slap his face with increasing force, that is to say softly at first, then a little harder as his prick grew firmer, and finally with all my strength as he came; I had so expertly grasped this character's mania that at the twentieth slap I made his come fly.'

'At the 20th!' said the Bishop. 'Golly, it wouldn't have taken that many to make my prick go limp in a flash.' 'You see, my friend,' said the Duc, 'to each his own mania – we must never condemn nor be surprised at anyone else's. Go on, Duclos, one more and then finish.'

'The one I have left to tell you this evening,' said Duclos, 'was relayed to me by a friend of mine: she had been living for two years with a man who would get hard only once his nose had been flicked twenty times, his ears pulled until they bled and his buttocks, prick and balls bitten. Excited by these brutal preliminaries, he would be as hard as a stallion and would come, swearing like a devil, almost always over the face of the woman who had dealt with him in this peculiar manner.'

Of all the things that had just been described, Messieurs' minds had been inflamed only by those related to male fustigation and that evening they emulated that fantasy alone: the Duc had himself flogged until he bled by Hercule, Durcet by Bande-au-ciel, the Bishop by Antinoüs, and Curval by Brise-cul; the Bishop, who had done nothing that day, came, so they said, at the orgies as he was eating Zélamir's turd, which he had kept aside for two days. And they went to bed.

19th day.

That morning, following some observations made regarding the shit of those subjects intended for lubricious acts, they decided they ought to try something Duclos had talked about in her tales, by which I mean withholding bread and soup from all the tables other than the gentlemen's own; these two items were removed – the provision of poultry and game, on the other hand, was doubled. Within a week they noticed a fundamental difference in the excrements: these were smoother, silkier, infinitely more refined, and they agreed that d'Aucourt's advice to Duclos was that of a libertine with true expertise in such matters. It was claimed there might be a slight alteration to the subjects' breath as a result. 'Eh? So what?' said Curval in answer to the objection raised by the Duc. 'It is utterly misguided to say the mouth of a woman or a young boy must be absolutely clean in order to give pleasure; putting all manias to one side, I shall grant you if you wish that a man who craves a stinking mouth does so only out of depravity, but you must in return grant me that a mouth without the slightest fragrance gives no pleasure at all when kissed – there must always be a certain spice, a certain piquancy to all such pleasures and this piquancy is found only in a little filth. However clean the mouth may be, the lover who sucks it is certainly doing something filthy, though he does not even suspect it is this very filthiness that pleases him. Make this impulse a degree stronger and you would have me believe there is something impure about this mouth; it may not stink of decay or death – fair enough – but if it were to smell of milk or babies then that would be beyond the pale as far as I'm concerned. So the regimen we shall impose will at worst lead to a slight alteration rather than any deterioration, and that's all that is required.'

The morning inspections did not turn up anything new ... the subjects were watching their step. No one asked for permission to go to the privy that morning and the friends sat down to eat; Adélaïde, who was serving, was asked by Durcet to fart into a glass of champagne and as she was unable to do so she was immediately put down in the fateful book by that barbaric husband, who, since the start of the week, had been looking for any excuse to find fault with her. They went through for coffee – it was served by Cupidon, Giton, Michette and Sophie; the Duc thigh-fucked Sophie while making her shit in his hand and smearing it over his face, the Bishop did as much to Giton, and Curval to Michette; as for Durcet, he put it in Cupidon's mouth, having just made him shit. They did not come and after a nap went off to listen to Madame Duclos.

*

'A man we had not seen before,' said this loveable whore, 'came to propose a rather peculiar ceremony: it entailed tying him to the 3rd rung of a stepladder. His feet were tied to this 3rd rung, his body where it rested, and his raised arms to the top of the ladder. He was naked in this position; he had to be roundly thrashed – with the birch handle once the tips had been worn out; he was naked, there was no need to touch him at all (he didn't even touch himself), but after a certain dose of this medicine his monstrous instrument began to soar into the air – one could see it swinging between the rungs like the clapper of a clock, and, not long after, forcefully spurting its come into the middle of the room; he was untied, he paid and there was no more to be said.

'The following day he sent us one of his friends, whose prick and balls, buttocks and thighs had to be jabbed with a gold needle; he would come only when he was covered in blood. I dealt with him myself and, as he kept telling me to do it harder, it was when I thrust the needle – almost to its eye – right into his glans that I saw his come spurt into my hand; as he spilled it, he pounced on my mouth, which he sucked prodigiously, and there was no more to be said.

'A third, also an acquaintance of the first two, ordered me to thrash him all over with thistles: I drew blood, he examined himself in the mirror and it was [only] when he saw himself in this state that he spilled his come – without touching anything, without fondling anything, without demanding anything of me.

'I thought those excesses highly entertaining, and it secretly thrilled me to serve them – what's more, all those who indulged in them were delighted with me. It was around the time of these three scenes that a Danish lord, who had been sent to me for pleasures of a different kind – and which do not fall within my purview – was foolhardy enough to visit my house with ten thousand *francs* worth of diamonds, as much again in jewellery, and five hundred *louis* in cash. This was too good a haul to let slip: between Lucile and myself, the gentleman was robbed to his very last *sol*; he wanted to lodge a complaint, but since I used to pay large bribes to the police, and as one could do anything one liked in those days with a bit of gold, the gentleman was

ordered to keep quiet and his belongings stayed in my possession
(with the exception of a few jewels I had to let the officers have
so I might enjoy the remainder in peace). I had never committed
a theft without a stroke of good luck coming my way the next
day: this particular good fortune was a new client, but one of
those regular clients one may regard as a brothel's meat and
drink. This one was an old courtier, who, weary of the tributes
he received in the royal palace, liked to switch roles and visit
whores. He wanted to begin with me: I had to make him recite
his lesson, and every time he made a mistake he was sentenced
to kneel down and suffer vigorous blows – sometimes to his
hands, sometimes to his backside – from a leather ferula[75] like
the ones used by schoolmasters in class. It was up to me to notice
when he was truly ablaze – I then grabbed hold of his prick and
tugged on it expertly, all the while scolding him, calling him a
little libertine, a rotten little scoundrel and other childish insults
that made him come sensually. This same ceremony was to be
performed five times a week at my house, but always with a new
girl in the know, and for that I received 25 *louis* a month. I knew
so many women in Paris that it was easy for me to promise him
what he asked for and to keep my word; I had this charming
schoolboy come to my house for ten years, until he decided to
pursue his studies in hell.

'Meanwhile, I was not getting any younger, and, though I had
the kind of face that retains its beauty, I was beginning to notice
it was now mostly out of whimsy that men would seek me out.
I still had pretty enough clients nonetheless, despite my 36 years
(and the remaining adventures I had a share in unfolded between
this age and 40).

'Although I was, as I say, 36 years of age, the libertine whose
mania I shall relate as I bring this evening to a close wanted to
deal only with me. He was an Abbé of about 60, for I only ever
entertained men of a certain age, and any woman who wants to
make her fortune in our trade will certainly follow my example.
This saintly fellow arrives, and as soon as we are together he
asks to see my buttocks. "Now there's the finest arse in the
world," he tells me, "but unfortunately this is not the one that
will provide me with the pittance[76] I shall devour. Here," he says

to me, placing his buttocks in my hands, "this is the one which will provide it . . . Help me shit, please." I grab hold of a porcelain chamber pot that I place on my knees, the Abbé positions himself above it, I squeeze his anus, I open it and in a word shake it about in any and every way I think might expedite its evacuation; this happens – an enormous turd fills the dish, I offer it to the libertine, he grabs it, pounces on it, devours it and comes after I spend quarter of an hour administering the most violent fustigation to the very buttocks which had just laid such a fine egg for him. Everything was wolfed down – he had gauged his task so well that his ejaculation came only as he finished his last mouthful. For the whole time I had been flogging him I had continued to spur him on with comments such as "Come on, you little rascal. You filthy swine! How can you eat shit like that?" I asked him. "Oh, I'll teach you, you little rogue, to indulge in such abominations." And it was with words and deeds such as these that the libertine reached the giddy heights of pleasure.'

At this moment, Curval wanted, before supper, to offer the company the actual spectacle of the scene Duclos had only painted in words: he summoned Fanchon, she had him shit and the libertine devoured it while that old witch roundly flayed him. As this lubricity had inflamed their minds, shit was demanded from all quarters, and then Curval, who had not come, mixed his turd together with that of Thérèse, whom he had shit on the spot. The Bishop, accustomed to adopting his brother's pleasures, did the same with Madame Duclos, the Duc with Marie, and Durcet with Louison. It was appalling – inconceivable – I say again, to use old tarts like these when they had such pretty objects at their beck and call, but as we know satiety springs from abundance[77] and it is in the midst of sensual pleasures that one takes delight in torments. Once all these foul acts were over, at the cost of just one ejaculation (and this was by the Bishop), they sat down to eat; in the mood for filth, they only wanted the 4 old women and the 4 storytellers at the orgies and the rest were sent away. They said and did so much that this time everyone let fly, and our libertines went to sleep in the warm embrace of exhaustion and intoxication.

20th day.

Something very amusing had happened the previous evening: the Duc, utterly drunk, instead of making it to his own bedroom, had got into young Sophie's bed, and as much as this child protested – for she knew full well that what he was doing was against the rules – he would not budge, and still maintained he was in his own bed with Aline, who was to be his wife for the night. But as he could take certain liberties with Aline that he was still forbidden with Sophie, when he tried to get the latter into position so he could have his way with her as he pleased, the poor child – to whom nothing of this kind had yet been done – suddenly felt the enormous head of the Duc's prick knocking at the narrow door of her young backside and trying to smash it in; the poor little thing uttered dreadful screams and bolted stark naked into the middle of the room. The Duc follows her, swearing after her like a devil, still taking her for Aline: 'Bitch!' he said to her. 'It's not like it's the first time!' And thinking he has caught hold of her as she was getting away, he tumbles on to Zelmire's bed, taking it for his own, and embraces this young girl, thinking that Aline has come to her senses. It is the same story with this girl as with the other, for the Duc was determined to have his way, but as soon as Zelmire realizes what he is up to she follows her companion's example, utters a piercing scream and bolts. Meanwhile, Sophie, the first to bolt, seeing all too well that there was no way of sorting out this case of mistaken identity other than to go and fetch some light and someone clear-headed to restore [order], had consequently gone to find Duclos; the latter, however, having drunk herself silly at the orgies, was now stretched out almost senseless in the middle of the Duc's bed and could not rule in her favour. Desperate, and not knowing who to turn to in such a situation, and hearing all her friends crying out for help, she ventured into Durcet's bedroom, where he was in bed with his daughter, Constance, and told her what was happening. Constance, in any case, ventured out of her bed despite the efforts a drunken Durcet made to hold her back – telling her he wanted to come again.

She took a candle and entered the girls' bedroom: she found them all in their nightshirts in the middle of the room, with the Duc chasing them one after the other – still believing it to be the same girl, whom he took for Aline and whom he declared to be a witch that night. Constance finally convinced him of his mistake, and begged permission to lead him back to his bedroom, where he would find Aline perfectly ready for everything he might demand of her; the Duc – very drunk, and very sincerely with no other intent than to bugger Aline – let himself be led away; this lovely girl received him, and they went to bed. Constance withdrew and calm was restored to the young girls' bedroom. This nocturnal adventure provoked much hilarity throughout the next day, and the Duc claimed that had he by some misfortune popped anyone's virginity in such circumstances, he would not have been liable for a fine as he was drunk. The others assured him that he was mistaken and that he would most certainly have paid. They took breakfast as usual in the quarters of the sultanesses, all of whom confessed they had been scared witless. None of them, however, were found to be at fault despite all the turmoil; everything was similarly in order in the boys' quarters, and as nothing out of the ordinary happened over lunch or coffee, they went through to the chamber of stories, where Duclos, fully recovered from the excesses of the previous night, entertained those assembled that evening with the following five tales.

'Once again it was I, Messieurs,' she said, 'who served at the tryst I shall describe to you: he was a doctor; his first concern was to inspect my buttocks, and as he thought them splendid he spent over an hour simply kissing them; finally he confessed his foibles to me – these were all about shitting; I already knew about them and had prepared myself accordingly. I fill a white porcelain chamber pot that I had set aside for these kinds of exploits; as soon as he is in possession of my turd, he pounces on it and devours it; no sooner has he set to work than I arm myself with a bull's pizzle – this was the instrument with which his backside had to be caressed; I threaten him, I strike him – scolding him for indulging in such abominations – and without listening to me, the libertine comes as he wolfs it down, and bolts as quick as a flash, throwing a *louis* on to the table on his way out.

'I placed another one soon after into Lucile's hands and she had no small difficulty in making him come: he had to be sure first of all that the turd he was to be presented with had come from an old pauperess, and in order to convince him, the old woman had to do her business in front of him. I offered him a 70 year old, riddled with ulcers and erysipelas, and who had not had a single tooth in her gums for the last 15 years. "That's good, that's excellent!" he said. "That's how I like them." Then, as he shut himself away with Lucile and the turd, this girl – as skilful as she was obliging – had to entice him into eating that vile shit: he smelled it, looked at it, touched it, but struggled to take the next step; so Lucile, resorting to drastic measures, sticks a shovel in the fire and, taking it out when it's red hot, declares she'll burn his buttocks to persuade him to do as she demands unless he makes up his mind there and then. Our man trembles, tries again, but is still repulsed so Lucile, holding back no longer, pulls down his breeches to reveal a foul, utterly withered arse, utterly scorched by similar operations, and lightly singes his buttocks. The lecher curses, Lucile redoubles her efforts – she ends up burning him right between his cheeks; the pain finally spurs him into action – he bites into a mouthful; he is egged on by more burns and the whole lot is polished off in the end. This was the moment he came and I have seen few do so more violently: he uttered piercing screams, he rolled on the floor – I thought he had gone mad or was having an epileptic fit. Delighted with our good manners, the libertine promised me his custom, but on condition that I would give him the same girl each time and always use different old women. "The more disgusting they are," he said, "the more I'll pay you. You cannot imagine," he added, "just how far I can take such depravities – I hardly dare admit to it myself."

'However, one of his friends, whom he sent me the following day, took things even further in my opinion, for with the sole difference that his buttocks had to be struck hard with red-hot tongs instead of being singed – with this sole difference, as I say, he required the turd of the oldest, filthiest and most disgusting porter who could be found. An old valet of 80, who had been in the house since time immemorial, appealed to him enormously for this operation, and he gobbled down his steaming hot turd while Justine battered him with tongs so burning hot one could barely touch them. And, what's more, she had to pinch great chunks of his flesh with the tongs and almost roast them.

'Another one used to have his buttocks, belly, balls and prick jabbed with a large cobbler's awl, and all this with more or less the same ceremony, that is to say until he had eaten a turd that I would present in a chamber pot without his wanting to know whose it was.

'One cannot imagine, Messieurs, the delirium to which men may be driven by the force of their imagination. Have I not seen one who, still following these same principles, demanded I flay his buttocks with a cane until he had eaten a turd drawn up from the cesspit before his very eyes? And his perfidious come only flowed into my mouth during this exploit when he had devoured that foul muck.'

'Everything is conceivable,' said Curval as he fondled Desgranges's buttocks. 'I am convinced one can go even further than all that.' 'Further?' said the Duc, who was playing rather roughly with the naked backside of Adélaïde, his wife for the day. 'And what the devil would you have one do?' 'Worse,' said [Curval], 'worse – for I find one never goes far enough in all these matters.' 'I quite agree with him,' said Durcet, who was being buggered by Antinoüs, 'and I feel my imagination might refine this filth still further.' 'I bet I know what Durcet means,' said the Bishop, who was not up to anything yet. 'And what the devil is that, then?' asked the Duc. So the Bishop stood up, spoke in a low voice to Durcet, who said that was it, and the Bishop went to tell Curval – who said 'Oh! Absolutely!' – and the Duc, who cried out, 'Oh, fuck! I would never have thought of that one.' As these gentlemen did not explain themselves further, we have been unable to discover what they meant. And, even if we did know, I think that out of decency we should do well to draw a veil over it, for there are a great many things one should do no more than suggest – prudence demands it. One might happen upon chaste ears, and I am utterly persuaded that the reader is already grateful to us for all the circumspection we are showing him; the further he progresses, the worthier we shall be of his most sincere praise in this regard – we can almost guarantee him of this already. In the end, whatever one might say, everyone has a soul to save, and what punishment, in this world or the next, would be too severe for the man who would, for instance, happily divulge without restraint all the whims, all the depravities, all the secret horrors to which men are subject by the force of their imagination? This would be to reveal secrets that should remain buried for the good of humanity; this would be to undertake the universal corruption of morals, and to plunge one's brothers in Jesus Christ into all the excesses such scenes can inspire – and God, who sees deep into our hearts, that almighty God who made heaven and earth, and who one day must judge us, knows if we would ever wish to hear Him reproach us for such crimes!

The friends finished off a few horrors they had started earlier: Curval, for instance, made Desgranges shit, the others either did as much with different subjects or got up to other things that were no better, and they all went to have their supper. Having heard these gentlemen hold forth on the new regimen described above, the aim of which was to make the shit more abundant and more refined, Duclos told them at the orgies she was astonished such connoisseurs seemed unaware of the true secret to very abundant and refined turds. Questioned as to how one should set about this, she said that the only method was to provoke a sudden bout of mild indigestion, not by having the subject eat anything harmful or unhealthy, but by making him eat his meals hurriedly at unaccustomed hours. The experiment was conducted that same evening: they woke up Fanny, who had been left alone that evening and had gone to bed after her supper; they promptly made her eat four very large biscuits, and the following morning she provided one of the largest and most handsome turds they had yet to lay their hands on. This system was therefore adopted, though with the condition (approved by Duclos) that no bread should be given, as withholding this could only improve the fruit the other secret would produce. Not a day passed without them thus provoking mild indigestion in these young girls and pretty little boys – and the results were unimaginable. I mention this in passing in case any connoisseur should wish to use this secret – he may be firmly convinced there is none better. As nothing out of the ordinary transpired for the rest of the evening, they went to bed in order to prepare the following day for Colombe and Zélamir's magnificent nuptials, which were to herald the festivities of the 3rd week.

21st day.

Preparations for this ceremony began in the morning, following their usual practice, but – and I do not know whether this was deliberate or not – but the young bride was found guilty that very morning: Durcet declared he had found shit in her chamber pot; she denied this, saying that it was one of the old women who had done this to get her punished and that they often played such tricks when they wanted to punish them; no matter what she said, she was not heard, and as her little groom was already on the list, the friends took great pleasure in punishing them both. After Mass the young couple were nonetheless conducted with much pomp to the great drawing room where the ceremony was to be completed before lunch. They were both the same age and the young girl was presented naked to her husband, leaving the latter to do whatever he wanted with her. Nothing is more persuasive than an example: a more dreadful or more contagious one could not have been given, so the young man pounced in a flash on his little wife, and as his prick was very hard – though he was still too young to come – he would doubtless have screwed her; as slight as that breach may have been, however, Messieurs made a point of honour of ensuring that nothing would disturb those tender flowers they themselves wanted to pluck. So the Bishop, curbing the young man's enthusiasm, took advantage of the erection himself by shoving up his own arse the very pretty and well-developed tool with which Zélamir had been about to screw his young bride. What a world of difference for this young man, and what a contrast between the old Bishop's capacious arse and a little 13-year-old virgin's tight young cunt! But there was no reasoning with such people: Curval grabbed hold of Colombe and thigh-fucked her from in front, licking her eyes, her mouth, her nostrils and her whole face; a few services were doubtless rendered in the meantime for he came, and Curval was not a man to spill his come for such child's play. They had lunch; the bride and groom were allowed to join them for coffee, as they had for the meal, and that day coffee was served by the finest of the subjects, namely Augustine, Zelmire, Adonis and Zéphire. Curval, who wanted to get hard again, absolutely had to have some shit, and so Augustine let drop the finest turd one could ever hope to produce; the Duc had himself sucked by Zelmire, Durcet by Colombe, and the Bishop by Adonis – who shat in Durcet's mouth once he had seen to the Bishop. But there was no come – it was becoming rare; they had not exercised any restraint in the first few days, and as they sensed the utmost need they would have of this towards the end, they kept themselves in check. They went through to the chamber of stories where the lovely Duclos, invited to bare her arse before starting, wantonly showed it off to the assembled audience before taking up the thread of her oration thus.

'And now for another of my character traits, Messieurs,' said this lovely whore, 'after which, once you have heard enough about it, you will be so good as to decide for yourselves what I may be concealing in what I am to tell you, and to allow me to say no more about myself.

'Lucile's mother had just fallen into dreadful penury, and it was by the greatest stroke of luck imaginable that this charming girl, who had not heard tell of [her] mother since running away from home, learned of [her] unfortunate distress. One of our walkers, on the lookout for a young girl one of my clients had been requesting along the same lines as the Marquis de Mesanges, meaning a girl who could be bought and never heard from again – one of our walkers, as I say, came to report to me (while I was in bed with Lucile) that she had found a little girl of 15, most assuredly a maiden, extremely pretty and resembling, so she said, Milli Lucile like two peas in a pod, but in such a state of penury she would need to be kept and fattened up for a few days before being sold; and she then described the old woman with whom she had found her, and the terrible poverty in which this mother was living. These features, these details of her age and appearance, and everything she said about the child led Lucile to the secret premonition that this might well be her mother and sister; she knew that, when she had run away, she had left this little one at a very young age with their mother, and she asked my permission to go and confirm her suspicions. My infernal imagination hatched a horrible little plan, the effect of which set my senses ablaze so suddenly that, sending the walker packing and unable to cool the fire in my veins, I began by asking Lucile to frig me; then, stopping halfway through this operation, I asked her, "What do you want to go see that old woman for – and what do you intend to do?" "Oh, but . . . ," said Lucile, whose heart was not yet like my own – far from it indeed . . . "to help her if I can, and especially if she's my mother." "You imbecile!" I said, pushing her away. "Go! Go along with those contemptible common prejudices of yours without me, and waste – just because you don't dare flout them – the most wonderful opportunity to excite your senses by an abomination that would make you come for ten long years!" Lucile looked at me in astonishment and so I saw I had to explain a philosophy she was far from grasping. I did so – I made her understand how contemptible are the bonds that tie us to those who created us; I showed her that a mother, far from deserving our gratitude for having carried us in her womb, deserved only our hatred, since, for her own pleasure and at the risk of exposing us to all the misfortunes that might beset us in this world, she gave birth to us regardless, with the sole intention of satisfying her brutish lust. I added everything that could be said in support of a system dictated by good sense and counselled by the heart when it is not consumed by childhood prejudices. "And what does it matter to you," I added, "if that creature is happy or wretched? Does her situation affect you in any way? Cast aside those contemptible bonds that I've just shown you to be absurd, and then, if you isolate yourself from that creature, if you completely separate yourself from her, you'll see not only that her misfortune should be indifferent to you, but that compounding it may provide you with quite a thrill. For in the end you owe her your hatred – as I have demonstrated – and you would therefore be taking your revenge; you would be committing what fools call a wicked act, and you know the hold crime has always had over the senses. So there are then two sources of pleasure in the outrages I want you to commit against her: the delights of vengeance and those one always tastes when doing evil." Either I was more eloquent with Lucile than I am here in describing the event, or her mind – already very libertine and very corrupt – immediately told her heart of the sensuality of my principles; she savoured them, and I saw her pretty cheeks colour with that libertine flame that never fails to appear whenever one breaks free of a restraint. "Well then," she said to me, "what should we do?" "Have our fun with her," I told her, "and make some money out of her. As for pleasure, you can be sure of that if [you] adopt my principles; as for money, you can be sure of that too as I can use both your old mother and your sister for two different deals that will be very lucrative for us." Lucile accepts – I frig her, the better to rouse her appetite for crime, and we then get to work on the arrangements. Let us turn to the first of these schemes since it fits into the category of tastes I have to tell you about (even if I am moving it from its proper place in order to follow the order of events) and once you are acquainted with this first part of my plans, I shall enlighten you as to the second.

'There was a gentleman of high society – terribly rich, terribly influential and with a dissolute mind that defies description; as I knew him only by the title of Comte at the time, you will allow me – well though I may know his name now – to refer to him by this title alone. The Comte's passions were at their peak – he was 35 years of age at most, with no faith, no law, no god, no religion, and above all endowed, as you are, Messieurs, with an insurmountable horror of so-called charitable sentiment; he said that this was beyond his comprehension, and that he could not understand how anyone could imagine outraging Nature to such a degree as to upset the order she had established between the different classes of individuals by helping one to rise up at the expense of another, and by spending to this end absurd and revolting sums that would be far more pleasantly spent on one's pleasures. Deeply convinced of these sentiments, he did not stop there – not only did he get a real thrill out of refusing succour, but he even enhanced this thrill by adding insult to injury. One of his greatest pleasures, for example, was to have a careful search carried out for those shadowy refuges where ravenous poverty eats as best it can a crust of bread sprinkled with bitter tears and earned though toil. He would get hard not only from the bitterness of those tears, but also from compounding their cause and snatching – if he could – the woeful sustenance that kept those wretches alive; and this taste – it was not a whim, it was an obsession; no delights were more intense than these, so he said, and nothing could excite, could inflame his soul quite like this excess. It was not, he assured me one day, born of depravity; this extraordinary mania dated from his childhood, and his heart, perpetually hardened to the plaintive tones of misfortune, had never experienced more exquisite sensations. As it is essential we acquaint you with this individual, you must first of all know that the same man had three different passions – the one I shall describe to you, one Madame Martaine will explain to you (with a reference to his title to jog your memory), and an even more appalling one Madame Desgranges will certainly save for the end of her tales, as it is doubtless one of the most extreme passions she has to relate. But let us begin with the one that concerns me: as soon as I had informed the Comte of the miserable refuge I had discovered for him, and its immediate environs, he was giddy with joy, but as matters of the greatest importance to his fortune and advancement, which he took all the more seriously as he saw these as laying the foundations for his depravities – because, as I say, these matters were going to occupy him for much of the next fortnight, and because he did not wish to miss out on this little girl, he preferred to sacrifice a little of the pleasure this first scene had promised him to be sure of the second. Consequently he ordered me to have this child abducted whatever the cost and to have her taken to the address he indicated to me; and, to keep you in suspense no longer, Messieurs, this was the address of Madame Desgranges, who supplied him for those secret trysts of the third kind. Next we settled on a day; in the interim we set about finding Lucile's mother, as much to prepare for her reunion with her daughter as to find a way of abducting her sister. Lucile, playing her part, only recognized her mother for the sake of insulting her, telling her that she was the reason for her descent into libertinage, and a thousand other such remarks that broke this poor woman's heart and ruined all her pleasure at finding her daughter again. I thought this opening might provide a way of getting to the matter in hand and impressed upon the mother that, having plucked her elder daughter from libertinage, I was offering to do the same for her second, but [this] gambit did not succeed – the wretched woman wept and said that nothing in the world could wrench from her the only succour she had left in this second daughter, that she was old, infirm, that this child looked after her and that it would kill her to be without her. To my shame, Messieurs, I must confess here that I felt something stir deep in my heart that told me my pleasure would only intensify with the horrid refinement I was going to add to my crime in this case, and, having informed the old woman that her daughter would pay her a second visit in a few days with an influential man who could be of considerable service to her, we left, and I busied myself with pulling the usual strings in order to become that young girl's mistress. I had examined her closely – she was worth the trouble: 15 years old, a lovely figure, a very beautiful complexion and very pretty features. Three days later she arrived and, having examined every part of her body and finding it all charming – all perfectly plump and perfectly fresh – in spite of the meagre fare to which she had been condemned for so long, I had her sent to Md. Desgranges, with whom I now had dealings for the 1st time in my life. Our man finally returned, having attended to his affairs; Lucile led him to her mother's home and it is here that the scene I am to describe to you begins. They found the old mother in bed, without a fire even though it was the middle of a very cold winter; by her bed she had a wooden bowl with a little milk in it – which the Comte pissed into the moment he entered. To keep any rabble from interfering and to

remain in complete charge of the hovel, the Comte had posted
two strapping knaves, both in his pay, in the stairwell, and they
were there to prevent – forcefully if necessary – any unwelcome
comings or goings. "You old bitch," the Comte said to her, "we've
come here with your daughter over there – who's a very pretty
whore indeed. We have come, you old witch, to ease your woes,
but you must describe them to us. Come now," he said as he sat
down and began to feel Lucile's buttocks, "come and tell us
everything you've suffered." "Alas!" said the good woman. "You
have come with that hussy to add insult to these injuries, not to
ease them." "Hussy?" said the Comte. "You dare insult your
daughter? Come now," he said, standing up and dragging the
woman from her pallet, "get out of your bed this instant, get
down on your knees and beg forgiveness for the insult you've
just paid her." There was nothing she could do to resist. "And
you, Lucile, hitch up your skirts, have your mother kiss your
arse – I want to be quite sure she'll kiss it and that the two of
you will make up your differences." The insolent Lucile rubs her
arse in her poor mother's old face, lambasting her with impertinences; the Comte let the old woman take to her bed again,
and resumed his conversation with her. "Let me say again, one
more time," he continued, "that if you tell me all your sorrows,
I will ease them." The wretched believe every word they are told
– they enjoy feeling sorry for themselves; the old woman
described all she had to bear and complained bitterly above all
that her daughter had been stolen from her, pointedly accusing
Lucile of knowing her whereabouts, since the lady accompanying her on her recent visit had offered to take care of the girl
– and she surmised from this, with good reason, that this was
the lady who had abducted her. Meanwhile the Comte – facing
Lucile's arse, for he had made her take her skirts off, and kissing
that fine arse from time to time and frigging himself – listened,
questioned, asked for details and attuned all the caresses of his
perfidious pleasure to the answers he was given. But when the
old woman said that the absence of her daughter, whose work
had been providing her with enough to eat, would lead her little
by little to the grave, since she now had nothing left and had for
the last four days survived only on the few drops of milk he had

just spoiled, he replied – "Well then, you slut!" – as he aimed
his come at the old woman and continued to squeeze Lucile's
buttocks – "Well then, you whore, you will croak and it will
be no great misfortune." And as he finished spilling his sperm
– "If that happens, I shall have only one regret, and that is not
to have hastened that moment myself." But all was not yet said
and done: the Comte was not a man to be appeased by a single
climax; as soon as he was finished, Lucile, who had her own
part to play, made sure the old woman could not see what he
was up to, and the Comte, rummaging everywhere, grabbed
hold of a silver goblet, the last remnant of the modest comforts
that poor wretch had once enjoyed, and put it in his pocket;
with this outrage upon another outrage making him hard again,
he pulled the old woman out of bed, stripped her, and ordered
Lucile to frig him over this old matron's withered body; once
again she had no choice but to let him have his way, and the
scoundrel spurted his come over that decrepit flesh, redoubling
his insults and telling the poor wretch she could take it for
granted he would not stop there and that she would soon hear
tell of him and her little girl, who, he was pleased to inform
her, was in his clutches; he proceeded to this final climax in
lubricious raptures sparked by the horrors his perfidious imagination was already concocting for this unfortunate family, and
then left. But so that we may leave this episode behind us once
and for all, Messieurs, listen to the lengths to which I went to
satisfy my wickedness. The Comte, seeing he could trust me,
told me of the second scene he was preparing for this old
woman and her little girl: he told me that I had to have her
abducted immediately and, what's more, that since he wanted
to reunite the whole family I had to hand over Lucile as well
– her beautiful figure had moved him profoundly and he did
not hide from me that he was planning her demise, along with
the other two. I loved Lucile, but I loved money even more; he
offered me a staggering price for these three creatures – I agreed
to everything. Four days later, Lucile, her little sister and the
old mother were reunited: it will be for Md. Desgranges to tell
you how.[78] As for me, I shall now take up the thread of my
tales – interrupted by this anecdote that should have been told

only at the end of my tales, as it is among my most extreme ones.'

'One moment,' said Durcet. 'I cannot hear these things with a cool head – they have a hold on me that is difficult to convey. I've been holding back my come since midway through the tale – be so good as to let me spill it now.' And, rushing into his closet with Michette, Zélamir, Cupidon, Fanny, Thérèse and Adélaïde, he could be heard roaring a few minutes later, and Adélaïde returned in tears saying that she was very unhappy her husband's mind was going to be inflamed yet again with such tales, and that the person telling these should by rights be the one to suffer. Meanwhile the Duc and the Bishop had not been idle, but since the manner in which they had proceeded was one of those that circumstances oblige us to conceal, we ask our readers to allow us to draw a veil over these and to turn at once to the four remaining tales with which Duclos was to conclude her 21st evening.

'A week after Lucile's departure, I attended to a lecher with a rather amusing mania. Forewarned several days in advance, I had let a great number of turds pile up in my close stool; I had asked one of my girls to add some of her own. Our man arrives, dressed as a Savoyard; it was morning – he sweeps my room, takes the pot from the close stool and goes to the latrine to empty it (a task that, incidentally, kept him busy for quite some time); he returns, shows me how carefully he has cleaned it and asks for his payment. But, forewarned about this charade, I lay into him with the broom handle. "Your payment, scoundrel?" I tell him. "Here's your payment!" And I deal him half a dozen blows at least. He looks to escape, I follow him, and the libertine – reaching the critical moment – spills his come as he flies down the stairs, yelling at the top of his voice that he is being maimed, that he is being murdered, that this is the house of a hussy and not a decent woman as he had thought.

'Another one wanted me to insert into his urethra a small, knotty stick that he carried in a case for this purpose; when it was three inches in, I had to shake the small stick vigorously and with my other hand frig his prick with the foreskin pulled back; as his climax approached, I pulled out the stick, hitched up the front of my skirts and he came all over my crotch.

'An Abbé I saw 6 months later wanted me to drip wax from a burning candle on to his prick and balls; he came from this sensation alone and there was no need to touch him; but he could never get hard, and to spill his come he had to be so completely covered in wax that his body was barely recognizable as that of a human being.

'A friend of this last one would have his bottom completely covered in gold pins, and when his backside, thus decorated, began to resemble a saucepan rather than an arse, he would sit down, the better to feel the pinpricks; one had to show him one's buttocks spread wide apart, he would frig himself and come over one's arsehole.'

'Durcet,' said the Duc, 'I should rather like to see your fine, podgy arse all covered like that with gold pins; I am convinced it would be most alluring.' 'Mr. le Duc,' said the financier, 'as you know, it has been my pride and my honour to emulate you for 40 years – be so good as to lead by example and I promise I shall follow your lead.' 'God be damned,' said Curval, from whom not a peep had yet been heard. 'The story of Lucile has made me hard – I kept quiet, but I didn't think any the less of it. Here,' he said, showing everyone his cock glued to his belly, 'see for yourself if you don't believe me. I am itching to know how the story of those three bitches ends – I do hope they'll be reunited in the same grave.' 'Slow down, slow down,' said the Duc. 'Let's not get ahead of ourselves. Just because you're hard, Mr. le Président, you want to hear about the wheel and the gallows straight away – you are just like those gentlemen of the bench whose pricks, so it's claimed, invariably spring up each time they condemn a man to death.' 'Leaving aside matters of state and justice,' said Curval, 'the truth is that I'm delighted with Duclos's exploits, that I find her to be a charming whore and that her story about the Comte has put me in a dreadful state – in such a state that I'd willingly head for the open road and rob a coach.' 'That has to be planned properly, Président,' said the Bishop, 'otherwise

we won't be safe here, and all you'll succeed in doing is condemn
us to a hanging.' 'No, not you – but I don't deny I'd gladly
condemn these young ladies, and above all Md. la Duchesse,
who's lolling about like a calf on my sofa over there and who
imagines, just because she has a little modified come in her
womb, that she's untouchable.' 'Oh!' said Constance, 'I'm far
from imagining I could count on any such respect from you for
my present condition – we know all too well how much you
hate pregnant women.' 'Oh, prodigiously so!' said Curval. 'That's
the truth.' And I do believe he was, in his fervour, about to
commit some sacrilege upon that fine belly when Duclos grabbed
hold of him. 'Come, come, M. le Président,' she said. 'Since it
was me who did the damage, I would like to repair it myself.'
And they went off together into the far boudoir, followed by
Augustine, Hébé, Cupidon and Thérèse. It was not long before
the Président was heard bellowing and, for all of Duclos's best
efforts, little Hébé returned in floods of tears; there was indeed
something more to it than tears, but we dare not yet say what
it was – circumstances do not allow it. A little patience, friendly
reader, and soon we shall hide nothing more from you. With
Curval back, muttering under his breath that all these rules
meant one could not come as one wanted, &c., they settled down
to eat. After supper they shut themselves away for the corrections;
there were few that evening – only Sophie, Colombe, Adélaïde
and Zélamir were at fault. Durcet, whose mind had since the
start of the evening been considerably inflamed against Adélaïde,
did not go easy on her; Sophie, who had been caught weeping
during the story about the Comte, was punished for her previous
offence as well as this one; and that day's young couple, Zélamir
and Colombe, were treated by the Duc and Curval with a severity bordering on barbarity. The Duc and Curval, in particularly
high spirits, said they did not wish to go to bed and, ordering
liqueurs to be brought to them, they spent the night drinking
with the four storytellers and Julie, whose libertinage – increasing day by day – marked her out as a most amiable creature who
deserved to be ranked among those objects treated with some
respect. The next day all seven of them were found dead drunk
by Durcet, who paid them a visit; the daughter was found naked

between her father and her husband, and in a position that evinced neither virtue nor even decency in libertinage. To keep the reader in suspense no longer, it seemed in a word that they had both enjoyed her simultaneously. Duclos, who had apparently served as second, was sprawled dead drunk beside them, and the rest were piled one on top of the other in another corner, facing the great fire that had been diligently tended throughout the night.

22nd day.

As a result of these nocturnal bacchanalia, the friends did very little that day: they forgot half of the ceremonies, grazed on their lunch, and only really began to return to their senses at coffee – served by Rosette and Sophie, Zélamir and Giton. To pull himself together, Curval had Giton shit, and the Duc swallowed Rosette's turd; the Bishop had himself sucked by Sophie, and Durcet by Zélamir, but no one came. They went through to the chamber: the beautiful Duclos, suffering greatly from the excesses of the previous evening, managed to appear but couldn't really give a shit, and her tales were so short, she mixed in so few episodes, that we have decided to take her place and summarize for the reader what she told the friends.

As usual, she recounted five passions. The first was that of a man who had his arse frigged with a pewter dildo filled with hot water, which was squirted into his fundament the moment he ejaculated and which he administered by himself without being touched.

The second had the same mania, but this operation required a great many more instruments: it began with a very small one, and – the size increasing little by little, a fraction of an inch each time – it ended with an enormous one, and it was only with this one that he came.

The 3rd required much more of a fuss: to start off with he had an enormous one inserted into his arse; next it was withdrawn; he shat, ate what he had just produced, and was then flogged. Once that was done, the instrument was inserted again in his backside and then withdrawn; this time it was the whore who shat and flogged him while he ate what she had just done. The instrument was thrust in a 3rd time: this time he spilled his come without being touched as he finished off the girl's turd.

Duclos spoke in her 4th tale about a man who had all his joints tied with string: to make his climax all the more delectable, even his neck was constricted, and in this state he spilled his come straight on to the whore's arse.

And, in her 5th, about another man who had a cord tied tight around his glans; at the other end of the room a naked girl threaded the end of the cord between her thighs and pulled it out in front of her as she displayed her buttocks to the patient; this was how he came.

The storyteller, truly exhausted now her task was complete, asked for permission to retire – this was granted. They horsed around for a short while, after which they went to eat, but in all this there were still signs of our two principal actors' previous excesses. The friends were as well behaved at the orgies as it was possible for such libertines to be, and everyone went quite calmly to bed.

23rd day.

'How can anyone bellow and roar as you do when you come?' the Duc asked Curval when he saw him again on the morning of the 23rd. 'Who the devil were you with to scream like that? I've never seen anyone come with such violence.' 'Oh, by God!' said [Curval]. 'That's a bit rich coming from you when you can be heard a league away. Those screams, my friend, are caused by the extreme sensitivity of our physiology: the objects of our passions give such a jolt to the electrical fluid flowing through our nerves, the shock received by the animal spirits which comprise this fluid is so violent that the whole machine is shaken by it, and one can no more suppress the screams provoked by these terrible convulsions of pleasure than one could those provoked by strong emotions of pain.' 'Now that is very well defined indeed, but what was the exquisite object that set your animal spirits vibrating so?' 'I was violently sucking the prick, mouth and arsehole of Adonis, my bedtime companion, disconsolate at still being unable to do anything more to him, and as I did this Antinoüs – assisted by your dear daughter Julie – strove, each in their own way, to expel the liquid which prompted those screams you heard as it poured forth.' 'With the result that today,' continued the Duc, 'you're worn to the bone.' 'Not at all,' said Curval, 'if you deign to follow me and do me the honour of examining me, you will see I shall conduct myself at least as well as you.' As they were saying this, Durcet came to announce that breakfast was served: they headed to the girls' quarters, where they saw those eight charming little sultanesses offering cups and black coffee; the Duc then asked Durcet, in charge that month, why the coffee was black that morning. 'You can have it with milk whenever you wish,' said the financier. 'Would you like some?' 'Yes,' said the Duc. 'Augustine,' said Durcet, 'serve some milk to M. le Duc.' So the young girl, prepared for this request, came and placed her pretty little arse over the cup and poured three or four teaspoons of very clear and perfectly unsoiled milk straight from her anus and into the Duc's cup. The friends laughed heartily at this stunt, and each asked for milk; all the arses were prepared as Augustine's was – a delightful surprise the friend in charge that month had wished to offer his friends. Fanny came and poured some into the Bishop's cup, Zelmire into Curval's, and Michette into the financier's; the friends called for a second cup, and the other four sultanesses came and performed the same ceremony with these new cups that their companions had with the old ones. The friends very much enjoyed this stunt – it inflamed the Bishop, who wanted something other than milk, and the beautiful Sophie came over to satisfy him. Although all the girls needed to shit, they had been strongly advised to restrain themselves during the milk exercise and to offer nothing but milk on this first occasion. The friends headed to the boys' quarters: Curval made Zélamir shit and the Duc made Giton do the same; the chapel's privies only yielded two subaltern fuckers, Constance, and Rosette – she was one of the girls on whom they had tested their theory about indigestion the night before; she had had dreadful difficulty restraining herself at coffee, and thus let drop the most splendid turd one could ever hope to see. Duclos was congratulated on her secret and from then on it was used every day with the greatest success. The stunt at breakfast enlivened the conversation at lunch and led them to imagine more of the same – including things we may have cause to speak of in due course. They went through for coffee, served by four young subjects of the same age: Zelmire, Augustine, Zéphire and Adonis – all four of them 15 years old; the Duc thigh-fucked Augustine while tickling her anus, Curval did the same to Zelmire, the Duc[79] to Zéphire, and the financier fucked Adonis in the mouth. Augustine said that she had been expecting them to make her shit at this hour, and that she could hold it in no longer – she was another one of those girls on whom they had experimented with indigestion the previous evening. At that moment Curval opened wide and the charming little girl let drop a monstrous turd that the Président gobbled down in three mouthfuls – not without spilling an abundant river of come into Fanchon's hands as she tugged on him. 'Well then,' he said to the Duc, 'you see – the night's excesses are not detrimental to daytime pleasures, and here you are lagging behind, M. le Duc.' 'Not for long,' said the latter as Zelmire, with just as pressing a need herself, performed the same service Augustine had just performed for Curval – and at that very moment the Duc falls over, screams out, swallows some shit and comes like a madman. 'That will do,' said the Bishop. 'Two of us at least should preserve our strength for the storytelling.' Durcet, who unlike these two gentlemen could not summon up his come at will, agreed wholeheartedly and after a brief nap they went to take their seats in the chamber, where the alluring Duclos took up the thread of her dazzling and lascivious tale in the following terms.

'How is it, Messieurs,' said this lovely whore, 'that we see people in this world whose hearts have been so numbed, whose feelings of honour and delicacy have been so dulled by libertinage that they can find pleasure and enjoyment only in their own degradation and debasement? It is as if they find satisfaction only in the depths of opprobrium, that it can exist for them only when it lures them into dishonour and infamy; in what I am about to tell you, Messieurs, in the different examples I shall give you as proof of this assertion, do not counter with physical sensation – I know this is a part of it, but be perfectly clear that this exists in some way only because of the powerful support moral sensation provides, and that if you give such people the same physical sensation without including all that they draw from morals, you will not succeed in moving them. A man whose name and title I did not know, but whom I could nevertheless tell was clearly a man of noble birth, was a very frequent visitor to my house; he was utterly indifferent to the kind of woman I would pair him with – beautiful or ugly, old or young, it was of no consequence to him. All she had to do was play her role well, and this is what that was: he would usually arrive in the morning; as if by mistake he would enter a room where there was a girl on a bed, her skirts hitched up to her waist in the pose of a woman frigging herself; as soon as she saw him enter, the woman – as if startled – would immediately spring from the bed. "What are you doing here, you scoundrel?" she would say to him. "Who gave you permission, you rascal, to disturb me?" He would beg for forgiveness, she would not listen, and as she rained down a torrent of the most brutal and stinging insults, she would fall on him with great kicks up the arse – and would find it increasingly difficult to miss her target as the patient, far from dodging her blows, would never fail to turn around and present his backside even as he seemed to be avoiding her and trying to flee. She would redouble her efforts, he would beg for mercy – all he would get in return were more blows and impertinences, and as soon as he felt sufficiently excited he would promptly take his prick from his breeches (which until then he had kept tightly buttoned up) and with three or four quick flicks of the wrist he would come as he was escaping, the insults and blows continuing all the while.

'A second, who was either tougher or more accustomed to this kind of exercise, only wanted to deal with a porter or carrier who would be counting out his money. The libertine would enter furtively, the knave would cry out that he was being robbed, and from that moment the blows and impertinences would rain down, as it did on the other, but with the difference that this one, leaving his breeches around his ankles throughout, would want the kicks that were aimed at him to land right in the middle of his bare buttocks – and the assailant would have to put on a large hobnailed boot covered in mud. At his moment of climax, this one would not dodge any blows: standing firm in the middle of the room, his breeches right down, tugging away with all his might, he would brave his enemy's kicks, and at the final moment would challenge the man to give quarter, insulting him in turn and swearing he was dying of pleasure. The more contemptible the man I offered him, the more he belonged to the dregs of society, the fouler and filthier his boot, the more I satisfied his desires; I had to take the same care over these refinements as I would dolling up and prettifying a woman for another man.

'A third wanted to be in a harem (as it is known in a brothel) at the very moment two men, paid and posted there for that purpose, would start quarrelling. They would turn on him, he would beg for mercy, he would drop to his knees, they would not listen, and one of the two champions would suddenly fall on him, assailing him with blows from his cane all the way to the doorway of a specially prepared room into which he would escape; there a girl would receive him, console him, caress him as one would a wailing child; she would hitch up her skirts, show him her backside, and the libertine would come all over it.

'A fourth demanded the same preliminaries but as soon as the blows from the cane started raining down on his back, he would frig himself in front of everyone. He would then pause for a moment, though the torrent of blows from the cane and the insults would continue, then, as soon as they saw that he was excited and that his come was ready to let fly, they would open a window, seize him by the waist and fling him on to a specially prepared dunghill on the other side – a drop of 6 feet at most. That was the moment he would come: the preceding preparations would excite his moral faculties, but it was only the thrill from the fall that would do the same for his body, and it was only on the dunghill that his come would ever flow. We would not see him afterwards – he had the key to a little door downstairs, and would promptly disappear.

'A man paid to kick up a racket would charge into a room where the man who provides our 5th example would be shut away with a girl whose backside he would be kissing as he waited for the action to begin. Turning on the trick, the troublemaker would insolently ask him as he broke down the door what right he had to steal his mistress like that, then, taking hold of his sword, would tell him to defend himself; the trick, utterly abashed, would fall to his knees, beg for forgiveness, kiss the ground, kiss his enemy's feet and swear to him that he could have his mistress back and that he did not want to fight over a woman. The troublemaker, made all the more insolent by his adversary's servility, would become even more imperious: he would call his enemy a coward, a weakling, a good-for-nothing, and would threaten to slash his face with the blade of his sword; and the nastier the first man became, the more the other would cower. Finally, after quarrelling for some time, the assailant would offer his enemy a compromise: "I can see full well you're a weakling," he would tell him. "I'll let you off, but on condition you kiss my arse." "Oh, Monsieur, whatever you want!" replied the other man delightedly. "I'd kiss it even if it were covered in shit, if you wanted me to, as long as you didn't hurt me." Returning his sword to its sheath, the troublemaker would immediately reveal his backside – the trick, only too happy at this, would pounce on it with great enthusiasm, and while the young man unleashed half a dozen farts in his face, the old lecher, beside himself with joy, would spill his come while dying of pleasure.'

'All these excesses are conceivable,' stammered Durcet, for the little libertine was hard from the tale of these depravities. 'Nothing could be simpler than to enjoy degradation and gain satisfaction from contempt – the man who passionately loves anything that brings dishonour will find pleasure in being dishonoured himself and is bound to get hard when he is told this is the case. Depravity is a well-known thrill for certain souls: they like to be called by the name they aspire to deserve, and it is impossible to know how far a man will go on this score when nothing makes him blush any more – this is what happens with certain sick people who relish their cacochymism.'⁸⁰ 'That's just a matter of brazenness,' said Curval as he fondled Fanchon's buttocks. 'Who doesn't understand that punishment itself produces raptures? And haven't people been seen getting hard at the very moment they were being publicly shamed? Everyone knows the story of the Marquis de . . . , who, as soon as he learned he'd been sentenced to burn in effigy,[81] pulled his prick from his breeches and cried out, "Holy fuck! Here I am just where I wanted to be, here I am covered in opprobrium and infamy – leave me be, leave me be, I need to come!" And so he did, there and then.' 'These are the facts,' the Duc said in reply, 'but explain their cause to me.' 'It is in our hearts,' continued Curval. 'Once a man has debased himself, has demeaned himself by these excesses, his soul is left with a kind of vicious bent that nothing can undo; in any other case, shame would serve as a counterweight to the vices his mind might be telling him to indulge, but that is no longer possible here – it was the first sentiment he snuffed out, the first he banished far away, and from a state in which he ceases to blush to one in which he enjoys anything that would make others blush, there [is] no more than a single step. Everything that had previously had an unpleasant effect, now meets a differently constructed soul and is transformed into pleasure, and from that moment on anything that reminds one of this newly adopted state will always be sensual.' 'But how far down the road of vice one has to travel to reach that point!' said the Bishop. 'I agree,' said Curval, 'but this path is travelled imperceptibly – it is always strewn with flowers whenever one follows it. One excess leads to another – the imagination, always insatiable, draws us on to the very end, and as it hardens the heart with every step, once it has reached its ultimate goal, this heart, which used to contain some virtues, no longer recognizes a single one. Accustomed to livelier things, the heart promptly shrugs off the dull and dreary first impressions that had previously intoxicated it and, sensing that its new impulses will bring infamy and dishonour in their wake, it begins to acquaint itself with them so as not to fear them. The heart no sooner embraces than loves them, as they stem from the nature of its new conquests, and it will never change again.' 'That's what makes correction so difficult,' said the Bishop. 'Impossible

you mean, my friend – for how could the discipline inflicted
upon the person you wish to punish succeed in converting him,
since, barring a few privations, this state of degradation – which
characterizes the one you have put him in by punishing him –
pleases him, amuses him, delights him, and deep down inside he
relishes being treated in a way he didn't deserve in the slightest?'
'Oh, what an enigma is man!' said the Duc. 'Yes, my friend,' said
Curval, 'and that's why a man of great intelligence said it was
better to fuck him than understand him.' And with supper interrupting our interlocutors, they went to eat without having got
up to anything that evening. But over dessert Curval, hard as a
devil, declared he wanted to pop someone's virginity even if it
cost him twenty fines, and, promptly grabbing hold of Zelmire,
who had been reserved for him, he was about to drag her into
the boudoir when the 3 friends, throwing themselves in his way,
begged him to submit to what he himself had prescribed, and
added that, since they wanted to break those laws at least as
much he did but were still obeying them regardless, he ought
to follow their example out of goodwill if nothing else; and
when Julie, whom he loved, was promptly summoned, she
grabbed hold of him along with Madame Champville and Brise-
cul, and the three of them went through to the chamber where
the other friends, joining them soon after for the start of the
orgies, found them all grappling each other, with Curval finally
spilling his come among the most lubricious poses and libertine
scenes. Durcet, at the orgies, had the old women kick him two
or three hundred times up the arse; the Bishop, the Duc and
Curval had the fuckers do the same, and no one failed to spill
at least some come, according to the ability with which Nature
had endowed him, before going to bed. Concerned that the
deflowering fantasy Curval had just announced would rear its
head again, they took the precaution of sending the old women
to sleep in the girls' and boys' bedrooms, but this precaution
was unnecessary and Julie, who had taken charge of him for
the whole night, restored him to the company the next day as
limp as a glove.

24th day.

Piety is a veritable malady of the soul – no matter what one does, one cannot mend one's ways. It penetrates the souls of the unfortunate more easily because it consoles them, because it offers them fantasies to console them for their woes, and so it is much more difficult to eradicate it from these souls than from others. This was the case with Adélaïde: the more the scene of debauchery and libertinage unfolded before her eyes, the more she threw herself into the arms of that consoling God she hoped would one day rescue her from the woes she could see all too clearly lying in wait for her. No one understood their situation better than she – her mind foresaw with perfect clarity all that was bound to follow the fateful beginning of which she had already been the victim (albeit in a small way); she understood all too well that as the tales would become more extreme, so the men's dealings with her companions and herself would become ever more ferocious. All this, despite everything she had been told, made her eagerly seek out her dear Sophie's company as often as she could; she no longer dared visit her at night – they had spotted her doing this once too often, and were adamant there should be no further exploits of this kind – but as soon as she had a moment she would fly off to see her, and on the very morning we are now recording in this journal, she had left the Bishop's side very early after spending the night in his bed, and had come to the young girls' bedroom to talk to her dear Sophie. Durcet, who because of his duties that month also rose earlier than the others, found her there and declared that he had no choice but to report this, and that the company would make its judgement as it saw fit. [Adélaïde] wept – this was her only weapon – and put up no resistance; the sole mercy she dared ask of her husband was to try to prevent Sophie from being punished – it was she who had sought out Sophie, not Sophie who had come to her bedroom, so her friend could not be guilty. Durcet said he would report the facts as they were and not dress them up in any way – no one is less moved to pity than a disciplinarian with the keenest interest in discipline. Such was the

case here: there was no prettier subject for punishment than
Sophie – why on earth would Durcet have spared her? The
friends gathered, and the financier provided his report: this was
a repeat offence; the Président recalled that when he was at the
law courts his ingenious colleagues would claim that as a repeat
offence proved Nature was a more powerful influence over a
man than either his education or his principles – that by committing a repeat offence he was thereby demonstrating he was not
master of himself so to speak – he had to be doubly punished;
he wished to reason as coherently and as cleverly as his former
fellow students, and so declared that both she and her companion had consequently to be punished to the full extent of the
statutes. But as these statutes carried the death penalty for such
cases, and as they wished to entertain themselves with these
ladies for some time yet before reaching that point, they simply
summoned them, made them kneel and then read out the clause
of the statute in question, driving home to them all the risk they
had run in exposing themselves to such a crime; once that was
done they imposed a penance upon them three times as severe
as the one they had endured the previous Saturday, made them
swear it would never happen again, assured them that if it did
happen again they would be treated with the utmost severity,
and put them down in the fateful book. Durcet's inspection
added three more names to the list – two from the girls and one
from the boys. This was the result of their latest experiments
with mild indigestion – these were progressing very nicely, but
it so happened that those poor children, unable to restrain themselves, were perpetually in danger of being punished. This was
the case with Fanny, with Hébé among the sultanesses, and with
Hyacinthe among the boys: the contents of their chamber pots
were enormous and Durcet enjoyed them for quite some time.
Never had so many permissions been requested in one morning,
and they all cursed Duclos for having revealed such a secret.
Despite the numerous permissions requested, these were granted
only to Constance, Hercule, 2 subaltern fuckers, Augustine,
Zéphire and Madame Desgranges; the friends entertained themselves with them for a moment and then sat down to eat. 'You
see,' said Durcet to Curval, 'how wrong you were to let your

daughter learn about religion? Now there's nothing we can do
to make her renounce those idiocies – I told you so at the time.'
'My word,' said Curval, 'I thought that knowing them would
be reason enough for her to detest them and that with age she
would be convinced of the idiocy of those vile dogmas.' 'What
you say is all well and good when it comes to reasonable minds,'
said the Bishop, 'but one should never delude oneself when dealing with a child.' 'We shall be obliged to resort to violent
measures,' said the Duc, who was well aware Adélaïde was listening to him. 'That will come,' said Durcet. 'I can tell her now that
if she only has me as her lawyer she will be poorly defended.'
'Oh, I can believe that, Monsieur!' said Adélaïde, weeping. 'Your
feelings towards me are clear enough.' 'Feelings?' said Durcet.
'I shall begin, my beautiful wife, by warning you I have never
had any for a woman, much less for you – who belong to me
– than for any other; I have a loathing for religion as I do for
all those who practise it, and I warn you that the indifference I
now feel for you will swiftly turn into the most violent aversion
if you continue to revere vile and execrable fantasies which I
have always held in contempt. One would have to lose one's
wits to believe in a God, and to become a complete imbecile to
adore Him. In a word, I declare to you – before your father and
these gentlemen – that there is no extreme to which I shall not
go if I catch you committing such an offence again. You should
have become a nun if you wanted to adore your good-for-nothing God – you could have prayed to Him to your heart's content.'
'Oh!' wailed Adélaïde. 'A nun, good God, a nun! Would to
heaven I had been!' And Durcet, sitting opposite her, irked by
this response, hurled a silver plate sideways at her face that
would have killed her had it struck her head, for the shock was
so violent it buckled against the wall. 'You are an insolent creature,' Curval told his daughter, who had leapt between her father
and Antinoüs to avoid the plate. 'It would serve you right if I
gave you a hundred kicks to the belly.' And sending her flying
with a punch – 'Get on your knees and apologize to your
husband,' he told her, 'or we shall subject you to the cruellest of
punishments later.' She threw herself in tears at Durcet's feet,
but having got very hard when throwing the plate and saying

he would not have wanted to miss his mark for a thousand *louis*, he now said there had to be a general and exemplary punishment right away, without taking anything away from the one scheduled for Saturday. He requested that on this occasion, and with no further consequences, the children should be dismissed from coffee, and that this venture should take place at the time they usually enjoyed themselves while they had their coffee; everyone agreed to this. Adélaïde and just two of the old women, Louison and Fanchon, the wickedest of the four and the most feared by the wives, headed to the coffee room, where circumstances require us to draw a curtain across what transpired there; what is certain is that our four heroes came, and Adélaïde was allowed to go off to bed. It is for the reader to imagine the scene as he sees fit and to be so good as to let us usher him, without further delay, to Duclos's narrations. With each friend sitting beside his wife except for the Duc, who should have had Adélaïde that evening and who had Augustine take her place, and with everyone in their places, Duclos took up the thread of her story thus.

'One day,' said this lovely whore, 'I declared to one of my fellow bawds that I had undoubtedly seen, in matters of passive flagellation, the most extreme things that could be seen, since I had flogged – and seen others flog – men with thorns and bulls' pizzles. "Oh, by God!" she said to me. "To convince you that you are far from having seen this practice at its most extreme, I shall send you one of my clients tomorrow." And sending me word in the morning of the time of this visit, and of the ritual to observe with the old Postmaster General[82] – whose name, I recall, was M. de Grancourt – I made all necessary preparations and waited for our man; it was me he was to deal with – that was the arrangement. He arrives and, once we had shut ourselves away – "Monsieur," I say to him, "I am mortified at being the bearer of such news, but you are now a prisoner and may no longer leave here; I am mortified that the Courts of Justice have looked to me to carry out your arrest, but such is their will and I have their order in my pocket. The person who sent you to my house has laid a trap for you, for she knew full well what all this was about and could certainly have spared you this scene;

in any case, you know the facts of your case – one cannot indulge with impunity in the dark and dreadful crimes you have committed and I consider you most fortunate to be getting off so lightly." Our man had listened most attentively to my harangue, and as soon as it was over he threw himself weeping at my knees, begging me to be gentle with him. "I know full well," he said, "that I have been deeply remiss – I have greatly offended God and Justice, but as it is you, my good lady, who are charged with my punishment, I urge you to be gentle with me." "Monsieur," I told him, "I shall do my duty. How do you know I am not under investigation myself or if I am free to indulge the compassion you inspire in me? Get undressed and do as you're told – that's all I can tell you." Grancourt obeyed and in a moment he was as naked as the day he was born. But, good God! What a body he offered to my sight! I can only compare it to taffeta chiné: every inch of his badly scarred body bore the trace of having been ripped open. Meanwhile I had put in the fire an iron scourge, covered in sharp tips, that had been sent that morning along with my instructions. The murderous weapon turned red hot at about the same time Grancourt had stripped naked; I grab hold of it and, starting to flay him with it – softly at first, then a bit harder, and then with all my might, all over from the nape of his neck down to his heels – in a few moments my man is drenched in blood. "You are a scoundrel," I said to him as I struck him, "a beggar who has committed all sorts of crimes – nothing is sacred to you and lately it's even been said you poisoned your mother." "That's true, Madame, that's true," he said as he frigged himself. "I'm a monster, I'm a criminal – there isn't a single abomination I haven't already committed and am not ready to commit again. Come – your blows are useless. I shall never mend my ways, I find crime too sensual – even if you were to kill me I should still not stop. Crime is my element, it is my life – I have lived in it and I want to die in it." And, as he spurred me on with these words, you can well imagine how I redoubled my curses and my blows. A *fuck* escaped his lips, however – this was the signal: at this word I redouble my efforts and try to strike him on his most sensitive parts; he skips, he leaps, he gets away from me and, as he comes, he plunges into a tank of warm water specially prepared to cleanse him after this bloody ceremony. Oh, after that I conceded to my fellow bawd the honour of having seen more than I had on this score, and I think we could certainly tell ourselves thereafter that we were the only two women in Paris to have seen so much, for our Grancourt never changed, and had been going to this woman's house every 3 days for the same escapade for more than twenty years.

'Soon after this same friend sent me to another libertine whose fantasy, I do believe, will strike you as no less peculiar: the scene took place in his *petite maison*[83] in Le Roule;[84] I am shown into a rather gloomy room where I see a man in bed and, in the middle of the room, a coffin. "You see before you," our libertine tells me, "a man on his deathbed, who did not want to close his eyes without paying tribute one last time to the object of his worship: I adore arses, and want to die kissing one. As soon as I have closed my eyes, you yourself will place me inside this coffin after first wrapping me in the shroud and then you will nail me in. It is my intention to die like this in pleasure's warm embrace and to be served at this final moment by the very object of my lust. Come," he continues in a weak and halting voice, "hurry up, for I am at my last gasp." I approach, turn around, show him my buttocks. "Oh, what a fine arse!" [he] says. "I am so glad to carry to the grave the memory of such a pretty backside." And he fondled it, spread it, kissed it as if he were the healthiest man in the world. "Ah!" he said after a while, abandoning his task and turning on to his other side. "I knew full well I would not have that pleasure for long. I am breathing my last – remember what I have told you to do." And with that he gives a great sigh, stiffens, and plays his role so well that the devil take me if I do not believe he is dead. I keep my wits about me: curious to see how such an amusing ceremony might end, I wrap him in the shroud; he was no longer moving and, whether he had uncovered some secret to appearing like this or whether my mind was playing tricks on me, he was as rigid and cold as an iron bar – only his prick gave some signs of life, as it was glued hard against his belly and some drops of come seemed to drip from it in spite of himself. As soon as he is wrapped up in a sheet, I pick him up, and this was far from easy as being rigid made him as heavy as an ox; I manage it in the end, however, and lay him in his coffin – once he is inside I recite the office of the dead and finally nail him in. This was his moment of climax: he no sooner hears the hammer blows than he cries out like a madman – "Oh! In the name of God – I am coming! Run away, whore, run away, because if I catch you, you're dead!" I am gripped by fear, I fly down the stairs where I meet a wily manservant, familiar with his master's manias, who gives me two *louis* and rushes into the patient's bedroom to rescue him from the state I'd left him in.'

'There's an amusing taste,' said Durcet. 'Well then, Curval, can you understand that one?' 'Marvellously well,' said Curval. 'That's a character keen to familiarize himself with the idea of death, and who has found no better way of doing so than to link it to a libertine idea – it is perfectly clear this man will die fondling arses.' 'What is certain,' said Champville, 'is that he is a proud heretic – I know him, and I shall have occasion to show you the way he treats religion's most sacred mysteries.' 'That must be the case,' said the Duc, 'he is a man who scoffs at everything and who wants to get used to thinking and acting in just the same way in his final moments.' 'For my part,' added the Bishop, 'I find something very piquant about this passion and I shall not conceal from you it has made me hard. Continue, Duclos, continue, for I sense I might do something foolish and I don't want to do so again today.'

'Well then,' said this lovely whore, 'here's a less complicated one: it concerns a man who visited me for over five years in a row for the unique pleasure of having his arsehole sewn up: he would stretch out on his belly across a bed, I would sit there between his legs and, armed with a needle and half a yard of thick waxed thread, I would meticulously sew up his anus all the way around – and this man's skin was so coarse there and so used to needle pricks that my operation did not draw a single drop of blood; he would frig himself in the meantime and come like a devil with the last stitch. Once his intoxication had dissipated, I would promptly unpick my needlework and there was no more to be said.

'Another one would have aqua vitae[85] rubbed into every part of his body where Nature had put hair, then I would light this alcoholic spirit, which would instantly consume every hair; he would come when he saw himself on fire as I showed him my belly, my crotch and the rest, for this one had the poor taste to examine only the front.

'But who among you, Messieurs, ever knew Mirecourt, now Président of the Supreme Court, and in those days ecclesiastical adviser[86] to the Crown?' 'I did,' replied Curval. 'Well then, Monsieur,' said Duclos, 'do you know what his passion was and, as far as I know, still is?' 'No, and as he passes or wishes to pass for a devout fellow, I should be very pleased to know.' 'Very well,' replied Duclos. 'He wants to be taken for an ass . . .' 'Oh, by God!' the Duc said to Curval. 'That, my friend, is a stately taste! I would wager that this man believes he is about to pass judgement. Well? What next?' said the Duc. 'Next, my Lord, he has to be led by the halter and walked around his chamber like this for an hour; he brays, he is straddled, and once one is on his back one has to whip him all over his body with a willow switch as if to quicken his step; he picks up his pace, and, as he frigs himself at the same time, the moment he comes he utters loud shrieks, kicks out, and sends the girl flying.'

'Oh! As for that one,' said the Duc, 'that's more amusing than lubricious – and pray tell, Duclos, did that man say to you he had a friend with the same taste?' 'Yes,' said the loveable Duclos, wittily joining in with this joke and stepping down from her rostrum as her task was complete. 'Yes, my Lord – he told me he had lots of them, but not all of them wanted to be straddled.' Now the session was over, they wanted to horse around before supper; the Duc clasped Augustine tight – 'I am not surprised,' he said, frigging her clitoris and making her grab hold of his prick, 'I am not surprised that Curval is sometimes tempted to try and break our pact and pop a virginity, for I feel that at this moment, for instance, I should gladly send Augustine's to the

devil.' 'Which one?' said Curval. 'My word, both of them!' said
the Duc. 'But we must behave – waiting for our pleasures makes
them all the more delightful. Come, little girl,' he continued,
'show me your buttocks – perhaps that will change my train of
thought . . . Good God, what a fine arse that little whore has!
Curval, what do you suggest I do with it?' 'A vinaigrette,'[87] said
Curval. 'God willing!' said the Duc. 'But patience . . . you'll see
that everything will come in due course.' 'My dearest brother,'
said the prelate in a halting voice, 'your words have a whiff of
come about them.' 'Oh, indeed – I have a great desire to spill
some.' 'Well, what's stopping you?' said the Bishop. 'Oh, all sorts
of things,' replied the Duc. 'Firstly there is no shit and I would
need some, and then – I don't know – I want all sorts of things.'
'Such as?' said Durcet, in whose mouth Antinoüs was shitting.
'Such as,' the Duc said, 'such as a little abomination I must
indulge in.' And heading into the far boudoir with Augustine,
Zélamir, Cupidon, Duclos, Desgranges and Hercule, a minute
later screams and curses were heard that proved the Duc had
finally soothed his mind as well as his balls. We are not too sure
what he did to Augustine, but despite his love for her, she was
seen returning in tears and with one of her fingers twisted
around; we deeply regret we are not in a position to explain all
of this, but it is clear that these gentlemen indulged, underhand-
edly and before it was really permitted to do so, in things that
they had not yet been told about, and in this they were formally
falling short of the conventions they had established – but when
an entire company commits the same faults, it generally forgives
itself. The Duc returned and saw with pleasure that Durcet and
the Bishop had not been idle, and that Curval, in Brise-cul's arms,
was taking every possible delight in all the sensual objects he
had managed to gather around him.

Supper was served. The usual orgies, and they went to bed;
as lame as Adélaïde was, the Duc, who was to have her that
night, wanted her, and as he had returned from the orgies a little
drunk as usual, they say he did not go easy on her. The night
finally unfolded like all the previous ones, that is to say in the
depths of delirium and debauchery; and when golden Aurora
had come, as the poets say, to open the gates of Apollo's palace,

this god – something of a libertine himself – mounted his azure chariot only to bring fresh lubricious acts to light.

25th day.

A fresh intrigue was nonetheless quietly brewing within the impenetrable walls of the castle of Silling, but its consequences were not as dangerous as the one between Adélaïde and Sophie. This new friendship was hatching between Aline and Zelmire: the conformity of temperament between the two young girls had done much to bring them together – both were sweet and sensitive, two and a half years apart in age at most, very childlike and good-hearted in temperament; in a word both of them had almost the same virtues and almost the same vices, for Zelmire, sweet and tender, was indolent and lazy like Aline. In a word they suited one another so well that on the morning of the 25th they were found in the same bed, and this is how that happened. Zelmire, being destined for Curval, was sleeping as we know in his bedroom; that same night Aline was Curval's bedfellow, but Curval, returning dead drunk from the orgies, only wanted to sleep with Bande-au-ciel, and as a result the two little doves, abandoned and brought together by this twist of fate, huddled together from fear of the cold in the same bed. And it was claimed their little fingers had scratched more than just an elbow there. Curval, when he opened his eyes in the morning and saw these two birds in the same nest, asked what they were doing there, and, summoning them both to his bed that instant, he sniffed them both below the clitoris and could clearly tell they were indeed both full of come. This was a serious case: the friends were perfectly happy for these young ladies to fall victim to indecent acts, but they demanded that among themselves there should be absolute modesty – for is there anything that libertinage does not demand in its perpetual inconsistencies? – and if on occasion they were allowed to be indecent among themselves, it had to be by order of these gentlemen and for their eyes only. As a result the case was brought to trial, and the two offenders, who could not or dared not deny the charges, were ordered to show how they went about it, and to demonstrate in front of everyone what their particular talent was. They did so while blushing deeply, weeping and begging forgiveness for what they had done, but the prospect of punishing this pretty little couple the following Saturday was too pleasant for there to be any thought of letting them off and they were immediately put down in Durcet's fateful book, which incidentally was filling up very nicely that week. Once this matter was dispatched, they finished their breakfast and Durcet carried out his inspections; the fateful indigestion produced another offender – little Michette. She could not hold it in any longer – she had been made to eat too much the previous evening, she said, along with a thousand other childish excuses that did not stop them from putting her name down. Curval, who was very hard, grabbed the chamber pot and devoured all its contents. And looking furiously at her – 'Oh yes, by God, you little hussy!' he said. 'Oh yes, by God, you'll be punished and by my hand once again: shitting like that is forbidden; you should have informed us at least – you know full well there's not an hour in the day when we're not ready to receive shit.' And he groped her buttocks roughly as he lectured her. The boys could not be faulted, no permissions for the chapel were granted, and they sat down to eat. Aline's actions were much discussed over lunch – they had thought her a hypocrite, and here all of a sudden was the evidence of her true character. 'So then, my friend,' said Durcet to the Bishop, 'should we set any store by girls' appearances now?' It was unanimously agreed that nothing could be more deceptive and that as girls were all so false, they only used their wits to deceive with greater skill. These remarks brought the conversation round to women, and the Bishop, who despised them, gave free rein to all the hatred they inspired in him: he brought them down to the level of the vilest animals, and proved their existence in this world to be so perfectly useless that they could all be wiped from the face of the earth without in any way harming the designs of Nature – who, having found a way in the past to create without them, would find one again when only men remained. They went through for coffee: it was presented by Augustine, Michette, Hyacinthe and Narcisse; the Bishop, one of whose favourite

simple pleasures was to suck little boys' pricks, had been enjoying this sport for a few minutes with Hyacinthe when all of a
sudden he cried out, pulling away with his mouth full – 'Oh,
good God, my friends – there goes a virginity! That's the first
time this little scamp has come, I'm sure.' And indeed no one
had seen Hyacinthe reach that point yet – they had even thought
he was too young to manage it, but he was well over 14, the age
at which Nature customarily showers her favours upon us, and
nothing was more certain than the victory the Bishop believed
he had won. They wanted to confirm the facts, however, and as
everyone wanted to witness the excitement they all sat in a
semicircle around the young man: Augustine, the harem's most
renowned masturbatrix, was ordered to manualize the child
before the company, and the young man was permitted to fondle
and caress whichever part of her body he desired; there can be
no spectacle more sensual than that of a young girl of 15, as
beautiful as the day is long, yielding to the caresses of a young
boy of 14, and spurring him to a climax with the most delicious
fondling. Hyacinthe, perhaps assisted by Nature but far more
probably by the examples before him, did not touch, fondle or
kiss anything other than the pretty little buttocks of his masturbatrix, and a moment later his beautiful cheeks blushed, he
heaved 2 or 3 sighs and his pretty little prick sent five or six
spurts of come – sweet and white as cream – 3 feet away to
land on Durcet's thigh (for he was closest and was having
himself frigged by Narcisse as he watched the operation). With
the facts now confirmed the child was caressed and kissed from
all sides – everyone wanted a small share of this young sperm,
and as it seemed that for his age and for his debut 6 climaxes
was not excessive, our libertines made him add to the two he
had already had one more for each of them, which he sprayed
into their mouths. The Duc, inflamed by this spectacle, grabbed
hold of Augustine and tickled her clitoris with his tongue until
she had come two or three times – which is just what this fiery
and passionate little minx soon did. While the Duc was fondling
Augustine in this manner, there was no sight more amusing
than Durcet, coming over to collect the symptoms of a pleasure
he had done nothing to elicit, and kissing that beautiful child's

mouth a thousand times and swallowing, so to speak, the ecstasy someone else had caused to flow through her senses. It was late – they were obliged to forgo their nap and head to the chamber of stories, where Duclos had been waiting for some time. As soon as everyone had taken their places, she continued the tale of her adventures in the following terms.

'As I have already had the honour of telling you, Messieurs, it is most difficult to comprehend all the torments man devises against his own interest as he seeks, in the debasement or agonies they provide, those sparks of pleasure that age or satiety have stolen from him. Would you believe that someone of this type, a man of 60 and singularly indifferent to all lubricious pleasures, could reawaken them in his senses only by having himself burned with a candle on every part of his body and particularly those parts Nature intends for these pleasures? It would be stubbed out firmly on his buttocks, prick, balls and above all his arsehole; he would kiss a backside in the meantime, and when this painful operation had been heartily performed fifteen or twenty times he would come as he sucked the anus exposed by his lady arsonist.

'I saw another one a little later who insisted I use a horse's curry comb and rub him down with it all over his body – just as one would the animal I have just mentioned. As soon as his body was drenched in blood, I would rub his skin with aqua vitae, and this second agony would make him come abundantly over my breasts – that was the battlefield he wanted to spray with his come. I would kneel down before him, squeeze his prick between my breasts, and there he happily sprayed the bitter surfeit of his balls.

'A third would have the hairs on his buttocks plucked one by one: throughout this operation he would frig himself over a hot turd I had just done for him. Then, when a *fuck* – our agreed signal – told me his climax was approaching, I had to prick each buttock with scissors and draw blood in order to seal the deal. His arse was covered in these wounds and I could barely find a spot that was unscathed to make my mark; at that moment his nose would plunge into the shit, he would smear his whole face in it and floods of sperm would crown his ecstasy.

'A fourth would put his prick in my mouth and order me to bite on it with all my strength; at the same time I would rip open both his buttocks with a very sharp-toothed steel comb; then as soon as I felt his tool was ready to ooze (as a very slight and very feeble erection indicated) – then, as I say, I would spread his buttocks prodigiously wide and bring his arsehole close to the burning candle placed on the floor for that purpose. It was the sensation of the candle scorching his anus that proved decisive; I would then bite twice as hard and my mouth would soon be full.'

'One moment,' says the Bishop. 'I cannot hear of someone coming in a mouth today without being reminded of the good fortune I've just had, and without my spirits being primed for more pleasures of the same kind.' As he says this, he pulls Bandeau-ciel – posted by his side that evening – closer and starts to suck his prick with all the lubricity of a true bugger; the come flies, he swallows it and soon repeats the same operation with Zéphire. He was hard, and women were rarely welcome by his side when he was in this critical state; unfortunately Aline, his niece, happened to be there. 'What are you doing there, you hussy,' he asked, 'when it's men I want?' Aline tries to slip away – he grabs her by the hair, and as he drags her into his closet with Zelmire and Hébé, the two girls from his harem – 'You shall see, you shall see,' he tells his friends, 'how I'll teach these beggars to bring me their cunts when it's pricks I want!' He ordered Fanchon to follow behind the 3 maidens and a moment later Aline's piercing screams were heard, his Lordship's bellowing climax merging with his dear niece's pained tones. They all returned . . . Aline was crying, squirming and clenching her backside. 'Come and let me have a look at that,' the Duc told her. 'Seeing the traces of Monsieur my brother's brutality drives me wild.' I do not know what Aline showed him as it has always been impossible for me to discover what went on in those infernal closets, but the Duc cried out, 'Oh fuck – that's delightful! I think I'll do the same.' But as Curval pointed out to him that it

was late and that he had a plan for their entertainment to share
with him at the orgies – one that would require all his wits and
all his come – Duclos was invited to tell the fifth tale which was
to bring the evening to a close, and she resumed in these terms.

'Among the ranks of these extraordinary people,' said this lovely
whore, 'with a mania for demeaning and debasing themselves,
there was a certain judge from the Court of Accounts called
Foucolet. It is impossible to imagine how far this man took his
mania – he had to be given a taste of every torment: I would
hang him, but the rope would break in time and he would land
on mattresses; a moment later I would stretch him out on a st.
Andrew's cross and pretend to break his limbs with a cardboard
rod; I would brand his shoulder with a warm iron that left a
slight mark; I would flog his back just like an executioner; and
I had to combine all this with vile insults, bitter reproaches for
various crimes – for which he would, during each of these operations, humbly beg forgiveness of God and Justice, wearing just
his shirt and holding a candle. Finally, the session would end
with my backside, where the libertine would spill his come when
his imagination was utterly ablaze.'

'Well then – will you let me come in peace, now that Duclos has
finished?' the Duc asked Curval. 'No, no,' said the Président,
'keep your come – I tell you I need it for the orgies.' 'Oh, you
must be joking,' said the Duc. 'Do you take me for someone
who's spent, and do you think that spilling a little come now
will prevent me from yielding or rising to all the abominations
that will cross your mind four hours from now? Fear not – I
shall always be ready, but Monsieur my brother was so good as
to give me a little example of brutality that I should be most
disappointed not to carry out with Adélaïde, your dear sweet
daughter.' And immediately pushing her into his closet with
Thérèse, Colombe and Fanny, the women of his quadrille, he
doubtless did there what the Bishop had done to his niece, and
came with the same accompaniments, for the young victim's
terrible scream and the lecher's roar were heard just as they had
been a moment previously. Curval wanted to determine which

of the two brothers had performed the better: he summoned the two women and, having examined both backsides at his leisure, decided that the Duc had only imitated the Bishop in surpassing him. They sat down to eat and, once they had by means of some drug filled the bowels of all the subjects – men and women – with wind, they had a game of fart-in-face[88] after supper. All four friends lay back on the sofas, their heads raised, and the subjects came one by one to fart in their mouths; Duclos was responsible for counting and keeping tally, and as there were 36 farteurs or farteuses against only 4 swallowers, some of the latter received up to 150 farts. This was the lubricious ceremony for which Curval had wanted the Duc to save himself, but there was no need to worry – he was too fond of libertinage for any new excess not to have the greatest effect upon him, no matter the circumstances in which it might be offered him, and indeed he came a second time purely because of Madame Fanchon's moist breezes. As for Curval it was Antinoüs's farts that cost him his come, while Durcet spilled his excited by those of Martaine, and the Bishop by those of Desgranges. But the young beauties received nothing, so true it is that everything must take place in the right order and that it takes depraved people to carry out abominations.

26th day.

As nothing was as delightful as the punishments, as nothing paved the way for as many pleasures – and those sorts of pleasures the friends had promised to taste only during these punishments, until the tales, elaborating these, allowed them to indulge in them with more freedom – they dreamt up everything they could to trick the subjects into offences that would offer them the thrill of punishing them. To this end the friends, convening an extraordinary meeting that morning to deliberate on this matter, added several clauses to the regulations, the infraction of which would necessarily result in punishments: firstly it was expressly forbidden for the wives, young boys and girls to fart anywhere other than in the friends' mouths; as soon as they felt

this need, they had to find one there and then and administer
what they were holding back – a harsh corporal punishment
was inflicted on the offenders. The use of bidets and the wiping
of arses were also absolutely forbidden: all subjects, universally
and without any exception, were ordered never to wash and
never to wipe their arses on anything after shitting; should any
arse be found to be clean, the subject would have to prove it
was one of the friends who had wiped it and would have to
name him; as a result the friend could deny the deed when
questioned if he so wished, thereby procuring himself two pleasures at once – that of wiping an arse clean with his tongue and
that of punishing the subject who had just given him this pleasure . . . we shall see examples of both of these. Next, a new
ceremony was introduced: at coffee in the morning, the moment
the friends entered the girls' bedroom, and similarly when they
went to the boys' bedroom afterwards, all the subjects had to
go up to each of them one after the other and say to him loud
and clear, *I don't give a damn about God! Do you want my arse?*
There's shit there, and those boys or girls who would not
pronounce both the blasphemy and the proposition out loud
would be put down there and then in the fateful book. One can
well imagine how difficult the devout Adélaïde and her young
pupil Sophie found it to pronounce such abominations, and this
is what the friends found so utterly entertaining; when all this
was settled, they agreed to allow denunciations – that barbaric
means of multiplying torments, used by all tyrants, was indeed
warmly embraced. It was decided that any subject bringing a
complaint against another would have the punishment for his
own first offence cut in half. This was in no way binding as the
subject who had just made an accusation never knew the extent
of the punishment they were promising to cut in half; as a result
it was very easy to mete out as much as one wanted while
persuading him he had still gained [by it]. It was judged and
decreed that denunciations would be given credence without
evidence, and next that one need only be accused – it did not
matter by whom – to have one's name put down that instant.
The old women were given even more authority and their slightest complaint, whether true or false, was enough to condemn

any subject there and then. In a word, the friends imposed every torment, every injustice imaginable, upon the rabble, confident they would derive ever greater pleasures once their tyranny had been perfected. Once that was done they visited the privies: Colombe was found guilty; she apologized, saying that the previous evening she had been made to eat between meals, that she couldn't help it, that she was most unfortunate and that this was the fourth week in a row she had been punished. This was indeed the case, and if there was a guilty party there was no need to look any further than her arse, which was the sweetest, prettiest and shapeliest arse one could ever hope to see; she objected that she had not wiped herself and that this at least should count in her favour a little – Durcet examined her and as he found a very large and thick layer of shit there, she was assured she would [not] be treated quite so severely. Curval, who was hard, grabbed hold of her and, having thoroughly wiped her anus, had the turd brought to him – which he ate as he had her frig him, interrupting the meal with many kisses on her mouth and clear instructions that she in turn should swallow the fruits of his labours. They inspected Augustine and Sophie, who, after the stools they had passed the day before, had been advised to remain in the foulest state. Sophie was by the book, despite spending the night in the Bishop's quarters, as her position demanded, but Augustine was absolutely spotless: sure of what she wanted to say, she boldly stepped forwards and said that they knew full well she had slept in M. le Duc's quarters as usual, and before falling asleep he had summoned her to his bed, where he had sucked her arsehole while she had teased his prick with her mouth. When questioned, the Duc said he did not remember that at all (though it was perfectly true), that he had fallen asleep with his prick up Madame Duclos's arse, and that they could probe the matter further. This matter was pursued with an air of the utmost seriousness and gravity: they sent for Duclos, who, realizing what was up, confirmed everything the Duc had claimed and declared that Augustine had been called over to his Lordship's bed only for a moment, when he had shat in her mouth only to return to eat his turd later. Augustine tried to defend her case, and disputed Madame Duclos's claim, but she was ordered to be silent and her name was put down even though she was perfectly innocent. They headed to the boys' quarters, where Cupidon was found to be at fault: he had left the most beautiful turd one could ever hope to see in his chamber pot; the Duc grabbed and devoured it while the young man sucked his prick. The friends refused all permissions to go to the chapel, and went through to the dining room. The beautiful Constance, who was sometimes excused from serving there on account of her condition, was feeling well that day and arrived naked – her belly, which was beginning to swell a little, greatly inflamed Curval's mind; and when they saw he was beginning to grope the poor creature's buttocks and breasts rather too roughly – one could see his loathing for her redoubling with each passing day – they allowed her, following her entreaties and their own desire to preserve her fruit until a certain time had come, to absent herself for the rest of the day until the narrations, from which she was never exempt. Curval started saying horrible things about baby-breeders again and swore that if he were in charge he would adopt the same law as the island of Formosa,[89] where pregnant women under the age of 30 are crushed in a mortar along with their fruit, adding that if that law were to be followed in France, the population would still be twice as large as it ought to be. They went through for coffee – it was presented by Sophie, Fanny, Zélamir and Adonis, but served in a most peculiar fashion: they had the friends swallow it directly from their own mouths. Sophie served the Duc; Fanny, Curval; Zélamir, the Bishop; and Adonis, Durcet: they took a sip, swilled it around their mouths and then poured it straight into the gullet of the person they were serving. Curval, who had left the table much inflamed, got hard again with this new ceremony and when it was over he grabbed hold of Fanny and came in her mouth, ordering her to swallow or suffer the most serious consequences – which this wretched child did without daring to bat an eyelid. The Duc and his two other friends made the subjects fart and shit, and after their nap everyone came to listen to Duclos, who resumed the rest of her tales as follows.

'I shall quickly run through,' said this lovable whore, 'the last two adventures I still have to tell regarding those peculiar men who only find a thrill in the pain they have inflicted on them, and then if it pleases you we shall change subject. The first one, whom I frigged as we stood naked, wanted floods of nearly boiling water to stream over our bodies through a hole in the ceiling for as long as our session lasted; try as I might to tell him that though I did not share his passion I was nonetheless going to be its victim, he assured me that I wouldn't feel any pain and that such showers were excellent for one's health. I believed him and let him have his way, and as we were at his house I had no control over the temperature of the water – it was nearly boiling. One cannot imagine the pleasure he felt as it washed over him; as for me, despite working away on him as quickly as I could, I confess I screamed out like a scalded tomcat – my skin peeled from this, and I firmly promised myself never to return to that man's house.'

'Oh, by God!' said the Duc. 'I feel the urge to scald the lovely Aline like that.' 'My Lord,' the latter humbly replied, 'I am not a pig.'[90] And once everyone had laughed at the innocent candour of her childish response, they asked Duclos for the second and final example she had to cite of this type.

'This one was not quite as painful for me,' said Duclos, 'it was simply a matter of pulling on a strong protective glove, then grabbing with this hand some burning-hot gravel from a pan on a chafing dish;[91] and with this hand now full, I had to rub my man down with this nearly blazing gravel from the nape of his neck down to his heels; his body had been so utterly toughened by this exercise it seemed to be made of leather. When it came to his prick, I had to grab it and frig with my hand full of this burning sand; he would get hard very quickly; then with the other hand I would place under his balls a specially prepared red-hot shovel. With this friction on the one hand, and this consuming heat consuming his testicles [on the other], and perhaps a little fondling of both my buttocks (which I had to keep in full view throughout the operation) – all this set him off and he came, taking great care to make his sperm flow on to the red-hot shovel and to watch it sizzle in delight.'

*

'Curval,' said the Duc, 'here is a man who seems to me no keener to populate the world than you are.' 'It looks that way to me,' said Curval. 'I won't hide from you I like the idea of trying to burn one's come.' 'Oh, I can see all the ideas this one is giving you,' said the Duc, 'and even if it had hatched[92] you would burn it with the same pleasure, would you not?' 'My word, I am rather afraid I would,' said Curval, as he did something or other to Adélaïde, who made him scream out loud.[93] 'What's got into you, whore,' Curval said to his daughter, 'to screech like that . . . ? Can't you see the Duc is telling me about burning, tormenting, disciplining come that's hatched? And what are you, pray tell, if not a little come hatched from my balls? Go on, continue, Duclos,' added Curval, 'for I sense that this slut's tears might make me come and I don't want to.'

'Now we come,' said this heroine, 'to details which, as they involve more piquant eccentricities, you may find more appealing. As you know it is the custom in Paris to display the dead at one's front door:[94] there was one gentleman who would pay me twelve *francs* for each and every one of these lugubrious ceremonies I could find for him in one evening; his pleasure consisted simply in getting as close to them as possible – right beside the coffin if we could – and there I had to frig him so that his come would ejaculate over the coffin. We would hurry to 3 or 4 of these in an evening, depending on the number I had discovered, and would carry out the same operation at all of them, without him touching anything other than my backside while I frigged him. He was a man of about 30 years of age and I enjoyed his custom for more than 10 years, during which time I'm sure I made him come over more than two thousand coffins.'

'But would he say anything as he proceeded?' said the Duc. 'Would he say something to you or the corpse?' 'He would hurl insults at the corpse,' said Duclos. 'He would say to it, "Take that, you rascal! Take that, you bugger! Take that, you villain! Take my come to hell with you!"' 'Now there's a peculiar mania,' said Curval. 'My friend,' said the Duc, 'be in no doubt that this man was one of our number and that this was not all he got up to.' 'You are right, my Lord,' said Madame Martaine, 'and I shall have occasion to portray this particular actor on the stage once more.' Duclos, availing herself of the silence, resumed thus.

'Another one, taking a more or less similar fantasy much further, wanted me to station spies in the countryside to send him word whenever a young girl, dead from something other than a dangerous disease (he was most adamant on that point), had been buried in a graveyard. As soon as I had found what he was after – and he always rewarded me handsomely for my discoveries – we would set out in the evening, slip into the graveyard as best we could and, heading straight to the spot indicated by the spy, where the earth had been freshly turned, we would promptly set to work, clearing away by hand everything covering the cadaver; and as soon as he could reach it, I would frig him over it and he would grope it all over, and especially its buttocks if he could. Sometimes he would get hard a second time, but in that case he would shit and have me shit on the cadaver and would then come over it, fondling every part of the body he could grab as he did so.'

'Oh, now that's one I can understand,' said Curval, 'and if I must offer my confession here and now, it's that I've done the same thing now and again in my life – it's true that I would sometimes add a few accompaniments that it is not yet time for me to share with you. In any case, it makes me hard – spread your thighs, Adélaïde . . .' And I don't know what happened, but the sofa groaned under the weight, the unmistakable sound of a climax was heard, and I believe that M. le Président, perfectly simply and very virtuously, had just committed incest. 'Président,' the Duc said, 'I wager you imagined she was dead.' 'Yes, in truth,' said Curval, 'for I would not have come otherwise.' And Duclos, seeing that they had fallen silent, brought her evening to a close as follows.

'So as not to leave you, Messieurs, with such lugubrious ideas, I am going to conclude my evening with the tale of the Duc de Bonnefort's passion. This young lord, whom I entertained five or 6 times and who, for the same operation, would often see one of my friends, requires a woman, armed with a dildo, to frig herself naked before him, both front and back, for three hours in a row without stopping. There is a clock that times you and if you abandon the task before the third hour is up, you are not paid; he is facing you, he watches you, turns you round and round in every direction, exhorts you to swoon with pleasure – and if, carried away by the effects of the operation, you really do end up fainting with pleasure, there is no doubt you will hasten his own. If not, at the very moment the clock strikes the 3rd hour, he draws close to you and comes in your face.'

'My word,' said the Bishop, 'I cannot see, Duclos, why you didn't choose to leave us with the previous ideas rather than this one; they had a certain piquancy that excited us immensely, whereas a mawkish passion – such as the one with which you have concluded your evening – leaves our minds blank.' 'She is quite right,' said Julie, who was with Durcet. 'Personally I thank her for it, and, without those horrid ideas Md. Duclos raised a moment ago filling our heads, we girls shall sleep easier.' 'Oh, you may be very much mistaken there, my lovely Julie,' said Durcet. 'As for me, when the new one bores me I only remember the old one – and, to prove it to you, be so good as to follow me.' And Durcet dashed into his closet with Sophie and Michette, coming I know not how, but in such a way, however, that displeased Sophie, for she uttered a terrible scream and returned as red as a cockscomb. 'Oh! As for that one,' said the Duc, 'you can't have wanted to take her for a corpse, as you have just made her give frantic signs of life.' 'She screamed in fear,' said Durcet. 'Ask her what I did to her, and have her whisper it.' Sophie approached the Duc to tell him. 'Oh!' the latter said out loud. 'That wasn't anything to scream about, nor to make one come!' And as the bell for supper rang, they broke off all these conversations and pleasures to go and enjoy those of the table. The orgies were celebrated rather peacefully and the friends virtuously went to bed, without the least sign of drunkenness – an extremely rare event.

Twenty-seventh day.

With the morning came the denunciations sanctioned the day before, and the sultanesses – having seen that with the exception of Rosette they were all 8 to be punished – did not fail to go and accuse her; they swore she had farted all night and, though this was pure spite on the part of the young girls, she had the whole harem against her and her name was put down there and then. Everything else went marvellously well and, aside from Sophie and Zelmire, who stammered a little, the friends were hailed from all sides with the new greeting, *Holy fuck! Do you want my arse? There's shit there.* And indeed there was plenty everywhere, as, for fear the subjects might be tempted to wash, the old women had removed all the chamber pots, towels and water. The regimen of meat but no bread was beginning to heat up all those unwashed little mouths; from that day the friends noticed a considerable difference in the subjects' breath. 'Oh, by God!' said Curval as he tongued Augustine's mouth. 'That at least means something – it makes you hard, kissing that.' Everyone agreed unanimously that this was infinitely better. As nothing new happened until coffee, we shall usher the reader there at once – it was served by Sophie, Zelmire, Giton and Narcisse. The Duc said he was perfectly sure that Sophie should be able to come, and that they absolutely had to put this theory to the test: he told Durcet to observe her and, laying her on a sofa, simultaneously fondled the sides of her vagina, her clitoris and her arsehole first with his fingers, then with his tongue; Nature triumphed – after a quarter of an hour this beautiful girl became agitated, she flushed, she sighed. Durcet pointed out all these movements to Curval and the Bishop (who could not believe she was already coming), and as for the Duc, he was better placed to judge than all the others, since this young little cunt was thoroughly soaked and the little minx had drenched his lips with come. The Duc could not resist the lubricity of his experiment: he stood up and, bending over the young girl, came all over her parted crotch, pushing his sperm inside her cunt with his fingers as best he could. Curval, his mind inflamed by this spectacle, grabbed her and demanded something other than come: she offered her pretty little arse, the Président sealed his mouth to it, and the intelligent reader will easily guess what he received. Meanwhile Zelmire was entertaining the Bishop: she was sucking him and fondling his fundament. And all this while Curval was being frigged by Narcisse, whose backside he was ardently kissing. It was only the Duc, however, who spilled his come – Duclos had announced tales more delightful than the previous ones for that evening and the friends wanted to save themselves to hear them; when the hour came, off they went, and this is how that alluring whore expressed herself.

'A man whose circumstances and identity, Messieurs,' she said, 'I have never discovered and whom as a result I shall be able to describe only most imperfectly to you, sent me a note inviting me to visit his house on the Rue Blanche du Rempart[95] at 9 o'clock in the evening. He told me in his note not to be suspicious in the slightest, and that although he had not made himself known to me I should have no cause to complain about him; two *louis* were enclosed with the letter and, despite my usual prudence – which certainly ought to have dissuaded me from this venture, since I didn't know who was putting me up to it – I nevertheless risked everything, putting my faith entirely in some kind of intuition that seemed quietly to tell me I had nothing to fear. I arrive: a valet instructs me to undress completely and adds that he can let me into his master's lodgings only in this state; I follow my orders and as soon as he sees me in the desired state he takes me by the hand and, having led me through two or three rooms, finally knocks at a door; it opens, I enter, the valet withdraws and the door closes again, but as far as daylight was concerned, the place to which I had been brought was no better than an oven, and neither daylight nor air entered this room from any side whatsoever. No sooner was I inside than a naked man comes up to me and grabs me without uttering a word: I keep my wits about me, convinced that all I have to do to get through this whole nocturnal ritual is help someone spill their come; I promptly reach down to his groin with the idea of swiftly draining this monster of a venom that made him so dangerous. I find a very large, terribly hard and utterly rampant prick, but my fingers are pushed away at once; it seems I am neither to touch it nor to inspect it, and I am seated on a stool instead. The stranger plants himself beside me and, grabbing my breasts one after the other, he squeezes and squashes them with such violence that I tell him brusquely, 'You're hurting me!' He then stops, pulls me up, lays me flat on my stomach upon a raised sofa and, sitting behind me, between my legs, he starts to do to my buttocks what he had just done to my breasts: he gropes and squashes them with unparalleled violence, spreads them apart, pushes them together, pummels them, kisses as he nibbles on them, sucks my arsehole – and as these repeated squeezes were less dangerous on this side than the other, I offered no resistance; and there I was, letting him have his way and wondering why all the mystery for things that seemed so straightforward to me, when all of a sudden I hear my man utter appalling screams. "Run away, you fucking whore, run away!" he tells me. "Run away, you slut, I'm coming and I can't be held responsible for your life!" You can well imagine my first impulse was to take to my heels: I make out a faint glimmer – it was daylight coming through the door by which I had entered – I hurl myself towards it, I find the valet who had received me, I rush into his arms, he returns my clothes to me, gives me two *louis* and I make myself scarce, very pleased to have got off so lightly.'

'You have every reason to congratulate yourself,' said Martaine, 'as that was merely the mild version of his usual passion. I shall show you the same man, Messieurs,' continued this matron, 'in a more dangerous light.' 'Not as deadly as the one in which I'll present him to these gentlemen,' said Desgranges, 'and I join Md. Martaine in assuring you that you were very fortunate to get off so lightly, for that same man had other passions that were far more peculiar.' 'Before we discuss those let us wait until we know his full story,' said the Duc, 'and tell us another one as quickly as you can, Duclos, to clear our minds of the kind of individual who would not fail to inflame them.'

*

'The one I saw next, Messieurs,' continued Duclos, 'wanted a woman with an exquisite bust, and, as this is one of my attributes, once I had shown it to him he preferred me to all my girls – but to what use did this flagrant libertine intend to put my breasts and my face? He lays me, completely naked, across a sofa, plants himself astride my chest, places his prick between my two breasts, orders me to squeeze it as best I can, and after a short ride this rogue drenches them in come as he gobs thick spittle into my face twenty times in a row.'

'Well,' grumbled Adélaïde to the Duc, who had just spat in her face, 'I don't see what need there is to imitate that particular abomination. Will you stop that?' she continued – as she wiped herself down – to the Duc, who had still to come. 'When I see fit, my sweet child,' the Duc told her. 'Remember once and for all that you're here only to obey and to let us have our way; come now – carry on, Duclos, for I might do something worse, and, as I adore this sweet child,' he said mockingly, 'I don't wish to offend her completely.'

'I do not know, Messieurs,' said Duclos as she took up the thread of her tales, 'if you have heard of the passion of the Commandeur de St. Elme. He had a gambling house, where all those who came to risk their money were mercilessly fleeced, but what was most extraordinary was that the Commandeur would get hard when stiffing them; with every sleight of hand he would come in his breeches, and a woman I knew very well, and whom he kept for a long while, told me that sometimes these tricks so inflamed him that he had to go off with her for some relief from the ardour devouring him. That was not all he did – every type of theft held the same appeal for him and no object was safe from him: if he was at your table, he would steal the cutlery; in your closet – your jewellery; near your pocket – your snuffbox or your handkerchief. It was all the same to him as long as he could snatch it, and every object made him hard – and even come – once he had snatched it.

'But for all that he was certainly less remarkable than the Président from the Courts of Justice with whom I had dealings

very soon after my arrival at Madame Fournier's, and whose
custom I enjoyed for many years, for this was a rather prickly
case and he wanted to deal only with me. The Président rented
a small apartment throughout the year on the Place de Grève:[96]
its sole occupant was an old servant who acted as housekeeper
and her only orders were to keep it tidy and inform the Président
at the first sign of preparations for an execution in the square;
the Président would immediately send me word to get ready,
would collect me in disguise in a hired carriage and we would
head to his little apartment. His bedroom window was positioned
so as to give directly on to the nearby scaffold; the Président and
I would place ourselves there behind a blind, he would rest a pair
of spyglasses on one of the slats, and as he waited for the victim
to arrive, Themis's[97] henchman would enjoy himself on a bed by
kissing my buttocks – a detail that, incidentally, utterly delighted
him. At last, with the hubbub heralding the victim's arrival, the
honourable judge would take his place by the window and bid
me take mine beside him – enjoining me to fondle and frig his
prick and to pace these tugs to coincide with the execution he
was about to witness, so that the sperm would let fly only at the
moment the convict gave his soul up to God. Everything would
be in place, the criminal would mount the scaffold, the Président
would look on; the closer the convict came to his death, the more
frenzied the scoundrel's prick would become in my hands; the
final blows would be delivered at last – this was the moment he
would come. "Oh, good God!" he would say. "Jesus fucking
Christ! How I'd like to be his executioner myself – and how much
better would I have struck him down." The impressions his pleasures made on him were moreover proportionate to the type of
execution: a hanged man would provoke only a very simple
sensation in him; a man broken on the wheel would send him
into delirium; but if the man were either burned or quartered he
would swoon with pleasure. Man or woman – it was all the same
to him: "Only a pregnant woman," he said, "might have more
of an effect on me, and unfortunately that cannot be."[98] "But,
Monsieur," I said to him one day, "because of your position you
are complicit in the death of this unfortunate victim." "Certainly,"
he replied, "and that is what amuses me all the more. In my thirty

years as a judge I have only ever pronounced in favour of the
death penalty." "And don't you think," I asked him, "that you
might have some reason to reproach yourself for the deaths of
these people – as you would with a murder?"[99] "Goodness!" he
said. "Must we dwell on this?" "But," I told him, "this is nonetheless what polite society would call an absolute horror." "Oh,"
he replied, "one must learn to accept the horror of anything that
makes one hard, and for one very simple reason – which is that
this thing, however appalling you would like to think it might
be, is no longer horrifying for you the moment it makes you
come;[100] it only remains so therefore in other people's eyes, but
who can tell me that the opinions of others – which are almost
always wrong on every score – are not equally so on this one?
Nothing," he continued, "is fundamentally good or fundamentally bad – everything is simply relative to our customs, opinions
and prejudices. Once this point is established, it is entirely possible that something perfectly indifferent in its own right might
nevertheless seem contemptible in your eyes and yet most
delightful in mine; and the moment I develop a liking for it – as
difficult as it may be to determine its true worth – the moment
it amuses me, would I not be mad to deprive myself of it just
because you disapprove? Come, come, my dear Duclos – the life
of one man is so unimportant that one may trifle with it to one's
heart's content, just as one would that of a cat or a dog; it is up
to the weakest to defend themselves, they have more or less the
same weapons we do. And since you have such scruples," my
man added, "what then would you say about the fantasy of a
friend of mine?" And if it pleases you, Messieurs, this taste he
described to me will provide us with our 5ᵗʰ and final tale this
evening.

'The Président told me this friend wanted only women who
are due to be executed. "The shorter the interval between the
moment they are delivered to him and the moment they are to
perish, the more he pays for them, but it must always be after
they have been notified of their sentence. As his office brings this
kind of prize within reach, he never lets one slip through his
fingers, and I have seen him pay as much as one hundred *louis*
for a tête-à-tête of this type; he does not, however, have his way

with them – he demands only that they show their buttocks and that they shit; he claims that nothing tastes like the shit of a woman who has just suffered such a reversal of fortune. There is no limit to his imagination when it comes to procuring these tête-à-têtes, and moreover – as you can well imagine – he does [not] wish to be identified by these women. Sometimes he passes himself off as the confessor, sometimes as a friend of the family, and in his overtures he always places great emphasis on his desire to be of service to them as long as they are willing to go along with him. And when he has finished, when he has had his way, how do you imagine he concludes his operation, my dear Duclos?" the Président asked me . . . "Just as I do, my dear friend. He keeps his come for the denouement and lets it go as he sees them die most delectably." "Oh, that is so wicked!" I told him. "Wicked?" he interrupted . . . "That's mere verbiage, my child. Nothing that makes one hard is wicked and the only crime in the world is to refuse oneself that pleasure."'

'Indeed there was nothing he refused himself,' said Madame Martaine, 'and Md. Desgranges and I shall, I dare say, have occasion to regale the company with some lubricious and criminal anecdotes about the same character.' 'Oh, so much the better!' said Curval. 'For there's a man I already like a great deal – that's how one should view pleasures and I like his philosophy immensely. The lengths to which man – already constricted in all his amusements, in all his faculties – will go to confine the scope of his existence out of unworthy prejudice is quite incredible. One cannot comprehend, for example, what possesses the man who makes a crime out of murder to impose such limits on all his delights: he has deprived himself of a hundred pleasures each more delicious than the last by having the audacity to adopt the odious fantasy of that prejudice; and what the devil does it matter to Nature whether there are one, ten, twenty, five hundred more or fewer men in the world? Do conquerors, heroes, tyrants submit themselves to that absurd law according to which we dare not do unto others anything we would not have them do unto us? In truth, my friends, I shall not hide from you that I tremble when I hear fools dare to tell me that that is the law of Nature, &c.

Heavens above! Craving murders and crimes, Nature passes her law to encourage and inspire us to commit such acts, and the only law she inscribes in the depths of our hearts is to satisfy ourselves at no matter whose expense. But patience – perhaps I shall soon have a more opportune moment to discuss these subjects more fully with you; I have studied these in great depth and I hope that sharing them with you will leave you as convinced as I am that the only way to serve Nature is to follow her desires blindly, whatever they may be, because as vice is as necessary as virtue to the preservation of her laws, she understands how to steer us at every turn towards that which she believes is necessary at that moment. Yes, my friends, I shall discuss all that with you another day, but right now I must spill some come, because that devil of a man overlooking the executions on the Place de Grève has utterly swelled my balls.' And heading into the far boudoir with Desgranges and Fanchon (his two good friends, because they were just as wicked as he), these three had Aline, Sophie, Hébé, Antinoüs and Zéphire follow behind; I am not too sure what the libertine dreamt up in the midst of these seven, but it took a long time. He was heard shouting several times – 'Go on, turn around, then! But that's not what I asked for!' – and other ill-tempered remarks littered with curses to which, as we know, he was much inclined in these scenes of debauchery, and at last the women reappeared very flushed, terribly dishevelled and looking as if they had been savagely groped from all sides. Meanwhile, the Duc and his two friends had not been idle, but the Bishop was the only one who had come – and in such an extraordinary manner that we are not yet allowed to say any more about it. When they sat down to eat, Curval philosophized a little more, as for him the passions had no influence on theoretical matters: firm in his principles, he was as heretical, as atheist and as criminal when he had just spilled his come as he was at his most inflamed, and that is how all wise people should be; come must never dictate or guide one's principles – it is for principles to govern the manner in which it is spilt. And whether one's prick is hard or not, philosophy – regardless of the passions – must always remain the same. The entertainment at the orgies consisted in ascertaining something the friends had not yet considered, and

which was interesting nonetheless: they wanted to determine who
had the finest arse of all the girls and of all the boys; consequently
they first made the boys stand in line, upright but leaning forwards
very slightly nonetheless – this is the only way to examine and
judge an arse properly. The examination was very long and very
severe: they fought for their opinions, they changed them, they
inspected the goods fifteen times in a row, and the prize was by
common assent awarded to Zéphire: they agreed unanimously
that it was physically impossible to find anything more perfect
or more shapely. Then the friends moved on to the girls: they
adopted the same poses; at first it took a long time to reach a
decision – it was almost impossible to decide between Augustine,
Zelmire and Sophie; taller and more finely proportioned than
the other two, Augustine would indisputably have won had she
been judged by painters, perhaps, but libertines prize grace over
perfection, portliness over proportion; what counted against her
was that she was a touch thin and delicate – the other two each
offered a complexion so fresh, so plump, buttocks so white and
so round, loins so sensually sculpted that they prevailed over
Augustine. But how to decide between the two who remained?
Ten times in a row opinions were split equally; finally Zelmire
prevailed. These two charming children were brought out: they
were kissed, fondled and frigged all evening; Zelmire was ordered
to frig Zéphire, who, coming like a dream, was observed in all
his ecstasy with the greatest pleasure; he in turn frigged the young
girl, who swooned in his arms, and all these unspeakably lubricious scenes made the Duc and his brother spill some come, but
only feebly stirred Curval and Durcet, who agreed that they
needed less mawkish scenes to stir their weary old souls and that
all these capers were only fit for young people. At last they went
to bed and Curval, wallowing in some fresh abominations, sought
to make up for the tender *pastourelles*[101] he had just witnessed.

28th day.

It was a wedding day and the turn of Cupidon and Rosette to
be united in the bonds of matrimony – and by a peculiar twist

of fate they were both to be punished that evening. As no one
was at fault that morning, all this part of the day was devoted
to the wedding ceremony and, once it had come to a close, the
two of them were brought to the drawing room to see what they
would get up to together. As the mysteries of Venus were often
celebrated in full view of the children, though none of them had
yet been put to use in them, they had a sufficient grasp of theory
in these matters to allow them to perform more or less what
was required. Cupidon, whose prick was very hard, thus placed
his little peg between Rosette's thighs and she acquiesced with
all the candour of the most perfect innocence; the young boy
was going about it so well that he might in all likelihood have
succeeded, when the Bishop, laying hold of him, thrust in himself
what the child would, I think, have much preferred to thrust in
his little wife: as he pierced the Bishop's ample arse he looked
over at her with eyes that betrayed his regret, but she was soon
occupied herself, as the Duc thigh-fucked her. Curval came over
to give the arse of the Bishop's little fucker a lubricious grope,
and as this pretty little arse was, following orders, in the desired
state, he licked it and stiffened a little; as for Durcet, he did as
much to the little girl whom the Duc was holding from in front;
no one came, however, and they went to eat – the young bride
and groom, who had been allowed in with them, went to serve
coffee with Augustine and Zélamir. And the sensual Augustine,
all upset at not having won the beauty prize the day before, had
– as if in a sulk – left her hair in a dishevelled state that made
her a thousand times more alluring. This stirred Curval and, as
he examined her buttocks, he said, 'I cannot understand how
this little minx failed to win the palm yesterday, for the devil
take me if there is a finer arse in the world than this one.' At the
same time he parted her cheeks, and asked Augustine if she was
ready to satisfy him: 'Oh, yes,' [she] said, 'and then some, because
I can't hold it in any longer.' Curval bends her over a sofa and,
kneeling before her beautiful backside, devours her turd in an
instant. 'In the name of God!' he said as he turned towards his
friends and showed them his prick glued to his belly. 'Now I'm
in a frenzy that might drive me to all sorts of things.' 'Like what?'
said the Duc, who liked to make him spout obscenities when he

was in this kind of state. 'Like what?' replied Curval. 'Any abomination you care to propose – even if it meant dismembering
Nature and dislocating the universe.' 'Come, come,' said Durcet,
who saw him casting furious glances at Augustine. 'Come, let's
go and listen to Duclos – it's time, for I am sure that if we were
to give you free rein now, that poor little chick would have a
wretched quarter of an hour.' 'Oh yes!' said Curval all ablaze.
'A most wretched one – I can promise you that much.' 'Curval,'
said the Duc, who also had a rampant erection having just made
Rosette shit, 'let the harem be surrendered to us now and we
shall answer for it in two hours.' The Bishop and Durcet, calmer
at that particular moment, took each of them by the arm, and
it was in this state – in other words with their breeches down
and their pricks aloft – that these libertines appeared before
those who had already assembled in the chamber of stories ready
to hear new tales from Duclos, who, anticipating from the state
of these two gentlemen that she would soon be interrupted,
nonetheless began in these terms.

'A nobleman at Court, a man of around 35 years of age, had
just asked me,' said Duclos, 'for one of the prettiest girls I could
possibly find; he had not informed me of his mania, and to satisfy
him I gave him a young dressmaker who had never taken part
in any trysts and who was unquestionably one of the loveliest
creatures it was possible to find. I left them to grapple with each
other and, curious to see what would happen, I rush to my
peephole. "Where the devil did Md. Duclos," he began by saying,
"find a nasty slut like you? . . . In the mire, no doubt . . . you
must have been trying to snare some soldiers when she came
looking for you." And the young lady, ashamed and utterly at a
loss as to what was happening, did not know how to respond.
"Come now – get undressed!" continued the courtier . . . "How
clumsy you are . . . never in all my days have I seen such an ugly
and stupid whore . . . Well then, come on! Will this take all day?
. . . Oh . . . so this is the body they made such a fuss about? . . .
What tits! . . . You'd take them for an old cow's udder." And he
groped them brutally. "And this belly – how wrinkly it is . . . you
must have had 20 children!" "Not a single one, Monsieur, I do

assure you." "Oh yes – not a single one, that's what all those sluts say – to listen to them, you'd think they were all virgins ... Come on, turn around – what a foul arse! ... such flabby and revolting buttocks – no doubt it's from all those kicks in the arse that your backside has turned out like that!" And you will note, if it pleases you, Messieurs, that this was the most beautiful backside one could possibly hope to see. Meanwhile, the young girl began to get flustered: I could almost make out the palpitations of her little heart, and could see her beautiful eyes cloud over. And the more flustered she appeared, the more that accursed rogue would mortify her; I should find it impossible to tell you all the nonsense he spouted at her – one would not dare make such cutting remarks to the vilest and foulest of creatures. Finally her stomach heaved and her tears fell: it was for this moment that the libertine, who was frigging with all his might, had reserved the final flourish of his litanies; it would be impossible for me to convey all the obscenities he aimed at her skin, her figure, her features, the rank smell he claimed she exuded, her clothes, her intelligence – in a word, he tried everything, dreamt up everything he could to shatter her pride, and came all over her, spewing abominations even a porter wouldn't dare utter. Something most amusing arose from this scene, which was that it had the effect of a sermon upon this young girl: she swore she would never again in all her life put herself through such an ordeal and I learned a week later that she had entered a convent for the rest of her days. I said as much to the young man, who found it enormously amusing and subsequently asked me for someone else to convert.

'Another man,' continued Duclos, 'ordered me to find him extremely sensitive girls who were awaiting news that – should it turn out badly – might overwhelm them with the most intense sorrow. I went to a great deal of trouble to satisfy this taste, because it was very difficult to trick him in any way. Our man had become a connoisseur in the time he had played this game, and could see with one glance if the blow he delivered had truly hit home. So I didn't deceive him and would always give him young girls who were absolutely in the state of mind he desired. One day I showed him one who was awaiting news from Dijon regarding a young man whom she idolized and who was called Valcourt. I left them to do battle. "Where are you from, Mademoiselle?" our libertine asks politely. "From Dijon, Monsieur." "From Dijon? Oh, good heavens! Here's a letter I've just received from there this minute that's told me some most upsetting news." "And what's that?' asks the young girl with interest. "As I know the whole town, this news might be of interest to me." "Oh no," our man replies, "it only concerns me. It's about the death of a young man in whom I took the keenest interest: he had just married a girl whom my brother, who lives in Dijon, had found for him – a girl with whom he was besotted – and the day after the wedding he suddenly died." "His name, Monsieur, if you please?" "He was called Valcourt – he was from Paris, from such and such a street, from such and such a house . . . Oh, you surely don't know him." And at that moment the young girl falls over backwards and faints. "Oh, fuck!" says our libertine, quite beside himself as he unbuttons his breeches and frigs himself over her. "Oh, good God, that's what I wanted! Now some buttocks, some buttocks! I just need some buttocks to make me come!" And turning her over and hitching up her skirts, with her lying there utterly prone, he lets fly seven or 8 spurts of come over her backside and rushes off, without worrying about either the consequences of what he said, or what might become of the unfortunate girl.'

'And did she croak as a result?' asked Curval, who was being roundly fucked from behind. 'No,' said Duclos, 'but she did fall ill for more than 6 weeks.' 'Oh, that's something!' said the Duc. 'But as for me,' continued this scoundrel, 'I wish our man had chosen to tell her this news when she had her period.' 'Yes,' said Curval, 'tell us what you really think, M. le Duc – I can see from here you're hard, and you would quite simply have preferred her to die on the spot.' 'Well, fair enough,' said the Duc. 'Since that's what you want I'll go along with it – as for me, I don't have many scruples when it comes to the death of a girl.' 'Durcet,' said the Bishop, 'if you do not send these two rascals off to come, there will be trouble this evening.' 'Oh, by God!' said Curval to the Bishop. 'You fear for your flock? What difference would two or three more or less make? Come on, M. le Duc, let's go into the boudoir and let's go there together, with some company, for I can see these gentlemen do not wish to be scandalized this evening.' This was no sooner said than done, and our two libertines were followed there by Zelmire, Augustine, Sophie, Colombe, Cupidon, Narcisse, Zélamir and Adonis, escorted by Brise-cul, Bande-au-ciel, Thérèse, Fanchon, Constance and Julie. After a while the screams of two or three women were heard, along with the roars of our two scoundrels, who were disgorging their come together; Augustine returned, holding her handkerchief to her nose, which was bleeding, and Adélaïde with a handkerchief over her breast; as for Julie, always libertine and adept enough to keep out of harm's way, she was laughing like a madwoman, and saying that without her they would never have come. The troop returned; Zélamir and Adonis had their buttocks still covered in come; and, having assured their friends that they had conducted themselves with all possible decency and modesty in order to be beyond reproach and that they were now perfectly calm and ready to listen, Duclos was ordered to continue and did so in these terms.

'I am sorry,' said that lovely whore, 'that M. de Curval was in such a hurry to relieve his needs, for I had two stories about pregnant women to tell him that might perhaps have given him some pleasure; I know his taste for these sorts of women and I am sure that if he were still to have a slight hankering, he would find these two tales entertaining.' 'Tell them – tell them all the same,' said Curval. 'Don't you know that come has never had the least impact on my feelings, and that the moment I am most in love with evil is always the moment I've just spilled some?'

'Well then,' said Duclos, 'I've seen a man whose mania was to watch a woman give birth: he would frig himself while observing her labour pains, and would come over the baby's head as soon as he could see it.

'A second man would plant a woman who was 7 months pregnant on a free-standing pedestal over 15 feet high: she had to stand straight and keep her head, because if she were unfortunate enough to lose it, she and her unborn fruit would be

crushed for ever. This libertine I'm describing, caring very little
for the plight of this poor woman (whom he'd pay for this),
would keep her up there until he had come and would frig
himself in front of her as he shouted, "Oh, the beautiful statue,
the fine ornament, the beautiful empress!"'

'You would have given the column a shake, isn't that so, Curval?'
said the Duc. 'Oh not at all, you're quite mistaken! I know all
too well the respect we owe Nature and her works – is not the
most interesting of all these the propagation of our species? Is
this not a kind of miracle that we should endlessly worship and
that should inspire in us the most tender admiration for the
women who do this? As for me, I can never see a pregnant
woman without feeling moved – do you realize what kind of
creature a woman is? One who can, like an oven, hatch some
snot deep inside her vagina? Is there anything more beautiful,
anything more moving than that? Constance, come here I beg
you, come so I may kiss you upon the altar within which such
a profound mystery is now unfolding.' And as she was indeed
in his alcove he did not have far to go to find the temple he
wished to serve, but there is reason to believe this did not happen
in quite the manner Constance was expecting (though she only
half-believed his words), for she promptly uttered a scream that
bore no resemblance to what normally followed an act of
worship or tribute. And Duclos, seeing that silence had descended,
concluded her tales with the following story.

'I once knew,' said this lovely whore, 'a man whose passion
consisted in listening to children cry out: he required a mother
with a child of 3 or 4 years of age at most; he would order this
mother to beat her child severely in front of him and when the
little creature, upset by this treatment, began to cry, the mother
had to grab hold of the lecher's prick and frig it hard in front
of the child, whose face he would come over as soon as he saw
it covered in tears.'

'I wager,' said the Bishop to Curval, 'that this man did not like
propagation any more than you do.' 'I can believe it,' said Curval.

'In any case, he must have been, according to the theory of a very intelligent lady (or so they say) – he must have been, as I say, a great scoundrel, for any man, according to her, who does not like animals, children or pregnant women is a monster who deserves to be broken on the wheel. So there's my trial over and done with at that old busybody's court,' said Curval, 'for I certainly don't like any of those three things.' And as it was late and the interruption had taken up a large part of the evening, they went to eat. At supper they debated the following questions, namely what purpose sensitivity served in man, and whether or not it was conducive to his happiness? Curval proved that it could only be dangerous and that it was the first sentiment that needed to be smothered in children, by familiarizing them from an early age with the most savage of sights; and with each one having debated the question differently they settled on Curval's opinion. After supper the Duc and he said that the women and young boys should be sent to bed and that there should be only men at the orgies; everyone agreed to this plan – they shut themselves away with the 8 fuckers, and spent almost the whole night getting fucked and drinking liqueurs. They went to bed for two hours at daybreak, and the following day brought with it both the events and the tales the reader shall find if he takes the trouble to read what follows.

29th day.

There is a proverb (and proverbs are a terribly good thing) – there is one, as I say, that claims that eating whets the appetite; this proverb, coarse though it may be, nonetheless has a very broad meaning: that by dint of committing atrocities one desires fresh ones, and the more one commits, the more one desires. This was the case of our insatiable libertines – out of unforgivable callousness, out of a despicable refinement of debauchery, they had, as we have said, condemned their unfortunate wives to perform the most foul and filthy services upon them as they left the privy. They did not stop there, and that very day a new law was proclaimed that seemed to be the product of the sodomitical libertinage of the day before – a new law, as I say, that stipulated that these wives would serve, starting from the 1st of December, in every respect as chamber pots for their needs, and that these needs – in a word, large or small – would only ever be relieved in their mouths; that any time Messieurs wanted to satisfy their needs, they would be followed by four sultanesses who would perform, once the need had been relieved, the service their wives had previously performed but could no longer perform any more as they were going to serve a far more serious purpose; that the four officiating sultanesses would be Colombe for Curval, Hébé for the Duc, Rosette for the Bishop and Michette for Durcet; and that the least mistake in either of these operations – the one regarding the wives or the one regarding the 4 young girls – would be punished with the utmost severity. These poor wives had no sooner learned of this new rule than they wept in despair – unfortunately without moving anyone. The only prescription was that each wife would serve her husband, and Aline, the Bishop, and that for this particular operation there could be no switching of roles. Two old women were also ordered to take it in turn to be present at this task, and the hour for this was unalterably fixed for the evening, at the end of the orgies; it was settled that they would always act in tandem, that during the operation itself the 4 sultanesses, while waiting to perform their service, would present their buttocks, and that the old women would go from one anus to the next, squeezing them, opening them up and indeed arousing them for the operation. Once this regulation was promulgated, they proceeded that morning with the corrections that had not been carried out the previous day, when they were taken with a desire for a male orgy: this operation took place in the sultanesses' quarters; all 8 of them were dispatched, and after them Adélaïde, Aline and Cupidon, all three of whom were also on the fateful list; the ceremony, with the particularities and all the formalities customary in such cases, lasted almost four hours, at the end of which the friends went down to lunch, their minds much inflamed – and especially Curval's, for he utterly cherished these operations and never took part in them without the most unmistakable erection. As for the Duc, he had come during them, as had Durcet. The latter, who was beginning to develop a very spiteful libertine streak when it came to Adélaïde, his dear wife, could not punish her without violent spasms of pleasure costing him his come. After lunch they went through for coffee; they would very much have liked a selection of sweet arses there, with Zéphire and Giton among the men and plenty of others should anyone have wanted them; this could have been arranged, but as for the sultanesses it would have been impossible, so, according to the order dictated by the table,[102] it was left to Colombe and Michette to serve everyone. Curval examined Colombe's arse, its motley hues – partly his own handiwork – inspiring some very peculiar desires in him, and put his prick between her thighs from behind as he gave her buttocks a good grope; his tool would occasionally, as it retraced its steps, knock – as if unwittingly – against the sweet hole it would dearly have liked to pierce. He watched it, he observed it. 'Good God!' he said to his friends. 'I'll give two hundred *louis* to the company this minute if I'm allowed to fuck this arse.' He contained himself nonetheless and did not even come; the Bishop made Zéphire come in his mouth and spilled his own while swallowing that of this delectable child; as for Durcet, he had himself kicked up the arse by Giton, made him shit and remained a virgin. They went through to the chamber of stories where each father, by a rather familiar arrangement, had his daughter with him on the sofa that evening, and listened with breeches dropped to our dear storyteller's 5 tales.

'It seemed that ever since the moment I diligently executed Madame Fournier's pious bequest, good fortune had rained down on my house,' said this lovely whore. 'I had never had so many rich acquaintances: one day the Benedictine prior, one of my best clients, came to tell me he had heard of a rather peculiar fantasy and, indeed, having seen it carried out by one of his friends who was smitten with it, he wanted to carry it out himself, and thus asked me for a girl who was very hairy. I gave him a tall creature of 28 years of age with tufts a yard long under her armpits and over her crotch. "That's what I need," he told me, and because he was particularly attached to me and we had enjoyed ourselves together many times, he didn't hide himself from view. He had the girl strip naked and lie halfway across a sofa with both arms raised, and, wielding a pair of very sharp scissors, he began to shear this creature's armpits right down to the skin; from the armpits, he moved on to the crotch – he sheared this as well, but so meticulously that it didn't seem there had ever been the least trace of hair in either of the spots he had tackled. When he had finished his task, he kissed the parts he had just cropped and sprayed his come over that shorn crotch, in ecstasy at his handiwork.

'Another man insisted on a ceremony that was undoubtedly far more bizarre: this was the Duc de Florville;[103] I was ordered to bring him one of the most beautiful women I could find. A manservant received us and we entered the mansion through a side door. "Let us prepare this beautiful creature appropriately," the valet said to me, "so that Monsieur le Duc may have his way with her ... Follow me." Around corners and along corridors as dark as they were endless, we finally reach a gloomy apartment lit by just 6 altar candles placed on the floor around a mattress of black satin; the whole room was decorated in mourning and we were deeply afraid as we entered. "Don't worry," our guide told us, "not the slightest harm will come to you – but go along with everything," he said to the young girl, "and above all do exactly what I tell you." He had the girl strip entirely naked, unpinned her hair and let her curls – which were magnificent – tumble down; then he laid her on the mattress surrounded by the candles, enjoined her to play dead and above all to make sure she moved and breathed as little as possible throughout the whole scene. "For if by some misfortune my master – who's going to believe you are truly dead – sees through this ruse, he will storm out in a rage and you certainly won't be paid." As soon as he had posed the young lady in the attitude of a cadaver on the mattress, he had her mouth and eyes assume pained expressions, let her hair fall over her naked breast, placed a dagger beside her, and smeared chicken's blood over her heart to make a wound the size of a fist. "Above all don't be scared," he told the young girl again. "There's nothing you need to say, nothing you need to do – it's just a matter of staying absolutely still and breathing only when you see he's not too close to you.

Let's withdraw now," the valet told me. "Come, Madame – so you won't be worried for your young lady, I'm going to place you in a spot where you'll be able to hear and see the whole scene." We go out, leaving the girl rather agitated at first, but somewhat reassured nonetheless by the valet's words; he leads me into a closet adjoining the room in which the rites were to be celebrated and, through a badly pointed partition wall covered in black drape, I could hear everything. It was even easier to see as this drape was made only of crêpe – I could make out all the objects through it as if I had been in the room itself. The valet tugged on a bell pull – this was the signal – and a few minutes later we saw a tall, wizened, gaunt man of around 60 years of age enter the room; he was completely naked underneath a loose dressing gown of Indian taffeta. He paused upon entering (I should say at this point that we were observing the Duc in secret, for he believed he was utterly alone and was very far from thinking he was being watched). "Oh, what a beautiful cadaver!" he exclaimed at once . . . "What a beautiful dead girl . . . Oh, my God!" he said as he saw the blood and the dagger . . . "She must have been murdered just a moment ago. Oh, good God! Whoever did this deed must be hard!" And, as he frigged himself – "I would love to have seen him deliver the blow." And, as he touched her belly – "was she pregnant? . . . Sadly not." And as he continued to touch her – "such fine flesh, still warm . . . what a beautiful breast!" And then he bent over her, and kissed her mouth with incredible fervour. "She's still drooling," he said . . . "How I love this saliva!" And he thrust his tongue down her gullet again. No one could have delivered a finer performance than this girl – she remained as still as a post, and whenever the Duc was near her she did not breathe at all. Finally he grabbed her and, turning her over on to her belly – "I must examine this fine arse," he said, and as soon as he had seen it – "Oh, good God! What beautiful buttocks!" And then he kissed them, spread them and we clearly saw him put his tongue into the sweet little hole. "My word! That," he cried out in absolute raptures, "is one of the most superb cadavers I've ever seen in my life! Oh, how happy the man who took this girl's life must be, and what pleasure it must have given him!" This idea made him come: he

[Say he fondled the dagger.]

was lying beside her, squeezing her, his thighs glued against her buttocks and he came over her arsehole with extraordinary signs of pleasure – and shrieking like [a] devil as he spilled his come. "Oh, fuck! Fuck! How I wish I had killed her!" This was the end of the operation; the libertine stood up and disappeared. It was time for us to come in and pick up our dying girl: she was exhausted; the confinement, the dread – it had all sapped her senses, and she was on the verge of playing in earnest the role she had just impersonated so convincingly. We left with four *louis* from the valet, who, as you can well imagine, had kept at least half the money for himself.'

'Christ alive!' exclaimed Curval. 'Now there's a passion that has some savour, some spice about it at least.' 'I'm as hard as an ass!' said the Duc. 'I wager that character didn't stop there.' 'You can be sure of that, M. le Duc,' said Martaine, 'sometimes he prefers a little more reality. Md. Desgranges and I shall have occasion to persuade you of that much.' 'And what the devil are you up to in the meantime?' Curval asked the Duc. 'Leave me be, leave me be!' said the Duc. 'I'm fucking my daughter and imagining her dead.' 'Oh, you scoundrel!' said Curval. 'So that's two crimes in your head at once.' 'Oh, fuck!' said the Duc, 'I should very much like them to be more real!' And his impure sperm flew into Julie's vagina. 'Come on, then – continue, Duclos,' he said as soon as he was done. 'Continue, my dear friend, and don't let the Président come, for I can hear him incestifying his daughter. That little rascal is filling his head with wicked ideas. His parents entrusted me with his care – I have to keep an eye on his conduct and I don't want him turning into a pervert.' 'Oh, it's too late!' said Curval. 'It's too late – I'm coming! Oh, God damn it! What a beautiful corpse!' And the scoundrel, as he fucked Adélaïde's cunt, fantasized he was the Duc fucking his murdered daughter – the incredible waywardness of the libertine imagination, which cannot hear or see anything without wanting to imitate it that very instant. 'Duclos, continue,' said the Bishop, 'for the example shown by these rascals might seduce me and in my current state I might do worse than they.'

*

'Some time after this adventure, I went alone to visit another libertine,' said Duclos, 'whose mania, though perhaps more humiliating, was not as sombre. He receives me in a drawing room, its parquet floor covered with a very beautiful rug, has me strip naked, then get on all fours: "Let's see," [he] says, talking about the two Great Danes he had by his side, "let's see who will be the most nimble – my dogs or you. Go fetch!" And at this he throws some large roast chestnuts across the floor – and, talking to me as if I were an animal, "Fetch! Fetch!" he tells me. I race on all fours after the chestnut, with the aim of entering into the spirit of his fantasy and of bringing it back to him, but the two dogs, dashing after me, soon overtake me; they snaffle the chestnut and bring it back to their master. "You are downright clumsy," the owner tells me. "Are you afraid my dogs will eat you? Don't be scared of them – they won't do you any harm, but inwardly they'll hold you in contempt if they see you're less agile than they. Go on – it's your chance to get even . . . Fetch!" Another chestnut thrown and another victory for the dogs over me; in the end the game lasted two hours, during which time I was only agile enough to grab the chestnut once and bring it back in my mouth to the man who had thrown it. But whether I triumphed or not, these animals – trained for this game – never did me any harm; they seemed on the contrary to toy and play with me as if I were of the same species as they. "Come," said the owner, "that's enough work – it's time to eat." He rang a bell and a trusted valet entered. "Bring food for my animals," he said, and at this the valet brought in an ebony trough that he put on the floor and that was filled with a very delicious type of minced meat. "Come," he told me, "dine with my dogs, and see to it that they are not as nimble when eating as they were when racing." There was nothing for me to say – I had to obey, and, still on all fours, I stuck my head in the trough and, as everything was very clean and very tasty, I began to graze with the dogs, who very politely left me my share without fighting over it in the slightest; this was the moment our libertine came – the humiliation, the degradation to which he reduced a woman inflamed his wits to an incredible degree. "The bitch!" he said as he frigged himself. "The slut! Look at her eating with my dogs – that's how all women should be treated, and if they were, they wouldn't be so impertinent. They're domestic animals just like these dogs – why should we treat them any differently? Oh, you slut! Oh, you whore!" he shouted as he approached me and sprayed his come over my backside – "Oh, you bitch! There – I made you eat with my dogs!" And that was that: our man disappeared, I promptly put my clothes back on and found two *louis* on my cape – the usual sum, and one the lecher was doubtless used to paying for his pleasures.

'Now, Messieurs,' continued Duclos, 'I am obliged to retrace my steps and, as I bring the evening to a close, to tell you about two adventures that happened to me in my youth; as they are rather strong, they would have been out of place in the series of mild events with which you ordered me to begin – I have thus been obliged to put them to one side and keep them for you until the denouement. I was only 16 years old at the time and still at Madame Guérin's house: I had been put in the inner closet of a very distinguished gentleman's apartment, and told simply to wait, keep quiet and obey the lord who was to come and take his pleasure with me – but they had been careful not to tell me any more than this; I would not have been so scared had I been forewarned, and our libertine would certainly not have been so pleased. I had been in the closet for around an hour when at last the door swung open. It was the master himself. "What are you doing here, you hussy," he asked me with a look of surprise . . . "at this hour in my apartment? Oh, you whore!" he cried as he grabbed me so hard by the collar I couldn't breathe. "Oh, you beggar – you've come to rob me!" He then calls for help – a trusted valet appears: "La Fleur,"[104] his master tells him in a rage, "here's a thief I found hiding – strip her naked, and then get ready to carry out the order I'll give you." La Fleur obeys – in an instant I am stripped bare, and my clothes thrown out as they are taken off me. "Right," the libertine tells him, "now go find a sack, sew this whore inside and go throw her in the river." The valet heads off to find the sack – I leave it for you to wonder whether I made use of this interval to throw myself at the master's feet and beg him to spare me, assuring him that it was Md. Guérin, his usual bawd, who had placed me there herself and that I was no thief.

But the lecher, turning a deaf ear, grabs both my buttocks and, pummelling them like a brute – "Oh, fuck!" he says. "So I'm going to feed this fine arse here to the fish!" This was the only lubricious act he seemed to allow himself, and even then he didn't reveal anything to make me think libertinage was playing any part in this scene. The valet returns, carrying a sack – despite my pleas I am stuffed inside, I am sewn in, and La Fleur heaves me on to his shoulders: suddenly I hear the signs of the libertine's approaching climax and in all likelihood he had starting frigging himself as soon as I had been put in the sack. The moment La Fleur heaved me up, the scoundrel's come let fly. "In the river, in the river ... do you understand, La Fleur?" he said, babbling with pleasure. "Yes – in the river, and be sure to put a rock in the sack so the whore drowns all the sooner." There was no more to be said: we left, we went into an adjoining room where La Fleur, having unstitched the sack, handed me my clothes, gave me two *louis* and some unequivocal proof of his own manner of pursuing pleasure (which was very different to that of his master), and I returned to Madame Guérin, whom I vehemently scolded for not having forewarned me, and who – to patch things up with me – sent me two days later to the following tryst, for which I received even less warning.

'Rather like the one I just told you about, I found myself in the closet of a farmer-general's apartment, but this time I was in there with the same valet who had come to fetch me from Madame Guérin's on behalf of his master. As we waited for his master to arrive, the valet passed the time by showing me several jewels that were in the desk of this closet. "By God!" this honourable pimp said to me. "What harm would it do if you took one? That old Croesus is rich enough – I bet he doesn't even know how many or what kind of jewels he has in this desk. Believe me, don't think twice about it – and don't worry about me betraying you." Alas, I was only too keen to follow this perfidious advice: you are well aware of my inclinations – I have told you about them – so without any further encouragement I laid my hands on a little gold box worth seven or eight *louis*, not daring to grab anything more valuable. That was all that rascal of a valet wanted and, lest there be any doubt about it, I learned afterwards

that had I refused to take anything, he would have slipped one of those possessions into my pocket without my noticing. The master arrives, he gives me a warm welcome, the valet leaves and we remain together: this man did not behave like the other one – he really enjoyed himself; he kissed my backside a great deal, had himself flogged, made me fart in his mouth, put his prick in mine and, in a word, gorged himself on every kind and type of lubricity (except any involving my front parts), but for all his efforts he did not come. That moment had not yet arrived: all the things he had just done were for him minor episodes; now you shall see the denouement. "Oh my God!" he said to me. "I completely forgot there's a servant waiting in my ante-chamber for a little jewel I just promised to send his master this instant – allow me to be as good as my word and as soon as I've finished we shall get back to work." Guilty as I was of the little crime I had just committed at the instigation of that accursed valet, I leave you to imagine how these words made me tremble; for a moment I wanted to hold him back, then upon reflection I thought I'd be better off putting on a bold front and taking my chances. He opens the desk, looks inside, rummages around, and, unable to find what he wants, he casts furious glances in my direction: "You hussy!" he says to me at last. "Only you, and a valet I trust, have been in here recently; my box is missing – it could only be you who took it." "Oh, Monsieur!" I say to him trembling, "rest assured that I am incapable of . . ." "Come on, for God's sake!" he says angrily (though you will note that his breeches were still unbuttoned and his prick glued to his belly – that alone should have enlightened me and stopped me from being so worried – but I saw and noticed nothing at this point). "Come on, bitch! My box must be found." He orders me to strip naked; I throw myself at his feet twenty times begging him to spare me the humiliation of such an examination – nothing softens him, nothing moves him; he tears off my clothes angrily himself and, as soon as I'm naked, he goes through my pockets – and as you can imagine it doesn't take him long to find the box. "Oh, you villain!" he says to me. "Now I am convinced, bitch – you come to people's houses to rob them." And promptly summoning his trusted valet – "Go!" he told him all ablaze. "Go fetch me the commissioner this instant." "Oh, Monsieur," I cried out, "take pity on my youth! I was enticed, it was not my idea – I was put up to it . . ." "Well, then," said the lecher, "you can explain all that to the officer, but I want justice." The valet leaves, while he throws himself into an armchair, still hard and still very agitated – and hurling a thousand insults at me. "That beggar, that villain!" he was saying. "When I was happy to pay her the going rate – to come to my house to rob me like that . . . Oh, by God, we shall see about that!" At that instant there is a knock at the door and I see a man in robes enter. "M. le Commissaire," said the master, "here's a little hussy I am handing over to you and handing over to you naked, as I stripped her in order to search her. Here's the girl, there are her clothes and, what's more, the stolen box – and have her hanged, M. le Commissaire, whatever you do!" This was the moment he threw himself back into his armchair, coming as he did so. "Yes, have her hanged, good God! Let me see her hanged, good God, Mr. le Commissaire! Let me see her hanged, that's all I ask of you!" The alleged commissioner leads me away with the box and my rags, takes me into an adjoining room, disrobes to reveal the same valet who had received me and put me up to this theft – and whom in my confusion I had been unable to recognize. "Well then," he said to me, "did you get a real scare?" "Alas!" I said to him, "I can't take any more of this." "It's over," he told me, "and here's your reward." And at the same time, on behalf of his master, he hands me the very box I had stolen, returns my clothes, gives me a stiff drink and takes me back to Md. Guérin's.'

'That's an amusing mania,' said the Bishop. 'One might put it to better use in other matters, and with fewer scruples, for I must tell you I'm not one for scruples in libertinage. With fewer of these, as I say, this tale may teach us the best way to prevent a whore from complaining – however unjust the measures one wishes to take with her may be: one has only to lay traps for her, make her fall into them, and, as soon as one has ensured her guilt, one can then do anything one likes; there is no longer any fear she will dare complain – she will be too frightened of being reported or accused.' 'There is no doubt,' said Curval, 'that had I been in this financier's position I would have gone further, and you might not, my charming Duclos, have managed to get off so lightly.' As the tales had gone on for a long while this evening, there was no time for any frolicking before supper, so they went to eat, firmly resolved to make up for this after the meal. With everyone gathered together, the friends then decided once and for all to establish which of the young girls and young boys could be classed as men and women; in order to settle the matter it was proposed to frig any of those of either sex whom they had cause to suspect. Among the women, they were sure about Augustine, Fanny and Zelmire – these three charming little creatures, aged between 14 or 15, all came at the slightest touch. Hébé and Michette, still only 12 years old, were not even worth trying, so that left, among the sultanesses, Sophie, Colombe and Rosette – the 1st of whom was 14 years old and the two others 13. Among the boys they knew that Zéphire, Adonis and Céladon spilled their come like grown men; Giton and Narcisse were too young to be tried, so that left only Zélamir, Cupidon and Hyacinthe. The friends formed a circle around a pile of large cushions arranged on the floor: Champville and Duclos were put forward for masturbatory duties – the first, in her capacity as tribade, was to frig the three young girls, and the second, as mistress of the art of frigging pricks, was to masturbate the boys; they entered the ring formed by the friends' armchairs, and which had been filled with cushions, and Sophie, Colombe, Rosette, Zélamir, Cupidon and Hyacinthe were handed over to them; and each friend, to excite himself during this spectacle, took a child between his thighs – the Duc took Augustine; Curval, Zelmire; Durcet, Zéphire; and the Bishop, Adonis. The ceremony began with the boys and Duclos – her breasts and buttocks bared, her sleeve rolled up to her elbow – used all her skill to masturbate each of those delightful Ganymedes one after the other; it was impossible to do so more sensually – her hand rubbed with such deftness, she moved with such delicacy and such violence, she offered these young boys her mouth, her breast or her buttocks so artfully that there was no doubt that those who did not come were not yet able to do so. Zélamir and Cupidon were hard, but for all her efforts nothing came.

As for Hyacinthe, the climax came immediately at the 6ᵗʰ flick of her wrist: the come spurted over her breast and the child swooned as he fondled her backside – a sight remarked upon all the more as throughout the operation it had not crossed his mind to touch her front. Next it was the girls' turn: Champville, almost naked, her hair arranged very beautifully and as elegant as ever, did not look a day over thirty even though she was 50; the lubricity of this operation – from which, as an inveterate tribade, she intended to extract the greatest pleasure – added a lustre to her large black eyes, which had always been very beautiful. She used at least as much skill in her round as Duclos had in hers: she fondled the clitoris, the entrance to the vagina and the arsehole all at the same time, but Nature had not ripened in Colombe or Rosette – there was not even the slightest semblance of pleasure. The same could not be said of the beautiful Sophie: at the tenth stroke of Champville's fingers she swooned against the whore's breast; some halting little sighs, her beautiful cheeks flushed with the most tender crimson, her lips parted and moist – everything confirmed the delirium with which Nature had just overwhelmed her and she was declared a woman. The Duc, who was extraordinarily hard, ordered Champville to frig her a second time, and at her moment of climax the scoundrel drew close to mix his impure come with that of this young virgin; as for Curval, his business had been conducted between Zelmire's thighs, and the two others with the young boys they were gripping between their thighs. They went to bed and, as the following morning produced no event worthy of a place in this collection, and neither did lunch nor coffee, we shall head straight for the chamber, where Duclos, magnificently dressed, appeared on her rostrum to bring to a close, with the following five tales, the round of 150 stories that had been entrusted to her for the 30 days of the month of November.

30ᵗʰ day

'I do not know, Messieurs,' said that lovely whore, 'if you have heard of the Comte de Lernos's fantasy (one as peculiar as it is

dangerous) but a liaison I happened to have with him gave me
a profound knowledge of his machinations, and, as I found them
to be most extraordinary, I thought they should be included
among the pleasures you have ordered me to describe to you.
The Comte de Lernos's passion is to ruin as many young girls
and married women as he can, and aside from the books he
employs to seduce them, there is no end to the methods he has
devised to deliver them up to men; either he indulges their inclinations by uniting them with the object of their desires, or he
finds them lovers if they have none. He has a house for this very
purpose, where all the couples he arranges meet; he brings them
together, assures them they will be left in peace to rest, and takes
his pleasure watching them grapple with each other from a secret
closet. But the extent to which he multiplies these disorders and
the efforts he makes to forge these little marriages is remarkable:
he has contacts in almost all the convents in Paris, and among
a great number of married women, and he goes about it so well
that not a day goes by without three or four rendezvous taking
place at his house; he never fails to spy on their pleasures, without them suspecting a thing, but because he is always alone at
the peephole of his observatory, no one knows how he proceeds
to his climax or what kind of climax it is – only the deed itself
is known, so there it is, and I thought it was worth describing
to you.

    'You may perhaps find the old Président Desportes's fantasy
more amusing: forewarned of the etiquette that was usually
observed at this lecher's house, I arrive there at around 10 o'clock
in the morning and, perfectly naked, I approach the armchair
in which he is sombrely ensconced, present my buttocks to be
kissed, and promptly fart in his face. Excited by this, my Président rises, grabs a handful of birches he had beside him and
starts to chase after me, while my immediate concern is to get
away. "You impertinent girl!" he says as he pursues me. "I'll
teach you to come to my house and behave so abominably!" It's
for him to pursue me, and for me to keep running away:[105] in
the end I make for the space between the bed and the wall, and
crouch down as if in an impregnable retreat, but I am soon
cornered there; the Président's threats redouble as he sees me in

his grasp, he brandishes his birch, threatens to strike me with it, I huddle up, I cower, I am no bigger than a mouse; this air of terror and humiliation finally prompts him to come and the lecher sprays my breasts as he roars with pleasure.'

'What? Without giving you a single blow with his birch?' asked the Duc. 'Without so much as brushing me with them,' replied Duclos. 'Now there's a very patient man,' said Curval. 'My friends – admit that we are less so when we have the instrument Duclos mentioned in our hands.' 'A little patience, Messieurs,' said Champville. 'I shall soon show you men of the same type who won't be as patient as the Président Md. Duclos is describing here.' And the latter, seeing that the silence the friends were now observing would allow her to resume her tale, proceeded in the following manner.

'Shortly after this adventure, I visited the Marquis de Saint-Giraud, whose fantasy was to place a naked woman in a swing and raise her to a very great height: with each push the woman flies past his nose; he waits for you, and at that moment you must either fart or get a slap on the arse; I satisfied him as best I could – I was slapped several times, but I offered him a great many farts. And when the lecher had at last come after an hour of this tedious and tiresome ceremony, the swing stopped and my audience with the Marquis was at an end.

'Around three years after I had become the mistress of Madame Fournier's house, a man came to me with a peculiar proposal: he wanted to find libertines who would have their way with his wife and daughter, but only on condition that he would be hidden in a corner in order to see everything that was being done to them; he would hand them over to me, he said, and not only would the money I earned from them be mine alone, but he would give me a further two *louis* for every tryst I arranged for them. There was just one other thing: for his wife he wanted only men with a certain penchant, and for his daughter men whose fantasy was of a different type; for his wife he required men who would shit on her breasts, and for his daughter he required men who, as they hitched up her skirts, would expose her backside in full view of the hole through which he would be watching (so that he might contemplate it at his leisure) and who would then come in her mouth; he would not hand over the goods for any other passions than these two. Having made this man promise that he would answer for any eventuality should his wife and daughter complain about being brought to my house, I agreed to everything he wanted and promised him that the individuals he was bringing me would be looked after just as he intended. The very next morning he brought me his goods: the wife was a woman of 36 years of age, not particularly pretty, but tall and shapely, with a very sweet and modest air about her; the young lady was 15 years old, blonde, a little chubby and with the most tender and appealing physiognomy in the world. "In truth, Monsieur," said the wife, "you are making us do things here . . ." "It mortifies me," said the lecher, "but it must be so, believe me – accept your fate, for I shall not waver, and should you put up the least resistance to the proposals and procedures to which you will be subjected, Madame, and you, Mademoiselle, I shall take you both to the furthest depths of an estate from which you will never return in all your days." At this the wife shed some tears and, as the man for whom she was destined was waiting, I invited her to go through to the room intended for her while her daughter would remain perfectly safe in another room with my girls until it was her turn. At this cruel moment there were a few more tears and I could clearly see that this was the first time this brutal husband had demanded such a thing of his wife – and unfortunately it would be a difficult debut, for aside from the baroque taste of the character to whom I was delivering her, this was a most imperious and brusque old libertine and one who would not treat her very honourably. "Come now, no tears," said the husband as he came in. "Remember that I'm watching you and that if you do not fully satisfy the gentleman to whom you have been delivered, I shall come in myself and force you to do so." She enters, and the husband and I go through to the room where we could see everything. One cannot imagine how inflamed that old scoundrel's imagination became as he observed his unfortunate wife fall prey to a stranger's brutality. He took great delight in each and every thing demanded of her: the modesty – the candour – of this poor woman, humiliated by the atrocious acts of this libertine having his way with her, offered him a delicious spectacle, but when he saw her brutally thrown to the floor and the old Barbary ape to whom I had given her shit on her breasts, and when he saw his wife's tears and disgust at the proposal and execution of this abomination, he could not hold back any longer and the hand with which I was frigging him was instantly covered in come. Finally this first scene came to an end and, as much pleasure as it had given him, his enjoyment of the second was something else altogether. It was not without great difficulty, and above all not without great threats, that we had managed to get the young girl into the room, as she had witnessed her mother's tears without knowing what had caused them. The poor little thing kicked up a dreadful fuss; finally we made up her mind for her. The man to whom I delivered her was perfectly aware of everything he had to do – I had chosen to reward one of my regular clients with this good fortune and to show his gratitude he agreed to everything I demanded of him. "Oh, what a fine arse!" exclaimed the libertine father, as soon as his daughter's trick had stripped it completely naked. "Oh, good God! What fine buttocks!" "Eh? What?" I replied. "Is this the first time you've seen them, then?" "Yes, indeed," he told me. "I needed this ploy in order to enjoy this spectacle, but if it's the first time I've seen this fine backside I promise you it won't be the last!" I frigged him vigorously – he was in ecstasy, but when he saw the indignity demanded of this young virgin, when he saw the hands of a consummate libertine roaming over that beautiful body which had never suffered such caresses, when he saw her ordered to her knees, saw her forced to open her mouth, saw a large prick thrust inside and saw it come there, he leapt back cursing like a man possessed, swearing that in all his days he had never tasted so much pleasure, and leaving between my fingers the irrefutable proof of that pleasure. There was no more to be said: the poor women withdrew in floods of tears and the husband, all too enraptured by such a scene, doubtless found some way to persuade them to offer him the spectacle of frequent repeat performances, as they came to my house for more than 6 years; and, following the orders

I would receive from the husband, I [submitted] these two unfortunate creatures to all the different passions I've been describing for you, with the possible exception of 10 or 12 that the women were unable to satisfy as these were not practised at my house.'

'What a palaver – over prostituting a wife and daughter!' said Curval. 'As if those sluts were fit for anything else! Are they not born for our pleasures and from that moment on must they not satisfy them no matter what? I have had many wives,' said the Président, 'three or four daughters, of whom, thank God, there remains only Milli Adélaïde – whom I believe M. le Duc is fucking at the moment; but if any of these creatures had refused the whoring to which I regularly subjected them, may I be damned alive – or worse, condemned to fuck only cunts for the rest of my life – if I had failed to blow their brains out.' 'Président, you are hard,' said the Duc. 'Your filthy words always betray you.' 'Hard? No,' said the Président, 'but I'm about to make Milli Sophie shit, and I'm hoping her delicious shit will perhaps have some effect.' 'Oh, my word – more than I thought!' said Curval, having gobbled down the turd. 'There – in the name of that God I don't give a damn about – there's my prick gaining in firmness! Which one of you gentlemen wants to join me in the boudoir?' 'I do,' said Durcet, dragging Aline, whom he had been pawing for an hour, behind him; and our two libertines – taking with them Augustine, Fanny, Colombe and Hébé, Zélamir, Adonis, Hyacinthe, and Cupidon, along with Julie and the two old women, Madame Martaine and Madame Champville, Antinoüs and Hercule – reappeared triumphant after half an hour, with each having spilled his come in the sweetest excesses of depravity and libertinage. 'Now,' Curval said to Duclos, 'give us your denouement, my dear friend, and if it gets me hard again you can pride yourself on a miracle for – my word! – I haven't spilled so much come at once in more than a year. It's true that . . .' 'Goodness!' said the Bishop, 'if we listen to him it will be far worse than the passion Duclos is to narrate, so rather than go from strong to mild, be so good as to keep quiet and let us listen to our storyteller.' Whereupon this beautiful whore concluded her tales with the following passion.

'It is finally time, Messieurs,' she said, 'for me to tell you about the passion of the Marquis de Mesanges, to whom you will remember I had sold the daughter of the hapless cobbler who was rotting away in prison with his poor wife while I enjoyed the bequest left him by his mother. As it was Lucile who dealt with him, you will hear this tale, if it pleases you, from her own lips: "I arrive at the Marquis's house," this charming creature told me, "at about ten o'clock in the morning. As soon as I am inside, all the doors close behind me. 'What are you doing here, you villain?' the Marquis asks me all ablaze. 'Who gave you permission to come and interrupt me?' And as you hadn't given me any warning, you can easily imagine how terrified I was by this welcome. 'Come now – strip naked!' continued the Marquis. 'Now I have you, you slut, you will never leave here again . . . you are going to die – these are your final moments.' I then burst into tears; I threw myself at the Marquis's feet but there was no way of swaying him. And as I was not undressing quickly enough, he tore my clothes himself as he forcibly ripped them from my body, but what filled me with horror was the sight of him throwing them into the fire as he removed them. 'None of this will be needed any more,' he said as he threw all the clothes he had gathered one by one into the great hearth. 'You don't need a dress any more, or a cape, or any finery – all you need is a coffin.' The next moment I was completely naked, then the Marquis, who had never seen me before, considered my backside for a moment, groped it as he cursed, spread it, squeezed it, but did not kiss it. 'Come now, whore,' he said, 'that's that – you're going the same way as your clothes, and I'm going to tie you to these andirons. Fuck yes! Damn yes! I'll burn you alive, slut – I'll have the pleasure of breathing in the smell of your burnt flesh!' And as he says this he falls swooning into his armchair and comes – spurting his seed over my clothes, which are still burning; he rings a bell, a valet leads me away, and in a neighbouring room I find all I need to get dressed – in finery twice as beautiful as that which he had destroyed."

*

'That was the tale Lucile told me – it remains to be seen now whether it was for this or for something worse that he used the young maiden I sold him.' 'For something far worse,' said Madame Desgranges, 'and you have done well to introduce the Marquis to these gentlemen, for I shall also have occasion to speak of him.' 'May you, Madame,' said Duclos to Madame Desgranges, 'and you, my dear colleagues,' she added, addressing her two other friends, 'do so with greater zest, wit and charm than I managed. It is your turn now – mine is finished – and all that remains for me is to beg these gentlemen to forgive me for the tedium I may have caused them, for there is an almost inevitable monotony with tales of this kind, which, merged together within a single frame, can barely stand out in their own right.' With these words, the lovely Duclos paid her respects to the company and stepped down from her rostrum to approach these gentlemen's sofas, where she was applauded and exalted by all and sundry. Supper was served and she was invited to join the friends – an honour not previously granted any woman. Her conversation was as charming as her story-telling had been entertaining, and as a reward for the pleasure she had given the assembled audience, she was made director-general of the two harems with a promise, given privately by the 4 friends, that no matter the extremes to which they might be driven against the women in the course of this expedition, she would always be looked after and would most certainly be returned to her house in Paris, where the company would amply compensate her for the time she had lost and the trouble she had gone to for the sake of their pleasures. Curval, the Duc and she got so utterly drunk over supper that all three were almost incapable of making it to the orgies; they left Durcet and the Bishop to enjoy these after their own fashion, and went off with Champville, Antinoüs, Brise-cul, Thérèse and Louison to enjoy themselves in [the] far boudoir, where one may be sure they committed and uttered at least as many atrocities and abominations as the two other friends were able to conceive. At two o'clock in the morning everyone went to bed, and so ended the month of 9ber and the first part of this lubricious and interesting narrative; we shall not make our

public wait for the second part if we see they have warmly
received the first.

Mistakes I have made.

I have revealed too much about the privy episodes at the beginning – these must only be developed after the tales that refer to
them.

Spoken too much about active and passive sodomy; conceal
this until the tales speak of it.

I was wrong to make Duclos sensitive to her sister's death – it
does not match the rest of her character – change that.

If I said that Aline was a maiden upon arriving at the castle
I was wrong – she is not and must not be; the Bishop has deflowered her from all sides.

And as I have been unable to reread myself, this must surely
be teeming with other mistakes.

When I make a fair copy, one of my first concerns should be
to have a notebook nearby at all times, where I shall need to
enter each incident and each portrait as I write them for without
that I shall become horribly confused because of the multitude
of characters.

Start, for the second part, from the principle that Augustine
and Zéphire are already sleeping in the Duc's bedroom in the
1st part, as Adonis and Zelmire are in Curval's, Hyacinthe and
Fanny are in Durcet's, Céladon and Sophie are in the Bishop's,
even though all this lot have yet to be deflowered.

Part Two.

The hundred and fifty passions of the second class, or dual passions, comprising 31 days in X^{ber} taken up by Champville's narration, to which is attached the detailed journal of the scandalous events at the castle during this month.

Plan.

The 1st of X^{ber}. Madame Champville takes over the storytelling and relates the following 150 stories. (The numbers precede the tales).

1. Only wants to deflower girls from three to seven years of age, but in the cunt. He is the one who deflowers Champville at five years of age.

2. He has a girl of nine years of age bound up into a ball and deflowers her from behind.

3. He wants to rape a girl of twelve to thirteen years of age and only deflowers her with a pistol to her throat.

4. He wants to frig a man against a maiden's cunt – the come serves as pomade; then he fucks her cunt, the maiden held down by the man.

5. He wants to deflower three girls in a row: one from the cradle, one of five years of age, and one of seven.

The 2nd. 6. He wants to deflower girls from nine to thirteen years of age only; his prick is enormous – four women are needed to hold down the maiden for him. It is the same man Martaine described, who buggers only three year olds – the man of Hell.[1]

7. He has girls from ten to twelve years of age deflowered in front of him by his valet and touches them only on the arse during this procedure; at times he fondles the virgin's arse, at times that of the valet – he comes over the valet's arse.

8. He wants to deflower a girl due to be married the following day.[2]

9. He wants the wedding to take place and to deflower the bride between the Mass and the wedding night.

10. He wants his valet, a very cunning fellow, to marry girls from all over and to bring them to him; the master fucks them, then traffics them to bawds.

The third. 11. He only wants to deflower two sisters.

12. He marries the girl, deflowers her, but he has tricked her and as soon as the deed is done he ditches her there.

13. He fucks the maiden only the moment after a man has deflowered her in front of him; he wants her cunt to be all smeared with sperm.

14. He deflowers with a dildo, and comes over the opening he has made without introducing his prick.

15. He wants only nobly born maidens and pays their weight in gold. This will turn out to be the Duc, who will admit to having deflowered more than fifteen hundred over the last thirty years.

[*The fourth.*] 16. He forces a brother to fuck his sister in front of him, and he fucks her afterwards; he has them both shit beforehand.

17. He forces a father to fuck his daughter after he has deflowered her himself.

18. He takes his daughter to a brothel when she turns nine and deflowers her there as she is held down by the bawd; he has had twelve daughters and has deflowered them all in this manner.

19. He wants to deflower only women from thirty to forty years of age.

20. He wants to deflower only nuns and spends enormous sums to have them – and have them he does.

This is the evening of the fourth, and that same evening at the orgies the Duc, assisted by Duclos, deflowers Fanny, who is held down by the four old women. He fucks her twice in a row; she faints – he fucks her the second time when she is unconscious.

The fifth. As a result of these stories, to celebrate the festivities of the fifth week, Hyacinthe and Fanny are married that day and the marriage is consummated in front of everyone.

21. He wants the mother to hold down her daughter; he fucks the mother first and then deflowers the child held down by the mother. This is the same one Desgranges describes on the twentieth of February.

22. He enjoys only adultery: he requires virtuous wives renowned for being happily married; he fills them with disgust for their husbands.

23. He wants the husband to prostitute his wife himself and hold her down while he fucks her. The friends will imitate this immediately.

24. He places a married woman on a bed and fucks her cunt while this woman's daughter, in full view above her, has him kiss her cunt; a moment later he fucks the daughter's cunt as he kisses the mother's arsehole. When he kissed the daughter's cunt he made it piss; when he kisses the mother's arse he makes it shit.

25. He has four legitimate daughters, now married; he wants to fuck all four of them – he gets all four pregnant so that one day he can have the pleasure of deflowering the children he has had with each of them and whom the husbands believe to be their own.

Whereupon the Duc tells of a case (but one that does not count towards the total because it cannot be repeated, and therefore cannot constitute a passion) – he tells, as I say, of a man he knew who fucked the three children he had by his mother, including a daughter whom he married to his son, so that by fucking this girl he was fucking his sister, his daughter and his daughter-in-law, while forcing his son to fuck his own sister and mother-in-law. Curval tells another one about a brother and sister who decided on a mutual exchange of children: the sister had a son and daughter, as did the brother; they mixed them up so that they alternated between fucking their nieces and nephews and fucking their own children, and the children alternated between fucking their first cousins and fucking their own brothers and sisters, while the father and mother, that is the brother and sister, also fucked each other. That evening Fanny's cunt is offered up to the company but as the Bishop and M. Durcet do not fuck cunts, she is fucked only by Curval and the Duc. From this moment she wears a little ribbon around her neck and after the loss of both her virginities she will wear a very broad pink one.

The sixth X^{ber}. 26. He has himself frigged while a woman's clitoris is frigged, and wants to come at the same time as the girl, but comes over the buttocks of the man who is frigging the girl.

27. He kisses a girl's arsehole while a second fondles his arse and a third his prick; they take it in turns so that each has her arsehole kissed, each fondles his prick and each fondles his arse. They must all fart.

28. He licks a cunt while he fucks a second girl in the mouth and a third licks his arse, and they take it in turns as above; the cunts must all come and he swallows the come.

29. He sucks on a shitty arse, has his own shitty arse stroked with a tongue and frigs himself upon another shitty arse, then all three girls switch round.

30. He has two girls frigged in front of him and by turns fucks those doing the frigging from behind while they continue to sapphotize each other.[3]

That day they discover that Zéphire and Cupidon frig each other but have yet to be buggered by each other; they are punished. Fanny's cunt is roundly fucked at the orgies.

The seventh. 31. He wants an older girl to corrupt a younger one, to frig her, to give her poor counsel and to finish by holding her down for him while he fucks her – whether she is a virgin or not.

32. He wants four women: he fucks two of them in the cunt and two in the mouth, taking care to put his prick in the mouth of one only at the very moment it comes out of the other's cunt; a fifth girl follows him around throughout, frigging his arse with a dildo.

33. He wants twelve whores: six young ones and six old ones, and if possible six mothers and six daughters; he gamahuches their cunts, arses and mouths; from the cunt he wants urine, from the mouth he wants saliva, and from the arse he wants farts.

34. He employs eight women to frig him, all from different positions. This will need to be described.

35. Wants to see three men and three girls fuck each other in different positions.

The eighth. 36. He forms twelve groups of two girls each, but they crowd around him in such a way that they show only their arses; the rest of the body is entirely hidden. He frigs himself as he observes all these buttocks.

37. He has 6 couples frigging at the same time in a hall of mirrors: each couple comprises two girls frigging each other in various lubricious poses; he is in the middle of the room, watching both the couples and their doubles in the mirrors, and he comes in the midst of all this as he is frigged by an old woman. He has kissed the buttocks of these couples.

38. He gets four common whores drunk and has them beaten up in front of him, and once they are very drunk he wants them to vomit in his mouth; he picks them as old and as ugly as possible.

39. He has a girl shit in his mouth but does not eat it, and meanwhile a second girl sucks his prick and fondles his arse; he shits as he comes in the hand of the one socratizing him; the girls switch places.

40. He has a man shit in his mouth and eats it while a little boy frigs him, then the man frigs him and he has the boy shit.

That evening at the orgies Curval deflowers Michette, following as ever the same routine as she is held down by the four old women and he is assisted by Duclos; we shall repeat this no longer.

The ninth. 41. He fucks a girl in the mouth having just shat in her mouth; a second girl lies on top of the first, with the head of the first between her thighs, and a third drops a stool on the face of the second – and he, thus fucking his own turd in the mouth of the first, will eat the turd offered by the third upon the face of the second, and then they switch places so that each girl performs all three roles in succession.

42. He receives thirty women in a day and has them all shit in his mouth: he eats the turds of three or four of the prettiest ones; he repeats this episode five times a week, which means that he sees seven thousand eight hundred girls each year. When Champville visits him he is seventy years old and has been occupying himself in this way for fifty years.

43. He sees twelve of them each day and swallows the twelve turds; he sees them all together.

44. He gets into a bath and thirty women fill the tub by pissing and shitting into it; he comes as it covers him and as he bathes in it all.

45. He shits in front of four women, insists that they watch him and help him do a turd; next he wants them to share and eat it, and then they each do one of their own – he mixes them together and eats all four, but the women have to be at least sixty years old.

That evening, Michette's cunt is offered up to the company. From this moment she wears the little scarf.

The tenth. 46. He has a girl A and another girl B shit. He then forces B to eat A's turd and A to eat B's turd. Next they both shit and he eats their two turds.

47. He wants a mother and three daughters, and he eats the girls' shit on their mother's arse, and the mother's shit on one of her daughters' arses.

48. He forces a girl to shit in her mother's mouth and to wipe her arse with her mother's breasts; next he eats the turd from

the mother's mouth, and afterwards makes the mother shit in her daughter's mouth – and will once again eat the turd from it. It would be better to put a son and his mother to distinguish it from the previous one.

49. He wants a father to eat his son's turd and he eats the father's turd.

50. He wants the brother to shit in his sister's cunt, and he eats the turd; then the sister has to shit in her brother's mouth, and he eats the turd.

The eleventh. 51. She warns that she will speak of impieties and tells of a man who wants a whore to proffer appalling blasphemies as she frigs him; he in turn says some appalling ones himself. His pleasure throughout consists of kissing her arse – this is all he does.

52. He wants the girl to come and frig him in the evening in a church, especially when the Blessed Sacrament is exposed. He places himself as close as he can to the altar and fondles her arse throughout.

53. He goes to confession solely to make his confessor hard: he tells him obscenities and frigs himself in the confessional as he is speaking.

54. He wants the girl to go to confession; he waits until the moment she leaves to fuck her in the mouth.

55. He fucks a whore during a Mass performed in his own chapel and comes at the elevation.

That evening the Duc deflowers Sophie's cunt and blasphemes a great deal.

The twelfth. 56. He pays off a confessor who gives him his seat for the confessions of his young boarders; he thus eavesdrops on their confessions and, as he hears them, gives them the worst possible advice.

57. He wants his daughter to go to confession with a monk in his pay, and is placed where he can hear everything, but the monk also orders his penitent to hitch up her skirts during confession, and her arse is positioned so that her father can see

it – he thus hears his daughter's confession and looks at her arse at the same time.

58. Has completely naked whores celebrate Mass. And he frigs himself over the buttocks of another whore as he looks on.

59. He makes his wife go to confession with a monk in his pay who seduces his wife and fucks her in front of her husband, who is hidden; if his wife refuses, he comes out and helps the confessor.

That day they celebrated the festivities of the sixth week with the marriage of Céladon and Sophie, which is consummated, and in the evening Sophie's cunt is offered up and she wears the scarf.

It is because of this event that only four passions are listed.

The thirteenth. 60. Fucks whores on the altar just as Mass is about to be offered; their arses are naked on the sacred stone.

61. He has a naked whore straddle a large crucifix: he fucks her cunt from behind as she holds this pose so that Christ's head rubs against the whore's clitoris.

62. He farts and has the other fart in the chalice, he pisses into it and has the other piss into it, he shits into it and has the other shit into it, and ends up coming into it.

63. He has a young boy shit on a paten[4] and he eats it while the child sucks him off.

64. He has two whores shit on a crucifix, he shits on it after they do, and they frig him over the three turds that now cover the idol's face.

The fourteenth. 65. He smashes up crucifixes, images of the Virgin and of the Eternal Father, shits on the debris and burns it all.

[ ][5] The same man has a mania for taking a whore to a sermon and having himself frigged during the Word of God.

66. He goes to communion and returns to have four whores shit in his mouth.

67. He makes her go to communion and fucks her in the mouth on her return.

68. He interrupts the priest during a Mass held in his own chapel – he interrupts him, as I say, to frig into the chalice, then orders the girl to make the priest come into it too, and forces him to swallow it all.

70. He interrupts him when the host is consecrated and forces the priest to fuck the whore with his host.

They discover that day that Augustine and Zelmire frig together; the two of them are severely punished.

The fifteenth. 71. He has the whore fart on the host, farts on it himself and swallows the host afterwards as he fucks her.

72. The same man who had himself nailed into a casket, and of whom Duclos spoke, forces the whore to shit on the host; he shits on it too and throws the whole lot into the latrine.

73. Rubs it against the whore's clitoris, has her come over it, then he thrusts it up her and fucks her with it there until he in turn comes over it.

74. He carves it up with a knife and has the crumbs thrust up his arse.

75. He has himself frigged over the host, comes over it, and, later, when he has regained his composure and his come has flowed, has a dog eat it all.

The same evening the Bishop consecrates a host and Curval deflowers Hébé with it: he thrusts it into her cunt and comes over it. They consecrate many more and the previously deflowered sultanesses are all fucked with the hosts.

The 16th. Champville announces that profanity, which earlier formed the principal element of her tales, will now only be incidental, and what is known in brothels as the little ceremonies of dual passions will form the main subject. She begs them remember that everything linked to this will only be incidental, but that there will nevertheless be a difference between her own tales and those of Duclos on the same subject, namely that Duclos never spoke of anything other than a man with a woman, whereas she – she will always combine numerous women with the man.

76. He has himself flogged during Mass by a whore, he fucks a second in the mouth, and comes at the elevation.

77. He has himself lightly flogged across the arse with a cat-o'-nine-tails by two women; they give ten lashes each and fondle his arsehole in between.

78. He has himself flogged by four different whores while they fart in his mouth; they switch so that each of them flogs and farts in turn.

79. He has himself flogged by his wife as he fucks his daughter, and next by his daughter as he fucks his wife; it is the same one of whom Duclos spoke and who prostitutes his daughter and his wife at the brothel.

80. He has himself flogged by two whores at once: one from in front and one from behind, and when he is ready he fucks one while the other flogs him, then the second while the 1st flogs him.

The same evening Hébé's cunt is offered up and she wears the little ribbon, as she cannot wear the large one until she has lost both her virginities.

The seventeenth. 81. He has himself flogged as he kisses a boy's arse while fucking a whore in the mouth; next he fucks the boy in the mouth as he kisses the whore's arsehole and continues to receive a whipping from another whore – then he has himself flogged by the boy, fucks the mouth of the whore who flogged him and has himself flogged by the whore whose arse he kissed.

82. He has himself flogged by an old woman, fucks an old man in the mouth, and has the daughter of this man and this woman shit into his mouth; then they switch so that each plays all three roles.

83. He has himself flogged as he frigs and comes over a crucifix pressed against a whore's buttocks.

84. He has himself flogged as he fucks a whore from behind with the host.

85. He has a whole brothel paraded before him: he receives

a whipping from all the whores as he kisses the bawd's arsehole and she farts and shits in his mouth.

The eighteenth. 86. He has himself flogged by some coachmen and stable boys – receiving them two by two – and always making the one without the whip fart in his mouth; he receives 10 to 16 of them each morning.

87. He has himself held down by three whores, a fourth straddles him on all fours and flays him; all four switch places and take turns straddling him.

88. He enters, naked, to find six whores around him: he begs forgiveness, throws himself to his knees, each girl orders a penance and for each penance he refuses he receives a hundred lashes of the whip; it is the whore he has refused who flogs him. These penances are moreover all utterly filthy: one wants to shit in his mouth, the other to make him lick her spit off the floor; this one here wants her cunt licked when she has her period, that one there between her toes, another her snot, &c.

89. Fifteen whores visit him, three by three: one flogs, one sucks him off, another shits, then the one who shat flogs him, the one who sucked him off, shits, and the one who flogged him sucks him off. He receives all fifteen this way; he sees nothing, he hears nothing, he is intoxicated – a bawd oversees everything. He repeats this episode six times a week. (This one is a charming one to carry out and I recommend it to you: it has to proceed at a very quick pace, each whore must give twenty-five lashes of the whip, and it is between these lashings that the first one sucks and the third shits. If he wants each whore to give fifty lashes, he will have received seven hundred and fifty, which is not too many.)

90. Twenty-five whores soften his arse by smacking and groping it; he is left alone only when his backside is completely numb.

In the evening they flog the Duc as he deflowers Zelmire's cunt.

The nineteenth. 91. He has himself tried by six whores – each has her role: he is condemned to be hanged; he is indeed hanged, but the rope breaks; this is the moment he comes. Link this to one of Duclos's that resembles it.

92. He has six old women placed in a semicircle; three young whores flay him in front of this semicircle of duennas who all spit in his face.

93. One whore teases his arsehole with a birch-handle, a second, standing in front him, flogs him across his thighs and prick; in this way he comes over the breasts of the flagellatrix in front of him.

94. Two women flay him with bulls' pizzles as a third, on her knees before him, has him come over her breasts.

She tells only four this evening because of the marriage of Zelmire and Adonis, which celebrates the seventh week and which is consummated since Zelmire's cunt was deflowered the day before.

The twentieth. 95. He does battle with six women whose flogging he pretends to wish to evade; he wants to strip the birches from their hands, but they are stronger and fustigate him despite his efforts; he is naked.

96. He runs the gauntlet[6] between two rows of twelve whores; he is flogged all over his body and comes after the ninth run.

97. He has himself flogged on the soles of his feet, on his prick, his thighs; while he is stretched out on a sofa three women straddle him and shit in his mouth.

98. Three whores whip him in turn, one with a cat-o'-nine-tails, another with a bull's pizzle, the third with a birch. A fourth, on her knees before him as her arsehole is fondled by the lecher's lackey, sucks his prick while he frigs that of his lackey, who comes over the buttocks of the whore sucking him off.

99. He is surrounded by six whores: one pricks him, another pinches him, the third burns him, the fourth bites him, the fifth scratches him and the sixth flogs him. All of this at once, all over his body – he comes surrounded by them all.

That evening Zelmire, deflowered the night before, has her cunt offered up to the company, meaning as ever just Curval and the Duc, as they are the only two of the quadrille[7] who fuck cunts. As soon as Curval has fucked Zelmire his hatred for Constance and Adélaïde redoubles; he wants Constance to serve Zelmire.

The twenty-first. 100. He has himself frigged by his lackey while the whore is on a pedestal, naked; she must neither move nor lose her balance for as long as he is frigged.

101. He has himself frigged by the bawd, fondling her buttocks while the whore holds in her hand the very short stub of a candle that she must not drop before the lecher has come – and he makes sure not to do so until she burns herself.

102. He has six whores lie down flat on their stomachs upon his dining table, each with the stub of a candle in their arse, while he dines.

103. He has a whore held down on her knees upon sharp stones while he dines, and if she moves at all during the meal she is not paid; above her are two overturned candles which drip hot wax on to her back and her breasts. The slightest movement and she is dismissed without being paid.

104. He forces her to remain in a very cramped iron cage for four days: she can neither sit nor lie down; he feeds her through the bars. This is the one at the turkey ballet of whom Desgranges will speak.[8]

That same evening Curval deflowers Colombe's cunt.

The twenty-second. 105. He has a naked girl dance in a blanket with a cat that claws, bites and scratches as it tumbles about; she must keep leaping regardless until the man comes.

106. He rubs a woman with a certain drug that causes such a violent itch that the woman scratches herself bloody; he watches her do so as he frigs himself.

107. He stops a woman's period with a drink and thereby risks making her seriously ill.

108. He gives her horse-medicine, which causes awful cramps; he watches her shit and suffer all day.

109. He rubs a girl all over with honey, then ties her naked to a column and releases a swarm of large flies.

*

That same evening Colombe's cunt is offered up.

The twenty-third. 110. He places the girl on a pivot that spins at a prodigious speed; she is bound naked to it and spins until he comes.

111. He hangs a girl upside down until he comes.

112. Has her swallow a strong dose of emetic, convinces her she has been poisoned and frigs as he watches her vomit.

113. He pummels her breasts until she is completely black and blue.

114. He pummels her arse nine days in a row for three hours each day.

The twenty-fourth. 115. He has a girl climb twenty feet high up a ladder: a rung breaks and the girl falls, but on to mattresses placed there specially; he comes over her body the moment she lands, and sometimes fucks her at that moment.

116. He slaps her with all his might and comes as he does so; he is in an armchair and the girl is on her knees before him.

117. Smacks her hands with a ferula.

118. Hard smacks across her buttocks, until her whole backside is on fire.

119. He inflates her with a blacksmith's bellows up her arsehole.

120. He gives her an enema of nearly boiling water; he enjoys her contortions and comes over her arse.

That evening Aline receives some slaps on the arse from the four friends until her arse turns scarlet; an old woman holds her by the shoulders. Augustine is given a few as well.

The twenty-fifth. 121. He seeks out devout women and flogs them with crucifixes and rosaries before placing them on an altar, like statues of the Virgin, in an awkward pose they are obliged to hold. She has to remain there for the duration of a very long Mass, at the elevation of which she must leave a turd on the host.

122. Makes her run naked on a freezing winter's night in the

middle of a garden, and there are ropes stretched across at inter-
vals to trip her.

123. He throws her, as if by accident, into a vat of nearly
boiling water as soon as she is naked, and prevents her from
climbing out until he has come over her body.

124. He has her stand naked upon a column in the middle of
a garden in the dead of winter until she has said five Our Fathers
and five Hail Marys – or until he has spilled his come, which
another girl excites as he faces this spectacle.

125. He spreads glue on the seat of a specially prepared close
stool: he sends her there to shit; as soon as she sits down her
arse sticks fast to the seat; meanwhile, from below, a small chafing dish is placed under her backside; she flees, leaving a layer
of skin in a circle on the seat.

That evening they make Adélaïde and Sophie, that devout pair,
commit profanities, and the Duc deflowers Augustine, whom he
has loved for a long time; he comes in her cunt three times in a
row. And that same evening he proposes having her run naked
in the courtyards in the freezing cold – he proposes this eagerly;
the others do not want to because she is very pretty and they
want to keep her for later, and because her arse has yet to be
deflowered in any case. He offers two hundred *louis* to the
company in exchange for having her taken down to the crypt
that same evening – they refuse. He wants her arse to be smacked
at least – she receives twenty-five smacks from each friend. But
the Duc strikes her with all his might and comes a fourth time
as he does so; he sleeps with her, and fucks her cunt three times
during the night.

The twenty-sixth. 126. He gets the girl drunk: she goes to bed;
as soon she is asleep her bed is taken away; she leans over to
reach for her chamber pot in the middle of the night; unable to
find it, she falls because her bed is in the air and it tips her out
as soon as she leans over; she falls on to mattresses placed there
specially; the man waits for her there and fucks her the moment
she lands.

127. He makes her run naked in the garden, pursuing her

with a driving whip just to threaten her; she must run until she collapses from exhaustion – that is the moment he throws himself upon her and fucks her.

128. He flogs the girl with a cat-o'-nine-tails with black silk knots, 10 lashes at a time, until he reaches a hundred; he kisses her buttocks a great deal with each lashing.

129. He flogs with a birch soaked in aqua vitae, and comes over the girl's buttocks only when he sees them covered in blood.

Champville tells of only four passions this day because of the festivities for the eighth week, which they celebrate with the wedding of Zéphire and Augustine, both of whom belong to the Duc and sleep in his bedroom, but before the celebration the Duc wants Curval to flog the boy while he flogs the girl. This takes place – they each receive a hundred lashes of the whip – but the Duc, who is more incensed against [Augustine] than ever because she made him come so often, flogs her until she bleeds. On this evening it will be necessary to explain what the penances are, how they go about them, and how many lashes of the whip are received – you can make a table of the offences with the corresponding number of lashes next to them.

The twenty-seventh. 130. He wants to flog only little girls from five to seven years of age and is always searching for a pretext to make it look like he is punishing them.

131. A woman comes to him for confession – he is a priest; she confesses all her sins and for her penance he gives her five hundred lashes of the whip.

132. He receives four women, and gives each of them six hundred lashes of the whip.

133. He has the same ceremony conducted before him by two valets who take it in turns: twenty women receive six hundred lashes each – they are not bound; he frigs himself as he watches the proceedings.

134. He flogs only little boys from fourteen to sixteen years of age and he has them come in his mouth afterwards. He gives them a hundred lashes each; he always sees two at a time.

*

That evening Augustine's cunt is offered up: Curval fucks it twice in a row, and, like the Duc, wants to flog her afterwards. Both of them hound this charming girl; they offer four hundred *louis* to the company for the two of them to become her masters that same evening – the others refuse.

The twenty-eighth. 135. He has a naked whore enter an apartment; two men then fall upon her and each flogs a buttock until it bleeds – she is tied up. When this is done, he frigs the men over the whore's bloody backside, and frigs himself too.

136. She is attached hand and foot to the wall: in front of her, also attached to the wall, is a sharp steel blade raised to the height of her belly. If she wants to avoid the whip she must throw herself forwards, cutting herself in the process; if she wants to avoid the machine, she has to submit to the whip.

137. He flogs a whore nine days in a row – a hundred lashes the first day, then doubling the number of lashes each day up to and including the ninth day.

138. He has the whore crouch on all fours, then straddles her facing her buttocks while squeezing her tightly between his thighs; in this position he flays her buttocks and cunt from above, and as he uses a cat-o'-nine-tails for this operation he finds it easy to aim his blows into the interior of her vagina, and so this is what he does.

139. He wants a pregnant woman: he has her bend over backwards upon a cylinder that supports her back; her head, hanging over the end of the cylinder, rests against the seat of a chair and is fixed there, her hair loose; her legs are spread as wide as possible and her fat belly stretched extraordinarily tight; beneath it, her cunt yawns with all its might; it is here and across the belly that he aims his lashes, and when he sees blood he crosses to the other end of the cylinder and comes over her face.

N.B. – *My drafts indicate the adoptions only after the deflowering, and, as a result, state that the Duc here adopts Augustine. Check that this is not wrong, and whether the adoption of the four sultanesses is not carried out from the very beginning,*

*and from that moment on whether it is not said that they sleep
in the bedrooms of those who have adopted them.*

The Duc that evening repudiates Constance, who falls into utter
disgrace – they protect her, however, because of her pregnancy,
upon which they have designs. Augustine assumes the role of
the Duc's wife, and now has only marital duties to carry out –
upon the sofa and at the privies. Constance's rank has now fallen
beneath that of the old women.

The twenty-ninth. 140. He wants only girls of fifteen years of
age and he flogs them with holly and nettles until they bleed; he
is very particular in his choice of arses.

    141. Flogs only with a bull's pizzle until the buttocks are
completely bruised; he sees four women in a row.

    142. He flogs only with a cat-o'-nine-tails with iron knots,
and only comes when the blood is dripping from everywhere.

    143. The same man of whom Desgranges will speak on the
twentieth of February wants pregnant women: he lashes them
with a driving whip, removing great lumps of flesh from the
buttocks, and lets fly from time to time with some stinging blows
across the belly.

They flog Rosette that evening, and Curval deflowers her cunt.
They discover that day the affair between Hercule and Julie – she
had got herself fucked; when they scold her for it she replies like
a libertine. They flog her stupendously; then, as she is well-liked
– as indeed is Hercule, who has always conducted himself well
– they pardon them and laugh the whole thing off.

The thirtieth. 144. He places a candle at a certain height; the
girl has, on the middle finger of her right hand, the stub of a
wax taper which is very short and which will burn her if she
does not hurry. With the stub of this wax taper she must light
the raised candle, but as it is placed at a height she has to leap
to reach it, and the lecher, armed with a leather-corded whip,
lashes her with all his might to make her spring higher, or catch

fire more quickly. If she succeeds, there is no more to be said; if not, she is roundly thrashed.

145. He flogs his wife and daughter in turn and prostitutes them at the brothel to be flogged before his very eyes, but this is not the same one that has already been mentioned.

146. He flogs with a birch from the nape of the neck down to the calves; the girl is bound – he drenches her whole back in blood.

147. Flogs only the breasts – he wants her to have very large ones. And pays double for pregnant women.

That evening Rosette's cunt is offered up; when Curval and the Duc have given it a good fucking, they and their friends flog her cunt – she is on all fours and with the cat-o'-nine-tails they aim their lashes into its interior.

The thirty-first. 148. He flogs only the face with a birch; they must have charming features – this is the one of whom Desgranges will speak on the seventh of February.

149. He indiscriminately flogs every part of her body with a birch – nothing is spared, the face, the cunt and breasts included.

150. Gives two hundred lashes of the bull's pizzle to young boys from sixteen to twenty years of age, all over their backs.

151. He is in a room: four whores inflame and flog him; when he is all ablaze he throws himself upon the fifth whore, naked in a room opposite, and assails her indiscriminately all over her body with great lashes of the bull's pizzle until he comes; but to ensure this happens sooner and that the waiting victim suffers less, the whores stop flogging him only when he is very close to coming. (*Check why there is one too many.*)[9]

Champville is applauded, she is given the same tributes as Duclos, and that evening both of them dine with the friends. That evening at the orgies Adélaïde, Aline, Augustine and Zelmire are condemned to be flogged all over except for their breasts, but as the friends want to have their way with them for at least another two months, they are handled with great care.

Part Three.

The hundred and fifty passions of the third class, or criminal passions, comprising thirty-one days in January, taken up by Madame Martaine's narration, to which is attached the journal of the scandalous events in the castle during this month.

The first of January. 1. He likes only to be buggered and it is difficult to find pricks large enough for him; but she does not dwell, she says, on this passion, as it is a taste all too simple and familiar to her listeners.

2. He wants to deflower only little girls from three to seven years of age – in the arse. This is the man who took her virginity of this kind: she was four years old; she falls ill as a result; her mother begs for the man's assistance – how obdurate he was! This is the same man of whom Duclos speaks last on 29th 9ber, the same as Champville's of the second of December, and also the man of Hell. He has a monstrous prick, he is an immensely wealthy man, he deflowers two little girls a day – one in the cunt in the morning, as Champville stated on the second of December, and one in the arse in the evening – and all this quite apart from his other passions. Four women held Martaine down while he buggered her. His ejaculation lasts six minutes, and he bellows throughout. A skilled and simple method of popping the virginity of her arse even though she is only four years of age.

3. Her mother sells Martaine's little brother's virginity to

another man who buggers only boys and who wants them to have just turned seven.

4. She is thirteen years old and her brother fifteen; they visit a man who forces the brother to fuck his sister, and who alternately fucks the boy and girl in the arse while they grapple with each other.

She brags about her arse – they tell her to show it: she displays it from atop the rostrum. The man of whom she has just spoken is the same as Duclos's of 21st 9ber, the Comte, and as Desgranges's of the twenty-seventh of February.

5. He has himself fucked as he buggers the brother and sister; it is the same man of whom Desgranges will speak on the twenty-fourth of February.

That same evening, the Duc deflowers Hébé, who is only twelve years old, in the arse: the pain is immeasurable; she is held down by the four old women, and he is assisted by Duclos and Champville; and to avoid any disruption, as there are festivities planned for the following day, Hébé's arse is offered up that same evening and all four friends have their way with it. She is carried out unconscious – she has been buggered seven times.

Martaine should not say that her vagina is obstructed.
This is false.

The second of January. 6. He has four girls fart in his mouth as he buggers a fifth, then he switches them around. All the girls fart and all are buggered; he comes only in the fifth arse.

7. He takes his pleasure with three young boys: he buggers and is shat on as he switches all three around, and he frigs the one who is unoccupied.

8. He fucks the sister in the arse while he has the brother shit in his mouth, then he switches them around and throughout each of these pleasures he is buggered.

9. He buggers only 15-year-old girls but always roundly thrashes them beforehand.

10. He mauls and pinches the buttocks and arsehole for an hour, then he buggers while he is roundly thrashed.

That day they celebrate the festivities of the ninth week. Hercule marries Hébé and fucks her in the cunt; Curval and the Duc take turns buggering the groom and the bride alternately.

The third of January. 11. He buggers only during Mass and comes at the elevation.

12. He buggers only while trampling a crucifix underfoot and while making the girl trample it too.

13. The man who enjoyed himself with Eugénie on Duclos's eleventh day has the girl shit, wipes her shitty arse, has an enormous prick and buggers her, with a host on the end of his tool.

14. Buggers a boy with the host, has himself buggered with the host – on the nape of the neck of the boy he is buggering is another host, upon which a third boy shits. He comes in this way without switching them around, but spouts appalling blasphemies.

15. He buggers the priest as he delivers Mass, and when the latter has performed the consecration the fucker withdraws for a moment; the priest thrusts a host up his own arse and is buggered again on top of this.

In the evening Curval deflowers the young and charming Zélamir's arse with a host. And Antinoüs fucks the Président with another host; while fucking, the Président thrusts a third one in Fanchon's arsehole with his tongue.

The fourth. 16. He likes to bugger only very old women while he is flogged.

17. Buggers only old men while he is fucked.

18. Has a long-standing affair with his son.

19. Wants to fuck only freaks, or negroes or the deformed.

20. To combine incest, adultery, sodomy and sacrilege, he buggers his married daughter with a host.

That evening Zélamir's arse is offered up to the four friends.

*

The fifth. 21. He has himself fucked and flogged in turn by two men, while he buggers a young boy and an old man drops in his mouth a turd, which he eats.

22. Two men fuck him in turn, one in the mouth, the other in the arse; this must last three hours by the clock – he swallows the come of the one who fucks him in the mouth.

23. He has himself fucked by ten men, paying them by the assault; he withstands as many as eighty assaults in a day without coming.

24. He prostitutes his wife, daughter and sister to be fucked in the arse, and watches them at it.

25. He surrounds himself with eight men: one in his mouth, one in his arse, one by his right groin, one by his left; he frigs another two with each hand; the seventh is between his thighs and [the] eighth frigs himself over his face.

That evening the Duc deflowers Michette's arse and causes her dreadful agonies.

The sixth. 26. He has an old man buggered in front of him: the prick is repeatedly withdrawn from the aged man's arsehole – it is put into the mouth of the observer, who sucks it, then sucks the old man, gamahuches him, buggers him, while the one who has just fucked the old man buggers him in turn and is flogged by the lecher's governess.

27. He violently throttles a young girl of fifteen in order to make her anus contract as he buggers her; he is flogged with a bull's pizzle throughout.

28. He has large balls of mercury combined with quicksilver[1] inserted into his arse – these balls rise and fall and, while they tickle him furiously, he sucks pricks, swallows the come, has girls' arses shit, swallows the turds; he spends two hours in this ecstasy.

29. He wants the father to bugger him while he sodomizes this man's son and daughter.

In the evening Michette's arse is offered up; Durcet takes Martaine to sleep in his bedroom, following the example of the Duc, who has Duclos, and Curval, who has Fanchon. This whore

exerts the same lubricious hold over him that Duclos enjoys over
the Duc.

The seventh. 30. He fucks a turkey whose head has been slipped
between the thighs of a girl lying on her belly, so that it looks
as if he is buggering the girl; he is buggered throughout and the
moment he comes the girl slits the turkey's throat.

31. He fucks a goat from behind while he is flogged; he has
a child with this goat, which he buggers in turn even though it
is a freak.

32. He buggers billy goats.

33. Wants to see a woman come, licked by a dog; and he shoots
the dog dead upon the woman's belly without injuring the woman.

34. He buggers a swan while putting a host up its arse; and
he strangles the animal himself as he comes.

That same evening the Bishop buggers Cupidon for the first time.

[*The eighth.*] 35. He has himself placed in a specially prepared
basket that has only one opening, against which he places his
arsehole, smeared with a mare's come; the basket is in the shape
of a mare and covered with that animal's hide. An ungelded
horse, trained for this purpose, buggers him and while it does
so he fucks a pretty white bitch inside his basket.

36. He fucks a cow, gets it pregnant and fucks the freak.

37. He has a woman placed in a similarly arranged basket to
receive a bull's member; he enjoys the spectacle.

38. He has a tame serpent which penetrates his anus and
sodomizes him while he buggers a cat in a basket – which, with
no room to move, cannot do him any harm.

39. He fucks a jenny[2] as he is buggered by an ass in specially
prepared machines that will be described.

In the evening Cupidon's arse is offered up.

The ninth. 40. He fucks the nostrils of a goat, which licks his
balls with its tongue as he does so; meanwhile he is by turns
flayed and has his arse licked.

41. He buggers a sheep while a dog licks his arsehole.

42. He buggers a dog, the head of which is cut off as he comes.

43. He forces a whore to frig an ass in front of him, and is fucked during this spectacle.

44. He fucks a monkey in the arse: the animal is trapped in a basket; it is tormented throughout to make its anus contract all the more.

That evening they celebrate the festivities of the tenth week with the marriage of Brise-cul and Michette, which is consummated and which causes great pain to Michette.

The 10ᵗʰ. 45.³ She announces that she is going to change passion and that the whip, which was the principal element above, in Champville's tale, is henceforth merely incidental.

He searches for girls guilty of some or other crimes: he frightens them, tells them that they will be arrested but that he will take care of everything if they are willing to receive a violent fustigation, and such is their fear they allow themselves to be flogged bloody.

46. Sends for a woman with beautiful hair under the sole pretext of examining it, but treacherously cuts it off and comes when he sees her lament this misfortune, which makes him laugh a great deal.

47. With great ceremony she enters a dark room: she sees no one but hears a conversation that concerns her, the details of which you will provide, and which is enough to scare her to death. Finally she suffers a barrage of slaps and punches without knowing where this is coming from; she hears the roars of a climax and is freed.

48. She enters a kind of sepulchre below ground which is lit only by lamps: she sees it in all its horror; the moment she is able to take stock everything goes dark; a horrifying noise of screams and chains is heard; she faints, or if not her fears are multiplied by some additional scenes until she does; as soon as she has passed out, a man falls upon her and buggers her; next, he leaves her and there are valets who come to her aid. He requires very young and callow girls.

49. She enters a similar place, but one that you will distinguish

in the detail: she is enclosed naked in a casket, she is nailed inside and the man comes at the sound of the nails being hammered in.

That evening, they had deliberately excluded Zelmire from the tales – she is taken down to the crypt mentioned earlier, which has been prepared in the same manner as those just depicted: the four friends are there, naked and all of them armed; she faints, and while she is unconscious Curval deflowers her arse. The Président has conceived for this girl the same feelings of love mixed with lubricious rage that the Duc has for Augustine.

The eleventh. 50. The same man, the Duc de Florville of whom Duclos spoke second on the twenty-ninth of November, and the same one also of whom Desgranges spoke fifth on the twenty-sixth of February – wants the beautiful cadaver of a freshly murdered girl to be placed on a bed of black satin; he gropes the body every which way and buggers it.

51. Another man wants two of them – that of a girl and that of a boy, and he buggers the young boy's cadaver as he kisses the girl's buttocks and thrusts his tongue into her anus.

52. He receives the girl in a closet full of very realistic waxwork cadavers:[4] they are all wounded in different ways; he tells the girl to choose, and says he is going to kill her like the cadaver whose wounds please her the most.

53. He ties her to a real cadaver, mouth to mouth, and flogs her in this pose until her back is completely covered in blood.

That evening Zelmire's arse is offered up, but beforehand they had put her on trial and told her she would be killed in the night; she believes this but instead, once she has been well buggered, they each content themselves with giving her a hundred lashes of the whip and Curval takes her to bed with him, where he buggers her again.

The twelfth. 54. He wants a girl who has her period: she approaches him, but he is positioned next to a kind of reservoir of icy water more than twelve feet square and eight in depth – it is hidden so that the girl does not see it; as soon as she is beside the man he shoves her in, and the moment she falls is the moment he comes; the girl is immediately pulled out, but as she has her period she is more often than not violently ill as a result.

55. He lowers her naked into a very deep well and threatens to fill it with stones; he throws down some clods of earth to frighten her, and comes into the well and on to the whore's head.

56. He has a pregnant woman brought to his house and terrifies her with threats and insinuations; he flogs her, renews his browbeating to make her miscarry either at his house or once she has returned home. If she gives birth at his house he pays her double.

57. He shuts her away in a dark dungeon, surrounded by cats, rats and mice; he convinces her that she is there for the rest of her life, and every day he frigs himself at her door as he taunts her.

58. He thrusts a bundle of fireworks up her arse and the sparks scorch her buttocks as they rain down on her.

That evening Curval has Zelmire recognized as his wife and weds her publicly – the Bishop marries them. He repudiates Julie, who falls into utter disgrace, but whose libertinage nevertheless sustains her and whom the Bishop protects a little until the time comes for him to give her his full backing, as we shall see.

Durcet's spiteful hatred for Adélaïde is more noticeable than ever that evening: he torments her, he harries her, she despairs. And the Président, her father, does not support her.

The thirteenth. 59. He attaches a girl to a st. Andrew's cross suspended in the air and roundly thrashes her all over her back; after that he unties her and throws her through a window, but she falls upon mattresses placed there specially – he comes as he hears her fall. Describe the lengths to which he goes to justify his behaviour.

60. He has her swallow a drug that makes her see a room full of horrible objects. She sees a pond closing in on her – she climbs on to a chair to avoid the water. She is told she has no choice but to leap in and swim – she jumps, but falls flat on the stone floor and often hurts herself badly. This is the moment our libertine comes, having enjoyed repeatedly kissing her backside beforehand.

61. He keeps her suspended by a pulley at the top of a tower

– he is within reach of the rope by a window above her: he frigs himself, tugs on the rope, and threatens to cut it as he comes; he is flogged throughout and has the whore shit beforehand.

62. She is held up by four thin ropes attached to her four limbs. Thus suspended in the cruellest pose, a trapdoor is opened beneath her to reveal a blazing brazier – if the ropes snap, she falls in; these are shaken, and the lecher cuts one of them as he comes. Sometimes he puts her in the same pose, places a weight on her back and pulls so vigorously on the four ropes that her stomach splits, so to speak, and her back breaks; she remains like this until he comes.

63. He ties her to a stool: one foot above her head is a finely sharpened dagger attached by a hair;[5] if the hair snaps, the razor-sharp dagger enters her skull; the man frigs himself in front of her and delights in the victim's terrified contortions; after an hour he releases her, and bloodies her buttocks with the point of this very dagger to show her how sharp it was; he comes over her bloodied arse.

That evening the Bishop deflowers Colombe's arse and, after he comes, flogs her until she bleeds, because he cannot bear that a girl should make him come.

The fourteenth. 64. He buggers a young and ignorant novice, and as he comes he fires two pistol shots close by her ears, singeing her hair.

65. He makes her sit in a spring-loaded chair: her weight triggers all the springs, releasing iron rings that pin her down; further springs reveal twenty daggers, all ready to plunge into her body; the man frigs himself as he tells her that the slightest movement of the chair will cause her to be impaled, and his come spurts all over her.

66. She falls by means of a counterweight into a closet lined in black and furnished with a prayer stool, a coffin and skulls: she sees six spectres armed with a club, a sword, pistols, sabres, a dagger and lances – with each poised to pierce a different part of her body; she reels, fear grips her, the man enters, seizes her, roundly thrashes her whole body, then comes as he buggers her.

If she has already fainted when he enters, as is often the case, he brings her back to her senses with blows from a birch.

67. She enters a chamber in a tower: in the middle of the room she sees a large brazier, some poison on a table, and a dagger – she is given the choice of three kinds of death.[6] Usually she chooses the poison: it is a specially prepared opiate that plunges her into a deep stupor during which the libertine buggers her. It is the same man of whom Duclos spoke on the twenty-seventh and of whom Desgranges will speak on the sixth of February.

68. The same man of whom Desgranges will speak on the sixteenth of February goes through the entire ritual of beheading the girl: when the blade is about to fall, a cord rapidly pulls back the girl's body, the blade lands on the block, and sinks in three inches; if the rope does not pull the girl away in time, she is dead; he comes as he lets the blade fall. But he has buggered her with her neck on the block beforehand.

In the evening, Colombe's arse is offered up; they threaten her and make as if to cut her throat.

[*The fifteenth.*] 69. He hangs the whore right up: her feet are resting on a stool; a rope is attached to the stool; he sits in an armchair opposite, where he has himself frigged by the woman's daughter; as he comes he pulls the rope; the whore, no longer supported, is left hanging; he leaves the room, valets arrive, untie the whore, and once bled she comes round, but this assistance is given without his knowledge; he goes to bed with the daughter and sodomizes her all night, telling her he has hanged her mother; he does not want to know that she has come round. Say that Desgranges will speak of this.

70. He pulls the girl by the ears, and walks her around in this manner, naked, in the middle of the room; then he comes.

71. He pinches the girl extraordinarily hard all over her body, except for the breasts; he leaves her black and blue.

72. He pinches her breasts, mauls them and pummels them until they are covered in bruises.

73. He traces numbers and letters with the tip of a needle on

her breasts, but the needle is poisoned, her bosom swells and she suffers a great deal.

74. Inserts one or two thousand little pins into her breasts and comes when her bosom is covered with them.

That day they catch Julie, more libertine than ever, frigging with Madame Champville; the Bishop protects her even more from this moment and allows her into his bedroom – just as the Duc has Duclos, Durcet has Martaine and Curval has Fanchon. She confesses that since her repudiation, as she had been condemned to bed down in the stables with the animals, Madame Champville had brought her into her own bedroom and was sleeping with her.

The sixteenth of January. 75. He inserts large pins all over the girl's body, including her breasts – he comes when she is covered with them. Say that Desgranges will talk about this – it is the one she explains fourth on the twenty-seventh of February.

76. He swells her with drink, then he sews up her cunt and arse; he leaves her like this until he sees her faint from the need to urinate or shit without being able to do so. Or until the force and weight of her needs finally tear apart her stitches.

77. There are four of them in a room and they assail the girl with punches and kicks until she falls; all four frig each other and come when she is on the floor.

78. Her air supply is turned off and on at whim inside a pneumatic machine.[7]

To mark the eleventh week they celebrate that day the marriage of Colombe and Antinoüs, which is consummated. The Duc, who gives Augustine's cunt a prodigious fucking, has since the night before been possessed by a lubricious rage against her: he had her held down by Duclos and gave her three hundred lashes of the whip from halfway down her back to her calves, and then buggered Madame Duclos as he kissed Augustine's whipped arse. Next he goes giddy for Augustine, wants her to dine beside him, eats only from her mouth and engages in a thousand other libertine trifles which reveal the character of those lechers.

*

The seventeenth. 79. He ties the girl face down to a table and eats a sizzling omelette off her buttocks, vigorously stabbing at the morsels with a very sharp fork.

80. He presses her head against a chafing dish until she faints, and he buggers her in this state.

81. He gently and little by little grills the skin of her breast and buttocks with sulphur matches.

82. He extinguishes a great many candles one after another in her cunt, in her arse and on her breasts.

83. He burns off her eyelashes with a match, which prevents her from getting any rest at night, or from being able to close her eyes to sleep.

That evening the Duc deflowers Giton, who falls ill as a result because the Duc is enormous, because he fucks most brutally and because Giton is only 12 years old.

The eighteenth. 84. He forces her – with a pistol to her throat – to chew and swallow a lump of burning coal, and then syringes aqua fortis[8] into her cunt.

85. He makes her dance the *olivettes*[9] stark naked around four specially prepared pillars, but the only path she can follow barefoot around these pillars is strewn with jagged metal scraps and sharp spikes, and with bits of glass, and there is a man placed by each pillar, a fistful of birches in his hand, who lashes her front or rear according to the part of the body she exposes each time she passes close by; she is forced to run like this a certain number of times according to how young and pretty she is, the prettiest always being the most tormented.

86. He punches her violently on the nose until she bleeds, and he carries on even though she is covered in blood; he comes and mixes his come with the blood she is losing.

87. He pinches her flesh and mainly her buttocks, crotch and breasts, with very hot iron tongs. Say that Desgranges will speak of this.

88. He places various little piles of gunpowder on her body, especially in the most sensitive parts, and he sets fire to them.

*

That evening Giton's arse is offered up and [he is] fustigated after the ceremony by Curval, the Duc and the Bishop, who have all fucked him.

The nineteenth. 89. He thrusts into her cunt a cylinder of untreated and unwrapped gunpowder; he sets fire to it and comes upon seeing the flame. Beforehand he kissed her arse.

90. He soaks her from head to toe in nothing but aqua vitae: he sets her on fire and delights in seeing this poor girl all ablaze until he comes; he repeats the same operation two or three times.

91. He gives her an enema of boiling oil.

92. He thrusts a red-hot poker into her anus as well as her cunt having roundly thrashed her beforehand.

93. He wants to trample a pregnant woman underfoot until she miscarries. He flogs her beforehand.

The same evening Curval deflowers Sophie's arse, but she is flogged bloody beforehand with a hundred lashes from each of the friends; as soon as Curval has come in her arse, he offers the company five hundred *louis* in exchange for taking her down to the crypt that same evening and having his way with her – they refuse. He buggers her again and, withdrawing from her arse after coming a second time, he kicks her backside so hard she lands on a mattress fifteen feet away. From that evening on he will have his revenge by roundly thrashing Zelmire.

The twentieth of January. 94. He looks as if he is caressing the girl who is frigging him – she does not suspect a thing – but at the instant he comes he seizes her head and dashes it hard against the wall; the blow is so unexpected and so violent she usually collapses unconscious.

95. Four libertines gather together: they judge a girl and condemn her by the book; her sentence is one hundred blows from a rod, with twenty-five blows delivered by each of the friends, the first beating her from her back to the top of her buttocks, the second from the top of her buttocks to her calves, the third from her neck to her navel, including her breasts, and the fourth from her loins to her feet.

96. He pricks a pin into both eyes, both nipples and her clitoris.

97. He drips sealing wax on to her buttocks, into her cunt
and on to her breasts.

98. He bleeds her from the arm and only staunches the blood
when she faints.

Curval proposes bleeding Constance because of her pregnancy:
this is done until she faints – it is Durcet who bleeds her. That
evening Sophie's arse is offered up and the Duc proposes bleeding her (saying that this can do her no harm – far from it) and
making black pudding from her blood for breakfast. This is done
– it is Curval who bleeds her. Duclos frigs him as he does so,
and he only makes the incision the moment his come escapes;
he makes a broad incision, but he does not miss his mark. Despite
all this the Bishop has taken a liking to Sophie, adopting her as
his wife and repudiating Aline, who falls into utter disgrace.

The twenty-first of January. 99. He bleeds her from both arms
and wants her to stand as the blood flows; from time to time he
staunches the blood in order to flog her. Next he reopens the
wounds, and so on until she faints – he only comes when she
collapses. He has her shit beforehand.

100. He bleeds her from all four limbs and from the jugular
and frigs himself as he watches these five fountains of blood flow.

101. He scarifies her flesh lightly, and above all her buttocks,
but not her breasts.

102. He scarifies her roughly, and above all her breast near
the nipple, and, when he gets to her buttocks, near her arsehole.
Next he cauterizes the wounds with a red-hot poker.

103. He is bound hand and foot like a wild beast – he is
covered in a tiger's pelt: in this state he is excited, aroused,
flogged, beaten, his arse is fondled; facing him is a very fat young
girl, naked and with her feet tied to the floor and her neck to
the ceiling so that she cannot move. As soon as the lecher is all
ablaze, he is released: he hurls himself like a wild beast upon the
girl and bites her flesh all over, and particularly her clitoris and
nipples, which he usually tears off with his teeth; he roars and

cries out like an animal, and comes as he roars; the girl has to shit – he will eat her turd off the floor.

The same evening the Bishop deflowers Narcisse; he is offered up the same evening so as not to disrupt the festivities of the twenty-third. Before buggering him the Duc has him shit in his mouth and thereby yield the come of his predecessors; once he has buggered him, he gives him a flogging.

The twenty-second. 104. He pulls out some teeth and scratches the gums with needles. Sometimes he burns them.

   105. He breaks a finger, sometimes several.

   106. He vigorously flattens a foot with a hammer.

   107. He dislocates a wrist.

   108. He smashes the front teeth with a hammer as he comes; his pleasure beforehand is to suck the mouth a great deal.

The Duc that evening deflowers Rosette's arse, and the very moment his prick enters her arse Curval pulls out one of the little girl's teeth so that she experiences two dreadful agonies at once. She is offered up the same evening so as not to disrupt the following day's festivities. Once Curval has come in her arse (and he is the last in line) – once he is done, as I say, he sends the little girl flying backwards with an almighty smack.

The twenty-third. Because of the festivities there are only four.

   109. He dislocates her foot.[10]

   110. He breaks an arm as he buggers her.

   111. He breaks a bone in her leg, with a blow from an iron bar, and buggers her afterwards.

   112. He ties her to a stepladder, her limbs pointing in peculiar directions: a rope is attached to the ladder, the rope is pulled, the ladder falls – she breaks one limb or another.

That day they held the wedding of Bande-au-ciel and Rosette to celebrate the 12th week. That evening they bleed Rosette, once she has been fucked, and Aline, whom they have Hercule fuck; both girls are bled so that their blood spurts over the thighs and pricks of our libertines, who frig themselves at this spectacle and come as both girls faint.

The twenty-fourth. 113. He cuts off her ear. (*Be careful to specify everywhere what all these people do beforehand.*)

114. He splits her lips and her nostrils.

115. He pierces her tongue with a hot poker, having sucked and bitten it.

116. He tears off several nails from her fingers or toes.

117. He cuts off her fingertip.

And as the storyteller said when asked that such a mutilation has no unfortunate repercussions if treated on the spot, Durcet that same evening cuts off Adélaïde's fingertip, his lubricious spite erupting against her more and more. It makes him come with indescribable ecstasy. The same evening Curval deflowers Augustine's arse even though she is the Duc's wife. The torment she suffers. Curval's rage against her afterwards; he conspires with the Duc to take her down to the crypt that same evening, and they tell Durcet that if they are permitted to do so they will permit Durcet to dispatch Adélaïde immediately too – but the Bishop harangues them and makes them promise to wait a little longer for the sake of their own pleasure. Curval and the Duc thus content themselves with flogging Augustine vigorously, each in the other's arms.

The twenty-fifth. 118. He trickles fifteen to twenty drops of bubbling molten lead into her mouth and burns her gums with aqua fortis.

119. He cuts off the tip of her tongue, having had his shitty arse licked by this same tongue, then buggers her once her mutilation is complete.

120. He has a circular machine made of iron which bores into the flesh, and which, once withdrawn, extracts a cylinder of flesh as deep as the machine has been allowed to reach; the machine keeps on boring if it is not held back.

121. He makes a eunuch of a boy of ten to fifteen years of age.

122. He grips and removes her nipples with pincers and cuts them up with scissors.

*

That same evening Augustine's arse is offered up; while buggering her, Curval had wanted to kiss Constance's breasts, and as he came he tore off a nipple with his teeth – but as they dress the wound immediately, they ensure this will have no effect on her unborn fruit. Curval says to his fellow libertines, who laugh at his rage against this creature, that he is not master of the feelings of rage she inspires in him; when the Duc takes his turn to bugger Augustine, his own fury against this beautiful girl bursts forth with unimaginable force – had the others not kept an eye on him, he would either have wounded her breast or throttled her with all his might as he came. He again asks of those assembled that he be made master of her fate, but they object that he must wait for Desgranges's stories; his brother begs him to wait patiently until he himself has set an example with Aline – that what he wants to do now would disrupt the whole structure of their arrangements. Nonetheless, as he can contain himself no longer, and as he absolutely must torture this beautiful girl in some way, they allow him to inflict a small wound on her arm; he does so in the flesh of her left forearm, sucks the blood from it, comes, and they dress the wound so no trace of it remains four days later.

The twenty-sixth. 123. He smashes a fragile bottle of clear glass on the face of a girl who is bound and defenceless; he sucked her mouth and tongue a great deal beforehand.

124. He ties both her legs down, binds one hand behind her back, places in her other hand a short rod for her to defend herself, then assails her with great blows from his sword, cutting open her flesh in several places, and coming over her wounds.

125. He stretches her out on a st. Andrew's cross, makes a show of breaking her bones, injures three limbs without dislocating them, and then actually breaks either an arm or a leg.

126. He has her stand in profile, and fires a pistol loaded with shot that grazes her two breasts; he aims to shoot off one of her nipples.

127. He places her on all fours at twenty paces, and fires his flintlock into her buttocks.

*

That same evening the Bishop deflowers Fanny's arse.

The twenty-seventh. 128. The same man of whom Desgranges will speak on the twenty-fourth of February makes a woman miscarry by flogging her across the belly; he wants to see her give birth in front of him.

129. He makes a eunuch of a boy of 16 to 17 years of age, slicing it clean off. He buggers him beforehand and flogs him.

130. Wants a maiden: he cuts off her clitoris with a razor, then deflowers her with a hot iron cylinder which he drives in with a hammer.

131. Makes her miscarry at 8 months with a potion that immediately makes the woman deliver her dead child; on other occasions he contrives a delivery through the arsehole. But the child emerges lifeless and the mother's life is put at risk.

132. He cuts off an arm.

That evening Fanny's arse is offered up; Durcet saves her from a torment that had been planned for her – he takes her as his wife, has the Bishop marry them, and repudiates Adélaïde, who is subjected to the torment intended for Fanny, which entailed having a finger broken. The Duc buggers her as Durcet breaks her finger.

The twenty-eighth. [133.] He cuts off both hands at the wrist and cauterizes with a hot iron.

134. He cuts off the tongue at the root and cauterizes with a hot poker.

135. He cuts off a leg and most often does so while buggering her.

136. He pulls out all her teeth and puts in their place a red-hot nail he drives in with a hammer; he does this having just fucked the woman in the mouth.

137. He removes an eye.

That evening they roundly thrash Julie and prick all her fingers with a needle. This operation is carried out while the Bishop buggers her, even though he is quite fond of her.

*

The twenty-ninth. 138. He blinds and melts both eyes by dripping sealing wax into them.

139. He slices a breast clean off, and cauterizes with a hot poker. Madame Desgranges will say here that this is the man who cut off her own missing breast and that she is sure he grilled and ate it.

140. He cuts off both her buttocks, having buggered and flogged [her]. He is said to eat them too.

141. He slices both ears clean off.

142. Cuts off all her extremities: her twenty digits, her clitoris, her nipples, the tip of her tongue.

That evening Aline, having been vigorously flogged by the four friends and buggered by the Bishop for the last time, is condemned to have a digit from each limb cut off by each friend.

The thirtieth. 143. He removes several pieces of flesh from all over her body, has them roasted, and forces her to eat them with him. It is the same man as Desgranges's of the eighth and seventeenth of February.

144. He cuts off a young boy's four limbs, buggers the torso, feeds him well and so keeps him alive; as the limbs were not cut off too close to the torso, he lives for a long time – he buggers him thus for more than a year.

145. He ties the girl up tightly by the hand and leaves her thus without feeding her: beside her is a large knife and before her an excellent meal; if she wants to feed herself, she must cut off her hand, if not she will die like this; he fucked her in the arse beforehand; he watches her through a window.

146. He ties the mother and the daughter together: for one to live and rescue the other, she must cut off her own hand; he enjoys watching the debate between them and seeing which of the two will sacrifice herself for the other.

She tells only four stories so that they may celebrate that evening the festivities of the thirteenth week, during which the Duc, as a bride, takes Hercule as his groom, and, as a groom, takes Zéphire as his wife. The young catamite, who is known to have the finest arse of the eight boys, appears dressed as a girl, and is as pretty as Cupid like this; the ceremony is consecrated by the Bishop and takes place in front of everyone. This young boy is deflowered only this day; the Duc takes great pleasure in this, and great pain too – he leaves the boy bleeding. Hercule fucks him throughout the operation.

The thirty-first of January. 147. He puts out both her eyes and leaves her locked away in a room, telling her that there is food in front of her and that she has only to search for it. But to do so she will have to walk across an iron sheet which she cannot see and which is always kept red hot; he enjoys watching through a window to see what she will do – will she burn herself or will she prefer to die of hunger? She has been severely flogged beforehand.

148. He subjects her to the rope torture,[11] which entails having all four limbs tied to ropes and being raised very high by them; he then leaves you to plummet from this great height – each fall dislocates and breaks every limb because it happens in mid-air and one is held up only by the ropes.

149. He makes deep wounds in her flesh into the middle of which he trickles boiling pitch and molten lead.

150. He ties her up naked and helpless at the very moment she has given birth: he ties up her child in front of her; it cries and she cannot rescue it; she must watch it perish like this; after this he roundly thrashes the mother's cunt, aiming his blows into her vagina. He is usually the child's father.

151. He swells her with water; next he sews up her cunt and her arse as well as her mouth and leaves her like this until the water breaks through the passages or she dies. (*Check why there is one too many, and if there is one to be omitted let it be this last one, which I think has already been done.*)[12]

That same evening Zéphire's arse is offered up and Adélaïde is condemned to a brutal flogging, after which she will be burned with a hot poker very close to the interior of her vagina and beneath her armpits, and gently singed beneath each breast. She endures all this like a true heroine and invokes God, which excites her torturers all the more.

Part Four.

The one hundred and fifty murderous passions or passions of the fourth class, comprising twenty-eight days in February taken up by Desgranges's narration, to which is attached the detailed journal of the scandalous events at the castle during this month.

Establish first of all that everything changes aspect this month. That the four wives are repudiated, that Julie has nonetheless found favour with the Bishop, who has taken her on as a servant, but that Aline, Adélaïde and Constance have neither hearth nor home – except, however, that Duclos has been allowed to shelter the last of these in her own room to keep her unborn fruit safe from harm. But as for Adélaïde and Aline, they sleep in the same stable as the animals destined for slaughter; it is the sultanesses – Augustine, Zelmire, Fanny and Sophie – who replace the wives in all their duties, including at the privies, at the lunch table, upon the sofas, and in Messieurs' beds at night. Accordingly at this stage this is how Messieurs' bedrooms are organized at night-time. Aside from the fuckers, with whom each takes his turn, they have as follows: the Duc – Augustine, Zéphire and Duclos in his bed with the fucker; he sleeps in the middle of the four, with Marie on the sofa. Curval sleeps likewise between Adonis, Zelmire, a fucker and Fanchon; no one else besides. Durcet sleeps between Hyacinthe, Fanny, a fucker and Madame Martaine (*check*), with Louison on the sofa. The Bishop sleeps between Céladon, Sophie, a fucker and Julie, with Thérèse on the sofa. All of which goes to show that the young couples, Zéphire and Augustine, Adonis and Zelmire, Hyacinthe and Fanny, Céladon and Sophie, who were all married together, belong to the same master. There are only four young girls left in the girls' harem, and four in the boys' harem. Champville sleeps in that of the girls and Desgranges in that of the boys, with Aline in the stable, as mentioned, and Constance on her own in Duclos's bedroom, as Duclos sleeps with the Duc every night. Lunch is always served by the four sultanesses standing in for the four wives, and supper by the remaining four sultanesses; a quadrille always serves the coffee, but the quadrilles for the tales, facing each mirrored alcove, now comprise only a boy and a girl. For each tale, Aline and Adélaïde are attached to the pillars in the chamber of stories of which we have spoken: they are bound there, their buttocks facing the sofas, with a little table strewn with birches beside them so that they are always perfectly ready to receive a flogging. Constance has permission to be seated with the storytellers. Each old woman stands by her couple, and Julie, naked, roams from one sofa to another to take orders and execute them there and then; in addition, as ever, one fucker for each sofa. It is in these circumstances that Desgranges begins her tales. Under a particular ruling, the friends have decreed that during the course of this month Aline, Adélaïde, Augustine and Zelmire would be sacrificed to the brutality of their passions, and that they may on the prescribed day either immolate them alone or invite any friend they wish to the sacrifice without offending the others; that, as for Constance, she would be used for the celebration of the last week, as will be explained at the appropriate time and place. Should the Duc and Curval, who by this arrangement would become widowers once again, require other wives to carry out marital duties for the rest of the month, they may choose one of the four remaining sultanesses. But the pillars will remain bare once the two women who had previously adorned them have gone.

Desgranges begins and, having warned that henceforth the only subject will be murder, she says that she will endeavour to enter into the most minute details, as she has been encouraged to do,

and above all to reveal the ordinary tastes which had preceded
the passions of these debauched murderers, so that those listening may judge the relations and links between the two and see
what form of straightforward libertinage may, if refined by minds
without morals or principles, lead to murder, and the kind of
murder to which it may lead. Then she begins.

The first. 1. He used to enjoy having his way with a pauperess
who had not eaten for three days, and his passion now is to
leave a woman to die of hunger down in a dungeon, without
offering the slightest assistance; he watches her and frigs himself
while observing her, but only comes the day she perishes.

2. He keeps her alive there for a long time, reducing her ration
a little each day; he makes her shit beforehand, and eats the turd
from a dish.

3. He used to enjoy sucking the mouth and swallowing the
saliva, and now he immures a woman in a dungeon, with food
for only a fortnight; on the thirtieth day, he enters and frigs
himself over the cadaver.

4. He used to make women piss, and now he kills one little
by little by preventing her from drinking and giving her a great
deal to eat.

5. He used to flog women, and now kills one by preventing
her from sleeping.

That same evening Michette, having eaten a great deal, is
suspended by her feet until she has vomited all of it over Curval,
who frigs himself beneath her and swallows.

The second. 6. He used to have a woman shit in his mouth and
would eat it as she did so; now he feeds one only breadcrumbs
and wine – she croaks after a month.

7. He used to enjoy fucking cunts; now he gives the woman
a venereal disease by injection, but of such an awful kind she
croaks very soon after.

8. He used to have a woman vomit into his mouth, and now
by means of a drink he gives her a malignant fever that does her
in very quickly.

9. He used to make a woman shit, and now he administers an enema of poisonous ingredients in boiling water or aqua fortis.

10. A famous fustigator places a woman on a pivot upon which she spins endlessly until her death.

In the evening they give Rosette an enema of boiling water the moment the Duc has finished buggering her.

The third. 11. He used to enjoy slapping women, and now he twists the neck all the way round so that she faces the same way as her buttocks.

12. He used to enjoy bestiality, and now he likes having a girl deflowered before him by a stallion that kills her.

13. He used to enjoy fucking arses, and now he buries a girl halfway up and feeds her until half her body is rotten.

14. He used to enjoy frigging the clitoris, and he now has one of his servants frig a girl's clitoris until she dies.

15. A fustigator perfects his passion by flogging every part of a woman's body until she dies.

That evening the Duc wants Augustine's clitoris – a particularly ticklish one – to be frigged by Duclos and Champville, who take turns until she faints.

The fourth. 16. He used to enjoy squeezing the neck, and now he ties a cord around a girl's neck; before her is a large meal but in order to reach it she must strangle herself or die of hunger.

17. The same man who killed Duclos's sister, and who had a taste for manhandling flesh, pummels the breasts and buttocks with such ferocious force that he kills by this torture.

18. The man of whom Martaine spoke on the twentieth of January and who used to enjoy bleeding women, now kills them through repeated bleedings.

19. The one whose passion was to make a naked woman run until she fell, and who was mentioned earlier, now likes forcing a woman into a scalding steam room, where she suffocates and dies.

20. The one of whom Duclos spoke, who enjoyed being swad-

dled like a baby and to whom a girl would feed her own shit instead of pap, now wraps a woman so tight in swaddling that he kills her this way.

That evening, shortly before heading to the chamber of stories, they found Curval buggering one of the kitchen maids – he pays the fine. The girl is ordered to attend the orgies, where the Duc and Bishop bugger her in turn, and she receives two hundred lashes of the whip at the hands of each; she's a robust Savoyard girl of twenty-five, quite fresh-faced and with a fine arse.

The fifth. 21. His first passion is bestiality, and for his second he sews a girl into a fresh donkey skin, with her head sticking out; he feeds her and leaves her inside it until the animal's hide suffocates her as it shrinks.

22. The one of whom Martaine spoke on the fifteenth of January, and who used to enjoy hanging girls and toying with them, suspends a girl by her feet and leaves her there until she has choked on her own blood.

23. Duclos's one of the twenty-seventh of November, who used to enjoy getting a whore drunk, now kills a woman by swelling her with water through a funnel.

24. He used to enjoy mauling breasts, and now improves on this by encasing a pair in two iron pots; her two breasts armoured thus, the creature is then placed over two chafing dishes and left to croak in these agonies.

25. He used to enjoy watching a woman swim, and now he throws one in the water, and pulls her out half-drowned; he then hangs her by the feet to let the water pour out of her – as soon as she comes to she is thrown back in, and this is repeated until she croaks.

That day, at the same time as the previous evening, they find the Duc buggering another maid – he pays the fine. The maid is summoned to the orgies where they all have their way with her – Durcet in her mouth, the others in her arse, and even in her cunt (as she is a maiden), and she is condemned to two hundred lashes of the whip by each of them; she is eighteen years of age, tall and shapely, a hint of red in her hair, and a very nice arse. The same evening Curval says it is essential for her pregnancy that Constance be bled; the Duc buggers her and Curval bleeds her while he is fucked and while Augustine frigs him over Zelmire's buttocks. He pricks her as he comes and does not miss the vein.

The sixth. 26. His first passion was for launching a woman into a brazier with a kick up the arse, but she would escape so quickly she would suffer only very little; he improves on this by forcing the girl to stand up straight between two fires, one of which grills her from in front and the other from behind – she is left there until her fat has melted.

Desgranges announces that she will speak of murders that bring about a swift death with barely any suffering.

27. He used to enjoy restricting her breathing with his hands, either by tightening them around her neck or by placing one over her mouth for a long time, and he now improves on this by suffocating her between four mattresses.

28. The one of whom Martaine spoke, and who used to offer a choice of three deaths (see 14ᵗʰ January), now blows their brains out with a pistol without offering them any choice; he buggers them and pulls the trigger as he comes.

29. The one of whom Champville spoke on the twenty-second of December, who used to have a girl leap about in a blanket with a cat, now throws her from the top of a tower on to stones, and comes when he hears her land.

30. The one who used to enjoy throttling as he buggered, and of whom Martaine spoke on 6ᵗʰ January, buggers the girl, a black silk cord tied around her neck, and comes as he strangles her; have her say that this thrill is one of the most exquisite a libertine can procure for himself.

On this day they celebrate the festivities of the fourteenth week and Curval, as a woman, takes Brise-cul for his husband, and as a man, takes Adonis for his wife; this child is not deflowered until this day, in front of everyone, while Brise-cul fucks Curval.

They get drunk over supper. And Zelmire and Augustine are flogged across their loins, their buttocks, the back of their thighs, their stomach, their crotch and the front of their thighs; next Curval has Adonis fuck his new wife, Zelmire, and buggers them both one after the other.

The seventh. 31. At first he used to enjoy fucking a sleeping woman and he now improves on this by killing his victim with a strong dose of opium; he fucks her cunt while she is in a deathly sleep.

32. The same man of whom she just spoke and who throws his victims repeatedly into the water, also has a passion for drowning a woman with a stone hanging around her neck.

33. He used to enjoy slapping a woman across the face, and now he drips molten lead into her ear while she sleeps.

34. He used to enjoy flogging a woman across the face; Champville spoke of this on the thirtieth of X^{ber} (*check*).[1] He kills the girl instantly with a vigorous hammer blow to the temple.

35. He used to enjoy watching a candle burn down to its end in a woman's anus; now he attaches her to the foot of a conducting rod, and has her struck down by lightning.

36. A fustigator, he positions her on all fours at the end of a small cannon; the ball takes her by the arse.

That day they found the Bishop buggering the third maid – he pays the fine. The girl is summoned to the orgies, the Duc and Curval fuck her cunt and arse as she is a virgin, then she is given eight hundred lashes of the whip – two hundred from each; she's a Swiss girl of 19, very fair-skinned, rather plump, with a very nice arse. The cooks protest and say the service cannot continue if the maids are harassed, and so they are left alone until the month of March. That same evening they cut off one of Rosette's fingers and they cauterize with a flame; she is between Curval and the Duc during the operation – one fucks her arse, the other her cunt. The same evening Adonis's arse is offered up, so that the Duc has on this evening fucked both a maid and Rosette in the cunt, the same maid in the arse, Rosette

also in the arse when he changed places with Curval, and
Adonis. He is spent.

The eighth. 37. He used to enjoy flogging every inch of the body
with a bull's pizzle – and this is the same man of whom Martaine
spoke, who tied his victims to the wheel, grazing three limbs but
only breaking one of them. He now enjoys completely breaking
a woman on the wheel, but then chokes her on the cross itself.

38. The one of whom Martaine spoke, who pretends to cut
the throat of a young girl only to have her pulled back by a cord
at the last moment, now does cut their throats as he comes; he
frigs himself.

39. Martaine's one of the thirtieth of January who used to
enjoy scarifying now condemns his victims to a dungeon.

40. He used to enjoy flogging the bellies of pregnant women,
and improves on this by dropping upon a pregnant woman's
belly an enormous weight that instantly crushes both her and
her unborn fruit.

41. He used to enjoy seeing a girl's bare neck, and squeezing
and mauling it a little; now he sticks a needle in at a certain
point close to the nape of the neck, killing her on the spot.

42. He used to enjoy gently burning different parts of her
body with a candle. He now improves on this by throwing her
into a blazing furnace so fierce she is instantly consumed.

Durcet, who is very hard and who twice got up to flog Adélaïde
at her pillar during these tales, proposes she be laid across the
fire, and when she has had time enough to tremble at the
proposal, which is very nearly accepted, they settle for burning
her nipples instead; Durcet, her husband, burns one, and Curval,
her father, the other – they both come during this operation.

The ninth. 43. He used to enjoy pricking with pins, and now
comes as he plunges a dagger into her heart three times.

44. He used to enjoy lighting fireworks in cunts; now he
attaches a young girl, slim and attractive, to serve as a rod for
a large rocket – she is carried off and falls back to earth with
the rocket.

45. The same one fills a woman with gunpowder in her every orifice, sets fire to it, and all her limbs break and fly off at the same time.

46. He used to enjoy sneaking an emetic into whatever the girl was eating, now he has her breathe in some powder sprinkled on her snuff or on a bouquet of flowers, and she keels over backwards stone dead on the very spot.

47. He used to enjoy flogging the breasts and neck; now he improves on this by striking her down with a vigorous blow of the rod to her gullet.

48. The same one of whom Duclos spoke on 27th 9[ber] and Martaine on the fourteenth of January (*check*):[2] [she] shits in front of the lecher, he scolds her, and pursues her with great lashes of his driving whip down a corridor; a door to a small staircase opens, she believes she has reached safety and flies down it, but a missing step plunges her into a bathtub of boiling water which traps her beneath and she dies there scalded, drowned and suffocated. He has a taste for making the woman shit and for flogging her as she does so.

That evening, at the end of this tale, Zelmire – made to shit that morning by Curval – is now asked for some shit by the Duc. She cannot – she is condemned on the spot to having her arse pricked with a gold needle until the skin is completely drenched in blood, and, as it is the Duc who has been wronged by this refusal, he is the one to operate on her. Curval demands some shit from Zéphire: he says that the Duc made him shit that morning – the Duc denies this; they call Duclos to bear witness and she denies it too, although she knows it to be true. As a result, Curval has the right to punish Zéphire even though he is the Duc's lover, just as the Duc has punished Zelmire even though she is Curval's wife. Zéphire is flogged bloody by Curval and is flicked 6 times on the bridge of his nose; he bleeds from it, which makes the Duc laugh a great deal.

The tenth. Desgranges states she will speak of treacherous murders, where the method is paramount and the effect, that is to say the murder, is no more than incidental. And consequently she states she will deal with poisons first.

49. A man with a taste for fucking arses and nothing else poisons all his wives – he is on his twenty-second; he only ever fucked their arses and never deflowered them.

50. A bugger invites his friends to a banquet and poisons a few of them each time he serves them something to eat.

51. Duclos's one of 26th 9^{ber}, and Martaine's of the tenth of January, a bugger, pretends to succour the poor; he gives them provisions, but these are poisoned.

52. A bugger employs a drug which, strewn on the ground, kills those who walk upon it stone dead, and he uses it often.

53. A bugger employs another powder that makes you die in inconceivable torments – these last a fortnight, and no physician can discern the cause; his greatest pleasure is to visit you while you are in this state.

54. A bugger of men and women alike employs another powder whose effect is to deprive you of your senses and render you as if dead; you are indeed believed to be so – you are buried and you die in despair in your coffin, where you immediately come to your senses. He endeavours to stand over the spot in which you are buried to see if he can hear any screams – if he does he faints with pleasure. He has some of his family killed in this way.

That evening they amuse themselves by having Julie take a powder that gives her awful cramps: they tell her she has been poisoned, she believes it, she despairs; throughout the spectacle of her convulsions, the Duc has himself frigged in front of her by Augustine – who is unfortunate enough to cover the glans with the foreskin, which is one of the things that most displeases the Duc; he was about to come and this prevents him; he says he wants to cut off one of the bitch's fingers and cuts one from the offending hand, while his daughter Julie, who believes herself to be poisoned, helps him come. Julie has recovered by the end of the evening.

The eleventh. 55. A bugger often used to visit friends or acquaintances, and never failed to poison the human being most cherished by any such friend. He employed a powder that would do away with its victim after two days spent in terrible agonies.

56. A man with a taste for mauling bosoms improved on this by poisoning children on the very breast of their wet nurses.

57. He used to enjoy receiving the contents of milk enemas in his mouth, and then gave poisoned enemas that killed his victims with a terrible colic in their intestines.

58. A bugger, of whom she will have occasion to speak again on the thirteenth and the twenty-sixth, used to enjoy setting fire to poorhouses, and always did so in a manner that ensured that many were burnt, and children above all.

59. Another bugger used to enjoy making women die in childbirth by coming to see them armed with a powder, the smell of which induced spasms and convulsions that ended in their deaths.

60. The one of whom Duclos speaks on her twenty-eighth evening wants to see a woman give birth; he kills the baby as it emerges from its mother's belly before her very eyes, pretending to caress it as he does so.

That evening Aline is first flogged until she bleeds with a hundred lashes from each friend, then asked for some shit; she had already given some that morning to Curval, who denies this. Consequently they burn her on both breasts and the palms of her hands, they let sealing wax drip on to her thighs and on to her belly, they fill the hollow of her navel with the same, and they burn the hair of her cunt with aqua vitae. The Duc picks a quarrel with Zelmire, and Curval cuts off two of her fingers, one from each hand. Augustine is flogged across her crotch and arse.

The twelfth. The friends gather in the morning and decide that as the four old women are no longer of use to them and can easily be replaced in their duties by the four storytellers, it is time to have their way with them and torture them one after the other, beginning that very evening. The storytellers are asked to take their place – they accept on condition that they will not themselves be sacrificed; the friends give their word on this.

61. The three friends – d'Aucourt, the Abbé and Desprès – of whom Duclos spoke on the twelfth of 9ᵇᵉʳ still gather together to enjoy this particular passion: they find a woman who is eight

or nine months pregnant, open up her belly, tear out the baby, burn it before the mother's eyes, put in its place a pile of sulphur combined with mercury and quicksilver,[3] which they ignite, then they sew up the belly and leave her to die in front of them in unimaginable pain as they are frigged by that girl they have with them (*check her name*).[4]

62. He used to enjoy deflowering virgins, and now improves on this by having a great number of children with various women; then, as soon as they are five or six years old, he deflowers them, girl or boy, and throws them into a blazing oven as soon as he has fucked them – at the very moment of his climax.

63. The same man of whom Duclos spoke on 27th November, Martaine on the fifteenth of January, and Desgranges herself on the fifth of February, who had a taste for hanging his victims as he joked at their expense and for watching them hang, &c. – this man, as I say, hides his possessions in his servants' coffers and claims they have stolen from him. He tries to have them hanged, and if he succeeds, the spectacle will bring him to a climax – if not, he shuts them in a room and strangles them to death; he comes during this operation.

64. A great connoisseur of shit, the one of whom Duclos spoke on the fourteenth of November, has a specially prepared close stool at home; he invites the person he wants to perish to use it, and as soon as she is seated, the close stool gives way and tips her into a very deep shitpit where he leaves her to die.

65. A man of whom Martaine spoke, and who used to enjoy watching a girl fall from the top of a ladder, improves on this passion (*but check which man*).[5] He has the girl placed on a small trestle facing a deep pond, beyond which is a wall that offers an escape all the more assured as there is a ladder leaning against it, but first she has to dive into the pond, and this is all the more urgent as behind the trestle upon which she is placed a slow-burning fire is gaining on her little by little – if the fire reaches her she will be consumed, and if she dives into the water to avoid the fire she will drown as she does not know how to swim; with the fire upon her, she nevertheless chooses to throw herself into the water and head for the ladder she sees against the wall. Often the girl will drown, and there is no more to be

said; if she is fortunate enough to reach the ladder she climbs it, but a sabotaged rung near the top breaks underfoot when she reaches it, tipping her into a pit covered over with earth, which she had not seen and which, buckling under her weight, drops her into a flaming brazier where she perishes. The libertine, within view of this spectacle, frigs himself as he looks on.

66. The same one of whom Duclos spoke on 29th 9ber, the same one who deflowered Martaine's arse when she was five years old,[6] and the same one of whom, she announces, she will speak again when she comes to the passion with which she will conclude her tales (the passion of Hell) – this same man, as I say, buggers a girl of 16 to 18 years of age, the prettiest that can be found for him; just before he comes he releases a spring that lets fly upon the girl's bare neck a machine with steel teeth that saws away little by little and with great precision at the girl's neck while he has his climax. Which always lasts a long time.

That evening the affair between one of the subaltern fuckers and Augustine is discovered – he had not fucked her yet, but in order to do so he had proposed an escape that he presented as very easy; Augustine confesses she was on the verge of giving him what he asked of her in order to escape from a place where she believes her life to be in danger. It is Fanchon who discovers all this and reveals it. The four friends promptly throw themselves upon the fucker, tie him up, garrotte him and bring him down to the crypt, where the Duc buggers him violently, without pomade, while Curval cuts his throat and the two others burn him with a red-hot poker all over his body. This scene took place after lunch instead of the usual coffee; everyone goes to the chamber of stories as usual, and at supper the four libertines discuss among themselves whether Fanchon, who had discovered the conspiracy, should not be reprieved despite the decision taken in the morning to torture her that evening. The Bishop is against sparing her and says it would be unworthy of them to give in to any feeling of gratitude, and that they would always find him in favour of anything that might provide a new thrill to their company, and opposed to anything that might deprive it of any such pleasure. Consequently, having punished Augustine for taking part in the conspiracy, first by making her attend the execution of her lover, then by buggering her and making her believe her head will be cut off, and finally by tearing out two of her teeth (an operation the Duc carries out while Curval buggers this beautiful girl), having in short given her a thorough flogging – after all this, as I say, Fanchon is brought out, made to shit, each friend gives her a hundred lashes of the whip and the Duc slices her left breast clean off. She rails bitterly against the injustice of these proceedings. 'If it were just,' says the Duc, 'it would not make us hard!' Afterwards, her wound is dressed so she can be used for other torments. The glimmer of a general revolt among the subaltern fuckers comes to light but is completely quelled by the sacrifice of one of their number. The other three old women are, along with Fanchon, stripped of their duties and replaced by the storytellers and Julie. They shudder, but how to avoid their fate?

The thirteenth. 67. A man with a great love of arses lures a girl, whom he professes to love, for a jaunt on the water; the rowboat is specially prepared – it splits in two and the girl drowns. Sometimes the same man takes a different approach: he has a balcony prepared outside a bedroom at a great height, the girl leans against it, the balcony collapses and she is killed.

68. A man who used to enjoy flogging followed by buggery now improves on this by luring a girl to a specially prepared chamber: a trapdoor gives way and she tumbles into a crypt where the lecher is waiting; he plunges a dagger into her breasts, her cunt and her arsehole the moment she falls; he then throws her dead or alive into another crypt, the entrance to which is sealed with a stone; she lands upon the piled cadavers of those who came before, and dies there in a frenzy if she is not already dead. And he takes great care to stab her only gently with his dagger to avoid killing her too quickly, so that she dies only in the last crypt. He always buggers, flogs and comes beforehand. It is with sangfroid that he proceeds thus.

69. A bugger mounts the girl on an unbroken horse that drags her along until she falls to her death in a precipice.

70. The one of whom Martaine spoke on 18th January, and

whose first passion was to burn using piles of gunpowder, improves on this by having a girl placed in a specially prepared bed. As soon as she lies down it collapses on to a burning brazier, but one from which she can escape; he is there and whenever she tries to escape he drives her back with great blows from a pole into her belly.

71. The one of whom she spoke on the 11th, and who used to enjoy torching poorhouses, endeavours to lure men or women to his home on a charitable pretext; he buggers them, men or women, then breaks their backs and leaves them crippled in this way to die of hunger in a dungeon.

72. The one who used to enjoy throwing a woman through a window and on to a dunghill, and of whom Martaine spoke, carries out the following for his subsequent passion. He lets a girl sleep in her usual bedroom, the window of which she knows is very low to the ground: she is given opium; when she is fast asleep, she is moved to another bedroom identical to her own save for a window far higher off the ground that opens on to sharp stones; next, he barges into her bedroom, terrifying her; he tells her he is going to kill her; knowing her window to be low to the ground, she opens it and leaps through in great haste, but she falls on to the sharp stones from over thirty feet high, killing herself without anyone laying a finger on her.

That evening the Bishop as a woman takes Antinoüs as his husband, and as a man takes Céladon as his wife, and this child is buggered for the very first time on this day. The ceremony heralds the festivities of the fifteenth week; the prelate wants to crown the celebrations by brutally tormenting Aline, against whom his libertine rage is silently erupting – they string her up and let her down very quickly, and everyone comes as they see her hanging there. A bleeding that Durcet carries out pulls her through, and although it does not show the next day, she has grown an inch in the process; afterwards she describes what she suffered during this torture. The Bishop, for whom anything goes that day, slices old Louison's breast clean off her chest. Hence the two others clearly see what their fate will be.

*

The fourteenth. [73.] A man whose simple pleasure was to flog a girl improves on this by removing a pea-sized ball of flesh from a girl's body day after day, but her wounds are not dressed and so she slowly dies this way.

Desgranges warns that she will now speak of the most agonizing murders, and that the utmost cruelty will take centre stage; she is thus advised more than ever to spare no detail.

74. The one who used to enjoy bleeding girls now drains half an ounce of blood each day until they die. This one is warmly applauded.

75. The one who used to enjoy sticking pins in arses now stabs a girl lightly with a dagger each day; the blood is staunched but the wound is not dressed and so she dies slowly.

A fustigator 75[7] gently saws off each limb, one after another.

76. The first passion of the Marquis de Mesanges, of whom Duclos spoke earlier and to whom she sold the daughter of Petitgnon, the cobbler, was to have himself flogged for four hours without coming; his second passion is to place a little girl in the hands of a colossus, who holds the child by the head over a large brazier that burns only very gently – the girls must be virgins.

77. His first passion is to burn the flesh of breasts and buttocks little by little with a match, and his second is to prick a girl's body all over with sulphurous fuses that he lights one after the other – and he watches her die this way.

'No death is more painful,' says the Duc, who admits to having indulged in this abomination himself and to having vigorously come because of it, 'it is said the woman stays alive for six to 8 hours.'

In the evening Céladon's arse is offered up – the Duc and Curval have a fine time with him; Curval wants Constance to be bled for the sake of her pregnancy, and he bleeds her himself as he comes in Céladon's arse, then he cuts off one of Thérèse's breasts as he buggers Zelmire, and the Duc buggers Thérèse as they operate on her.

*

The fifteenth. 78. He used to enjoy sucking mouths and swallowing the saliva, and now he improves on this by having a girl swallow each day, for nine days, a small dose of molten lead through a funnel; she croaks on the ninth day.

79. He used to enjoy twisting fingers, and now he breaks every limb, tears out the tongue, gouges out the eyes, leaving her in this state while feeding her a little less each day.

80. A desecrator, the second of whom Martaine spoke on the third of January, ropes a handsome young boy to a cross raised very high, and leaves him there to be eaten by crows.

81. One who used to smell armpits and fuck them, and of whom Duclos spoke, now binds a girl hand and foot, hangs her by the armpits, and pricks her every day on some part of her body so that the blood will attract flies; he leaves her thus to die little by little.

82. A man with a passion for arses improves on this by entombing the girl in a crypt where she has enough to live on for three days; he injures her beforehand to make her death more painful. He wants them to be virgins and kisses their arses for a week before submitting them to this torture.

83. He used to enjoy fucking mouths and very young arses – he improves on this by ripping out the heart of a girl while she is still alive: he makes a hole in it, fucks this nice warm hole, then puts the heart back with his come still inside; her wound is sewn up and she is left without succour to her fate. Which is not long in coming in this case.

That evening Curval, still incensed against the beautiful Constance, says one can still give birth with a broken limb, and consequently they break the wretched girl's right arm. Durcet, the same evening, cuts off one of Marie's breasts, after flogging and making her shit beforehand.

The sixteenth. 84. A fustigator goes further by delicately hollowing out bones; he sucks out the marrow and pours molten lead in its place.

*

Here the Duc proclaims he will never fuck another arse if this is not the very torture he has in store for Augustine; the poor girl, whom he was buggering at the time, screams out and sheds a torrent of tears. And as she prevents him from coming by this scene, he gives her – as he frigs himself and comes on his own – a dozen slaps that ring out around the room.

85. A bugger minces a girl into small pieces on a specially prepared machine; this torture is from China.

86. He used to enjoy deflowering girls, and now likes mounting a maiden upon a sharpened stake by the cunt; with a cannonball tied to each foot, she straddles it like a horse as [it] is driven further in, and is left thus to die slowly.

87. A fustigator – flays a girl three times; he coats her fourth layer of skin in corrosive acid and she dies in terrible pain.

88. A man whose first passion was to cut off a finger, for his second now likes pinching a piece of flesh between red-hot pincers; he cuts this piece of [flesh] off with scissors then sears the wound. He spends four or five days stripping the flesh, little by little, from her body, and she dies from the pain of this cruel operation.

That evening they punish Sophie and Céladon, who are found enjoying themselves together: the two of them are flogged all over by the Bishop, to whom they belong; Sophie has two fingers cut off, as does Céladon, but, promptly healed, they nonetheless attend to the Bishop's pleasures. Fanchon is summoned to the stage once again and, after flogging her with a bull's pizzle, they burn her on the soles of her feet, her thighs front and rear, her forehead, the palms of both hands, and pull out her remaining teeth; the Duc almost always has his prick in her arse while they operate on her. Say that it has been prescribed by law that buttocks are not to be spoiled until the very day of the last torture.

The seventeenth. 89. Martaine's one of the thirtieth of January, whom she also described on the fifth of February, cuts off the breasts and buttocks of a young girl, eats them, then places dressings on her wounds that burn the flesh with such violence that she dies. He also forces her to eat her own flesh, which he has just cut from her body and which he has grilled.

90. A bugger – has a little girl boiled in a pot.

91. A bugger – has her roasted alive on a spit just after buggering her.

92. A man whose first passion was to have boys and girls buggered before him by very large pricks now impales a girl through the arse and lets her die this way as he observes her contortions.

93. A bugger – ties a woman to a wheel and, without having laid a finger on her beforehand, leaves her to die a natural death.

That evening the Bishop, all ablaze, wants Aline to be tormented – his rage against her is at its peak. She appears naked, he makes her shit and buggers her, then, without coming, he withdraws full of rage from her fine arse and gives her an enema of boiling water she is forced to expel, still boiling, in Thérèse's face; next they cut off all of Aline's remaining fingers and toes, they break both her arms, they burn them with a red-hot poker beforehand; then they flog and slap her until the Bishop, all ablaze, cuts off one of her breasts and comes. Then they turn to Thérèse – they burn the inside of her cunt, her nostrils, her tongue, her feet and her hands, and give her 600 lashes with the bull's pizzle. They pull out her remaining teeth and burn her gullet through her mouth. Augustine, a witness to this scene, starts to cry – the Duc flogs her bloody across her belly and cunt.

The eighteenth. 94. He used to have a passion for scarifying flesh, and now he likes to have a girl quartered by tying her between four young trees.

95. A fustigator hangs a girl from a machine that plunges her into a great fire before extracting her immediately, and this lasts until she is completely burnt.

96. He used to enjoy snuffing out candles on her flesh; now he covers her in sulphur and turns her into a torch, observing that the smoke fails to suffocate her.

97. A bugger – tears out the intestines of a young boy and a

young girl, puts the young boy's intestines in the girl's body, and the girl's intestines in the boy's body, then sews up the wounds, ties them back to back against a pillar and watches them die.

98. A man who used to enjoy gently burning his victims, now improves on this by having them roasted on a grill, as he turns them over and over.

That evening Michette is exposed to the full fury of the libertines: she is first flogged by all four, then each of them pulls out a tooth; they cut four fingers off (they each cut one off); they burn her thighs front and rear in four places; the Duc pummels her breast until it is black and blue while he buggers Giton. Next, Louison is summoned: she is made to shit, they give her eight hundred lashes with the bull's pizzle, they pull out all her teeth, they burn her tongue, arsehole, cunt and remaining breast, as well as 6 places on her thighs. As soon as everyone is in bed the Bishop goes to fetch his brother: they take Desgranges and Duclos with them; all four take Aline down to the crypt; the Bishop buggers her, as does the Duc; they pronounce her death sentence then carry it out with excessive torments that last until dawn. As they return upstairs they sing the praises of the two storytellers and counsel the other two always to make use of them in their tortures.

The nineteenth. 99. A bugger – he places the woman's rump on a stake with a diamond-shaped tip, her four limbs suspended in the air by string alone; the effect of this pain is to provoke laughter, and the torture is dreadful.

100. A man who used to enjoy cutting a little flesh from the buttocks improves on this by having a girl very gently sawn in half between two planks.

101. A bugger of both sexes has a brother and sister brought before him: he tells the brother he will die in dreadful torment, and shows him what lies in store, but adds that he will save his life if he is willing to fuck his sister then strangle her in front of him; the young man accepts, and while he fucks his sister the libertine buggers both the boy and the girl. Then the brother, out of fear for the death revealed to him, strangles his sister, and

the very moment he dispatches her a trapdoor opens and the two of them, in full view of the lecher, fall into a burning brazier.

102. A bugger – demands that a father fuck his daughter in front of him; he then buggers the girl in her father's arms. Next he tells the father his daughter absolutely must die but that he has a choice: either he can kill her himself by strangling her, so that she does not suffer, or, if he does not want to kill his daughter, then he, the bugger, will do it himself in front of the father by the most appalling tortures; the father prefers to kill his daughter with a cord around the neck rather than see her suffer dreadful agonies, but as he prepares to do so he is tied up, garrotted, and his daughter skinned in front of him; she is then rolled over red-hot iron spikes and thrown into a brazier, and the father is strangled to teach him a lesson, says the libertine, for agreeing to strangle his own daughter; afterwards he is thrown into the same brazier as his daughter.

103. A great connoisseur of arses and flogging summons a mother and daughter: he tells the daughter that if she does not agree to have both her hands cut off he will kill her mother; the little girl agrees and they are indeed cut off; he then separates these two creatures, stringing the girl up by the neck with her feet perched on a stool; tied around the stool is another cord that leads into another room, where the mother is held; the mother is told to pull the cord – she does so without knowing what she is doing; she is promptly shown the fruits of her labour and as she is overcome by despair she is felled by a sabre to the back of the head.

That same evening Durcet, jealous of the pleasures enjoyed the previous night by the two brothers, wants them all to torment Adélaïde, whose turn he insists it will soon be anyway: consequently Curval (her father) and Durcet (her husband) pinch her thighs between red-hot pincers while the Duc buggers her without pomade; they pierce the tip of her tongue, they cut off the tops and bottoms of both ears, they pull out four teeth, then they give her an almighty flogging. That same evening the Bishop bleeds Sophie in front of Adélaïde, her dear friend, until she faints; he buggers her as he bleeds her, remaining in her arse the whole time. Narcisse has two fingers cut off while Curval buggers him, then Marie is brought out and they thrust a red-hot poker into her arse and cunt, burn her with a hot poker in 6 different places on her thighs, her clitoris, her tongue and her remaining breast, and pull out her remaining teeth.

The twentieth of February. 104. Champville's one of the fifth of December, who had a taste for making a mother prostitute her son for him to bugger, improves on this by summoning both mother and son: he tells the mother he is about to kill her, but that he will spare her if she kills her son. If she does not kill him the child's throat is cut in front of her, and if she does kill him she is bound to his corpse and left to die slowly upon the cadaver.

105. A great devotee of incest summons two sisters he has just buggered: he binds them to a machine, each of them holding a dagger; the machine starts, the girls are pressed together, and each kills the other.

106. Another devotee of incest requires a mother and four children: he locks them in a room where he can observe them; he gives them no food so that he may see the effects of hunger upon the woman and see which of her children she will eat first.

107. Champville's one of the twenty-ninth of December, who used to enjoy flogging pregnant women, wants both mother and daughter to be pregnant: he binds them both to iron plates, one above the other; a spring is released, and the two plates slam against each other with such violence that the two women are reduced to powder along with their unborn fruit.

108. An inveterate bugger takes his pleasure in the following manner. He summons a lover and his mistress: 'There is only one person in the world,' he says to the lover, 'who stands in the way of your happiness – I shall deliver him to you.' He leads him into a dark room where someone is lying asleep in a bed: wildly excited, the young man goes over and runs the person through; the moment he has done so he is shown that it is his mistress he has killed; out of despair he kills himself – if he does not the libertine shoots him dead, not daring to enter the bedroom where the young man, armed and enraged, remains. Beforehand he had fucked both the young boy and

the young girl, promising to help their cause and bring them together, and it is only once he has done so that he lays this trap.

That evening, to celebrate the sixteenth week, Durcet as a woman takes Bande-au-ciel as his husband, and as a man takes Hyacinthe as his wife; at the wedding, however, he wants to torment Fanny, Hyacinthe's female wife. Consequently they burn her arms and 6 places on her thighs, they pull out two teeth, they flog her, they force Hyacinthe, who loves her and is her husband according to the sensual arrangements described above – they force him, as I say, to shit in Fanny's mouth, and her to eat it. The Duc pulls one of Augustine's teeth out and fucks her in the mouth straight after. Fanchon reappears – they bleed her and, as the blood drips from her arm, they break it; next they remove her toenails and cut off her fingers.

The twenty-first. 109. She announces that the following are buggers who murder male victims only. He thrusts a gun barrel loaded with heavy grapeshot up the arse of a boy he has just fucked and pulls the trigger as he comes.

110. He forces the young boy to watch his mistress being carved up before his very eyes, and he makes him eat the flesh. And mainly from her buttocks, breasts and heart. He must either eat these dishes or die of hunger; as soon as he has eaten, if this is the choice he makes, he is wounded all over his body and left thus to bleed to death, and if he does not eat he dies of hunger.

111. He rips off his balls and has him eat them without telling him so, then replaces these testicles with balls of mercury, quicksilver and sulphur that cause such violent agonies that he dies from them; he buggers him during these agonies and adds to them by burning him all over with sulphur fuses, and by scratching and burning all the wounds.

112. He nails him by his arsehole to a very narrow stake, and leaves him thus to die.

113. He buggers him, and during this act of sodomy he opens the skull, removes the brain and replaces it with molten lead.

That evening Hyacinthe's arse is offered up and he is vigorously fustigated before they proceed. Narcisse is brought out – they cut off his 2 balls. Adélaïde is summoned – they press a red-hot shovel against the front of her thighs, they burn her clitoris, they pierce her tongue, they flog her breasts, they cut off her nipples, they break both her arms, they cut off her remaining fingers, they pull out the hair of her cunt, six teeth and a handful of hair from her head. Everyone comes, except the Duc who, as hard as a madman, asks permission to execute Thérèse himself – this is granted; he removes all her nails with a penknife and burns her fingers with a candle for good measure, then breaks an arm and, yet to come, he fucks Augustine's cunt and pulls out one of her teeth as he finally lets his come spurt into her cunt.

[*The twenty-second.*] 114. He breaks the bones of a young boy then ties him to a wheel upon which he is left to die; he is rotated to show his buttocks up close, and the scoundrel who torments him has his dining table placed beneath the wheel, and eats there every day until the patient has died.

115. He peels the skin from a young boy, rubs honey all over him, and leaves him to be devoured by flies.

116. He cuts off the boy's prick and nipples, places him on a stake to which he is nailed by his foot, and props him up against another stake to which he is nailed by his hand; he leaves him thus to die a natural death.

117. The same man who had made Duclos eat with his dogs has a young boy devoured by a lion in front of him, giving him just a flimsy pole with which to defend himself and this only enrages the beast further against him; he comes when the boy is completely devoured.

118. He turns a young boy over to an ungelded horse trained for this purpose, and the horse buggers him to death; the child is covered in a mare's skin, and has his arsehole smeared with a mare's come.

That same evening Giton is offered up for torture: the Duc, Curval, Hercule and Brise-cul fuck him without pomade; he is roundly thrashed, has four teeth pulled out, four fingers cut off (it is four of everything as all four officiate), and Durcet crushes one of his balls between his fingers. Augustine is roundly thrashed by all four, her fine arse bleeds, the Duc buggers her while Curval cuts off a finger, then Curval buggers her while the Duc burns her thighs with a red-hot poker in 6 places; the Duc cuts off another finger at the moment of Curval's climax and despite all this [she] still has to spend the night with him. They break Marie's arm, pull out her fingernails, and burn her fingers. That same night Durcet and Curval take Adélaïde down to the crypt, assisted by Desgranges and Duclos. Curval buggers her for the last time then they have her die from dreadful tortures you will describe in detail.

The twenty-third. 119. He places a young boy in a machine that stretches him, sometimes from above, sometimes from below, as it dislocates his limbs; his bones are broken into small pieces, and he is by turns removed and placed back inside for several days in succession until his death.

120. He has a young boy masturbated to the point of exhaustion by a pretty girl; he is soon completely spent, is not fed at all, and dies in terrible convulsions.

121. He carries out on the same day and on the same patient a gallstone operation, trepanning, the removal of a fistula from the eye, and another from the anus; all these operations are carefully botched, and he is abandoned in this state without succour until he dies.

122. Having sliced the prick and balls clean off, he forms a cunt for the young man with a red-hot instrument that creates the hole and cauterizes instantly; he fucks him in this opening and strangles him with his bare hands as he comes.

123. He rubs him down with a currycomb; when he has drawn blood this way, he rubs in aqua vitae which he then lights; he then rubs him down again, rubs in more aqua vitae which he again lights, and so on until he dies.

That same evening Narcisse is brought out to be tortured: they burn his thighs and prick, they crush his two balls.[8] Augustine is brought out again by order of the Duc who has it in for her:

they burn her thighs and armpits, and thrust a hot poker into her cunt; she faints – this only infuriates the Duc even more; he cuts off a breast, drinks her blood, breaks both her arms, pulls out the hair of her cunt, all her teeth, and cuts off all her fingers, cauterizing them with a flame. He nevertheless takes her to bed and, according to Duclos, fucks her in the cunt and arse all night, telling her he will finish her off the following day. Louison is summoned: they break her arm, they burn her tongue and her clitoris, they pull out all her nails and they burn the ends of her bloodied fingers. Curval sodomizes her in this state and in his rage crushes and pummels one of Zelmire's breasts with all his might as he comes. Not content with this excess, he grabs her again and roundly thrashes her.

The twenty-fourth. 124. The same one as Martaine's fourth of the first of January wants to bugger a father between his two children, and as he comes he stabs one of these children with one hand and strangles the second with the other.

125. A man whose first passion was flogging pregnant women across the belly, for his second now gathers six of them together eight months along: he ties them all up back to back in pairs, presenting their bellies; he splits open the stomach of the first, pierces that of the second with blows from a knife, kicks that of the third a hundred times, strikes that of the fourth a hundred times with a rod, burns that of the fifth and grates the skin from that of the sixth – and then he bludgeons the belly of any who have survived his torture.

Curval interrupts with some frenzied scene of his own making, this passion having greatly inflamed him.

126. The seducer mentioned by Duclos gathers two women together: he exhorts the first to save her life by renouncing God and her religion, but she has been prompted beforehand not to do anything of the sort and told that if she does she will be killed, while if she does not no harm will come to her. She stands firm and he blows her brains out – 'There's one for God!' He summons the second woman who, struck both by this example and by

what she was told on the sly – that the only way to save her life was to renounce God – does everything that is asked of her. He blows her brains out – 'There's another for the Devil!' The scoundrel plays this little game every week.

127. A prodigious bugger enjoys hosting balls, but the floor is specially prepared to collapse when the room is full, and almost everyone perishes. If he were always to remain in the same town he would be discovered, but he changes town very often; he is only discovered on the fiftieth occasion.

128. The same one as Martaine's of 27th January, who has a taste for inducing abortions, places three pregnant women in three cruel poses to form three pleasing compositions; he watches them give birth in these circumstances, then he ties their babies around their necks until they die or are eaten, for he leaves the mothers in this pose without feeding them.

[ ]9 The same one also had another passion: he would have two women give birth in front of him, would blindfold them while he switched their babies (whom he alone could distinguish by a birthmark) and would then order them to identify their own child. If they made no mistake he would let them live, if they did make a mistake he would cleave them with a sabre over the body of the child they had taken for their own.

The same evening Narcisse is brought out for the orgies: they cut off his remaining fingers while the Bishop buggers him and Durcet operates on him; a red-hot needle is thrust into his urethra. Giton is summoned: they knock him about, playing ball with his body, and break his leg while the Duc buggers him without coming. Zelmire appears: they burn her clitoris, tongue, and gums, they pull out four teeth, they burn her thighs front and rear in six different places, they cut off both nipples, all her fingers, and Curval buggers her in this state without coming. Fanchon is summoned and they put out an eye. During the night the Duc and Curval, escorted by Desgranges and Duclos, take Augustine down to the crypt: her arse, which had been kept in pristine condition, is flogged; they each bugger her but do not come, then the Duc inflicts fifty-eight cuts on her buttocks and pours boiling oil into each of them; he thrusts a hot poker into her cunt and arse, and fucks her wounds with a condom made from dogfish skin[10] that tears open the burns; this done, they lay bare her bones and saw them apart in different places, then they lay bare her nerves in four places to form a cross, they attach a tourniquet to the end of each of these nerves and they twist them, stretching these tender fibres and causing her to suffer unspeakable agonies; they give her brief respite to make her suffer all the more, then they resume the operation and this time they scrape her nerves with a penknife as they stretch them; this done, they make a hole in her gullet through which they pull her tongue; they slowly burn her remaining breast, then they thrust a hand wielding a scalpel into her cunt, cutting apart the septum separating the anus from the vagina; they leave the scalpel to one side and thrust a hand in again to rummage around in her bowels and force her to shit through her cunt; next, through the same opening, they split her stomach sac open, then they return to her face; they cut off her ears, they burn the inside of her nose, they put out her eyes by letting molten sealing wax trickle into them, they score her skull all around, they hang her up by her hair with stones attached to her feet so that she falls and the top of her skull is pulled off. When she fell from this height she was still breathing and the Duc fucked her in the cunt in this state – he came, only to withdraw even more frenzied than before; they cut her open, they burned her intestines in her belly, and with a hand bearing a scalpel stabbed her heart from within in different places. Only then did she give up the ghost; thus perished at fifteen years and 8 months one of the most heavenly creatures ever formed by Nature, &c. Her eulogy.

The twenty-fifth. 129. (From this morning, the Duc takes Colombe as his wife and she carries out her duties accordingly.) A great connoisseur of arses buggers the mistress in full view of her lover and her lover in full view of his mistress, then he nails the lover to his mistress's body and leaves them thus to die mouth to mouth one on top of the other.

This will be the torture for Céladon and Sophie, who love each other, and there is an interruption as Céladon is forced to drip sealing wax on to Sophie's thighs – he faints; the Bishop fucks him in this state.

130. The same one who used to enjoy throwing a girl into the water and then fishing her out, now enjoys throwing seven or eight girls into a pond and watching them struggle; he has a red-hot iron rod dangled in front of them, they try to grab hold, but he forces them back, and to make sure they perish he cuts off a limb from each of them as he throws them in.

131. His first taste was for making others vomit; he improves on this by using a secret method by which he spreads the plague across a whole province; it is extraordinary how many people he has already killed. He also used to poison fountains and rivers.

132. A man who used to enjoy the whip now has three pregnant women and three of their children put together in an iron cage: a fire is lit beneath the cage; as its base heats up the women skip and hop about, taking their children into their arms, and eventually fall down and die. (*This has been mentioned somewhere earlier – see where.*)[11]

133. He used to enjoy pricking the flesh with an awl, and he now improves on this by enclosing a pregnant woman in a barrel filled with spikes; he then has the barrel vigorously rolled around a garden.

Constance was as distressed by these tales of the torture of pregnant women as Curval was delighted by them – she sees her fate all too well; as it is indeed looming, they decide her torments may now begin. They burn her thighs in six places, they drip sealing wax on to her navel and they prick her breasts with pins. Giton is summoned: they thrust a red-hot needle through his rod, they prick his balls, they pull out four teeth. Next to appear is Zelmire, whose death is approaching: they thrust a red-hot poker into her cunt, they wound her breast in six different places and her thighs in twelve, they prick her navel deeply, she receives twenty slaps from each friend; they pull out four teeth, they prick one eye, they flog her and they bugger her; as he sodomizes her, Curval, her husband, informs her she will die the following day – she is delighted at this, saying it will mean an end to her woes. Rosette is summoned: they pull out four teeth, they brand her with a red-hot poker on both shoulder blades, they cut her thighs and calves, then they bugger her as they pummel her breasts. Thérèse is summoned: they put out an eye and they give her a hundred lashes across her back with a bull's pizzle.

The twenty-sixth. 134. A bugger stands at the foot of a tower in a spot covered in iron spikes: from the top of the tower a number of children of both sexes, whom he has buggered beforehand, are hurled down; he delights in seeing them impaled and in finding himself spattered with their blood.

135. The same one of whom she had spoken on 11th and 13th February, and who has a taste for arson, also has a passion for shutting six pregnant women away in a place where they are tied to inflammable material; he sets fire to it and if they try to escape he lies in wait with an iron pole, beats them with it and drives them back into the fire. Meanwhile, as they are half-roasted, the floor collapses and they fall into a great vat of boiling oil specially prepared beneath for them, where they finally perish.

136. The same one of whom Madame Duclos spoke, who so despises the poor, who bought Lucile, her mother and her sister, and who was cited by Desgranges (*check this*),[12] also has a passion for gathering a family of paupers together over a landmine and watching it explode.

137. A devotee of incest and a great connoisseur of sodomy, in order to combine the latter with the crimes of incest, murder, rape, sacrilege and adultery, has himself buggered by his sons with the host up his arse, rapes his married daughter and kills his niece.

138. A great lover of arses strangles a mother as he buggers her; when she is dead he turns her over and fucks her in the cunt; as he comes he kills the daughter on her mother's bosom by knifing her repeatedly in the breast, then he fucks the girl in the arse even though she is now dead – next, utterly convinced they are not yet dead and can still be made to suffer, he throws the cadavers on to a fire and comes as he watches them burn. He is the same one of whom Duclos spoke on the twenty-ninth of November, who used to enjoy observing a girl on a bed covered

in black satin; he is also the first one Martaine describes on the eleventh of January.

Narcisse is brought out to be tortured: they cut off his hand at the wrist, and do the same to Giton. They burn the inside of Michette's cunt, do the same to Rosette, and both of them are burned on their bellies and breasts, but Curval, who is no longer master of himself despite the statutes, cuts off Rosette's whole breast as he buggers Michette. Next comes Thérèse, who is given two hundred lashes of the bull's pizzle all over her body and whose eye is put out. That night Curval comes to fetch the Duc and, escorted by Desgranges and Duclos, they take Zelmire down to the dungeon, where the most refined torments are employed to put her to death; these are all far more formidable even than those suffered by Augustine, and they are found still operating on her at breakfast time the next day. This beautiful girl dies aged 15 years and two months. Hers was the finest arse of the girls' harem. And the following day Curval, who no longer has a wife, takes Hébé.

The twenty-seventh. The festivities of the seventeenth and last week are deferred to the following day so that they coincide with the conclusion of the storytelling, and Desgranges recounts the following passions.

[139.] A man of whom Martaine spoke on the twelfth of January and who used to burn fireworks up the arse, now has a passion for binding two pregnant women together in the shape of a ball, and firing them from a mortar.

140. One with a taste for scarifying forces two pregnant women to fight each other in a room (they are observed without any risk) – to fight, as I say, armed with daggers: they are naked; he threatens them with a rifle he aims at them in case they do not put their hearts into it. If they kill each other he has what he wants; if not, he storms, sword in hand, into the room where they are, and once he has killed one of them he eviscerates the other and burns her intestines with aqua fortis, or with red-hot pieces of iron.

141. A man who used to enjoy flogging the bellies of pregnant women improves on this by attaching the pregnant girl to a wheel, beneath which, strapped to an armchair and unable to move, is this girl's mother, her mouth wide open, and forced to catch in her mouth all the filth that drips from the cadaver – and the baby if she gives birth to it.

142. The one of whom Martaine spoke on the sixteenth of January, and who used to enjoy pricking arses, attaches a girl to a machine completely covered in iron spikes: he fucks her upon it so that each thrust nails her to it all the more; next he turns her over and fucks her in the arse so that she is pricked equally on her other side, and he pushes down on her back so that her breasts are also skewered. When he is done he places over her a second panel, similarly prepared, then screws the two panels together; she dies thus, crushed and pierced all over. The panels are screwed together little by little – she is given all the time in the world to die in agony.

143. A fustigator – places a pregnant woman upon a table: he nails her to this table by first driving a red-hot nail through each eye, another through her mouth, and another into each breast, then he burns her clitoris and nipples with a candle, and slowly saws halfway through her knees, breaks her leg bones and finally drives an enormous red-hot nail through her navel which finishes off her baby as well as herself; he wants her to be about to give birth.

That evening Julie and Duclos are flogged, but only for sport as they are both among the protected few; despite this, Julie's thighs are burned in two places and she is depilated. Constance, who is to perish the next day, is summoned but still remains ignorant of her fate: they burn both her nipples, they drip sealing wax on to her belly, they pull out four teeth and they prick the whites of her eyes with a needle. Narcisse, who is also to be sacrificed the next day, is summoned: they pull out an eye and four teeth. Giton, Michette and Rosette, who must also accompany Constance to the grave, each have an eye and four teeth pulled out; Rosette has both nipples cut off, and 6 lumps of flesh gouged from her arms and thighs in equal measure; they cut off all her fingers and they thrust a red-hot poker into her cunt and into her arse. Curval and the Duc each come twice. Next to appear is Louison: they give her a hundred lashes of the bull's pizzle, and pull out her eye – which they force her to swallow; and she does.

The twenty-eighth. 144. A bugger – sends for two women who are firm friends: he ties them together mouth to mouth; in front of them is an excellent meal but they cannot reach it and he watches the two of them devour each other when their hunger becomes unbearable.

145. A man who used to enjoy flogging pregnant women shuts six of this sort within a ring formed by iron hoops: this forms a cage within which they all sit facing each other inside. Little by little, the ring contracts and tightens and all six are flattened and suffocated together with their unborn fruit. But beforehand he cut off a buttock and breast from each of them and arranged these around their necks like a stole.

146. Another man who used to enjoy flogging pregnant women ties two of them to poles attached to a machine that hurls and crashes them against each other. With these shocking blows each kills the other and he comes. He tries to use a mother and daughter, or two sisters.

147. The Comte, of whom Duclos spoke, and of whom Desgranges also spoke on the 26th (the one who bought Lucile, her mother, and her little sister), and the 4th of whom Martaine also spoke on 1st January, has one last passion, which is to hang three women over three holes: one of these is hanged by the tongue, and the hole beneath her is a very deep well; the second is hanged by the breasts, and the hole beneath her is a brazier; the third has her skull scored all around and is hanged by her hair, and [the] hole beneath her is covered in iron spikes. When the bodyweight of these women pulls them down, the hair tearing off with the scalp, the breasts ripping apart and the tongue shearing off, they escape from one torture only to begin another; when he can he procures three pregnant women, or a family if not, and this is the use he made of Lucile, her sister and her mother.

148. The final one. (*Check why these two are missing – they*

were all there in the drafts.)[13] The noble lord who indulges in the final passion, which we shall give the name of Hell, has been cited four times. He is Duclos's last one of 29th 9[ber], he is Champville's one who deflowers only nine year olds, Martaine's one who deflowers the arses of three year olds, and the one Desgranges spoke of herself a little earlier (*check where*).[14] He is a man of 40 years of age, of enormous stature and hung like a mule – his prick measures almost 9 inches around by a foot long; he is very wealthy, a very great nobleman, very obdurate and very cruel. For this particular passion he uses a house, utterly isolated, on the edge of Paris. The apartment he devotes to this pleasure includes a large and simply furnished reception room, but thickly padded throughout; a window is the only visible opening in this room – it overlooks a vast dungeon twenty feet beneath the floor of the room where he lies in wait, and, below the window are mattresses upon which the girls land when he hurls them into this crypt, as we shall describe a little later. He requires fifteen girls for this entertainment, all between fifteen and seventeen years of age, no older and no younger; six bawds in Paris and twelve in the provinces are hired to look for the most charming creatures of this age who can possibly be found, and they are cooped together as they are found in a rural convent of which he is the master – and from these he picks the fifteen subjects for his passion, which is carried out without fail every fortnight. He examines the subjects himself the day before: the slightest flaw rules them out – he wants them to be absolute models of beauty. They arrive escorted by a bawd and wait in a room adjoining his chamber of delights; they are shown to him first in this room, all fifteen of them naked; he touches them, fondles them, examines them, sucks on their mouths, and has them shit one after the other into his mouth, but he does not swallow. This first procedure is executed with terrifying gravity; he brands a number upon the shoulder of each with a red-hot iron according to the order in which he wants them to be sent in; this done, he enters the chamber alone, and remains there alone for a moment but no one knows how he spends this moment of solitude. Next he knocks on the door: the girl numbered 1 is thrown to him, but thrown with great precision;

the bawd hurls her towards him and he catches her in his arms
– she is naked. He closes the door, takes a birch and begins to
flog her arse; this done, he sodomizes her with his enormous
prick and never requires any assistance; he does not come; he
withdraws his erect prick, takes the birch again and flogs her
back, her thighs front and rear, then lays her back down and
deflowers her in front; next he takes the birch once more and
roundly thrashes her across her breasts, then grabs both of them
and pummels them with all his strength; this done, he wounds
her flesh with an awl in six different places, including one on
each of her battered breasts. Next, he opens the window that
overlooks the dungeon, stands the girl straight with her arse to
him near the middle of the room and facing the window; from
there he gives her such a brutal kick up the arse that she flies
through the window and falls on to the mattresses below – but
before he sends them falling in this way, he ties a ribbon around
their neck and this ribbon represents the torture he deems the
most appropriate or which he will find the most sensual to inflict,
and his subtlety and discernment in such matters is extraordinary. All the girls are shown in, one after the other, and all submit
to exactly the same ceremony, so that he takes thirty virginities
in a single day – all without spilling a drop of come. The crypt
into which the girls fall is furnished with fifteen different instruments of appalling torture, and executioners bearing the mask
and symbol of a demon preside over each torture, dressed in the
colour assigned to that particular torment; the ribbon the girl
wears around her neck corresponds to one of the colours assigned
to these tortures, and as soon as she hits the floor the executioner
bearing that colour seizes her and leads her to the torture over
which he presides – but the torments only begin when the last of
the fifteen has fallen there. As soon as she is down there, our man,
in a frenzied state having taken thirty virginities without coming,
descends, almost naked and with his prick glued to his belly, into
this infernal den. All is now in motion and all the tortures are
executed, and executed at the same time.

The 1st torture is a wheel to which the girl is attached and
which turns endlessly, brushing against a ring covered in razor
blades, upon which the unfortunate girl scratches and cuts herself

every which way with every turn, but as she is only lightly brushed by the blades she goes round for at least two hours before dying.

The 2nd. The girl is laid out two inches from a red-hot iron plate that melts her slowly.

3. Her rump is pinned to a red-hot piece of iron and each of her limbs contorts and is horribly dislocated.

4. Her four limbs attached to four springs that stretch little by little, slowly tugging on them until they finally come away and the torso falls into a brazier.

5. A red-hot iron bell serves as a bonnet for her but without any downward pressure applied, so her brain slowly melts and her head fries little by little.

6. She is chained up inside a vat of boiling oil.

7. Standing straight in front of a machine that fires stinging darts at her body 6 times per minute, always at a different spot; the machine stops only when she is covered in them.

8. Her feet in a furnace, and a leaden weight on her head pushes her down as she burns.

9. Her executioner pricks her constantly with a red-hot poker; she is tied up in front of him; little by little he wounds every inch of her body thus.

10. She is chained to a pillar beneath a glass dome, and little by little twenty ravenous serpents devour her alive.

11. She hangs by one hand with two cannonballs tied to her feet; if she falls it is into a furnace.

12. She is impaled through her mouth, with her feet in the air; a relentless deluge of flying sparks showers her body.

13. Her nerves pulled out of her body and tied to cords that stretch them, and pricked with red-hot iron spikes throughout.

14. Tortured and flogged by turns across the cunt [and] arse with iron cat-o'-nine-tails with red-hot steel spurs, and, from time to time, scratched with red-hot iron claws.

15. She is poisoned with a drug that burns and shreds her intestines, causes dreadful convulsions, makes her utter dreadful screams, but which is not intended to kill her until she is the last one alive; this is one of the most terrible tortures.

The scoundrel strolls around his crypt as soon as he arrives down there; he examines each torture for a quarter of an hour, blaspheming like one of the damned and hurling insults at each victim. When at last he can no longer take any more, and his come, trapped for so long, is ready to escape, he throws himself into an armchair from which he can observe all the torments: two of the demons approach, show their arses and frig him, and he spills his come while his screams drown out those of the fifteen victims; this done, he leaves; the *coup de grâce* is given to those who are not yet dead, their bodies are buried and there is no more to be said for that fortnight.

Here Desgranges ends her tales; she is complimented, acclaimed, &c.

Since the morning of this day terrible preparations had been underway for the planned festivities. Curval, who despises Constance, had gone to fuck her in the cunt first thing in the morning, and informed her of her sentence as he fucked her. Coffee was served by the five victims, namely Constance, Narcisse, Giton, Michette and Rosette. Horrors were committed throughout. During the tale that has just been read, what could be assembled of the quadrilles was naked there. And as soon as Desgranges had finished, Fanny was first to be summoned: they cut off her remaining fingers and toes, and she was buggered without pomade by Curval, the Duc and the four senior fuckers. Sophie appeared: Céladon, her lover, was obliged to burn the inside of her cunt; they cut off all her fingers, and they bled her from all four limbs; they tore off her right ear and pulled out her left eye; Céladon was compelled to assist throughout and often to carry out the torments himself, and at the slightest grimace he was flogged with a cat-o'-nine-tails with iron spikes. Next, they had supper: the meal was sumptuous and they drank only sparkling champagne and liqueurs. The torture took place at the hour of the orgies: as Messieurs ate their desserts they were approached and informed that all was ready; they went down and found the crypt well decorated and very well prepared. Constance was laid out on a kind of bier and the four children graced the four corners. As their arses were very fresh, great pleasure was taken in mauling them. Finally the torture began:

Curval himself opened Constance's belly as he buggered Giton, and ripped out her unborn fruit, which was already very developed and clearly of the male sex; then the torments, as cruel as they were varied, continued upon these five victims.

On 1st March, seeing that the snows had not yet melted, they decide to dispatch all those who remain one by one; the friends contrive new domestic arrangements in their bedrooms, and decide to give a green ribbon to all those who are to be brought back to France, on condition they lend a hand in the tortures of the remaining few. They say nothing to the six women working in the kitchen, but decide to torture the three maids who are well worth the trouble, and to spare the three cooks because of their talents. Consequently they draw up a list and see that at this point the following have already been sacrificed:

> wives: Aline, Adélaïde and Constance 3
> harem girls: Augustine, Michette, Rosette
> and Zelmire 4
> catamites: Giton and Narcisse 2
> fuckers: one of the subalterns 1
> *Total* 10

Skip to the mark on the last sheet of the recto.[15]

Here begins the end and the continuation of the verso.

The new domestic arrangements are thus put in place: the Duc takes with him or under his protection

> Hercule, Madame Duclos and a cook 4
> Curval takes Brise-cul, Champville and a
> cook 4
> Durcet takes Bande-au-ciel, Martaine
> and a cook 4
> and the Bishop, Antinoüs, Madame Desgranges
> and Julie 4
> 16

and it is decided only at that very moment and by agreement between the four friends, the four fuckers and the four story-tellers (the cooks not being wanted for this task), that all who remain shall be seized, with the utmost treachery, except for the three maids who shall not be seized until the last few days, and that the rooms of the upper floors shall be transformed into four prisons; that the three subaltern fuckers shall be put in the most secure of these and chained there; in the second, Fanny, Colombe, Sophie and Hébé; in the third, Céladon, Zélamir, Cupidon, Zéphire, Adonis and Hyacinthe; and in the fourth, the old women. And as a subject is to be dispatched each day, when it is time for the three maids to be arrested they shall be put in whichever of the prisons is empty. This done, each storyteller is made a prison warden. And Messieurs shall enjoy themselves whenever they wish with these victims, either in their prison or in the other rooms or in their own bedroom – it shall be entirely as they please. Consequently, as has just been stated, one subject is thus dispatched each day in the following order.

On 1st March, Fanchon. – On the 2nd, Louison. – On the 3rd, Thérèse. – On the 4th, Marie. – On the 5th, Fanny. – On the 6th and 7th, Sophie and Céladon together as lovers, and they perish, as has already been said, nailed one above the other. – On the 8th, one of the subaltern fuckers. – On the 9th, Hébé. – On the 10th, one of the subaltern fuckers. – On the 11th, Colombe. – On the 12th, the last of the subaltern fuckers. – On the 13th, Zélamir, on the 14th, Cupidon, on the 15th, Zéphire. – On the 16th, Adonis. – On the 17th, Hyacinthe. – On the 18th, in the morning, they seize the three maids and shut them away in the prison where the old women were, and dispatch them on the 18th, 19th and 20th.

Total 20

This summary shows the roles of all the
subjects as there were in total 46, namely

masters 4
old women 4
in the kitchen. 6

storytellers 4
fuckers 8
young boys 8
wives 4
young girls 8
Total 46

that, of these, 30 have been sacrificed while 16 return to Paris.

Total count.

Slaughtered before 1st March in the 1st orgies . . 10
since 1st March 20
and those returning . . . . 16 people
Total 46

As regards both the torture of the last twenty subjects and the life led up to the day of departure, you will detail these at your leisure; you will say first that the remaining 12 all ate together, and describe the tortures as you choose.

Notes.

Do not deviate in the slightest from this plan, everything within it has been worked out several times and with the greatest precision.

Describe the departure. And throughout add above all some moral instruction to the suppers.

When you come to copy it all out have a notebook, in which you will place the names of all the principal characters and all those who play an important role, such as those with numerous passions and those of whom you have spoken several times, like the one of Hell; leave a large margin by their names and fill this margin with everyone you find who resembles them as you make your copy – this note is utterly essential and it is the only way you will be able to see your work clearly and avoid repetitions.

Tone down considerably the 1ˢᵗ part: everything goes too far – it cannot be too mild or too veiled; above all do not have the four friends do anything that has not been related, and you have not taken care over this.

In the 1ˢᵗ part, say that the man who fucks the mouth of the little girl prostituted by her father is the one who fucks with a filthy prick and of whom she has already spoken.

Do not forget to place in December the scene of the little girls serving supper and squirting liqueurs into the friends' glasses with their arses; you announced this, but did not talk about it in the plan.[16]

Supplementary Tortures.

By means of a pipe, they introduce a mouse into her cunt; the pipe is withdrawn, they sew up the cunt, and the animal, unable to escape, devours her intestines.

They make her swallow a serpent which will in turn devour her.

In general, portray Curval and the Duc as two fiery and reckless scoundrels – this is how you describe them in the 1ˢᵗ part and in the plan – and portray the Bishop as a cold, rational and hardened scoundrel; as for Durcet, he must be spiteful, false, treacherous and perfidious. Have them do, accordingly, all that is appropriate to such temperaments.

Review with care the name and rank of all the characters described by your storytellers, to avoid repetitions.

In the notebook with your characters, with the plan of the castle, room by room, add a page with a blank left to one side to be filled with the kind of things you will have them do in one room or another.

All this great scroll was begun on 22ⁿᵈ 8ᵇᵉʳ 1785 and finished in 37 days.

Notes

[INTRODUCTION]

1. *the Regent . . . the Chamber of Justice*: When Louis XIV died in 1715 his nephew Philippe d'Orléans overturned the late monarch's will and assumed power as Regent for Louis XV, who was five years old. The Regent's edict of March 1716 established the *Chambre de justice* to investigate whether financiers had acted illegally, for example by breaking usury laws; punishment included severe fines, imprisonment or both.

2. *four among them*: The text is confused here. Of Sade's four libertines only Durcet is a tax-collector (*traitant*).

3. *Président*: The title conferred on judges in the *parlements*, or Courts of Justice in *ancien régime* France. There were twelve such courts in the provinces and one in Paris, whose jurisdiction covered at least a third of the country. The *parlement de Paris* was divided into chambers, the most prestigious one being the *Grand'chambre* (roughly equivalent to the Supreme Court), which had a *premier président* and ten *présidents à mortier* (which equate to Chief Justice and Lord Justices); the seven lower chambers also had *présidents*. Curval would no doubt have served in the *Grand'chambre*.

4. *among the uncivilized*: According to natural law, as it was generally understood in the eighteenth century, individuals had innate and universally shared notions of justice, though these were inflected by cultural differences. The article 'Droit de la nature, ou droit naturel' ('Law of nature, or natural law') in the *Encyclopédie* (published between 1751–72) states, 'More frequently, we mean by *natural law* certain rules of justice and equity which natural reason alone has established among men, or to put it better, which God has engraved in our hearts. Such are the fundamental precepts of *law* and of all justice: to live honestly, to offend no one and to render unto every man what belongs to him. From

these general precepts are derived many other particular rules, which nature alone, that is to say reason and equity, suggests to men.' Sade subversively substitutes moral relativism and egotism for natural justice and equality.

5. *all three*: Sade seems to have made an arithmetical error here.

6. *broken on the wheel*: This capital punishment involved the criminal being strapped to the spokes of a large wheel and his limbs being broken with an iron bar; he was left to die of his injuries. This form of punishment was not uncommon in the eighteenth century – Jean Calas notoriously died on the wheel in 1762. See Paul Friedland, *Seeing Justice Done: The Age of Spectacular Capital Punishments in France* (Oxford: Oxford University Press, 2012).

7. *the Conciergerie's dungeons*: Part of the former royal palace on the Ile de la Cité in Paris, the Conciergerie had been used as a prison since the late fourteenth century.

8. *resume thus*: Sade's short notes to himself are given in italics; longer notes are given in plain text. This missing portrait, apparently to be recopied from one of Sade's notebooks, would no doubt have followed the pattern of the preceding portraits in containing an anecdote to illustrate Durcet's libertine credentials. As a later reference suggests, this is likely to have involved the murder of a character called Elvire (see note 15 below).

9. *two lustres*: A lustre is a period of five years.

10. *Praxiteles*: Greek sculptor of the fourth century BC. Sade saw the Venus de' Medici in Florence during his travels around Italy (1775–6) and wrote in his *Voyage to Italy* that it was 'the most beautiful work I have seen in my life'. He considers the possibility that it may have been the work of Praxiteles, but adds, 'we are still completely unsure about who made this accomplished work.'

11. *she had never caused a port-wine stain*: Sade's expression 'elle n'avait jamais fait d'envie' has its origins in the popular belief that a birthmark (*envie*) was a manifestation on the child's body of objects imagined or craved by the mother during pregnancy. This belief in the monstrous power of the mother's imagination is also expressed by Julien Offray de La Mettrie in his *Machine Man* (1747): 'Since there is obviously communication between mother and child [. . .] we believe that it is by the same means that the foetus feels the effect of its mother's impetuous imagination, as soft wax receives all sorts of impressions, and that the same traces or desires of its mother can be imprinted on the foetus

in a way which we do not understand' (*Machine Man and Other Writings*, trans. and ed. Ann Thomson (Cambridge: Cambridge University Press, 1996), p. 29).

12. *her vagina was obstructed*: Madame Bois-Laurier, the storytelling prostitute of *Thérèse the Philosopher* (1748), also has an obstructed vagina.

13. *Cythera*: Reputed to be the birthplace of Aphrodite, the goddess of love, this Greek island featured significantly in the French erotic imagination of the eighteenth century, as, for example, in Watteau's painting *The Embarkation for Cythera* (1717).

14. *tribade*: Deriving from the Greek *tribein* ('to rub'), 'tribade' was a word designating a woman who engages in erotic acts with other women. The term 'lesbian' did not come into usage to describe same-sex female desire until the late nineteenth century.

15. *that same castle in Switzerland . . . little Elvire*: The references here to 'that same castle' and to the murder of a previously unmentioned character probably relate to an anecdote Sade intended as part of Durcet's missing portrait (see note 8 above).

16. *bourgeoisie*: In eighteenth-century France the bourgeoisie was an urban citizenship with particular rights and responsibilities. The Parisian bourgeoisie was forbidden from doing manual work and not allowed to sell anything except for the fruit of their properties; in return they enjoyed similar, though not as many, fiscal and honorific privileges as the nobility.

17. *Hébé*: The Greek goddess of youth and cup-bearer to the gods of Olympus.

18. *Senanges*: A name rich in libertine connotations, evoking the ageing coquette Madame de Senanges in Crébillon fils's influential libertine novel *The Wayward Head and Heart* (1736–8), as well as the title character of Dorat's *The Sacrifices of Love, or The Letters of the Vicomtesse de Senanges to the Chevalier de Versenai* (1771).

19. *Here are the names they gave*: It was common practice in the eighteenth century for servants to adopt new names when entering a different household. Given the extreme violence to come, however, the erasure of past identities and imposition of new ones in this context inevitably brings to mind the systematic depersonalization of prisoners in concentration camps during the Second World War.

20. *Albani*: Francesco Albani (1578–1660) was an Italian baroque painter, ten of whose paintings Sade saw while in Italy.

21. *La Flèche*: Located in the Loire region; the Jesuits founded a college there in 1604; their most famous student was the philosopher René Descartes. Following their expulsion from France in 1764, the college was transformed into a military academy to train young noblemen for admission to Paris's École militaire.

22. *Knight of Malta*: Also known as the Knights Hospitaller, a Roman Catholic military order that gained fixed quarters on Malta in 1530.

23. *Louis-le-Grand*: One of the most prestigious schools in France, which Sade himself attended from 1750 to 1754.

24. *Zéphire*: A Greek god of wind; according to one legend he blew a gust of wind at a discus thrown by Apollo, causing it to strike and kill Hyacinth, with whom he was jealously in love.

25. *Céladon*: A character in Honoré d'Urfé's pastoral romance *L'Astrée* (1607–27), whose name became a byword for a faithful and sentimental hero.

26. *Collège du Plessis*: One of the colleges of the Sorbonne.

27. *Hyacinthe*: The lover of Apollo (see note 24 above).

28. *Giton*: From Petronius' *Satyricon*, the name of the hero Encolpius' handsome if unfaithful young servant and lover. In erotic fiction of the seventeenth and eighteenth centuries, the name came to signify a catamite.

29. *Avenue de St. Cloud*: Where the Great Stables at Versailles were located.

30. *Antinoüs . . . Hadrian's catamite*: Antinous, the Emperor Hadrian's lover, drowned in the Nile in AD 130.

31. *Brise-cul*: Literally translates as 'Break-arse'.

32. *Bande-au-ciel*: Literally translates as 'Erect to the sky'.

33. *close stool*: A chair or box with a hole, beneath which a chamber pot was concealed.

34. *hanged 6 times in effigy*: Execution by effigy, usually a painting of the condemned, was common in eighteenth-century France in cases where the criminal had fled from justice. The *Encyclopédie* describes the practice: 'In Paris, the paintings that serve as *effigies* are simply a rough sketch in ink, which represents a man hanged or on the wheel, according to the sentence; but in the provinces where executions are more rare, *effigies* are usually painted and coloured to resemble the accused as far as possible' ('Effigie'). As Paul Friedland clarifies, 'effigies appear to have been not simply a representation of the condemned, but a representation of the condemned *being* executed [. . .] On occasion, however, instead of representing the execution within the painting, it was the painting itself that was, so to speak, executed' (*Seeing Justice Done*, p.

107). Sade himself was burned in effigy following the 'Marseille affair'.

35. *erysipelas*: Also known as Saint Anthony's fire, a skin infection that results in swelling, rashes and lesions.

36. *the Black Forest*: Durcet's castle appears to have moved from Switzerland to Germany. The earlier reference to Switzerland seems to have been based on the missing anecdote from Durcet's portrait (see notes 8 and 15 above).

37. *colliers and foresters*: Colliers is used in the old sense of those who produce and sell charcoal. Forestry and charcoal production were key industries in the Black Forest in the eighteenth century.

38. 9^{ber}: An abbreviation for November.

39. *Mont St. Bernard*: Sade may be thinking of the Great St Bernard Pass ('Col du Grand-Saint-Bernard'), the most ancient pass through the Western Alps and whose elevation is 2,469 metres.

40. *communicating directly with the kitchens*: This seems to be a system of dumb waiters connecting the dining room with the kitchens below.

41. *dressing room*: The French here is *garde-robes*, a term used in the eighteenth century for both dressing rooms and privies. Sade subsequently uses the word *cabinets* for these private spaces and *garde-robes* to refer to the privies in the chapel. The reference a few lines below to the *garde-robes* in the four friends' quarters is ambiguous, but privy here seems more likely than dressing room, given that these suites of rooms already include boudoirs. The phrase *aller aux garde-robes* is the eighteenth-century equivalent of 'to go to the toilet'.

42. 8^{ber}: An abbreviation for October.

43. X^{ber}: An abbreviation for December.

44. *likewise to capital punishment*: Sade seems to have made a mistake here in alluding to capital rather than corporal punishment, as neither the boys nor the girls are fatally punished for such transgressions.

45. *quartet*: The French is *quatrain*, the equivalent to the English 'quatrain' or four lines of verse. Sade seems to be drawing on the older *quatraine*, which Godefroy's *Dictionary of Old French Language* (1881) defines as 'an assemblage of four objects'. Sade later uses the term 'quadrille' instead (see Part 1, note 2 below).

46. *Grey Sisters*: The sense is ambiguous. The Grey Sisters were nuns who cared for the poor; Louis-Sébastien Mercier devotes a chapter ('Sœurs grises') to them in the *Tableau de Paris* (1781), but the juxtaposition of this particular order to the generic 'nuns'

(*religieuses*) in Sade's text seems odd. Sade may alternatively be alluding to the Graeae or Grey Sisters of Greek mythology, three aged sisters who shared one eye and one tooth between them; they were sisters to the Gorgons. The old women dress again as Grey Sisters on the first day of Part One.

47. *incestify*: Sade uses the verb *incester*, an Old French term that had fallen out of use; Godefroy's *Dictionary of Old French Language* attests to its usage in 1552. Similarly Sade's use of the term *adultérer* in the sense of 'to commit adultery' was already an archaism by the eighteenth century.

48. *incense*: Sade often uses 'incense' to mean ejaculate or sperm.

49. *each of these passions . . . given to the passion*: Sade does not appear to have systematically marked his manuscript in these ways.

50. *fructus belli*: The fruits of war.

51. *Tourville*: Zelmire's father was previously named the Comte de Terville.

52. *12 years old*: Giton was previously described as being thirteen years old.

53. *Hercule . . . very knavish*: In his initial character portrait, however, Sade describes Hercule as being 'moreover very sweet' (see p. 40).

PART ONE

1. *dodged*: The original French is *esquicher*, but Sade seems to confuse or conflate two verbs here: *esquiver* ('to dodge') and *s'esquicher* (figuratively, 'to avoid a quarrel').

2. *quadrille*: Sade henceforth uses the term *quadrille* rather than *quatrain* to describe his groups of four. A quadrille (a term he also adopts in his *History of Juliette*) was originally a team of four horsemen participating in a tournament or joust. Although it also referred in the eighteenth century to a popular card game (and, subsequently, a square dance for four couples), it is upon the original meaning which Sade draws here.

3. *the Recollect friars in Paris*: The Recollect friary was on the Rue du Faubourg Saint-Martin, opposite the church of Saint-Laurent in the north of the city.

4. *12 sols*: Not a large amount, considering that in the middle of the century a baker could earn thirty *sols* a day, which was enough to feed himself.

5.   *F's and B's*: *Foutre* ('fuck') and *bougre* ('bugger'). Sade self-censors here.

6.   *a little écu*: An *écu* was worth three *livres*; it was about half of what a wet nurse might earn in a month.

7.   *Comus*: A god of festivities in Greek mythology.

8.   *monks*: Sade uses the word *moines* here, rather than *religieux*, the word he uses elsewhere for the Recollect friars.

9.   *ten louis*: This equated to 240 *livres*; given that an assistant at a clothes shop would earn up to 200 *livres* a year, Duclos's sister has a tidy sum in her purse.

10. *poulard*: A young hen fattened for eating.

11. *Rue Soli*: This street was in the vicinity of Saint-Eustache, an area where prostitution was rife.

12. *As young as this girl may seem to you*: On 11 July 1750 the famous bawd Jeanne Moyon was whipped, branded and exiled from Paris for having attempted to corrupt a ten-year-old girl on behalf of a distinguished client. Guérin's recruitment of nine-year-old Duclos would thus have been regarded by the authorities as a serious offence.

13. *manualizing*: From the French *manualiser*, 'to masturbate'.

14. *she came when she was fucked*: The long-standing belief that the woman's orgasm was vital for conception persisted well into the eighteenth century, but towards the end of the period there was, in the words of historian Thomas Laqueur, a 'dramatic revaluation of the female orgasm' (see 'Orgasm, Generation and the Politics of Reproductive Biology', *Representations*, 14 (1986), pp. 1–41).

15. *in petto*: 'In the breast' (and by implication 'in secret') in Italian, used when the Pope, after creating cardinals in consistory, reports he has appointed others whom he reserves *in petto* and whom he will make known in due course.

16. *Abbé*: The position of *abbé* ('abbot') was by the eighteenth century only nominally clerical and had become an honorary title that allowed the holder – often the younger son of an aristocratic family – an income.

17. *had my first fruit ... in his mouth*: Duclos strikingly represents her first orgasm, rather than any act of penetrative sex, as a loss of virginity here. Her narration contains no mention of what would conventionally have been considered her loss of virginity, or indeed of any acts of vaginal or anal penetration. This is to prevent the four libertines from prematurely carrying out any deflorations of their own.

18. *dressed ... as a Savoyarde*: Sade writes that Augustine is *vêtue en marmotte* ('dressed as a marmot'). In the streets of eighteenth-century Paris, Savoyards often entertained passers-by with a marmot; see Mercier's chapter 'Savoyards' in the *Tableau de Paris*. The Metropolitan Museum of Art holds a drawing by Antoine Watteau (*c*.1715) of a 'Standing Savoyarde with a Marmot Box'.

19. *this delectable child's sperm*: There was some debate in eighteenth-century physiology as to whether women were able to produce seminal fluid. The *Encyclopédie*'s article 'Semence' ('Semen') states: 'Hippocrates says that a woman's semen is weaker than a man's, but that it is necessary. Aristotle barely admits that women produce semen; he thinks that the libidinous humour that they produce during coitus is not semen and that it does not contribute to conception. Galen grants that women produce semen, but less than men do.'

20. *gamahuches*: According to the *OED*, the French term *gamahucher*, signifying oral sex in general and cunnilingus in particular, was first used in 1783; that year saw the publication of Mirabeau's *My Conversion or The Libertine of Quality*, in which that word does indeed appear.

21. *spite*: The French word here, *taquinisme*, is Sade's own coinage and is used rather differently to the commonly used *taquinerie* (which had various senses, including teasing, miserly or quarrelsome behaviour). Sade's neologism implies cruelty and aggression.

22. *Mother*: The French *maman* was a term for a brothel-keeper or madam.

23. *Tuileries*: The Tuileries Gardens, adjoining the Louvre in the centre of Paris, were a notorious site of male and female prostitution; in 1734 Sade's father was arrested there for attempting to pick up a man who turned out to be an undercover police agent.

24. *brazenly*: The French term is *cyniquement*, deriving from the reputation of Cynics for public indecency; Diogenes (*c*.410–*c*.323 BC), one of the founders of this group of philosophers, was notorious for masturbating in public. The noun *cynisme* is used a few lines below, where the libertines' minds are described as 'inflamed by acts of brazenness'.

25. *contre-dances*: The English country dance was introduced to France in the early eighteenth century and was later reintroduced into England as the 'contre-danse' or 'contra-danse'. The formation of the partners into two opposite lines of indefinite length

(men on one side, women on the other) allows for the easy confusion between 'country' and 'contre-' or 'contra-'.

26.   *surcoat*: A close-fitting overcoat, often of rich material, worn by soldiers.

27.   *a porter or Savoyard*: Some jobs were closely, though not systematically, associated with people from particular provinces in eighteenth-century Paris. Water carriers, for instance, were associated with Auvergnats, and chimney-sweeps were often Savoyards. Of 'Savoyards' Mercier writes in the *Tableau de Paris*: 'They pace the streets from morning to night, their faces smeared with soot, their teeth white, an innocent and jolly air about them: their cry is long, plaintive and lugubrious.' Also finding work as lamplighters, shoe-shiners and *décrotteurs* (those who scraped mud off people's shoes), Savoyards were stereotyped for their poverty and became a by-word for those who performed dirty and menial tasks.

28.   *Say this better*: This is Sade's note.

29.   *a V and an* M: The 'V' stands for *vol* ('theft') and the 'M' for *maquerellage* ('pandering'). The usual punishment for pandering was to be sent to the workhouse or to be banished; in aggravated cases (involving forced prostitution) the punishment included being branded with an 'M' or a fleur-de-lis.

30.   *taffeta chiné*: A warp-printed fabric of woven silk, given a soft, blurry design (usually floral or striped), which became fashionable in the latter part of the eighteenth century. It involved a method of printing the warp before weaving.

31.   *grisettes*: Young women of modest means who worked as hat-makers, dressmakers and linen girls, with a reputation for easy virtue.

32.   *they both vomit . . . what they have borrowed*: This scene echoes one in *Thérèse the Philosopher* (1748) in which a prostitute and a monk, both drunk, vomit into each other's mouths (see *Thérèse philosophe* in *Romanciers libertins du XVIIIᵉ siècle*, 2 vols, ed. Patrick Wald Lasowski (Paris: Gaillimard, 2000), 1. 952).

33.   *farmer-general*: *Fermiers généraux* were private citizens under the *ancien régime* who had bought a licence from the King to raise an agreed amount of tax in a particular district. If they raised funds in excess of this agreed amount, they would keep the difference; they were renowned – and despised – for their often immense wealth.

34.   *aniseed . . . balsamic liquor*: The *Encyclopédie* notes that aniseed can induce wind and aid digestion; and that balsamic-based medi-

cines 'make fluids more volatile' and can be used to treat a host of ailments, including those of the stomach (see the 'Anis' and 'Balsamiques' articles).

35. *Morpheus*: The Roman god of dreams.

36. *Master of Requests*: The *maître des requêtes* was a high-ranking magistrate who served on the *Conseil du Roi* ('King's Council'), chaired by the Chancellor.

37. *mooncalves*: A mooncalf was a 'malformed, imperfect and entirely defective foetus' ('Faux-germe', *Encyclopédie*); the English term evokes the popular belief that such false conceptions were caused by the influence of the moon.

38. *goosing around*: The French here is *la petite oie* or 'little goose': an expression of culinary origin signifying sexual contact that stops short of – and provides an alternative to – penetrative intercourse.

39. *public treasurer*: The *payeur des rentes* was an official charged with paying annuities on the king's behalf; for a full definition, see the *Répertoire universel et raisonné de jurisprudence civile et criminelle, canonique et bénéficiale* (Paris, 1781).

40. *Daphnis to this Chloe*: The hero and heroine of a Greek romance by Longus, written in the second century AD.

41. *barbet*: A French water dog.

42. *a thousand times more than I have carried out*: In his *grande lettre*, written to his wife on 20 February 1781 from Vincennes, Sade states: 'Yes I am a libertine, I admit; I have imagined everything that can be imagined of this kind, but I have surely not done everything I have imagined and will surely never do so. I am a libertine, but I am not *a criminal* or *a murderer*' (italics in original).

43. *tax-collector*: The *sous-fermier* was junior to the *fermier-général*; the latter had the same privileges and rights over the former as the king had over the *fermier-général*.

44. *electrify himself*: Sade's term *s'électriser* evokes a theory of animal spirits, as also described by Curval at the start of the twenty-third day.

45. *reverse of this strip*: At this point Sade begins writing on the reverse of the scroll.

46. *Milli*: The Provençal equivalent of *Mademoiselle* and a term of address Sade often used in his correspondence with close friends, such as 'Milli de Rousset'.

47. *carrying his hod*: It would take the typical labourer three days to earn an *écu*.

48. *assembly room*: Earlier in the novel the assembly room (*salon d'assemblée*) was described as the place 'intended for the story-

tellers' narrations' (see p. 45), but here they appear as two distinct spaces. It seems that Sade has made a mistake and meant to allocate the drawing room (*salon de compagnie*) to the Bishop.

49. *Champville*: From this point on, Sade changes the spelling to Chanville.

50. *chincara*: In his edition of the *120 Days* for the Bibliothèque de la Pléiade (1990), Michel Delon suggests *chipola*, but Sade may mean *chinchard*, a mackerel from the coast of the Morbihan. There are two further possibilities, however. Heine may have mistranscribed the word *chicorée* ('chicory'), a plant which according to the *Encyclopédie* had health benefits. Alternatively, given that Pierre-Augustin Boissier de Sauvages's Languedoc–French dictionary (1785) refers to the verb *chinca*, meaning 'taste', Sade might be using *chincara* as a term for 'snack'.

51. *socratize*: Sade defines the verb *socratiser* in the *New Justine*: 'All libertines know that this is the name given to the action of putting one or two fingers in the patient's arsehole. This accompaniment, one of the most essential in lubricity, is suited above all to old and worn-out men; it promptly stimulates an erection and causes unbelievable pleasure at the moment of ejaculation.' The verb also appears in Fougeret de Monbron's libertine novel *Margot la ravaudeuse* (1753), when the eponymous heroine, despairing at the impotence of one of her clients, decides as a last resort 'to tickle his perineum and to socratize him with her finger tip'.

52. *tea*: The nearest English equivalent to a *goûter*, a light meal taken in the late afternoon.

53. *The guests arrived*: This is a *mise en abyme* of the situation described at the start of the novel, with four friends representing the Church, the military, the law and finance, and meeting for supper four times a week.

54. *d'Erville*: The spelling of names in this section is inconsistent, changing from d'Erville to Derville, du Cange to Ducange, and d'Aucourt to Daucourt.

55. *Vin d'Aï*: Until the 1860s the name *Champagne* rarely appeared on bottles of the sparkling wine produced in the region; instead, the names of prestigious vineyards – such as Aÿ (the modern spelling of Aï), Sillery or Bouzy – were generally used.

56. *Master of Accounts*: Guy Miège's *New Dictionary of French and English* (London, 1677) translates *maître des comptes* as 'an auditor or overseer of accounts', who was employed at the *Chambre des comptes* ('Court of Accounts'), a sovereign court dealing with financial affairs.

57. *He enters: I was naked; he looks*: Here, as elsewhere in the text, Sade's tenses are highly erratic, switching from past to present to future within the space of a sentence. Switching between past and present is, however, a common feature of fiction in this period – the use of the present to convey immediacy of action in this way is known in French as the *présent historique*.

58. *Aesculapius*: The Latin form for Asclepios, the Greek god of medicine.

59. *Iris*: In Greek mythology, the personification of the rainbow and a messenger of the gods.

60. *Salerno*: A city in southern Italy famous for its Schola Medica Salernitana, the first medical school in the world.

61. *Phaeton*: In eighteenth-century France a coachman might be ironically termed Phaeton, after Helios' son, who died while driving his father's chariot.

62. *Capuchin monks on the Rue St-Honoré*: This monastery, originally constructed in the sixteenth century, was the Order's most substantial house in France.

63. *Rue du Bouloir*: Now known as the Rue du Bouloi, this street was a few hundred metres north-east of the Capuchin monastery.

64. *Treasurer of France*: The *trésoriers de France* were at once magistrates, officers of police administration and high-ranking financiers; their responsibilities were therefore numerous, including passing judgement on financial matters involving the king's estate, oversight for street lighting and prison repairs.

65. *the Marquis*: The title changes in the original manuscript.

66. *I let him . . . one hundred louis*: It was not uncommon in the eighteenth century for parents to sell their daughters' virginity to madams, who would then sell them on to wealthy buyers. The sum paid by the Comte de Mesanges is much higher than that normally paid for virginities in the 1750s and 1760s, however. Grimod de la Reynière, an exceptionally wealthy farmer-general, paid 50 *louis* (1,200 *livres*) for the virginity of Mère Dumont's daughter; Madame Varenne sold Marie Boujard's virginity to the Marquis de Bandol for just 4 *louis* (96 *livres*); and Dame Perrin sold her niece's virginity twice, the second time to an Italian prince for 30 *louis* (720 *livres*). The usual sum seems to have been a cash payment of between 240 and 720 *livres*, often with additional 'gifts' of dresses, jewels and furniture. See Nina Kushner, *Erotic Exchanges: The World of Elite Prostitution in Eighteenth-Century Paris* (Ithaca and London: Cornell University Press, 2013), pp. 76–7.

67. *he said*: The repetition is in the original text.

68. *conclude the story of this beautiful girl*: There is, however, no explicit mention of Eugénie in Desgranges's narration in Part 4.

69. *an old salt-tax-collector*: The original French title is *receveur des gabelles*; the *gabelle* was a tax on salt in *ancien régime* France.

70. *Curval*: Sade presumably means the Duc rather than Curval here.

71. *myrtle leaves*: A symbol of Venus.

72. *commissioner*: The *commissaires* were some of the most important figures in what might be termed the police force of eighteenth-century Paris. They were trained in law and acted as magistrates in each of the city's districts; their duties were administrative, judicial and investigative. As in this case, an individual with a grievance would first go to the local *commissaire*, who – if unable to resolve the matter – would initiate court proceedings.

73. *whiff of burning faggots*: Sodomy was officially a capital offence and although punishment was rarely enforced, some offenders were burned at the stake; Benjamin Deschauffors was executed in 1726, and Jean Diot was executed in 1750.

74. *registrar*: The *greffier* was the clerk who transcribed the judges' sentences and maintained the archives where these registers were held.

75. *ferula*: A flat piece of leather or wood used to punish school-children by striking them on the hand.

76. *pittance*: The small portion of food or drink given at mealtimes to a monk or other member of a religious community.

77. *satiety springs from abundance*: An allusion to the phrase 'fit fastidium copia' in Livy's *History of Rome* (Book 3, section 1).

78. *Md. Desgranges to tell you how*: She does so in Part 4, passion 147.

79. *the Duc*: Sade confuses the Duc and the Bishop here.

80. *cacochymism*: Sade's term *cacochimisme* evokes *cacochymie* ('cacochymy'), a medical term referring to the unhealthy or degenerate state of the four humours. See William Black, *An Historical Sketch of Medicine and Surgery from their Origin to the Present Time* (London: J. Johnson, 1782), pp. 92–4.

81. *Marquis de . . . burn in effigy*: Sade is alluding to himself here: in 1772 he was burned in effigy, following his conviction for sodomy and poisoning in what became known as the 'Marseille affair'.

82. *Postmaster General*: The single office of *fermier des postes* replaced the *maîtres des courriers* (who were regional directors) in 1672, when François-Michel le Tellier, Marquis de Louvois,

created the *ferme générale des postes*. The Postmaster General purchased from the king the exclusive right to run the postal service and draw revenue from it.

83.   *petite maison*: A private, luxurious setting used for erotic encounters. These retreats flourished in the areas immediately surrounding Paris (such as Passy and Clichy). They regularly appear in eighteenth-century fiction, such as Bastide's *La Petite maison* (1758), and, while the owners were almost exclusively male, Madame de Merteuil has one of her own in *Dangerous Liaisons* (1782).

84.   *Le Roule*: Reached by the Rue Saint-Honoré, this village was just outside the city limits; it was formally made a *faubourg* of Paris in 1722.

85.   *aqua vitae*: A term for unrefined alcohol.

86.   *ecclesiastical adviser*: The *conseiller clerc* was an adviser to a royal court of law, a post always assigned to an ecclesiastic.

87.   *A vinaigrette*: The sense is unclear. Two possible interpretations are: either the Duc will ejaculate inside her, leaving his semen as a kind of sauce, or he will 'take her for a ride' (a *vinaigrette* was a little two-wheeled carriage, pulled by a man).

88.   *game of fart-in-face*: There was indeed an old game called *la pète-en-gueule*. It is described in *Beliefs and Legends of France: Memories of Bygone Times, Customs and Traditions* (1875): 'Fart-in-face, which Rabelais mentions in his catalogue of Gargantua's games [. . .] is a very ancient entertainment. There must be four people to take part. Two of the participants, facing in opposite directions, crouch beside each other and stay still, their hands and knees resting on the ground. Meanwhile, the two other participants – one standing up, the other upside down – clasp each other tight and form a seesaw, sitting with their buttocks on those of their friends, such that with each tilt of the seesaw they change position and find themselves, one after the other, with their feet in the air. Since the position of the two main participants forces them to place their faces between each other's legs, one can guess why this rather coarse game has been called *fart-in-face*. One of the engravings in an old illustrated edition of Scarron's *Virgile travesti* gives a very clear idea of the game.' Sade offers a far more rudimentary version.

89.   *island of Formosa*: The former Portuguese name for Taiwan. Here Sade amalgamates two distinct passages from Helvétius's *On the Mind* (1758), the first of which states that on Formosa 'it is a crime for pregnant women to give birth before the age of thirty-five. If they are pregnant, they stretch out at the feet of the

priestess, who, to execute the law, tramples upon them until she causes a miscarriage.' The second passage states: 'Among the Giagues, a cannibal people who devour their conquered enemies, one may, says Father Cavazi, pound one's children in a mortar, with roots, oil and leaves; boil them and form the whole into a paste with which to rub one's body and to render oneself invulnerable.'

90. *scald . . . I am not a pig*: The Richelet Dictionary (1735) gives as an example of the verb *échauder* ('to scald') 'to remove the hair of a suckling pig with hot water'.

91. *chafing dish*: A portable grate, often used for cooking on a low heat or for keeping food warm.

92. *hatched*: Sade's libertines appear to subscribe to the animalculist belief, derived from Aristotle, that sperm contains homunculi and that the mother's only role in reproduction is to hatch those minute creatures in her womb. Madame de Saint-Ange, one of the libertines of Sade's *Philosophy in the Boudoir* (1795), tells her pupil Eugénie, 'it is nonetheless proven that this foetus only owes its existence to the man's come; spurted forth, without mixing with that of the women, however, it would not succeed; but that which we provide only allows it to develop; it does not create – it helps creation without being its cause. Many modern naturalists even claim it is useless.' Sade may be thinking here of La Mettrie, whose *Machine Man* (1747) he greatly admired: 'It is so rare for the two seminal fluids to meet in intercourse that I am tempted to consider the woman's to be useless for reproduction.' This view – challenged by scientists such as the Comte de Buffon and Pierre Louis Maupertuis – was outdated by the 1780s.

93. *who made him scream out loud*: Sic. The next sentence suggests that Sade must have meant 'whom he made scream out loud'.

94. *the custom . . . at one's front door*: This fantasy derives from an exaggerated version of the actual ceremony, as described in the English translation of Bernard Picart's *Religious Ceremonies and Customs of the Several Nations of the Known World*, 7 vols (London, 1731–9): the officiating priest and associates 'all set out towards the house of the deceas'd, whose corps must be either set at the church-door, or in some apartment near it, with his feet turned towards the street, which the rituals say must be observed, tho the deceas'd were a priest' (2.99).

95. *Rue Blanche du Rempart*: Situated at the northern edge of Paris, on the current Boulevard de Clichy; at least ten *petites maisons* were located there in the mid-eighteenth century.

96.   *Place de Grève*: The main site of public executions in Paris.

97.   *Themis*: The Ancient Greek personification of law and order.

98.   *unfortunately that cannot be*: Under eighteenth-century law, a pregnant woman could not be executed and would be put to death only once her baby had been delivered.

99.   *as you would with a murder*: One of the arguments put forward in 'Frenchmen, Yet Another Effort if You Want to Be Republicans', a political pamphlet that forms part of *Philosophy in the Boudoir* (1795), is that the state must allow its citizens complete liberty, and has no right to impose the death penalty even if murder has been committed.

100. *no longer horrifying . . . makes you come*: Duclos's Président here echoes the narrator's logic in the Introduction: 'No doubt many of the various excesses you shall see depicted shall displease you, we know, but there shall be others that inflame you to the point of spilling your come, and that is all we require.' Both the Président and the narrator imply that arousal strips the subject of any moral high ground. Michel Tort describes this as the 'Sade effect' (see 'L'effet Sade', *Tel Quel*, 28 (1967), pp. 66–83).

101. *pastourelles*: A genre of Old French lyric poetry, in the classic form of which the narrator, sometimes identified as a knight, recounts his meeting with and attempted seduction of a shepherdess.

102. *according to . . . dictated by the table*: A reference to the 'Table of plans for the rest of the expedition' detailed on the third day.

103. *Florville*: The name also appears in Sade's short story 'Florville and Courval', where it is given to the doomed heroine.

104. *La Fleur*: According to the testimony of one of the prostitutes who took part in the orgy at Marseille in 1772, Sade's valet (and sexual partner) Latour called his master 'Lafleur', while Sade called him 'Monsieur le Marquis'.

105. *him to pursue me . . . keep running away*: This passion resembles a scene in *Thérèse the Philosopher* (1748) where a fifty-year-old lecher chases a prostitute named Bois-Laurier around a room (see *Thérèse philosophe* in *Romanciers libertins du XVIIIᵉ siècle*, I. 942–3.

PART TWO

1.   *the man of Hell*: The reference is to the final passion described by Desgranges in Part 4.

2.   *to deflower a girl . . . married the following day*: This passion recalls the *droit du seigneur*, the supposed (and historically unproven) right of the nobleman to take the virginity of his vassal's bride. This subject is taken up in several eighteenth-century works, including Voltaire's *The Lord's Right* (1762) and Beaumarchais's *The Marriage of Figaro* (1784).

3.   *to sapphotize*: Sade's use of the neologism *saphotiser* evokes the poet Sappho and denotes masturbation between women.

4.   *paten*: The plate or shallow dish on which the host is laid during the Eucharist.

5.   *[ ]*: The numbering of this section is confused, with this passion unnumbered and the number 69 omitted.

6.   *runs the gauntlet*: Originally a military punishment, running the gauntlet involves an individual being forced to run between two rows of soldiers who repeatedly strike him.

7.   *quadrille*: The only time in the novel Sade uses this term to describe the four libertines, rather than the groups of children serving them.

8.   *turkey ballet*: The *ballet des dindons* was a popular fairground entertainment in Paris from 1739 to 1844. Live turkeys were fenced in on a raised metal sheet which was progressively heated. As the heat rose the turkeys would move their feet in a macabre dance accompanied by a hurdy-gurdy. The practice was banned in 1844. Desgranges describes a human equivalent in Part 4, passion 132.

9.   *Check why . . . one too many*: This is because the numbering on 14 December is muddled.

PART THREE

1.   *mercury combined with quicksilver*: Mercury and quicksilver are one and the same; the accumulation is rhetorical.

2.   *jenny*: A female donkey or ass.

3.   *45*: Sade has inserted the number for the passion a sentence too soon as he does also on p.379 and p.384.

4.   *very realistic waxwork cadavers*: In his *Voyage to Italy* Sade writes of seeing such waxworks in Florence: 'In one of these cabinets one sees a sepulchre filled with an infinite number of cadavers, in each of which one may observe the different gradations of decomposition, from a cadaver fresh this morning to one entirely devoured by worms. This bizarre idea is the work of a Sicilian

named Zummo.' Sade also praises the work of Gaetano Giulio Zummo, or Zumbo (1656–1701) in the *History of Juliette*.

5. *dagger attached by a hair*: Sade's version of the Sword of Damocles, albeit one which dispenses with any reflection on the fragility of power in favour of simple torture.

6. *three kinds of death*: Sade would return to this scenario almost thirty years later in his historical novel, *The Marquise de Gange*, based on the true story of the gruesome murder in 1667 of the eponymous *belle Provençale*, Diane de Joannis de Chateaublanc. Confronted with the same choice by her two brothers-in-law, the Marquise picked the poison; although she managed to make her escape afterwards, she died a few days later. The tale was retold several times in the eighteenth and nineteenth centuries and a Provençal noble such as Sade would have known this story from an early age. There is another echo of this scenario in Sade's darkly comic short story, 'The Successful Ruse'.

7. *pneumatic machine*: The *Encyclopédie* describes this air pump – also known as 'Boyle's machine' after its inventor Robert Boyle – at some length (see the article entitled 'Pneumatique, machine'). Joseph Wright of Derby depicts the apparatus in *An Experiment on a Bird in the Air Pump* (1768), and the eponymous heroine of Revéroni Saint-Cyr's novel *Pauliska, or Modern Perversity* (1798) finds herself trapped in one.

8. *aqua fortis*: A term for nitric acid.

9. *olivettes*: 'A kind of dance practised by the inhabitants of Provence after they have gathered the olives. It features three dancers who chase after each other, weaving around three olive trees' (*Dictionnaire de l'Académie française*, 1762).

10. *her foot*: In passions 104–111 and 118–119 the gender of the victim is not specified. The immediate context, including passions 99–103 and 112, nevertheless suggests that a female victim is far more likely here.

11. *rope torture*: This is the strappado, described in the *Encyclopédie*'s 'Estrapade' article: 'a form of military punishment, by which the criminal, once his hands have been tied behind his back, is hoisted by a rope up to the top of a high wooden beam, from where he is dropped to just above ground level, so that his body weight dislocates his arms as he falls. Sometimes he is even condemned to endure three bouts of the *strappado*. [. . .] The *strappado* is no longer in use, at least in France.'

12. *has already been done*: Sade may be thinking of passion 76.

PART FOUR

1. *check*: Champville did speak of a man who 'flogs only the face with a birch', but this was on 31 rather than 30 December.
2. *check*: Desgranges has already mentioned this man; see Part 4, passion 28.
3. *sulphur . . . mercury and quicksilver*: Mercuric sulphide or cinnabar was used as a medicine. It was taken internally for skin diseases, epilepsy, convulsions and hysteria, and externally by fumigation for venereal diseases. See the 'Cinnabre artificiel' article in the *Encyclopédie*.
4. *check her name*: Sade presumably means Marianne.
5. *but check which man*: See Part 3, passion 112.
6. *five years old*: Martaine previously states that she was four years old at the time (p. 337).
7. *A fustigator 75*: Sade's numbering goes awry here.
8. *they crush his two balls*: Sade makes an error here: Narcisse's testicles have already been cut off (see above, p. 380).
9. *[ ]*: Sade forgets to number this passion, no doubt because it features the same libertine as the previous one.
10. *dogfish skin*: Dogfish skin is extremely rough and hard-wearing; the *Encyclopédie*'s 'Chien de mer' article notes that it was used as a kind of sandpaper.
11. *This has been . . . see where*: This refers to Part 2, passion 104.
12. *check this*: See Part 4, passions 58 and 71.
13. *they were . . . in the drafts*: This is no doubt because Sade numbers two passions as 75 and forgets to number the passion that directly follows 128.
14. *check where*: See Part 4, passion 66.
15. *last sheet of the recto*: At this point Sade has reached the end of the scroll, so he adds an extra page and continues writing on the other side.
16. *but did not talk about it in the plan*: Sade does not in fact announce this scene; there is, however, a comparable scene involving milk (see p. 251).